ON THE FRONT LINES OF PASSION

Quintin took Lily's chin in his hand and lifted her face. Lily's heart skipped a beat.

"I should like to kiss you, Lily Radford," he said.

"Well, you may not," Lily answered, a hesitancy in her voice.

Quintin lowered his lips slowly to cover hers. He still held her chin in his left hand, but his touch was light. She could move away, but she didn't.

Lily closed her eyes and marveled at the feelings the simple kiss aroused.

Quintin was looking down at her with a slight frown on his face. "I'd like to see you again, Miss Radford."

Lily glanced to the ground. "I...I can't." She steeled herself, knowing what she had to do, hating it all the same. "You'll learn soon enough, I suppose," she said. "I'm involved with someone else: Captain Sherwood. It's quite scandalous, I know, but that's just the way it is. You're a charming gentleman, Mr. Tyler. I'm certain you'll have no trouble finding yourself a young woman who will succumb to those charms."

"And you are immune?" He jested with her.

"Most definitely," she said too sternly.

IN ENEMY HANDS

LINDA WINSTEAD

LEISURE BOOKS **NEW YORK CITY**

This is for my sister, Sandy, and her crew—
Mike, Craig, Matthew, and Alan

A LEISURE BOOK®

May 1996

Published by

Dorchester Publishing Co., Inc.
276 Fifth Avenue
New York, NY 10001

Printed in the United States of America.

In Enemy Hands

Prologue

Spring, 1862

Past the tall window, beyond the barrier of glass, the soldiers—grave-faced men in blue coats—swarmed over the well-tended grounds. Before today, this house had seemed to be buffered from the war, but now Lily watched the horde of Yankees stake claim to her home with their threatening weapons always at hand—sabers that hung at their sides, pistols strapped to their thighs, rifles that even she recognized as all but obsolete, they were so old.

She watched through the window for a long moment, trying to shut out the argument that was taking place in this very room. If she didn't calm herself, she would surely say or do something stupid and get them all killed.

When her heart rate had returned to near normal, Lily turned her attention to the captain who was standing so formally in her father's study. His eyes had carefully examined the old books, the well-oiled wood, and her father's favorite leather chair, but now it was her father himself who commanded the captain's full attention.

"Those horses are my property," her father insisted, his accent not that of a Southern gentleman, but of an Englishman who had long lived in the South. He had railed fruitlessly for over an hour, and still the captain's men removed the horses from their stables and carried food from the house, everything from flour and bacon to her father's favorite rum.

"They are being confiscated for the use of the Union Army, Mr. Radford." The captain was stern, but his eyes were dull, his face haggard, even though he appeared to be a fairly young man—younger than her father, James Radford, in any case.

"If you cooperate, we will leave you and your family be." The captain glanced at her as he spoke, then turned his eyes to Elliot.

Lily's anger was, at that moment, directed at her brother. Elliot was old enough to be a soldier, but was not. He had avoided any confrontational stance or word, being almost polite to the invaders. He had a genteel way about him that at times infuriated Lily, from his softly curling hair, too long and too well styled, to the thin, elegant hands that were, even now, pale and soft. His eyes were vacant and washed-out as he observed the invasion of their home.

It was too much, and as if he knew what she was thinking, Elliot took her arm, his firm fingers warning her to hold her temper. How could she, while these men tore her home apart?

"You'll not hurt my children?" Her father's anger had faded, and as he spoke the captain turned his attention away from Lily and Elliot.

"We only want the horses and a few supplies," the captain repeated. "I regret the necessity, but our horses are being shot out from under us, and keeping a mount healthy in these conditions is difficult, sometimes impossible." To Lily, it sounded as if the captain was trying to rationalize his actions. "I need those horses," he said in a low voice.

James Radford moved to the window and watched the soldiers removing his prize mounts from the stable. Lily wanted to go to him, but Elliot continued to hold her back. It was tearing her up inside, but how must it be for her father, watching a lifetime of work whisked away in a single afternoon?

He was a wonderful father, taking on the raising of two children after his wife's death. Lily had been only four, Elliot seven, when their mother died. He had never pressured her to marry, even though she was twenty-four and considered herself an old maid. A happy old maid, with no wish to ever marry.

It was no wonder. James Radford had raised Lily to be the son he'd wanted Elliot to be. It was she who studied fencing with him, who raced the most spirited stallions across their fields. She beat her father at chess on a regular basis, and he'd told her more than once that she had the makings of a fine sailor in her blood.

James Radford raised his eyes to the portrait

that hung high on the wall. He had told Lily so often that she was the picture of her mother, but Lily didn't see herself in the serene countenance of the woman who watched over them all. True, she had her mother's unruly dark blond hair and blue-green eyes, and her father had told her that her mother had been tall for a woman, like Lily.

Perhaps she did look like the mother she didn't remember, but in her heart she was like her father. She could never be as content as the pale woman in the portrait.

James Radford turned to her and smiled, a half-hearted smile that told her to be still, to be patient—two virtues that were never easy for her to practice. But Lily ceased her mild struggle against Elliot's hold.

She saw the resignation on her father's face as he accepted the loss of his prize stock, ceded to the superior forces that overran his home.

He slid open the top drawer of his desk, and Lily knew he was reaching for his pipe. So many nights he had sat in that chair and puffed away, claiming that the smell of the tobacco soothed him after a hard day, that the feel of the smooth wooden bowl in his hand was a balm. The pipe had been a gift from his father, the last thing William Radford had given James before his death.

Lily heard the shouted warning and turned her eyes toward the raised voice just as an eager private, standing behind his captain and just to the left of the door, drew his pistol and fired as James Radford pulled his pipe from the drawer and raised it. The roar of the shot was deafening in the small room, and no one but Lily seemed to know what had happened.

Even the captain seemed to be surprised as the blood spread across James Radford's chest, and he spun toward a white-faced private, who sputtered some nonsense about her father reaching for a weapon.

Lily wrenched away from Elliot and ran to her father as he fell, clutching the pipe in one hand and covering his wound with the other.

"Father?" she whispered, dropping to the floor and laying her hand over his.

He blinked several times, as though trying to clear his vision. "Lily," he muttered. "Don't frown so. You're always so serious, and if I've told you once I've told you a thousand times, you can't take on the world." His voice was fading, and Lily placed her face close to his.

"Don't talk. Save your energy . . ."

"It will be all right, Lily," he assured her. Those were his last words as he slipped away from her. His hand opened, and the pipe rolled off his fingers and onto the floor.

For a long moment she didn't move, couldn't move. Each breath was an effort. The room was silent. No one moved; no one dared even to breathe.

Lily laid her father's head gently against the floor and stood to face the captain. "You bloody bastard." She stalked away from her father's body until she stood toe-to-toe with the captain. "Your man has killed my father."

She saw several hints of emotion on the captain's face—surprise, perhaps, that she was not hysterical, that she dared to face him, that she didn't speak with the simpering and honeysweet accent of a Southern woman. That influence was there, but it was tempered with a bit of her father's English manner.

There was also wariness, as he wondered what she would do. He'd spared only a glance for Elliot. There would be no trouble there.

Sadness, regret. Lily pushed away that conclusion. The man was a monster.

"The private made a tragic but understandable mistake." The captain defended the soldier who had shot her father, all the while seeming to stare at her nose. Was he afraid to meet her eyes? Afraid of what he would see?

"You are responsible." Lily jabbed him in the chest with a strong finger. "He is your man, and therefore whatever he does falls on your head. I demand that your soldiers return our stock to the stables and get off our land. Now." Her voice was strong and unyielding. "And I want your bloody head on a platter," she added in a low voice.

He cut his eyes away from her to watch Elliot stand over their father's body. He was stunned and helpless, an ineffectual man who had no backbone.

"I'm terribly sorry," the captain said, still not looking at her. "I'll have my men bury your father . . ."

"You'll not touch my father," Lily whispered. For the first time, the full force of what had happened hit her, and unwelcome tears welled up in her eyes. "I'll bury him with my bare hands before I allow you to touch him."

Behind her, Elliot sighed loudly. "We would be grateful if you would undertake that chore, Captain," he said wistfully. "You must forgive my sister. She can be quite difficult."

Lily turned on her brother, her anger changing direction like a swift underwater current. "You spineless coward," she hissed, and before he could stop her, she ran for the fireplace and reached for the saber that hung above it. Her fingers closed over the hilt, and the metal of the blade sung as she drew it from the housing. By the time she turned around to face the captain, she was staring at three pistols, all aimed directly at her. Elliot stood to one side, a horrified look on his normally impassive face.

Lily stood fearlessly before them all, the saber that had been her father's pointed at the captain's heart. She held the blade as steady as her unwavering eyes. Never had she imagined that she might hold the weapon trained on another human being. The war had seemed, until today, so remote, so unreal.

The captain lifted a hand to still his men. He held his hand aloft, and Lily could see something she didn't want to see—that regret she'd denied moments earlier, a pain that couldn't be expressed.

If he was waiting for her strength or her resolve to wane, he was in for a long wait. If he waited for her arm to tremble, for the tears to return, then he was a fool.

"Lily." Elliot moved toward her, obviously intending to take the saber from her hand. His pale hand was outstretched, his eyes locked on hers. "We've lost our father today. I don't want to lose you as well. Give me the saber. Please, Lily."

Lily could not disguise her disgust for her brother. "How can you stand there and do nothing?" There was a pain born of hopelessness in her voice. No matter how deep her grief, how great her anger, she knew she couldn't possibly take on the captain and all of his men, the damned Federals who swarmed over the house and grounds like great blue locusts. Lily lowered the saber and heard the captain's sigh of relief as he dropped his hand.

Elliot placed his arm around her shoulder and, with his free hand, took the saber from her. Lily allowed him to take it, reluctantly loosing her grip. "Father never should have argued. If he had only given them what they wanted, this never would have happened." His voice was tortured and gruff, but Lily couldn't believe that even Elliot would blame James Radford for his own senseless death.

Lily ignored her brother and glared at the captain. "I hope you choose Star as your own personal mount. He'll throw you so fast and so hard, you'll break your bloody neck."

She saw a flicker of some emotion in his eyes, doubt or pain or desperation. With a narrowing of his eyes, the captain bowed crisply, then turned on his booted heel to escape the confines of the room.

This room, her father's retreat, had been filled with laughter and tears over the years, but never this. Never violence. It had changed in an inkling into a corner of hell, where nothing was as it should have been, where lives were ended or changed in a heartbeat.

Lily pulled away from Elliot, shrinking from his touch even as he directed the two soldiers who lifted their father's body from the floor. Elliot had always been sweet and gentle, but sometimes he was too sweet. Too gentle.

"I'm going to join the army," Lily hissed when the soldiers were gone and she found herself alone with her brother. "I'm going to cut off all my hair and dress like a man and join the cavalry. Then I'll find that damned captain and cut his liver out."

"Lily," Elliot admonished, speaking to her as if she were a naughty child. "You'll do no such thing."

Elliot paced the small room, head down, hands behind his back. Lily saw him glance at her again and again with a frown on his face.

She knew very well what her brother thought of her, that on occasion, he detested her as much as she detested him. He enjoyed the finer aspects of the life their father's money allowed them to live, but Lily had never, in Elliot's opinion, been suitably impressed with their place in society.

Of course, if she had married as any respectable young lady should have by the age of twenty-four, if she had made any effort to conform to the rigid society they lived in, Elliot wouldn't be pacing the floor bemoaning the fact that he was suddenly and unpleasantly in charge of not only his life, but Lily's as well.

He stopped in the middle of the room and lifted his head as if he'd just experienced a striking idea.

"We're going to England," he declared finally. "We'll wait out the war there." He almost smiled. "It makes perfect sense. London. We've plenty of money, but if we don't take it and escape this madness now, who knows when we might have another chance."

"I'm not going," Lily said sternly, her early tears returning with a vengeance. Her beloved father. Dead. One moment he had been standing there, and the next . . . "You can go to England if you want. Gamble away your half of the money . . ."

Elliot grimaced and raised an eyebrow. Elliot, who avoided confrontations at all cost—especially with Lily—was evidently dreading what came next.

"It's all mine, Lily. Father had assumed you'd be married before his death. Certainly none of us expected . . . that it would come like this." He lifted his chin and faced her defiantly. "I'll make you a bargain. Come to England with me. You'll get half of whatever I have. Then, heaven help you, if you want to return to this godforsaken place, you can. I think you'll find London very pleasant."

He was so certain that she would prefer the

safety and comfort of England . . . he didn't know her at all.

Lily sat on the floor and buried her face in her hands. "He's dead, Elliot. He's really dead." Her anger was gone, replaced in a twinkling by a deep, unbearable sadness.

"I know." Elliot sat beside her and placed a brotherly arm around her shoulder. He was in shock, too, she knew, from witnessing their father's death. Lily leaned her head against his shoulder and closed her eyes. He was infuriating, most of the time, but she did love her brother.

And he loved her. Even when she didn't act like a proper lady. Even when she scared away any of his friends who had been foolish enough to attempt to court her.

They clashed so often because they approached life differently. Elliot always chose the easy path. He accused Lily of going out of her way to find the hard one.

"England, Lily," he whispered in her ear as he pulled her closer. "England."

Chapter One

December 1863

"Lieutenant Tyler!" The voice rose, tremulous and frightened, above the gradually slowing assault of gunfire. Private Louis Medfield was trapped, sheltered behind the stiff corpse of a cavalryman's abandoned horse. "I can't move!"

Quintin Tyler could see no more than a patch of blue from his position behind a stand of fallen trees. He and his men were retreating under attack of superior forces, as the Rebs bore down on them. For three days the battle had raged, and it looked to be a decisive victory for the Union and General Burnside. But a sizeable Confederate contingent had managed to pin down Quint and his men.

"Are you hit?" Quint shouted. The distance separating Private Medfield from the rest of his unit was probably no more than sixty feet—but it was a dangerously open sixty feet of nothing more than scrubby grass and sporadic patches of snow.

"Yes!" Louis Medfield was nothing more than a kid, a seventeen-year-old farm boy who hadn't seen battle before this winter. His voice trembled even as he shouted. "Don't leave me here!" he pleaded. "I can't move!"

Quint cursed under his breath as the men around him watched and waited. They were waiting for him to make a decision. Most of his soldiers were no older than Medfield, and few had any more experience with the hardships of battle. Quint didn't think of himself as a soldier at heart, any more than the men and boys who looked to him for answers.

He cast his eyes downward as he loosened the saber at his side and laid it on the ground. The patches of snow that dotted the landscape were remnants of a late November snowstorm. This was his third winter with the Union Army, and he still couldn't get accustomed to the cold. Clouds blocked the sun that might have warmed his skin, and the cold seemed to penetrate his layers of clothing and travel through his very skin to the bone. Of course, he hadn't seen snow until he was nearly thirty years old, and what he had called cold growing up would have been considered mild by many of the Northerners he fought alongside. It was hard to believe that he was actually in the South—Tennessee, to be exact. As close to home as he'd been in over two and a half years.

With a grimace and a slow exhale that fogged the air, Quint checked his pistols, two Colt Model 1860s, weapons he kept meticulously clean. With a Colt in each hand, he turned to the silent man at his side.

"Cover me, Candell."

Quint burst from shelter and sprinted over the frozen ground. With his appearance, the enemy fire increased once again, and he heard the whistle of the balls in the air around him as well as the sharp reports of the weapons themselves. With a final burst of energy, he leapt over the dead horse and landed nearly on top of Medfield. He descended on the wounded man and waited for the enemy fire to stop. Then Quint took a deep breath and rolled to one side, quickly looking over the private, who was trembling badly.

"Where are you hit?" Quint asked briskly.

"My leg." There were tears in Medfield's eyes, tear tracks down his dirty cheeks.

Quint assessed the wound in Medfield's calf without emotion. Painful, but not life-threatening as long as infection didn't set in.

"Listen to me, Private," he said sternly. There was no time for sympathy. Not now. That would come later. If they made it. "We're going to make a run for it."

"I can't . . ."

"You will, soldier!" Quint shouted as he placed a stony face close to the terrified private's. He couldn't allow Medfield to see any warmth or uncertainty. "It's going to hurt like hell, but you *will* move your goddamn feet!"

Quint reloaded one Colt and shoved the other into his waistband. He slid an arm around a suddenly less tearful private and looked into the young man's pale blue eyes. Eyes too young and innocent to see what they had seen today. Eyes that looked to his lieutenant to save him, to take care of him.

"Ready, soldier?" Quint felt a tightening in the pit of his belly. The attempt to rescue the private had been helpless, hopeless, but he could no sooner leave the boy there to be slaughtered or captured than he could shoot one of his own men.

They burst from the shelter of the dead horse, Quint's right side facing the fire that increased as he ran, practically dragging the wounded private as the young man attempted to move his legs. Quint raised his arm and fired aimlessly toward the invisible enemy, the Colt so natural in his hand that it felt like an extension of his arm.

He felt the sharp sting in his arm and dropped the pistol. Twenty more feet to go. He heard Medfield gasp in surprise and knew that somehow, even though the private was almost completely shielded by Quint's body, he had been hit again. Just a few more steps. Medfield was almost a dead weight, though Quint could hear the young man breathing raggedly.

The ball ripped into Quint's leg when he thought they were finally safe, tearing into his thigh and forcing him over the barricade in an awkward tumble. Medfield went first, and together they landed almost on top of the waiting soldiers.

"Lieutenant Tyler?" Candell hovered over him, panic in his voice as he gripped Quint's arm and leaned close to see if a breath stirred. A constant exchange of gunfire kept the Rebs at bay, though for how much longer no one could say.

Quint forced his eyes open, pushing away the comfort of darkness that threatened. The wound in his arm was little more than a scratch, but he recognized that the injury to his right thigh could be deadly. The wound was bleeding freely, and the ball was buried deep. He forced himself into a crouching position, with Candell's help, putting all of his weight on his left leg. Immediately his eyes fell on Medfield's body, that lifeless form not three feet away. The second ball had entered the private's back, and the farm boy was dead.

Quint closed his eyes and breathed a curse. All for nothing. But he had no time for recriminations, no time to wonder if there might have been another way.

"Let's go, Candell."

Two men carried Medfield's body, sharing the weight between them, and Candell placed a supporting arm around Quint.

Quint wanted to drop to the ground and let the darkness overtake him. He wanted to cry and scream for the boy who had died. But he showed no outward sign of giving in to either impulse. It was up to him to see that these boys survived another day.

He ordered the soldiers who continued to fire on the Rebs to retreat, and he and Candell brought up the rear, disappearing through the brush like pale, silent ghosts.

* * *

Quint sat up in the hospital bed, a place he had come to hate in the past weeks. He was in a large room full of hospital beds, a place where men died in the night and screamed in pain when there wasn't enough morphine. And this place was paradise compared to the field hospital.

He flexed his left leg, then his injured right leg. The pain shot through him like another bullet.

He was lucky to have his leg, and he knew that, though the knowledge did nothing to ease his mental anguish. It had been days after the skirmish before he'd heard the story, days he'd spent in a dark limbo. Weak from loss of blood, he'd passed out, and his unit had taken him to the field hospital. There they had gathered around him and shielded him from the surgeon who had decided that it would be simplest and safest to saw off the injured leg. Gangrene could set in. Death would follow. The lieutenant would be grateful to have his life. The surgeon's arguments had been delivered in a tired and lifeless voice, Candell had later told Quint. Surrounded by soldiers whose limbs had been cut away, Candell and the rest of the unit would not be swayed.

Even when they were threatened with severe discipline, the men had stood by him, and a colonel who had been called in to handle the situation was so impressed by their loyalty, and their story of his failed attempt to save Louis Medfield, that he'd sided with them, and Quint's leg was saved.

General Burnside's personal physician had seen to Quint that first week, at the Colonel's request, removing the ball that was buried deep in his thigh. And then Quint had been sent to this place.

He had his leg, but the physicians assured him that the damage was severe. And permanent. He would regain the use of his leg, but he would always have a limp. Possibly a debilitating one. The wound in his arm wouldn't have kept him away from his unit for even a day. He could have cleaned it and wrapped it himself and continued on. But the leg . . . his thigh had been pierced by a minie ball, a soft lead slug one-half inch in diameter and one inch long. It expanded on impact, producing a severe injury. Only time would tell if he would ever be able to return to battle. It would be a long time, at any rate, and even then he might be forced to transfer to the cavalry. A foot soldier with a disability that slowed him down endangered not only his own life, but the lives of the men around him.

Quint had been told by the physician, a man with an incongruous smile on his face and dead gray eyes, that he could count himself lucky. In a few days he would be able to go home to recuperate. Every soldier's dream.

But Quintin Tyler had no home to go to. He had left everything behind when he'd joined the Union Army. Everything. His family, his fiancée, his home. It was the latter that, surprisingly, he missed the most—the warm moist air, the towering oak trees, the big white house he had been born and raised in.

"Lieutenant Tyler." He had even come to hate

the sound of the ever-cheerful nurses' voices. Wives and widows of servicemen, most of them, doing what they could. Deep down, he admired them for what they did. The hospital could be a hellish place, yet they held a trembling hand or penned a letter to a patient's loved one without any visible reaction to the horror they saw every day. But he had seen their own hands tremble even as they smiled, and seen smiles fade as they turned from a dying man's bed.

In spite of his admiration, it was a fact that he had always lacked patience, and being confined to the bed made his impatience worse. Much worse.

"You have a visitor." The nurse, a pretty enough middle-aged woman with fair hair and honey-brown eyes, smiled. "Colonel Fairfax, Lieutenant Tyler is our most genial patient." She continued to smile even as she told the blatant lie, casting a sideways glance at the scowling man on the bed. "He's a delight to us all. I certainly hope you won't be taking him from us any time soon. Why, he's the sunshine of this ward."

"Sarcasm is never appreciated in the medical profession, Mrs. Nelson," Quint said in a low voice.

Colonel Fairfax ignored the exchange and stared at Quint intently, studying him, it seemed. Mrs. Nelson placed a chair at the colonel's side, and pulled a curtain around the bed to give them some privacy from the other patients who watched openly.

"Lieutenant Tyler. Good to see you looking so

fit." The colonel sat languidly in the straight-backed chair.

"Thank you, sir." Quint's voice was as dark as ever, suspicious and low.

"Where are you from, son?" The colonel continued to watch as if judging, openly curious.

"Mississippi, sir." Quint narrowed his eyes. What was this officer doing here? He'd never met Colonel Fairfax, and it certainly wasn't a social call. Quint knew his military career was all but over. That was painfully clear to everyone.

"Yes." The colonel nodded slightly. "I did wonder at the accent. To be honest, I have heard a good deal about you. The loyalty you instilled in your men is admirable, especially given that you're a Southerner. You were leading some of the greenest troops I've ever seen."

Quint ignored the insult to his men, since the offhand comment was probably true. "There are a number of Southerners serving in the Union Army, sir."

The colonel leaned forward, his eyes sharp and clear. "Why are you here, young man?"

Quint gave a short, derisive laugh. At thirty-two, he had ceased to think of himself as a young man. "That's rather personal, sir." A memory he had tried to bury flooded over him, as it sometimes did when he least expected it. Those unanticipated thoughts of Jonah always managed to surprise him.

"Your father is a planter, is he not?" the colonel pressed. "A slave owner?"

"If you knew that, then why did you bother to

26

ask where I was from . . . sir?" The pause was just long enough to be a mild insult, but the colonel didn't seem to mind.

"I just wanted to listen to you for a while. What you said is true. There are plenty of Southern boys in our army, each here for reasons of his own. A hatred for slavery, for the most part. But there are few Southerners of your . . . breeding . . . at our disposal."

Quint gave the colonel a wry smile, and felt suddenly lighter. He'd never been one to resign himself easily to defeat, and the colonel's words were oddly stimulating.

"Would you care to elaborate, sir?"

"The sooner we can stop supplies from reaching the Southern states, the sooner this damned war will be over." The colonel's easy manner was gone, and he was an officer again, giving instructions to an able soldier. "The blockade is successful in some areas, an abysmal failure in others. Those damn pilots can slip into the Cape Fear River almost at will. It's a lucrative business for the captains of these ships. A business they're not likely to give up easily."

"What does that have to do with me, sir? I'm no sailor." Quint's earlier anger had faded, and he was listening with interest to what the colonel had to say. He didn't understand it yet, but he knew there was a chance for him in it. A chance to continue his service in spite of the injury that had him bedridden.

Without the army, he was nothing, had nothing.

"The surgeons tell me you won't be soldiering for a while. That's a damn shame, a fine soldier like yourself. But you can still serve your country, Lieutenant Tyler. You can come to work for me and make a bigger difference than you ever dreamed."

"How is that, sir?" Quint was sitting up straighter and taller than he had been when the colonel had arrived. There was a wicked bent, he knew, to the smile that touched his lips, and the pain in his leg had subsided. He was ready to do whatever Colonel Fairfax asked of him.

The colonel grinned, deepening the wrinkles around his eyes. The smile passed quickly.

"Lieutenant Tyler." The colonel's voice was lowered, and he leaned close to the bed. "Have you ever been to Nassau?"

Chapter Two

Lily stood at the bow of the ship, the wind in her hair, the spray on her face. She was clad in black trousers, a loose linen shirt, and black boots that came nearly to her knees. It was the garb she always wore aboard the *Chameleon*.

They were almost home, and as they approached the island of New Providence she felt her heart lift in eagerness. It was such a beautiful place. Nassau had truly become her haven, and now, after an exhausting run, she had a place she could truly call home. A house in that quaint town, bought with the profits from her second run.

The *Chameleon* was a successful blockade runner, an iron-hulled screw steamer, painted slate gray and riding low in the water. Slipping past the Union blockaders was a dangerous game, one that always made Lily's heart beat faster, that always made her feel more alive than before. There was no more triumphant feeling than slipping past the Union ships, the crew silent, the throb of the engines muffled by the dank air and the waves crashing against the rocks as the *Chameleon* eased at a dead slow speed into the mouth of the Cape Fear River.

But it was more than a game. It was revenge. Revenge for her father's death.

If Elliot hadn't been so useless, Lily wouldn't have felt compelled to act. But it had become a matter of family honor. Honor meant nothing to Elliot. He was perfectly content to wait out the war at the London gaming tables, dining with the elite Englishmen who sympathized with the Southerners' cause.

So it was left to Lily. Elliot had been true to his word and had presented her with her inheritance once they were in London. She had been at a loss, not knowing what to do with the money. She wouldn't ensconce herself in London with Elliot and pretend that the war was nothing more than a nuisance. But it would be foolish for her to return home alone.

Tommy had shown her what to do. Actually, they had developed the plan together as they sat at Tommy and Cora's kitchen table, a pot of tea shared between them as Lily told Tommy of her father's death. He was as outraged as she, and Lily cried for the first time since she'd left her home. She cried as if her heart were broken, finally finding someone who mourned her father as she did.

Tommy Gibbon was her father's illegitimate half-brother, a fact that had been kept a deep, dark secret for many years. When James Radford discovered that he had a brother, he had approached the man himself, and James and Tommy had been close ever since. They didn't see one another often, and of course Elliot had always been embarrassed by Tommy's humble lifestyle. But Lily loved her uncle and his wife, the warm and pretty Cora. She saw in Tommy a bit of her father, though her uncle was rough around the edges, never having had the advantages his older brother had taken for granted.

It was not a good time for Tommy Gibbon when Lily found him in Liverpool. A sailor for most of his life, Tommy had fallen on hard times. He no longer wanted to stay away from his wife for weeks or even months, and the merchant ships he had served on were often at sea for that length of time. That hadn't been a problem when he was a bachelor, but once he found Cora, he changed.

So Tommy started his own business, a small mercantile in Liverpool. In spite of his good intentions and hard work, the business failed. Tommy had sorely underestimated the fierceness of his competition and the large amount of funding it would take to sustain his young business.

He was about to join the merchant fleet again and to leave Cora behind. They had no children, much to their dismay, and he hated to leave Cora at home alone. And she hated to be left behind.

It was Tommy's idea at first, though he quickly dismissed it as impractical. But a seed had been planted in Lily's brain, and she refused to let it die. Together they had hammered out the details, and the very next day they'd found themselves at the shipyards. Lily's inheritance was well spent.

When Elliot learned of her venture, he protested weakly, calling her plan insane, impossible, and improper. But in the end he had relented, as Lily had known he would. He couldn't stop her, so he didn't even make much of an effort.

Tommy had been a fine teacher, instructing her not only on how to operate her ship, but on how the engines worked and how to navigate using only the night sky as her guide. Lily was a quick study, and her love for the sea enhanced her ability to absorb what Tommy taught.

They'd made nearly a dozen runs since then, most of them uneventful, all of them extremely profitable. One summer night, they had been caught in a storm just hours from Nassau, but had managed to ride it out with no losses or injuries, and once they'd had to outrun a Union blockader off the coast of the Carolinas. A shot had been fired across the bow of the *Chameleon* before she disappeared into the fog, leaving the slower Union ship behind.

The *Chameleon* was not equipped with guns. Lily had no illusions about the dangers of her venture and had thought often of the possibility of capture. All of her crew were British, and if captured they would eventually be sent home. The British government would see to that. With no show of force from the *Chameleon,* she would be treated as the merchant ship she was.

As for Lily herself . . . there was a plan. A well thought-out plan for such a contingency.

The profits were made primarily on the luxury items that filled the cargo hold—and on the cotton that was carried out. The rest of the space was reserved for supplies for the Confederacy. Blankets, medicine, shoes, material for uniforms, Enfield rifles, gunpowder, cartridges, percussion caps . . .

"Cap'n?"

Lily turned and faced the young sailor who approached warily. "Aye?"

"The chief engineer says we're goin' to be needin' coal before much longer." The youth had a strong cockney accent, one Lily had become familiar with. "'E wants to know if we're goin' straight on to Cuba, or if . . ."

"There's enough coal to get us to Nassau to unload this cotton first, before the *Lady Anne* sails for England, and to sail to Cuba to take on coal tomorrow." Lily suppressed the urge to smile. She was always somewhat reserved around her crew, but had come to know them all well. Reggie Smythe was a damn fine engineer, but he always became testy toward the end of a run. And Lily couldn't blame him. The engine room was an unbearably hot and uncomfortable place to spend the better part of a week.

"Aye, Cap'n." The young sailor bowed slightly and turned away. It had taken him a while, as it had all of them, to accept Lily as their captain. She knew that very well. But they did accept her, each for his own reason. Every one of the crew helped to perpetuate the myth of the mysterious Captain Robert Sherwood as well. It had even

33

become an enjoyable game for them.

Captain Sherwood had been Lily's own invention, a fictional captain for the *Chameleon*. She was certain the idea of a woman captain would be too much for most people to accept, and too tempting to the Union blockaders. It was one thing to be bested by a legendary British captain, but quite another to be beaten by a woman. Lily was certain that the knowledge that she was captain of her own ship would cause the Union to single her out for capture, and she couldn't do that to her crew.

But she looked forward to the day when she could let her adversaries know that it was she who had slipped past them in the night.

It was amazing how many residents and visitors to Nassau now claimed to know Captain Sherwood. When Lily went shopping, the merchants often asked her to give the Captain their best, and they would swear to anyone who asked that they had met the man. It was difficult at times to keep a straight face when confronted with this phenomenon, but Lily managed. She was becoming quite an actress.

"Captain." Tommy's deep voice startled her. "You should be resting." Tommy always expressed concern at how little Lily slept during their voyages. A couple of hours a night were all she could manage, between taking the wheel and setting the course, seeing that the cargo was properly secured and that the crew functioned well. Many of the tasks she took on could have been handled by others, but that was not Lily's way.

"I'll sleep for two days once we get home." She allowed herself a small smile for her uncle. Tommy would have made a wonderful captain, and she sometimes wondered if he might not decide to buy his own steamer someday and strike out on his own. He had offered to captain her ship, while she stayed at home and collected most of the profits. That didn't seem fair to Lily, and she had a deeply ingrained sense of what was fair. Her crew received a better share of the profits than did most blockade runners' crews. It was a dangerous business, and Lily was well aware of that. She made certain that her crew was aware of that also. Her own profits were still outrageous, but that wasn't what compelled her. It was the vision of her father that drove her, the vision of him standing there holding his pipe, wondering what had gone wrong.

Tommy watched his niece as she turned to once again stare at the sea before her. James had once said that Lily had salt water in her veins, and that he had never met another woman who loved the sea as she did. She seemed to gain life from the salt air itself, from the spray that rose and rained on her. Lily turned her face upward to the sun and grasped the polished rail with strong hands—hands that were capable of taking the wheel of the steamer and guiding her through the narrow channels or holding her steady through a summer squall.

"Another good run," he said to her back.

"Aye, that it was," she agreed, her thoughts evidently elsewhere. Probably on the next run, if Tommy knew her as well as he thought he did.

"You're beginning to sound like a Liverpool dock rat," he said with affection. If he and Cora had been able to have children, he couldn't imagine that he would have loved them any more than he loved his niece Lily. With a smile, his thoughts turned to his wife. Cora awaited their arrival in Nassau. His voyages now kept him away from her for days, not months, and the profits were much grander. It was a good life they were living, thanks to Lily.

He knew that what they were doing was perilous, and that for a woman to dress in trousers and take command of a ship was unheard of—especially in the society Lily had been raised in, a courtly society where the pirate Anne Bonny was probably dismissed as a legend. If he could have convinced Lily to stay home and let him take the risks for her, he would have.

But he couldn't, so he became her right-hand man, her first mate, and this was where he would stay. Until the war was over. Until her mission was done.

Quint limped down the walkway, the picturesque shops he passed becoming familiar to him after four days in Nassau. He paid them little mind. It was a bad day as far as his leg was concerned, the pain shooting through his thigh with each step. The surgeon had said it would take some time—though how much time he'd refused to guess—and that for the rest of his life Quint would have days when his leg pained him. Damn it all! Months had passed, and he still felt like an invalid. Quint leaned on the hated cane, the sleek black cane with the gold handle—a serpent's head—grasped in his right hand.

At last he came to the house he was looking for. His contact's home. There was nothing about the cottage to set it apart from the surrounding houses. They were all tidy and well tended, and everyone had attempted to fight the native foliage that sought to encroach on their homes.

For the past four days, Quint had done nothing but establish himself in the best hotel in town and seek out the readily available games of chance. He had lost on one night as much as he had won the night before, and had readily identified the Confederate partisans he was expected to befriend.

The whole damn island was coursing with Southern sympathizers. Quint fit right in, with his cultured accent and the well-cut gentleman's clothes the colonel had provided for him. It was hard not to fit in, on an island populated almost entirely with Southerners, an island that had become a sanctuary for the blockade runners and their crews.

A uniformed servant opened the door quickly after Quint's knock, and he wondered if he was expected. Colonel Fairfax had only told him to make contact when he felt it was safe to do so.

"Quintin Tyler to see Mrs. Slocum." He presented himself to the woman, distancing himself with the scowl that had become a natural part of his countenance, a look that warned others to leave him alone. He had to work to remove that grimace from his face when he sat across from the Rebel sympathizers and the blockade runners who supplied the South. He didn't think he had the makings of a very successful spy.

The maid ushered him into a well-stocked library, a semi-dark room where every wall was lined with books and the furnishings were dark and masculine. He noted that there was not a single cut flower, not a speck of lace in the room to show that the house was inhabited by a woman.

Mrs. Slocum rose to meet him, and he was surprised once again. He had been expecting an older woman. Colonel Fairfax had told him that Eleanor Slocum was a widow, and Quint had pictured a gray-haired old lady dabbling in the spy game. But the lovely dark-haired woman who greeted him couldn't be much older than he was. He really didn't want to know how many young widows the war had produced.

"Thank you, Naomi." She dismissed the servant with an even smile and in an accent much like his own, deep and slow. She never took her eyes from him, never glanced at the servant who left silently, or dropped her gaze to the desk. She was studying him critically, and with a satisfied smile on her handsome face.

Quint didn't attempt to hide his impatience from her, and he didn't return her smile.

"Mr. Tyler," she said, circling around the desk, holding the voluminous skirt of her black silk dress in both hands. "Lieutenant Tyler," she corrected herself softly. "Welcome to Nassau."

Quint bowed at the waist, a curt and almost insolent greeting. "Mrs. Slocum. I suppose you know why I'm here. Shall we get on with it?"

She didn't seem at all put out by his attitude, but remained placid. "Please call me Eleanor, Quintin."

She sighed with what might have been resignation and returned to her desk. "We will be spending quite a bit of time together in the next several weeks. All information you collect is to be delivered to me." She was suddenly curt, businesslike, and she offered Quint a chair with a wave of her slender hand. "Have you met any of our colorful blockade runners yet?" Her tone was sardonic, and she gave Quint a half-smile. "The heroes of the South?"

"I met a Captain Dennison, and a bull of a man named John Wright." Quint took the chair, grateful to be able to take the weight off of his bad leg. He extended it before him gingerly. "I lost a bit of money to them both."

"Good. Lose a bit more. I can replenish your funds when you deliver your information." She placed her elbows on the desk in little-girl fashion and rested her chin in her hands. "Have you heard of a Captain Robert Sherwood?"

"I heard his name mentioned once or twice, but I haven't met him."

"His ship has been out for eight days, so you

wouldn't have had the opportunity. Not yet. He might be difficult to get close to. Captain Sherwood doesn't show himself around town like the other captains do. He . . . keeps to himself, he and his woman."

"His woman?"

"Yes. I've heard rumors that he has a wife in England, but he lives on this island with a Southern woman. Miss Lily Radford."

There was pure dislike in her voice, almost venomous, and Quint wasn't certain if it was for Miss Radford or for Southern females in general. Odd, since Eleanor Slocum was so obviously of Southern heritage herself.

"Miss Radford comes to town on occasion, and the Captain apparently makes an appearance now and again, but I have never seen him."

Quint leaned back in his chair, for a moment able to forget the pain in his leg. "That seems strange. He doesn't have to hide. No one on this island bothers to conceal their involvement with the blockade-running enterprise. On the contrary. They're local icons who feed the economy."

Eleanor shrugged. "Sherwood's very successful. It would be a notable distinction for us if we could aid in his capture."

"He doesn't live in the hotel, I take it."

Eleanor smiled. "Lily Radford owns a house just south of here. A lovely two-story white house with a private path to the beach. Sherwood has been seen, on occasion, walking that path draped in a hooded cloak. Depending on who you talk to he's short, he's tall, he's fat, he's thin. The man is a regular chameleon." Her smile widened. "That's the name of his ship. The *Chameleon*."

"Should I concentrate on Captain Sherwood?"

Eleanor shrugged her shoulders. "Not necessarily. But keep your eyes open. I'd like to get this one." She gave Quint a misty-eyed look. "This war won't be over until we can stop the blockade runners. When the South is starving and they have no ammunition . . . then this nightmare can end."

Quint wanted to ask her what had motivated her to become involved. Was she really a widow, or was that simply her cover? If she was a widow, had her husband's death driven her to become a spy?

"Our story is that you and I are old friends, who are going to become lovers." Eleanor smiled at Quint's raised eyebrows and the questioning tilt of his head.

"Don't worry," she said quickly. "I don't plan to carry my dedication to the Union quite that far. But the appearance of our involvement will give you an opportunity to come and go at any time, day or night. Discreetly, of course," she added wryly. "I have my reputation to think of."

Eleanor stood, and Quint knew that he was dismissed. Leaving his troops behind and becoming a spy still didn't sit well with him, but he was beginning to see what he might be capable of. If the blockaders knew when and where to expect the smaller and faster steamers, they could set up an effective trap and make blockade running unprofitable for their captains.

He walked back to the hotel less conscious of the pain in his leg than he had been earlier. His mind was on other concerns. Captain Sherwood. For some reason the man intrigued Quint . . . a mysterious captain who hid from the rest of the world.　.

With a new purpose, Quint entered his fine hotel with a reluctant grin on his face. Sherwood wasn't even on the island, if Eleanor's information was correct. But she would be—his mistress. The Lily Radford that Eleanor had spoken of with such obvious distaste. She was undoubtedly still on the island. Perhaps that was the way to proceed. Meet the man through his mistress.

Quint spotted James Dennison in the doorway to the dining room and approached with his friendliest smile set in place. "Captain," he called when he was a few feet from the tall, thin seaman. "Please tell me you'll give me an opportunity to win back some of the money I lost to you last night."

Captain Dennison grinned at Quint, flashing straight, white teeth set in a sun-bronzed face as he straightened his royal blue jacket. His joy at the opportunity presented him was evident in twinkling blue eyes.

"Aye, Tyler. I'd be happy to take a bit more o' your gold." Dennison sounded like a pirate of old, his accent as strange to Quint as his own well-bred Southern accent most likely was to the Englishman.

"I met an interesting woman this afternoon," Quint said as they walked to their table together.

They'd share a meal and a few glasses of rum before the gambling began. "I was wondering if you might be acquainted with her. A Miss Lily Radford."

Dennison smiled wickedly. "Ah, so you've finally met Miss Lily. She's a beauty, that one."

Quint nodded, though he had no idea what Lily Radford might look like.

"I'll warn you, though," Dennison continued as he folded his tall frame into a comfortable chair. "She's Captain Sherwood's woman, and he's a right jealous one, he is."

"Really?" Quint managed to look disappointed. "His woman, you say. Not his wife?"

"Don't be gettin' ideas, Tyler," Dennison warned, his grin fading and the sparkle leaving his pale eyes.

They were silent as a waiter placed, without asking, two full glasses of rum before them. The dining room would soon be full, but at the moment most of the tables were unoccupied. Quint was always more comfortable later in the evening, when the room was full and smoky and he felt almost invisible.

"Is Captain Sherwood a friend of yours?"

Dennison hesitated before answering, but only briefly. "Aye, he is. Take caution, mate. He wouldn't like you showin' an interest in Miss Lily. He'll run you through, cut out your heart, and have it for breakfast." Dennison lowered his voice as he finished delivering his warning. "Forget about Miss Lily."

Quint raised his glass in salute to the gregarious captain across from him. "Thank you for the warning, my friend. I've never met a woman I'd literally lose my heart for."

They both laughed heartily and moved on to other subjects of interest, but Quint's mind was never very far from the mysterious Captain Sherwood and his woman, Lily Radford.

Chapter Three

Lily strolled down the sidewalk at a leisurely pace, a parasol shading her face from the sun. It wasn't evident to those who watched that it was an effort for her to maintain the slow pace, that she wanted to stride quickly into town and get this chore over with. Her lavender gown was fussy and uncomfortable, but Lily controlled the urge to squirm in the scratchy petticoats and to crane her neck against the lace that brushed her throat. She'd drawn the line at the corset Cora had laid out for her and had left the torturous device where she'd found it, draped across a chair in her bedroom.

These appearances in town were necessary, though she dreaded the excursions. Lily smiled widely and vacantly at everyone who passed and nodded to those gentlemen who tipped their hats, but she never stopped to chat. On occasion she used her parasol like a shield, dipping it down to come between her face and the eyes of a passerby who stared too hard, too openly. She never stopped to chat. It would be foolish to invite friendship, closeness of any kind, when Nassau was swarming with spies.

She closed her lavender parasol that so perfectly matched her dress, and stepped into the fashionable shop, closing the door gently behind her. There was, fortunately, only one other patron present, a gossipy middle-aged woman Lily had met several times. Perfect.

"I simply must have that stunning hat you have displayed in your window." Lily smiled at the shopkeeper. It had taken her months to remove the English influence from her voice, but she had accomplished that quite well. She wondered what Elliot would say if he could hear her, and if he would realize that she was mimicking all the girls he had so admired. No. He wouldn't comprehend that at all. He would think that she had finally become a lady. A real Southern lady.

"I know I shouldn't purchase a single thing. The Captain brings me more gowns and hats than I will ever be able to wear, but . . ." She positively simpered. "I simply must have that hat."

The shopkeeper, an elderly man named Terrence who had lived on the island for years, removed the hat from the window with great care and handed it to Lily with a slight bending of his waist in a courteous bow. She was always treated well here, but then, she was one of his best customers. In spite of her *Captain's* gifts.

Lily placed the hat on her head. She studied her image in the mirror from the front, from each side, and over her shoulder. Terrence and

Mrs. Greene watched her closely. It was a hideous hat.

"How is the Captain, Miss Radford?" Mrs. Greene asked boldly.

"How very kind of you to ask, Mrs. Greene." Lily fluttered her lashes as she glanced over her shoulder at the nosy woman. "He's quite well. Exhausted, as he always is when he returns from one of his jaunts. What do you think of this hat?"

Mrs. Greene's eyes widened as she studied the wide-brimmed hat that was festooned with ribbons and bows in several different colors. "It's lovely, dear. Just lovely." Mrs. Greene was a poor liar. "Will you and the Captain be at the ball on Saturday?"

"Perhaps," Lily answered coyly. Another bloody ball. "I'm afraid the Captain might not be feeling up to it, so soon after a tryin' voyage."

"But surely . . ."

"I'll take this fabulous hat." Lily withdrew a silver coin from her bag. "The Captain will understand."

She heard the door open and braced herself to face another of Nassau's citizens. With the ridiculous hat still perched on her head, and a practiced and insipid smile on her face, Lily turned away from the shopkeeper.

"Mr. Tyler," Terrence greeted the new customer, reaching under the counter and withdrawing a box of cigars. "These just came in this morning."

Lily found herself staring into the eyes of a stranger. He didn't look away, but held her gaze with his dark eyes, eyes that announced his interest and suggested at mischief in their depths. The man ignored Terrence's offered cigars and smiled at her as if she were some wharf-side doxy.

There was something mesmerizing about the stranger. His black suit fit him well, but was perfectly ordinary. It was his eyes that were so fascinating. He should have had black hair, with those dark eyes and lashes, but he didn't. His full hair was an ash brown, without a touch of red or gold, and an errant lock fell across his forehead. It only made his eyes seem darker, deeper, and more powerful.

She lifted the hat from her head and turned away from the man. Stupid, stupid girl, Lily chided herself. She had expected to find herself face to face with someone like Mrs. Greene. Safe. Familiar. Easy to fool. The man with the cane and the dark eyes that seemed to see right through her had given her a start. Handsome and tall, dark and powerful, he had forced her to turn away. Lily didn't like being caught off guard.

She was about to make a quiet escape when he stopped her.

"Terrence," the stranger chided the shopkeeper. "Surely you're not going to allow this young lady to leave without first introducing us properly. I'm a newcomer here, and it can be so difficult to meet all the residents of your lovely town."

Lily took a deep breath, steeling herself, and turned with her vacant smile in place. He was staring at her—no, through her—and it was harder than ever to keep up her carefully crafted masquerade.

"Quintin Tyler," Terrence began, "this is Miss Lily Radford. Miss Lily, Mr. Tyler is a new resident of Nassau. He plans to stay for a while, I believe."

Quintin Tyler's eyes widened, just slightly. He must have heard of her and of her scandalous relationship with "the Captain." That moment of surprise passed quickly, and he stepped forward and took her offered hand in his left. Lily's hands were gloved, as they always were when she ventured into town, even though the day was warm.

He pressed that hand to his lips and held it there a moment longer than was necessary or proper. Lily could feel his breath on her skin, through the thin white cotton that covered her hand, and a faint tremor made its way up her spine.

"How charming," she managed to say as he rose to stare at her again. The man had no manners at all! "Have you met Mrs. Greene?" Lily smiled at the matron, who approached them anxiously. "She's one of the very most important people in Nassau. Why, everyone who's anyone knows Mrs. Greene."

As Tyler reluctantly turned to meet Mrs. Greene, Lily made her escape, spinning away from the man who had kissed her hand and held it just a bit too long. As she stepped out of the store and closed the door quietly behind her, Lily took a deep breath and sighed with relief. She hated these trips. It was easier to outrun a Union blockader than it was to paste that silly smile on her face and pretend to be the kind of woman she detested.

Lily barely had time to open her parasol and take two steps before Quintin Tyler emerged from the shop. She wanted to run, but knew she could not.

"Might I walk you home, Miss Radford?" He joined her, his steps matching hers, his limp not slowing him down as she increased her pace slightly.

"That's not necessary, Mr. Tyler," Lily answered without looking at him.

"It would be my pleasure."

Lily resigned herself and slowed her pace. "How kind you are, Mr. Tyler."

"Quint."

Lily giggled. It sounded forced and inane even to her own ears. "Why, Mr. Tyler. We've only just met. I couldn't possibly call you by your given name."

"Does that mean I can't call you Lily?"

She felt a sudden chill at the way he said her name. She liked it, and immediately regretted her weakness. "Yes, it does. What are you doing in Nassau, Mr. Tyler?"

"Gambling, mostly," he answered with an unconcerned shrug, watching her closely with those dark eyes. Lily tensed, and perhaps he saw it, because his wicked smile faded. "Unsuccessfully, if it makes you feel any better."

Lily smiled in spite of herself, and for a moment it was her own, true smile, unrestrained. Then she caught herself and it was gone.

"Gamblin' is a sin, Mr. Tyler."

"Not the only sin I've ever committed," he answered cryptically.

Lily gave him a sidelong glance. He had a strong profile, and his nose had apparently been broken at one time and had healed improperly, leaving a slight bump on the bridge of his otherwise perfect nose. It should have made him less attractive, but it suited him somehow, as did the dimple that appeared when he smiled. She knew it was time to mention "the Captain," to make certain he knew that she was the Captain's lady. But she didn't.

"You seem to have forgotten your cigars, Mr. Tyler." She spoke to him in a lightly chastising voice.

"I left in rather a hurry, Miss Radford." He didn't have to say that he'd left Terrence's shop quickly in order to catch up with her. They both knew that and avoided the fact smoothly. "I'll pick them up later this afternoon."

Lily took a deep breath and pulled her eyes away from his face. There was something very natural about walking home with Quintin Tyler.

"Do you like Nassau, Mr. Tyler?"

He smiled at her again, and her stomach did a funny little twist that she definitely did not like. She was not a silly little flirt, looking for an afternoon's entertainment in this man's company!

"It's beautiful, of course," he answered. "The weather is perfect, and at night you can smell the

51

sea if you leave your windows open."

"I always do," Lily answered too quickly. "I like the smell of the salt air."

They fell into a comfortable stride, silent much of the time, though Tyler asked Lily questions about the houses they passed before they turned onto the stone path. The path to Lily's house was tree-lined and abandoned, shaded and fragrant. Lily found it discomforting to be alone with Quintin Tyler, really alone, though she knew that when they turned the bend and the house was in view, Cora would be watching from a window. Watching and waiting.

Usually, Tommy was there also, but he and the *Chameleon* were on their way back from Cuba, freshly supplied with anthracite coal.

Lily's home was a small two-story house, painted white with dark green shutters and a red door. Blooming plants grew along the path and against the house itself, and lace curtains wafted through open windows. It was a warm and inviting place, a real home.

"What a lovely house," Tyler said as they approached, stopping on the walkway that led to the red door.

"Thank you." Lily gazed at the ground, purposely avoiding those dark eyes. He looked at her as if he could see through her disguise. But that was impossible.

Tyler took her chin in his hand and lifted her face. He gave her the most devilish grin she had ever seen, then leaned just a little bit closer. Lily's heart skipped a beat.

"I should like to kiss you, Lily Radford," he said in a low voice.

"Well, you may not," Lily answered, but there was a hesitancy in her voice. And she didn't draw away. She wanted to know, just this once, what it was like to be kissed by a man like Quintin Tyler.

Tyler lowered his lips slowly to cover hers. He still held her chin in his left hand, but his touch was light, caressing even. She could have moved away, but she didn't. She was tense when his lips first touched hers, shocked at the intense sensation the contact stirred, but then she relaxed, and her lips parted slightly.

Lily closed her eyes and marveled at the feelings the simple kiss aroused. The wonderfully soft pressure of his lips against hers. A tightening in her chest, a fluttering in her belly. And then he released her as gently and easily as he had taken her.

Quintin Tyler was looking down at her with a slight frown on his face. "I'd like to see you again, Miss Radford." His voice was low. Low and too intimate.

Lily glanced to the ground. "I . . . I can't." She was a fool, even after all this time. She steeled herself, knowing what she had to do and hating it all the same. "You'll learn soon enough, I suppose," she said, raising her head to meet Tyler's questioning stare. His eyes were a dark brown, almost black. Deep enough to fall into and get lost.

"I'm involved with someone else. Captain

Sherwood. It's quite scandalous, I know," she said in a chiding voice. "But that's just the way it is. You're a charming gentleman, Mr. Tyler." She said the word gentleman as if it were meant to be an insult, reminding herself of Elliot and men like him. "I'm certain you'll have no trouble finding yourself a young woman who will succumb to those charms."

"And you are immune?" He jested with her, a smile on his face and in his voice once again.

"Most definitely," she said too sternly.

Tyler took her gloved hand in his and kissed it, allowing his lips to linger. She felt the heat of those lips through the gloves and pulled her hand away.

"Good afternoon, Mr. Tyler." Lily turned away from him and, silly hat in hand, entered the house without a backward glance. Once inside, she flattened her back against the door and dropped the hat to the floor.

She waited there for several minutes before she went to a window, a window off the parlor. He was still there, staring at the red door as if she were going to appear there and request another kiss.

"Bloody hell," she whispered under her breath. He couldn't have heard her, but his head turned in her direction and she spun away from the window, only to find herself face to face with Cora.

"And who were you kissin' on the front lawn?" her aunt asked testily.

"Quintin Tyler." Lily spat the name as she impatiently yanked off her gloves and tossed them onto a table. She stared down at her hands. They were not the hands of a lady. Her nails were filed short, and there were calluses on her palms. "Some degenerate gambler who's hiding here the way Elliot is hiding in London."

"Well, why didn't you invite 'im in for a cup o' tea?" Cora asked contemptuously, hands on her hips.

Lily stepped back to the window, but stood far enough away that he couldn't possibly see her. She could still feel the warmth of his kiss on her lips. He was a stranger, and she had allowed him to kiss her. Had *wanted* him to kiss her. Less than an hour ago she hadn't known Quintin Tyler existed, but he had stormed into her life with the force of a hurricane.

"God help me, Cora, I almost did." Her voice was so soft, she wasn't certain her aunt could hear her. They both watched as Tyler finally turned away from the house and walked slowly away from them, his limp more pronounced now. Some of his swagger was gone, and Lily was almost certain she saw a hint of defeat in the way he leaned against his cane as he disappeared along the shaded path.

Quint stopped when he could no longer see Lily Radford's charming house. He stepped off the stone path and leaned his back against the trunk of a tall tree, one of the many that shaded the walkway.

He closed his eyes and saw her face. He saw turquoise eyes the color of the water that surrounded the island . . . an indescribable blue-green, clear and bright. He saw dark blond hair that refused to be completely tamed, those curls streaked as though bleached by the sun. He saw freckles, an unlikely sprinkling across her nose, and lips . . . lips that looked as if they'd been sculpted by a master.

Quint brought his palm to his forehead. Damn it all, this was the last complication he needed. When he'd seen her in Terrence's shop, he'd been entranced. In spite of her overdone dress and that hideous hat. In spite of a vapid smile that could not disguise the spark of intelligence in her eyes. She had been, during those moments, a bright spot in his dark life, solace of beauty and spirit.

He hadn't known, then, that she was Lily Radford. Dennison had been right. She was a beauty, but not like his sisters or their friends, or even Alicia, the woman he'd once been engaged to marry. Why couldn't she have been someone else? Anyone else? Why did he have to remind himself that she was Captain Sherwood's mistress . . . the enemy?

She spoke with that Southern influence that reminded him too much of his sisters and Alicia—cloyingly sweet and insincere. That voice and her vacant smile didn't fit her, didn't fit with the flash of fire he had seen in her eyes so briefly. Had he imagined it?

He hadn't imagined that kiss. If he didn't know better, he would swear she had never been kissed before . . . at least, not like that. Sweet and passionate. Simple and perfect. Lily had stood before him as if she hadn't known what to expect. But that was impossible. She was the Captain's mistress.

And she was the enemy. Damn it all, what was he supposed to do now?

Chapter Four

Lily sat at the vanity table in her bedroom while Cora styled her hair, pulling a bit too roughly at times and muttering under her breath.

"I didn't make an appearance last time, Cora," Lily defended herself unnecessarily. "We can't have people getting too suspicious."

"Humph." Cora coiled a strand of dark blond hair atop Lily's head. "Your decision wouldn't 'ave anything to do with that bloke who walked you 'ome the other day, would it?"

Lily glanced over her shoulder at her aunt, momentarily halting the styling process. "Don't be ridiculous. I can't possibly afford to get interested in a—in a man at this point. It would be too dangerous."

Cora Gibbon was in her mid-thirties, several years younger than her husband Tommy, and was as frail and feminine-looking as any English lass could be. She'd made it clear on more than one occasion that she didn't understand her husband's niece. But Cora had taken her place beside Tommy, and that meant beside Lily as well.

She'd tried to be a feminine influence in Lily's life, while loudly bemoaning Lily's lack of decorum. Several times she'd sworn that her husband's niece was a lost cause and would never be a lady. Lily merely smiled at that insult. She didn't want to be a lady. She never had.

"I'm afraid one o' these days you'll make a mistake, and then where will we be?" Cora asked. "You won't 'ave just the Yanks to worry about, but the people o' this island as well. Do you think they'll take kindly to the news that you've been making fools o' them all this time? I think not. And if you're so certain that going to this ball 'as nothing to do with that young fella, then wear the pink gown instead o' the blue."

Lily faced front and Cora resumed styling the locks that were usually left unrestrained. Her aunt had all but issued a challenge. Lily, when in public, made it a point to wear bright, fussy clothing. People tended to look at the gaudy dresses instead of her, and she was better able to play her part. Bright pinks and lavenders were her favorites, and the more rosettes and flounces, the better.

"I wore the pink last time. Even in a time of war, a proper young lady must not be seen in the same gown twice." Lily used her whining voice for that last statement, and her aunt burst into laughter.

But there were other gowns to choose from—gowns gaudier and fussier than the sapphire blue Lily had laid out for the evening. And, though she would never admit it to Cora, she did wonder what Quintin Tyler would think of her in the fashionable gown.

In the days since he'd walked her home, she hadn't been able to close her eyes without seeing his dark eyes and that dimple in his cheek. She was becoming obsessed, and she couldn't afford to let that happen. Not now. Maybe later, when the war was over and her days as captain of the *Chameleon* came to an end, she could think of marriage and a family. If she could find a man who wouldn't mind being married to a woman who dared to throw herself into the thick of a war. Lily knew she wouldn't marry any man without telling him the truth. All of it.

Marriage. The idea had popped into her head so easily, but in the past Lily had never stopped to think of it for herself. The men her father had presented for her inspection hadn't interested her at all, and in truth she realized that she interested them even less. They wanted women like the Lily Radford she pretended to be, sweet and not too intelligent. Willing to be led. Decorative and ultimately useless, in Lily's opinion. Of course, that was the woman Quintin Tyler believed her to be. That was the woman he had kissed.

She leaned closer to the mirror, studying the freckles that were sprinkled lightly across her nose. "Should I powder my face to cover these freckles, Cora?"

Cora clucked and rolled her eyes. "You've never thought it necessary before. This must 'ave something to do with that—"

"Don't say it," Lily warned, meeting her aunt's eyes in the mirror. Cora chuckled and laid her hands on Lily's shoulders.

"You've a beautiful complexion, Lily dear. Don't cover it with 'eavy powder just to hide a few freckles that are, in fact, quite lovely."

"Men don't like freckles."

Cora raised her eyebrows. "And since when 'ave you given a fig for what men like?"

Since Quintin Tyler kissed me, Lily thought, but she didn't answer her aunt. It was just a kiss, for God's sake. A kiss from a gambler who was too much like Elliot for her tastes. Were some people just better kissers than others? She'd never thought of that, but no kiss had ever stirred her the way his had. She could close her eyes and almost feel his mouth against hers, and it was frustratingly real. All she had to compare it with were a few clumsy and awkward attempts from young beaux, and her response to those kisses had been mild, to say the least. Perhaps Quintin Tyler was just a well-practiced womanizer, skilled in the art of seduction.

Damn his eyes! Why had he kissed her?

Lily stepped down from the carriage in front of the hotel. The sounds of the ball that was already in progress wafted through the doors and filled the dark night with echoes of laughter and music. As soon as she was safely down and clear of the carriage, it pulled away, before anyone had a chance to study the cloaked figure inside. It was only Tommy, of course, but anyone who caught a glimpse of the figure would believe that it was Captain Sherwood.

The ballroom was awash with bright light, and a sight to behold with the ladies in their fine gowns and the gentlemen in their evening wear, black and blue and burgundy. The musicians were playing a waltz, and brightly clad figures whirled across the floor, laughing and spinning, full skirts floating around the dancing ladies as they smiled up at their gentlemen.

Lily stood in the wide doorway and searched the room quickly, looking for Quintin Tyler. She saw many familiar faces, but not the one she was hoping, was dreading, to see. A wave of relief mixed with regret washed over her. Perhaps he wouldn't even attend.

"Why, Lily Radford." She was approached by a young woman whose name escaped Lily, a flighty girl with pale hair and white skin who always commented on how much she admired Lily's taste in clothes. "Where is that Captain of yours?" she drawled. "I was so hopin' that we might have a dance this evenin'."

Lily returned the girl's vacuous smile. "The Captain has some . . . something to check on his boat." Lily waved her gloved hand as if annoyed. "I declare, sometimes I think he likes that little ol' boat better than he likes me. He'll be here later. He promised me that he would be."

The men descended on Lily then, and she began the charade of dancing across the floor in their stiff arms, chatting about her Captain and smiling until she thought her face would crack.

Cora had been right. She never should have come here. Not tonight. At least her partners looked at her, and not through her, the way Quintin Tyler would have, had he been dancing with her.

Quint stood in the open doorway that led to the balcony, watching her. He tapped his cane restlessly against the floor and leaned against the doorjamb. His evening clothes were black, all but the white linen shirt he wore. Some of the men were dressed almost as gaily as the women, but Quint was not in a festive spirit. His somber clothing reflected that mood.

Lily Radford had danced one waltz after another, moving effortlessly across the floor in the arms of a succession of men, none of them the infamous Captain Sherwood. As he watched Lily, his black mood festered. Why her? He couldn't take his eyes from her, not from the moment he'd stepped into the room. The bodice of her sapphire dress clung to her seductively, free of the lace and ruffles so prominent in the room. Her gown was modestly cut, compared to some of the daring necklines that had danced past him during the evening, but he found hers the most enchanting. He found *her* the most enchanting.

He wasn't cut out for this spy business. In the days since he'd met her, he hadn't been able to get Lily Radford out of his mind. And he was supposed to use her to get to Captain Sherwood.

Lily was looking up into the face of some adoring sailor, a young man who leaned close to speak to his dance partner and was rewarded with a smile and a giggle. Her sapphire blue gloves came to her elbows, a perfect match to her gown, and Quint's eyes were fixed on her fingers as they rested against her partner's arm. As the sailor spun her around again, she saw him standing there. Lily's bright smile faded, but only briefly, as their eyes met. Quint gave her a brief bow, a curt and silent greeting as he grinned crookedly. Their eye contact was broken only when her dance partner spun her away again.

Dancers passed between them, a blur of color, and with a grunt of displeasure Quint stepped onto the large balcony, grateful to find it deserted for once. Damn it all, he should have known that he would have to watch her dance with other men.

The music stopped, and a few dancers joined him to enjoy the fresh, cool air. They whispered, lovers' whispers in the semi-dark seclusion. Quint looked away from them, over the railing to the sea that sparkled in the moonlight.

"Mr. Tyler."

He would have known that voice anywhere, and he put his grin in place before he turned to face her.

"Miss Radford." She stood alone in the doorway, her face shadowed and her stance hesitant. "You look splendid this evening."

"How gracious of you to say so, Mr. Tyler." She stepped toward him. "I do wish you would save me from these ever-vigilant and energetic young men. They seem determined to exhaust me before the evenin' is done." Lily stood next to him on the balcony and gripped the rail, closing her eyes and taking a deep breath of the sea air she'd claimed to love so much. Her lips parted slightly as she exhaled slowly, and Quint saw her visibly relax. The tension left her face and her stiff shoulders, and she looked remarkably content.

"I wish I were able to dance with you myself, Miss Radford," Quint said truthfully.

"I'm ever so glad that you cannot," Lily said, and she turned to face him just as he frowned at her statement. "Don't take that the wrong way, Mr. Tyler. It's just that I hate to dance, and I—"

"You hate to dance? How odd. And you dance so well. You're not saying that just to make me feel better, are you?"

Lily shook her head. "No. All the while I'm dancing, in my head I'm thinking one, two, three, one, two, three, don't step on toes, one, two, three." Off guard, she gave him a genuine smile, and he saw the flicker of intrigue in her eyes. But she was still wary of him. It would not be easy to win her trust.

"How did you hurt your leg?" she asked, changing the subject. "In the war?"

"No," he said adamantly. "I fell from a rather spirited horse several years ago and managed to break my leg in three places. It didn't heal quite right." He recited the story the surgeon had provided him with. If anyone were to see the scar on his thigh, they would know the story was false, but that was not likely to happen. "Rather embarrassing, for a Southern gentleman to fall from his own steed, though to be honest I had imbibed a bit too much just before deciding to take the beast out."

"A drunkard as well as a gambler?" Lily asked, more than a small hint of humor in her voice. "What a reprobate you are, Mr. Tyler."

The two couples who shared the balcony with Lily and Quint left to return to the dance floor, and they found themselves suddenly alone.

"I still wish I could dance with you, though I must admit I feel better knowing that while you were out there on the ballroom floor you were looking at those men and thinking one, two, three, one, two, three . . ." A balmy breeze gusted and then died, and there was a moment of awkward silence.

"And how did you break your nose?" Lily reached out and touched the bump, her gloved fingers brushing lightly against his flesh.

"You've noticed all my imperfections," Quint said, taking her gloved hand as she lowered it away from his face.

"It's not exactly an imperfection, Mr. Tyler. Aren't you going to answer my question?"

Quint pulled her gently into a shadow, where no light from the ballroom fell. "I cornered a beautiful woman at a ball, and I kissed her. It was most disgraceful. I barely knew her."

"And she broke your nose? What a silly girl," Lily whispered, and a bit of her Southern accent fell away.

"Actually, it was her husband who broke my nose." Quint lowered his face closer to Lily's, drawn there by her tempting mouth and soft, inviting voice. He was going to kiss her. He couldn't have helped it even if he wanted to. And he didn't want to.

Lily didn't want him to stop either. She didn't pull away, didn't giggle like a simpleton.

"Is that true?" Lily asked, her voice no more than a breath that passed between rose-colored lips. "Is that really how you broke your nose?"

"No," Quint answered.

"So, you're a liar as well?" There was no censure in her hushed voice.

"Sometimes," Quint said truthfully. It felt comforting to tell even a portion of the truth for a change, especially to Lily.

Their lips came together as they had before, softly, with a tentative tenderness that surprised Quint. Lily's eyes drifted shut, and she moved her mouth against his, testing, soft.

Quint's back was to the rail that encircled the balcony, and he wrapped one arm around Lily's back, pulling her closer. She didn't falter, didn't pull away or seem to think twice about falling into his arms.

It was not enough. Quint thrust his tongue between Lily's parted lips, and she parried with her own, probing, answering him.

Lily wrapped her arms around his neck and brushed her silk-gloved fingers against the back of his neck. Gone was the coy flirt he had seen dancing with other men. God, he felt like he was falling . . . falling into the deepest, darkest part of the ocean . . . drowning in its depths, but liking it. Loving it. Needing it. He could almost feel the currents washing over his body.

It was Lily who finally pulled away. Slowly, reluctantly, confusion in her wide eyes.

"Lily." Quint reached out his hand and brushed her cheek with the back of his hand. "Things like this aren't supposed to happen."

"Things like what?" she asked breathlessly.

Quint frowned. He couldn't tell her anything. She was the Captain's woman. She was the enemy. What he felt for her shouldn't be, couldn't be more important than the lives that were endangered every time Captain Sherwood ran the blockade. With a resigned sigh, he leaned forward and kissed her nose lightly, and he was rewarded with a low laugh, real and artless.

"What was that for?"

"I've wanted to do that since the first moment I saw you . . . kiss your freckles."

"You like freckles?"

"On you, I do," he admitted.

His back remained at the rail, and Lily backed away a half step. She seemed reluctant to move too far away, as if distance would break the spell that bound them. "This is most improper, Mr. Tyler," she said as if she didn't have a care for their impropriety. Her gloved fingers danced across his chest, then straightened his crumpled jacket.

Lily lifted her face to his, a bold invitation, and Quint leaned forward to kiss her again. At the moment, there was no time for pretending, no time for hesitation. . . .

"Miss Lily." Captain Dennison's booming voice

startled them both, and Lily jumped back.

"Why, Captain Dennison." She stepped toward the Englishman, instantly in control once again. "How handsome you look this evenin'."

Dennison gave her a deep bow. "And where is Captain Sherwood tonight?"

"Oh, I reckon he's around here somewhere," Lily drawled. "You know how the Captain is. He's so restless, he just comes and goes as he pleases, taking off on that silly little ol' boat . . ."

"Ship, Miss Lily," Dennison corrected.

"Ship, boat . . ." Lily waved her hand, dismissing the light-hearted censure. "Same thing."

Quint watched the scene with a deepening frown. This was not the woman he had kissed, the woman who had kissed him with such passion.

"Might I have this dance, Miss Lily?" Dennison offered Lily his hand.

"I'd just love to dance with you, Captain. You know how I love to waltz."

She didn't look back at Quint as she took Dennison's arm, but the captain did. How much he had seen, Quint didn't know, but it had been enough. Dennison glared at Quint, and his mouth formed silent words.

I warned you, Tyler.

Quint turned back to the ocean. Damn it all, he'd gladly allow Captain Sherwood to eat his heart for breakfast in exchange for another kiss like that.

Chapter Five

Eleanor Slocum always wore black. Quint had never seen her anywhere but in the gloomy half-light of her study, her black silk dresses as fashionable as was proper for a grieving widow, her dark hair invariably restrained in a severe bun. Still, she was a beautiful woman, and black was becoming on her, with her dark hair and eyes. The gowns she wore emphasized her tiny waist and full bosom, and her movements were slow and sensual—the swish of a skirt, the narrowing of her eyes.

She darted her eyes to Quint as she crossed the room and closed the heavy drapes, shutting out much of the afternoon light. The silk of her wide sleeves and full skirt rustled softly, the only sound to be heard as Quint took a seat and extended his bad leg gingerly.

"You're making wonderful progress, Quintin," Eleanor said as she resumed her seat behind the desk. "Did she tell you anything we can use?"

"What?"

"Lily Radford," she prompted. "The ball on

Saturday?" Eleanor relaxed and gave him a tender smile. "The balcony?"

Quint almost jumped from his chair, bad leg or no, but he didn't. He managed to remain remarkably still.

"What is this? Do you have spies spying on your spies?" His anger was restrained, but barely beneath the surface. He'd been able to gather small tidbits of information about the blockade runners—slips they made about their cargo, their schedules, their occasional passengers. It hadn't taken him long to separate the cautious, close-mouthed captains from the ones who tended to chatter when they drank too much.

Captains Dennison and Wright were the most gregarious, and they had introduced Quint to their fellow profiteers. When they were away, Quint joined in other card games and lost there as well. He played the part of an expatriated gambler to the hilt, caressing the cards, drinking, listening much more closely than he appeared to. And to think that someone had been watching *him* all the while he had been on the island.

"Occasionally," Eleanor admitted. "You're not the only operative in Nassau. Not by a long shot. But no one has ever been able to get close to Captain Sherwood or his lady, Lily. Wonderful plan, Quintin. When are you going to see her again?"

"I'm not."

Eleanor laughed lightly at his feigned indifference. "My God. I never would have pegged her as your type, Quintin. She's pretty, but a tad . . . empty-headed. Really, I'll never understand why men are so invariably attracted to stupid women, to addle-brained females who can't manage to think for themselves." Her smile faded.

"If Lily Radford is so empty-headed, then there's not much I can do." Quint had his doubts about Lily's apparent lack of intelligence. "I can't harvest an empty field."

"You must see her again," Eleanor insisted, a sparkle in her dark eyes.

"She doesn't know anything," Quint insisted, leaning back in his chair and trying to appear relaxed. "I imagine the Captain keeps her around for decoration, for amusement." An unwanted knot formed in his chest, but he ignored it and continued to smile. "I doubt that he keeps her informed of the workings of his business. I'll concentrate on Dennison and Wright."

"No," Eleanor argued. "Keep working on the Radford woman. I have a good feeling about this." She nodded and smiled at his scowling face. "And let me give you a piece of advice. Don't get involved. It can only complicate matters."

Quint showed no visible reaction to her warning, but his gut tightened. "Don't worry, Mrs. Slocum. I have no intention of getting involved."

"Good." She placed her elbows on the desk and cupped her chin in her hands. "And you'd better call me Eleanor. We're supposed to be lovers, remember?"

He smiled at her, a slow half-grin that was forced. If he wasn't mistaken, their cover story could easily become real. She was an attractive woman, and in any other time, any other place, he would have pursued her.

But he found that he wasn't interested.

"We're also supposed to be discreet," he countered.

Eleanor opened the top drawer of her desk and reached inside. "You need money?"

Quint shook his head. "I won big last night."

"Don't win too big. Dennison and Wright will quit playing with you."

"If I never win, they'll wonder why I continued to let them take my money."

Eleanor remained seated as Quint rose impatiently. "Don't give up on the Radford woman just yet," she said, obviously distracted as she slammed the drawer shut. "Pay her a call now and again. Maybe you'll get to meet the Captain."

Quint left more agitated then he'd entered, and he'd been in a state of disquiet for three days . . . since that damned ball . . . since Lily Radford had kissed him. Witless and frivolous one minute. Sparring with him and dazzling him with that fire in her eyes the next. If Captain Dennison hadn't interrupted them, he would have kissed her again, and maybe again, and in the end he would have forgotten why he was in Nassau in the first place. With Lily in his arms, he could forget anything . . . everything. He didn't like it. He'd realized, as Lily walked away from him without a backward glance, that he didn't want to use her. He liked her too much, too damned much, and she stirred feelings in him that he'd thought were long dead.

He didn't want to lose the control he'd gained

by locking those feelings away, and deep down he didn't want to betray Lily by using her the way Eleanor suggested. Ordered.

He couldn't stop the deep frown that crossed his face. The Captain's woman. Did she love Sherwood? Did she kiss her Captain the way she'd kissed him on the balcony? Of course she did. That and more. He didn't want to think about it, but visions entered his mind, unwanted but persistent. She'd said herself that it was scandalous . . . and it was. Lily and Captain Sherwood should be married, but Quint was glad they were not. At the same time, he was furious with the Captain for disgracing Lily that way.

The war, the Captain's precarious profession, perhaps the island itself, made their situation more palatable, easier for the residents of Nassau to accept. Lily had certainly not been scorned or ostracized, as she would have been back home. In the Old South, there would have been no invitations for Lily, no friendly greetings like the ones she'd received at the ball. Mrs. Greene and that vapid blonde he'd seen her talking to would have lifted their noses into the air and turned their backs on Lily. But the Old South was dead. They wouldn't admit it. Maybe they didn't even know it yet, but it was over.

Quint looked up and found that he'd wandered to the path that led to Lily's house, that peaceful place with the flowering plants and lace curtains. He couldn't see the house from where he stood; for that he would have to follow the winding path through the trees. Damned if that place wasn't calling him.

He tapped his cane absently, then suddenly turned on his heel and stalked back toward the hotel. Not today. He wasn't prepared to face her today.

"What's the matter with you, Lily?" Cora sat on the loveseat in the parlor, sewing on a bright green gown that Lily detested already. "I've never seen you pace about so much before."

"I'm nervous about the next run," Lily lied. The next run was more than a week away, and she was never nervous about the *Chameleon*.

Cora laughed. "Not likely. Is it that bloke you were kissing on the lawn last week?" Cora's eyes remained on her work as her fingers flew gracefully. " 'E's a right good-looking fella, at least from a distance."

"From up close, too," Lily said under her breath. "But you know as well as I do that I can't allow myself to get involved. . . ."

"The 'eart 'as a mind o' its own," Cora said cryptically. "The first time I saw Tommy, I knew 'e was the one for me. 'E wasn't much to look at, neither, all dirty and just in from the sea. But 'e gave me the most wonderful smile." Cora set her sewing aside. " 'E stole my 'eart with that smile o' his. Made it plumb stop." She said the words as if she were still amazed.

"Well, my heart doesn't have a mind of its own," Lily declared stubbornly. "I am in control—"

"You're always in control," Cora snapped. "You seem to think the world would stop revolving if you didn't give it a spin now and again. That ship, the war, those boys—"

"My crew is made up of men, not boys," Lily insisted.

Cora raised a disbelieving eyebrow. "They may be men to you, but as far as I'm concerned, most o' them are lads who should still be in knickers. Good boys, and loyal, but lads just the same."

Lily didn't argue. It was true. Most of her crew, with the exception of Tommy, the pilot, and the chief engineer, were young—seventeen, eighteen, not many over twenty-two.

None of them were men. At least, not like Quintin Tyler. He was a real man, tall and strong, a determined gleam in his eyes, a sureness in his lips against hers. His hands were brown and powerful, steady against the small of her back. There was no trepidation in those hands, no hesitation when he cupped her chin and stared into her eyes.

Maybe her heart did have a mind of its own, but that didn't mean she had to allow it to rule her, to sway her in any way. It was just a kiss . . . two kisses . . .

"This never should have happened," Lily snapped.

"What's that, dear?" Cora had returned to her sewing and didn't even lift her eyes.

"I'm supposed to be the Captain's *mistress,* for God's sake. I shouldn't be invited to balls, or expected to socialize with the locals. I should be an outcast. No one should even want to acknowledge my existence."

"A part o' your flawless plan went awry?" Cora smiled knowingly. "People aren't always predictable, Lily. Sometimes they surprise you."

"Pearls of wisdom, Cora," Lily said wryly, returning to the window for what could have been the hundredth time that day.

"Is 'e walking down the path this time?" Cora asked in a whispery voice.

"No. And that's not why I'm . . . I just feel a bit restless, that's all." Lily sounded too defensive, and she knew it as she turned back to the window. "Bloody hell." She breathed the curse.

"I 'eard that," Cora accused. "It's not fitting for a lady to use such language."

"I'm not a lady," Lily insisted. "I'm a sailor."

"Humph." Cora plied her needle swiftly. "You might not like the idea o' being a lady, but you can't 'elp being a woman. All the sailing and captaining and fencing in the world won't change that, my dear. If your Mr. Tyler—"

"He's not *my* Mr. Tyler," Lily snapped.

"All right. If Mr. Tyler disturbs you so, you can 'ave Tommy and a couple of the lads rough 'im up a bit. Tell 'im that Captain Sherwood wants 'im to stay away from 'is woman."

"No!"

Cora smiled contentedly. "Then sit down and relax. If your—pardon me, if Mr. Tyler comes calling—"

"He wouldn't dare!"

Cora looked up and stabbed herself with the

needle, pulling away a finger dotted with a drop of blood. "It's becoming quite difficult to carry on a conversation with you." She frowned and sucked on her injured finger. "And it's rude of you to interrupt your elders."

"You're not my elder. You're my friend," Lily said, forcing herself to relax and take a chair close to Cora. "I don't know what to do. I like him, Cora. I like him a lot. I've never . . . He kissed me," she confessed. "And I can't stop thinking about it."

"I see." Cora frowned. "Your father taught you swordplay and sailing and horseback riding, but your mother wasn't around to teach you about . . . other things. You're twenty-six years old. Old enough to be married and 'ave children, but you know nothing."

"I'm not ignorant of what happens between a man and a woman, Cora," Lily said, insulted and embarrassed at the same time.

Cora raised her eyebrows. "You're not a virgin, then?"

"Of course I'm a virgin!" Lily blushed, a rare occurrence for her, but she had already felt that warm flush in her cheeks twice since her conversation with Cora had begun. "That doesn't mean I'm ignorant."

Cora set her sewing aside and folded her hands in her lap. "I've tried to be like a mother to you," she said softly. "But you don't make it easy." She bit her bottom lip, and her arched brows came together.

"Some men are more . . . attractive than others," Cora continued. "Attractive in . . . in an animal way, almost." The look that crossed Cora's face was one of consternation. "I don't want you to be hurt. Women swoon over these men from the time they're out o' their knickers and don't stop until the day they die."

She shook her head dismally. "Your Mr. Tyler seems to fall into that category. 'E probably leaves broken 'earts wherever 'e goes. If you really like this man as much as you claim, I don't want you to approach 'im blindly. 'E might be playing with you. 'E might simply find you attractive and challenging." Cora sighed deeply. "Or 'e might like you as much as you like 'im."

"How do I tell? How do I know?" Lily leaned back in her chair, more confused now than when the conversation had begun.

Cora shrugged her shoulders. "Be wary, my dear. The 'eart is fragile."

Lily laughed. "Not my heart."

Cora studied her with a frown. "Especially yours," she warned, and then she returned her attention to the atrocious green dress in her lap. Her fingers flew furiously, and her frown deepened.

"Don't worry about me," Lily said softly, and Cora lifted her face. The frown didn't fade.

"I want you to be happy," Cora said. "I've known men like Quintin Tyler all my life . . . before Tommy, o' course. Pretty faces and wicked smiles, practiced 'ands and lips. Vague promises scattered among their sweet words. I don't want this man to break your 'eart."

Lily gave her aunt a bright smile that didn't come naturally. "I know how to take care of myself."

Cora sighed and returned to the chore at hand. "If 'e came at you with a sword, I wouldn't be worried." She turned a bright red. "What I mean is . . . be careful, Lily."

Lily took the warning to heart. She was nothing if not careful.

Chapter Six

Quint rapped against the red door with the gold head of his cane. It was still a bad idea, but his brain hadn't been able to transmit the message to his body as he'd walked from the hotel. He was excited about seeing Lily again. His heart was beating too fast, and he found himself nervously tapping his cane against the ground. He felt like an adolescent working up the nerve to speak to the prettiest girl in the county. How had she come to have this power over him? It irritated and puzzled him, but he couldn't deny that the power was real.

The door was finally opened by a solemn and almost disapproving woman, fairer in coloring than Lily, but attractive in her own way. At least, she would be if she didn't stare at him so sternly.

"Is Miss Radford in?" Quint asked when the servant maintained her stony silence.

"Whom may I say is calling, sir?" Her voice was cold, but held a trace of amusement, as if she knew perfectly well who he was.

"Quintin Tyler."

The rude woman closed the door in his face, and Quint stood there waiting as patiently as he could. It was several minutes later before the door was opened again, and the surly woman grudgingly invited him inside.

Lily was in the parlor, seated on a loveseat with a serpentine back. She was wearing a simple dress made of green linen, and the color made her eyes look bright and luminous. To his consternation, she was also wearing plain white gloves. If he didn't see her hands soon, he was going to go insane. It made no sense, to become obsessed with a woman's hands. But he was.

"Mr. Tyler." Lily greeted him sweetly, rising slowly and gracefully. Carefully, it seemed. "Whatever brings you here?" She was giving him her vapid smile, and it annoyed him. Where was the Lily he had kissed?

"I just happened to find myself on your path, and before I knew it I was at your doorstep. To be honest, my leg is bothering me, and I was hoping I might rest here for a while before starting back." He hated to lie to her. It had taken him a full three days after his meeting with Eleanor to work up the nerve to face Lily. Three days since he'd found himself at her path and turned away. Three days in which he'd fortified himself as best he could.

"By all means, have a seat." She directed him into a chair that was placed beside the loveseat and moved an ottoman so he could prop up his bad leg. She didn't cluck and coo, didn't offer any sweet sympathy, and for that Quint was grateful.

The truth was, his leg was healing nicely, perhaps even better than the surgeons had anticipated. He would always have a limp, but he wouldn't be carrying the damned cane forever.

When he was settled, Lily took the cane from him and propped it against the wall, and when she positioned herself on the loveseat, Quint found that he had the best seat in the house. The sunlight from the open window fell across Lily's face, soft and warm, and the highlights in her hair shone like gold. All the promises he had made to himself over the past three days—promises to stay detached, to remain uninvolved, to keep his composure—went out the window.

"You're more beautiful than ever, Lily." Quint spoke in a low voice. The ill-natured woman who had so reluctantly opened the door for him stood on the opposite side of the room, a vigilant guard. He didn't think she could hear him, but he didn't really care.

"Cora?" Lily lifted her eyes to the frowning woman. "Would you please prepare a pot of tea for my guest? Some sandwiches, also, and perhaps some of your marvelous sweetcakes."

"Miss, I don't . . ."

· A suddenly stern glare from Lily silenced the woman, and she left the room in a huff.

"Insolent servant," Quint observed when the woman was gone.

"I despair of ever findin' a decent housekeeper again," Lily said in a sweet drawl. "Cora's a simply marvelous cook, but her attitude—"

"Stop it," Quint ordered.

"Stop what?" Lily turned wide, innocent eyes to him and pouted. "Mr. Tyler, you—"

"Quint," he corrected her. "Call me Quint, Lily."

He saw it then, the flash of intelligence in her eyes, the fire that told him she was not the simpering female she sometimes pretended to be. "It's not proper, Mr.—"

"Proper? What do you care about proper, Lily? Is your Captain here? Is he listening at the door, or pacing upstairs waiting for a report from Cora?" His impatience made his voice sharper than he'd intended.

Lily sighed and looked away from him, gazing into her lap at folded, gloved hands. "The Captain's not here." Her smile had vanished.

Quint cursed himself. He was off to a bad start, but Lily had rattled him somehow. Start again, fool, he reminded himself. Start again. He began with a smile.

"Forgive me. When my leg is acting up, I can be quite a bear. I would, however, very much like for you to call me Quint." That was true. He wanted to hear her say his name, just once. "Even if only when we find ourselves alone."

"Very well, Quint," she obliged. "What have you been doing with yourself since I saw you last?" There was a spark in her eyes as she asked, perhaps as she chastised herself for reminding him of the last time they had found themselves alone together.

"Everything that has happened to me since

Saturday has been dull. You've spoiled me, Lily Radford."

"I can't believe that." Lily tried to smile brightly, but didn't quite succeed. That wariness he had come to expect from her was dimming her response.

"It's true, Lily." He couldn't take his eyes from her face. "You hurt my feelings, you know, when you didn't even say good-bye."

"The Captain was ready to leave . . ."

"You didn't want to introduce us?"

Lily sighed. "Not particularly." There was an almost wistful resignation in her voice.

Quint recognized her discomfort and relaxed his efforts. At least she had called him Quint. His gaze wandered around the parlor, a warm room filled with bowls of flowers and scattered books. He saw Sir Walter Scott's *Ivanhoe* and a collection of Shakespeare's sonnets. But there were also books on naval warfare and navigation, a dog-eared copy of Thoreau's *On the Duty of Civil Disobedience*, Melville's *Moby Dick*, and *Narrative of the Life of Frederick Douglass, An American Slave*. Quint was becoming more and more curious about this Captain Sherwood, an obviously learned man.

His gaze fell on the chessboard, the ebony and ivory men dusty and neglected. "Does Captain Sherwood play chess? Perhaps we could arrange for a game some evening."

"No," Lily answered quickly and sharply. "Actually, that's mine."

Quint lifted one eyebrow. "You play?"

Lily straightened her spine and looked Quint in the eye. There was a challenge there, a liveliness that she tried to hide. "I do play occasionally," she drawled.

"I've never known a woman to make a decent chess opponent," Quint said, knowing that would goad her on.

"Would you like to play, Quint?" She smiled, but there was mischief in her grin. He liked it.

Lily placed a small table between the loveseat and Quint's chair, then set up the chessboard with nimble fingers, her white-gloved hands almost caressing the game pieces. She had the most graceful hands, with long fingers and delicate wrists. Her movements were slow, but strong and confident. It crossed Quint's mind that she might remove her gloves to play.

He was disappointed in that respect, as she sat across from him and insisted that, as her guest, he move first. She had placed the ivory men in front of him and dusted her own black figures lovingly.

Lily hummed to herself and smiled vacantly. She giggled once and said she just didn't know what to do next. Cora appeared soon after they began to play and laid out a table of tea and finger foods. She stopped near the doorway and resumed her guardian stance, but Lily shooed her out of the room with an agitated wave of her hand as she studied the board. Fifteen minutes later, Lily had Quint in checkmate.

"Well, look at that," she said as she moved the

black queen to complete her strategy. "Little ol' checkmate."

Quint laughed. He had been paying little attention to the game, instead concentrating on watching Lily's face as she planned her moves. He didn't even mind her exaggerated accent, not when she was having so much fun with it.

"I believe I underestimated you, Lily."

She met his eyes then and managed to startle him. Those eyes were bold, daring, and vibrant. "Quintin Tyler, I do believe you've probably underestimated every woman you've ever met."

"That may be true, but you're the first woman who's ever surprised me." This revelation pleased her. He could see it in her face. "A rematch. I must regain my honor."

"Is it dishonorable to be beaten?"

"By a woman?" he scoffed.

She took that as a challenge and they set up the board again. Lily insisted on keeping her black figures and allowing Quint to move first once again. This time he paid more attention to the game, and he beat her soundly.

"Checkmate," he said, watching her face closely. He'd caught her off guard, and she twitched her freckled nose slightly.

"Bloody hell," she said under her breath.

"I beg your pardon?" Quint leaned across the board, and Lily looked up, startled.

"Sorry. A nasty habit I'm picking up from . . . from the Captain." She blushed, and he liked the color in her cheeks. But he hated being reminded of Captain Sherwood. "Would you like some tea and sandwiches now?"

"And leave this in a tie?" he asked incredulously, waving his hand over the gameboard.

"After we eat," she said, standing suddenly. "I'm starving, and I don't play well on an empty stomach."

"All the more reason for me to insist that we finish the game immediately," he teased.

Lily put a spoonful of sugar into her tea and piled two plates high with sandwiches and cakes. She cleared away the game and placed Quint's plate in front of him, then sat on the loveseat with her own plate in her lap.

She ate slowly and without dropping so much as a crumb, but she didn't pick at her food the way his sisters and Alicia had, as though eating was unnatural and distasteful. Quint liked that, the fact that Lily ate well. It didn't fit her image as a brainless self-absorbed female. Maybe she didn't realize that she was giving herself away.

For all their apparent distaste for food, none of his sisters had ever been as trim as Lily, a fact the gown he had seen her in that first day hid well. But her sapphire ballgown had shown him how finely shaped she was, and the simple green dress she wore as she sat across from him now molded to small, firm breasts, a tiny waist, and long, slender arms. She was taller than most women he knew, but no more than five-seven. At six-two, he could still look down at her. He remembered all too well doing just that.

Lily was eager to get back to the chessboard,

and so was Quint. He liked the sparkle in her eyes, the challenge she accepted. He knew, no matter what front she presented to others, that she would not allow him to win simply to feed his male ego. She was an honest woman, beneath the facade. An anomaly. A mystery.

"Who taught you to play?" Quint asked as she removed their plates and set the game in front of him once again.

"My father." A sweet sadness crossed her face as she answered him. "He said I learned quickly because I hate to lose. I suppose that's true. He meant it kindly enough, but it's not an admirable trait in a woman."

"I wouldn't say that." Quint spoke softly. He was afraid to break the spell that was revealing what he was certain was the real Lily Radford. "Your father sounds like a smart man."

"He was." Lily's voice was low as well. A host of emotions flowed across her face. Anger. Sadness. A poignant look that broke Quint's heart. "He . . . died a couple of years ago. A little more than two years ago, actually."

"Do you want to talk about it?"

Lily lifted her eyes to him. He saw a moment's hesitation, a fragment of time when she perhaps considered showing him something beneath her careful charade. He wanted to see more of the woman behind the mask.

"No," she finally answered, but he had seen the warring emotions on her face.

The final game was the longest, the most fiercely competitive, but in the end Lily beat him fair and square, and the victory lit up her face. It was worth defeat, Quint decided, to see that look.

Cora's continued and increasing interruptions reminded Quint that it was time to depart. He didn't want to leave Lily. The thought of returning to his hotel room left him empty. The room would be cramped and lonely, and Dennison and Wright suddenly seemed poor companions for the evening. But he stood, and Lily handed him his cane.

"It's been a most enjoyable afternoon," he said sincerely. "I hope you'll allow me a rematch."

"Of course," Lily answered with a smile.

Quint wanted to kiss her good-bye. It didn't have to be a passionate kiss like the one on the hotel balcony. Just a brief touching of their lips—that was all he wanted. That would satisfy him.

Liar, he chided himself. Cora was hanging over her mistress, a warrior-like chaperone, so he couldn't enjoy even that simple touch. But he knew it wouldn't have been enough.

He wanted her. All of her. He wanted to kiss her hands, the hands she hid from him. He wanted to feel her breasts under his palms, in his mouth. He wanted to lock her in a room, any room with a bed, and make love to her until neither of them could move. His visit had done nothing toward ridding his thoughts of Lily Radford. If anything, he suspected his obsession with her was only stronger than before. He would dream about her tonight, again.

There was a stirring in his loins even as he walked away from Lily Radford's house, and he cursed his own imagination.

He wanted her.

But he couldn't have her.

Quint leaned back in his chair and studied the cards he held. He'd lost a fortune, but he couldn't keep his mind on the game. Dennison was winning big, and John Wright had won a fair amount as the evening passed. The other two sailors had lost almost as much as Quint. Almost.

It was Lily Radford. She was forever in the back of his mind, smiling at him over the chess pieces, leaning toward him ever so slightly. He wanted to kiss her again, more than he'd ever wanted anything.

It was insane. He barely knew the woman, and she was another man's mistress. It was scandalous, as she'd admitted, but Quint found that he couldn't think less of her for it. She was beautiful, but not, Quint admitted to himself, the most beautiful woman he'd ever seen. Her mouth was a little too full, and her hair seemed to curl with a mind of its own. She was too tall, not at all dainty.

No matter how hard Quint tried to convince himself that Lily was not perfect, he couldn't quite accomplish his goal. He liked her mouth too full, he liked her curling hair, and she fit perfectly in his arms, so she couldn't possibly be too tall. He was drawn to her, and there was nothing he could do about that. Why couldn't she be a simple shopkeeper's daughter? Why did she have to be Captain Sherwood's mistress?

It was the island. An island so beautiful, so enchanting, it would have been a wonder if he didn't find himself entranced by some woman. After the years of fighting, of seeing death and bloodshed until he was sick of the sight, Nassau was a real paradise. He'd left behind the chill of the North for the balmy breezes of the island, the snowstorms and cold winds for gentle afternoon showers that fell to earth so softly, they seemed to be a gift from above, never a curse.

It was a good place to fall in love.

The thought shook him. He hadn't imagined himself in love since he'd left his home and Alicia. He hadn't imagined that he would ever find himself caught up in that emotion again. It was a trap that clouded a man's thinking, and Quint didn't want to fall in love . . . with Lily Radford or anyone else.

"Come on, Tyler," John Wright prompted. "You can join us any time." The burly captain leaned toward Quint and waved a big hand in his face. "It's your bid."

Quint tossed a coin absently into the pot and looked at his cards. There was nothing there. He was going to lose again.

Dennison was frowning slightly, and he leaned closer to Quint. "I seen the same look on your face as when I surprised you and Miss Lily at the ball," he said in a low voice. "It's a sad state of affairs when a man allows a woman to muddle his brain. I like you, Tyler," he added. "I don't want to have to bury you when Sherwood gets his hands around your bleedin' neck."

Quint ignored Dennison's dire warnings.

He lost everything he had on him, then threw his cards onto the center of the table. Wright poured Quint a drink and slapped him on the back as he attempted to console the loser.

"Better luck next time," Wright drawled, his Texas accent setting him apart from the British captains who frequented the hotel. "Have a drink on me, Tyler."

Quint lifted the glass to his lips and emptied it in one toss. The other players, the other losers, had drifted away one at a time, and there were just the three of them remaining at the table. They hovered over their drinks in the smoke-filled room.

Quint tried to remind himself that this was why he was in Nassau. Not to get blindsided by a woman, but to gather information.

Dennison was moodily silent, as he sometimes was, but John Wright had had a bit too much to drink, and he started to talk in a loud whisper. Boasting. Telling secrets.

For the first time that evening, Quint was able to forget Lily, as he leaned forward and listened carefully to Captain Wright.

Chapter Seven

Quint waited a few days before returning to Lily's house. He didn't want to appear too eager, and in truth he wanted to allow himself time to cool off and come to his senses. He couldn't possibly allow the woman to affect him the way she did.

Captain Wright, after winning the last two big hands and downing enough rum for three thirsty men, had started bragging about the special cargo he would be transporting within the week. Quint had listened intently, keeping his eyes half closed and occasionally allowing his gaze to wander over the room, as if he were not quite paying attention.

No one questioned that Quint was a loyal Southerner, and Wright was looking for approval, even a measure of respect, when he told Quint about the machinery he would be taking out in a few days. Marine engines for Confederate ironclads that were being built in Charleston. Two pairs of direct-acting steam engines. A marine engine works was under construction somewhere in Georgia, but until it was complete the South was dependent upon the British manufacturers and the blockade runners.

Eleanor had been delighted with the information, not only about what Wright was carrying in his cargo hold, but when his ship would be leaving Nassau and that his destination was Charleston. The Union blockaders would be waiting for Wright and would confiscate the engines.

Quint tried to push all that from his mind as he rapped his cane against Lily's door. The red door was opened by a frowning Cora. Quint gave her his most charming smile, flashing dimples and white teeth, but she was evidently unmoved.

"Is Miss Radford at home?" Quint asked when Cora showed no intention of inviting him in.

"Miss Radford is busy," Cora answered him curtly, and then she attempted to close the door in his face.

Quint stuck out his cane to stop the door. "Could I wait? I'm afraid I've overdone it again, and my leg is killing me." He tried to look pitiful and must have succeeded, because Cora sighed heavily.

"She's in the garden," Cora snapped. "Follow the stone path around back and you'll find 'er."

Quint turned away as the door slammed shut, and he tapped his cane against the stone walk that wound its way around the house and down a gentle incline. He could see a profusion of brightly colored flowers in the distance, red and pink and coral against a sea of lush green foliage. He passed Cora on the path. She was heading back toward the house, out of breath and giving him the same hateful glare she had given him when she'd first opened the door. She must have run from a back entrance to warn her mistress that he was coming. Quint was disappointed. He would have been pleased to catch Lily unaware, just to see what she was like in an unguarded moment.

Lily was waiting for him, seated on a wrought-iron bench amidst the almost wild flora. He would have thought she'd prefer a well-tended and orderly garden, rows of roses and lilies carefully trimmed and contained, but this garden was a wild paradise, the plants encroaching over the stone walkway, the leaves of the flowering vines and bushes mingling, fighting as they reached for the sun.

The garden that surrounded her was wild, but Lily herself was composed, more distant than usual, with a determined set to her face and her gloved hands folded primly in her lap.

"Mr. Tyler, what a pleasant surprise." From the tone of her voice, he wondered if she really and truly found the surprise pleasant. There was an uncomfortable strain in her voice, and a stubborn firmness of her mouth that he didn't like at all.

"It's Quint, remember? I came to challenge you to a rematch." He tried the charming smile he had bestowed on Cora, with dismal results. There was no softening of Lily's lips, no easing of the tension on her face. Perhaps his smile wasn't as charming as he'd imagined.

"A rematch," Lily repeated. "You must mean our chess game."

Quint frowned. She was playing the coquette for him again, smiling absently and looking everywhere but at his face.

"Of course our chess game. You promised me a rematch."

Lily lifted the fan that lay at her side, and Quint took advantage of her move, lowering himself beside her and stretching out his right leg. She fanned herself furiously and gave him a sidelong glance as he pretended to study the vine that meandered along the side of the wrought-iron bench. When he turned back to her, she lowered her eyes and seemed to concentrate on the buttons of his gray waistcoat.

"I really don't enjoy chess all that much," she whined. "It gives me such a headache. I don't know why I got all excited over a little ol' game of chess. I much prefer to work on my samplers and to read poetry in my spare time."

Quint wanted to shake Lily and call her the liar she was, but he controlled the urge, gripping the serpentine head of his cane. He hadn't mistaken the joy on her face when she'd beaten him, the cunning in her eyes as she planned her strategy against him.

"I'm sorry to hear that. I enjoyed our games very much." Quint wanted to take her chin in his hand and lift her face to his. She was hiding from him, averting her eyes and reverting to her defensive position. But he kept his hands to himself.

97

"Perhaps you could . . . read some of your favorite poetry to me." Mentally, he cringed. He hated poetry, but if that was what it took to be close to Lily . . .

"I don't think you should come here anymore, Mr. Tyler," Lily said quickly, the words rushing out of her mouth.

This time he couldn't resist the temptation, and he lifted her face gently. "Why?" His voice was little more than a whisper, a hint of confusion and hurt in it that he couldn't disguise.

Lily didn't jerk away from him or try to avert her eyes. She met his gaze with a determined strength in her own turquoise stare. "That's just the way it has to be. I don't want you to come here again."

Quint looked for some sign that she was lying and was disappointed when he didn't see one. "Is it Captain Sherwood?"

"Yes," Lily said, and he could see the truth of the answer in her eyes.

"Do you love him?" It was a whispered question, hesitant and probing. God help him, if she said no he just might carry her away with him. Leave Nassau, leave the business of spying that he was beginning to detest, leave everything behind.

Lily hesitated, and that gave him a moment of hope. But when she answered, her voice was sure and unwavering.

"I'm committed to the Captain." That was the truth. Lily didn't like lying to Quintin Tyler. It was somehow harder than deceiving the entire

98

town. So far she had told him nothing but the truth. She couldn't see him again because of the Captain, and she was committed . . . until the war was over.

She didn't move away from him until he lowered his head to kiss her, and then she backed away with a jerk and rose from her seat. She liked it too much, wanted it too much, and he would be able to tell. It would be much easier if they could make a clean break.

Lily's heart did a flip in her chest, but she gave no outward sign. She had made up her mind after a long and sometimes heated discussion with Cora and Tommy.

She couldn't see Quint again. If she ran into him in town—well, that was unavoidable. But she couldn't allow herself to let down her guard as she had that afternoon when he'd appeared on her doorstep. Not now. What she was doing was more important than a passing attraction to a charming gambler, a man too like her lackadaisical brother for her tastes. A handsome face, a practiced womanizer. That was all Quintin Tyler was.

"Please behave yourself, Mr. Tyler," she drawled.

"Quint."

"I'm afraid you've misinterpreted my actions, Mr. Tyler." Lily wrung her gloved hands. "You see, I do find you quite attractive, and a pleasant diversion on a quiet afternoon. But I must confess that I am sometimes peeved with Captain Sherwood, and I do try unmercifully to attract his attention." She was unable to look at him as she delivered this lie. "I sometimes accuse him of likin' his little ol' boat more than he likes me."

Quint tapped the end of his cane against the stone walk at his feet as he stared at her unmercifully. "You were trying to make Captain Sherwood jealous?" he asked testily.

Lily smiled coyly. "Why, yes, and it worked quite well, thank you."

"You're welcome, Lily," he said bitterly, rising with little difficulty. "I'm happy to be of service."

The look of thunder on his face was so startling that she turned away from him and ran up the winding path.

She ran from him as if he were the devil himself, her skirt in her hands as she fled swiftly, and not with the delicate, tiny steps of a twittering, silly girl, but with long strides that carried her away from him quickly.

Lily slowed her steps as she approached the house. Cora was standing in the back doorway, an entrance that led to the kitchen. She was waiting, steadfast and unsmiling, and she closed the door behind Lily and then peered through the pane of glass that was set in the kitchen door, watching the path. Lily didn't watch. She stepped away from the door, keeping her back to Cora.

Cora made a small noise of disgust, an unladylike grunt, and Lily knew that her aunt was watching Quint climb the hill. Lily left the kitchen, afraid even to turn around and risk glimpsing Quint.

Cora followed Lily into the parlor. "So, it's done?" she asked.

"Aye, it's done," Lily answered, so little of her Southern accent left in her voice that Quint wouldn't have recognized it as her own. She turned to face Cora with grim resolve. "You were right. I can't afford to get involved at a time like this."

Cora nodded sympathetically. "You've done what you 'ad to do to preserve us all. Tyler'll soon find another woman to charm. Men like 'im always do."

Lily accepted the decision she had been forced to make without a tear or an enraged word. There would be no sniffles, no quiet tears, but that didn't mean it didn't hurt.

"After the war, there will be time for such fanciful notions as 'andsome gamblers and 'eart-stopping kisses," Cora said in a lightly teasing voice. Lily knew her aunt was only trying to make her feel better, but her light-hearted words only made the pain deeper and sharper.

"I'm sorry," Cora said softly, her smile fading. "You really liked the bloke, didn't you?"

"Aye." Lily smiled at her aunt's choice of words, a small, sad smile. "I really liked the bloke. Bloody hell, what if I never meet another man I like so much?" She was certain that by the time the war ended, Quintin Tyler would have moved on to some other place, some other woman.

"The world is full o' men," Cora exclaimed. "Each one built much like another, though not many as finely put together as your gambler."

"Thanks for reminding me of that, Cora," Lily snapped. Of course, Cora was right. Tommy was right. There was no time in her life for entanglements of the heart, no time to waste on thoughts of warm lips and charming dimples. And it was true enough that the dark-eyed man who had bedeviled her from the moment she'd seen his face was not the only attractive man on the face of the earth.

But Lily had a sinking feeling that she would never again meet a man who made her feel the way Quintin Tyler did.

Quint banged on Eleanor Slocum's door with a quiet vengeance, the constant tapping of his cane against the door stopping only when it was opened to him, the door swinging back swiftly.

He was pacing in the gloomy, semi-dark study where he always met Eleanor Slocum when she entered the room. There was a gleam of excitement in her eyes. Was she wondering what news had brought him to her so soon after his last visit? Was she expecting some brilliant piece of information from him? She was in for a surprise.

Eleanor seated herself at her desk, back straight and eyes alight as she stared at Quint. Instead of taking his usual chair, Quint placed his hands on the edge of her desk and leaned forward. Her smile and the light in her eyes dimmed, and she pulled back slightly.

"I quit," he muttered, his eyes half closed, his mouth grim. To her credit, Eleanor didn't flinch at his obvious anger, didn't even blink as he stared at her.

"You can't quit," she reasoned, her voice and demeanor as calm as ever.

"Watch me." Quint backed away from the desk, but he didn't sit. He couldn't. "I'm getting nowhere with Captain Sherwood. Hell, I've never even seen the man. I've sucked all the information out of the captains who are willing to gamble and drink the night away . . ."

"You've given up on Sherwood?" Eleanor's eyes narrowed slightly as she watched him. Quint turned away from her and resumed his pacing.

"Lily told me she didn't want to see me again."

"Lily," Eleanor repeated. "You're on a first-name basis?"

"When she damn well feels like it."

Eleanor shrugged, seemingly unconcerned. "She'll change her mind."

Quint shook his head. "I don't think so."

"Even if she doesn't," Eleanor reasoned, "you've accomplished a lot. You can do more."

Quint snorted in disgust.

"In a matter of days, Captain Wright's ship will be intercepted, thanks to you. Do you know what would happen if that shipment reached the Confederacy? If those ironclads went to sea powered by those engines and fitted with the armaments that very well could be aboard as well?" Eleanor half rose, then seated herself again.

"And John Wright?" Quint asked.

"The foreign crewmen are usually detained no

more than a few weeks, until the prize court is held." Eleanor drummed her fingers on the desk, and her eyes hardened.

"John Wright is from Galveston," Quint said quietly.

"Then he will probably be sent to the prison at Fort Warren in Boston, or perhaps Fort Lafayette in New York Harbor." She dismissed his distressed look with a shrug. "Either of them is a sight better than Point Lookout Prison."

"I like John Wright," Quint said quietly, as much to himself as to Eleanor. Many nights the man had talked about his family rather than his lucrative and risky shipping venture. He had a mother and four sisters in Texas, and he sent them money and food and bolts of fabric. The youngest sister was only twelve, Quint remembered. How would they survive while he was in prison?

Eleanor leaned forward, giving Quint a stern and almost angry look. "You can't afford to like Captain Wright, or any of the others. They'd kill you without a second thought if they knew you were a spy. You can't afford to let Lily Radford lead you around by what you've got hanging between your legs, either."

Quint simply raised his eyebrows at the proper widow's sudden vulgarity.

"Don't tell me you don't realize that's exactly what she's doing." Eleanor leaned back and relaxed visibly. "It's the way women like her operate. Come hither. Go away. Come hither. Go away."

Quint finally took his usual chair. "Do you really think that's what she's doing? Playing with me? Leading me along?" He tried to remember all the changes he had seen in Lily. Her apparent vulnerability that came and went like the tides. One minute she was a simpering idiot, the next an expert chess player. He felt like a foolish boy, and his chagrin must have showed on his face, because Eleanor laughed kindly.

"Don't feel so bad. We Southern women are taught from a very early age how to wrap a man around our little finger. Lily Radford may not be very bright, but I have a feeling that she was raised to know exactly what I'm talking about. I wish you could see yourself. You look like a whipped puppy."

Quint's anger with himself grew. She was right. He should have recognized the signs. Just like Alicia. His frown deepened at the thought of the woman who had been his fiancée for three years. Beautiful Alicia, with her dark hair and eyes so like his own. He had believed that she was as close to perfect as a man could ask for, even as she continually postponed their wedding. They were young and had all the time in the world. Or at least they had believed that was true.

But his decision to leave his home, to leave the plantation that should have become his one day, had shown him a side of Alicia he had never even suspected. She refused to join him, refused to leave behind the security of her home. She had wanted, had planned for years, to one day be mistress of Quint's father's plantation when it passed to him, and she wanted no part of what she called Quint's foolish gesture.

Foolish gesture.

A year later, she married Quint's younger brother, Dalton. Quint had been in Baltimore when he'd received the news. The sense of betrayal he'd felt had filled him with bitterness and had made it impossible for him to completely trust anyone.

Alicia had gotten what she wanted all along. She was mistress of the plantation that had once been his home.

"You'll reconsider?" Eleanor asked softly.

"Yes," he agreed.

"Wonderful. We have it on good authority that the *Chameleon* is putting out to sea tomorrow night. Perhaps with the Captain away, Miss Radford will be more receptive to your persistent attentions."

"How do you know he's sailing? I haven't heard . . ."

"I told you that you're not the only operative on this island." Eleanor smiled brightly. "There's a pretty redhead who works in the cathouse across the street from your hotel. A young seaman from Sherwood's crew is quite taken with her and has been bemoaning the days he will be away from her bed."

Quint massaged his aching head. "All right. I'll give it another try." His voice had the ring of defeat, but deep inside he was glad of the excuse to pursue Lily a while longer. Playing with him, was she?

Well, she didn't have him in checkmate yet, and it was his move.

Chapter Eight

Lily leaned into the wind that brushed across her face, and she raised her hand, a signal for the engines to be cut to dead slow. With the hinged mast down, the gray-painted hull low in the water, and a mist of fog surrounding her, the *Chameleon* was almost invisible as she neared the coast. The pilot, Cyril, had the wheel, having taken over from Lily as they neared the Cape Fear River to enter via New Inlet.

There was not a sound from her crew, not a sniffle or a sigh, not a single whispered word. The engines had earlier been cut to half-speed, and then, at Lily's command, to the dead slow. Even the sound of the hull pushing against the water was lost in the roar of the surf.

As always, Lily felt a surge of excitement. They had spotted the Union blockaders in the distance, but had remained unseen. It was an exciting game, profitable and exhilarating, and she felt almost as if she were thumbing her nose at the Union Navy. It was a thought she dismissed as childish and unlike her, simply a product of her competitive nature. But the gesture was perhaps more like her than she cared to admit.

What would they say when they discovered, as one day they would, that a woman had commanded a ship that had been so easily able to elude their navy? Sometimes Lily imagined what it would be like to stand before her enemy and declare to him what she had done. In her daydreams it was always the captain who had been present at her father's slaying whom she faced.

Once under the protection of Fort Fisher, the entire crew relaxed. You could almost hear the release of their collective breath, the quiet sighs and satisfied murmurs slowly building as they threaded their way toward Wilmington.

Lily enjoyed the voyage from Nassau to Wilmington and back, in spite of the dangers, much more than she enjoyed the days spent in Wilmington. In port, it was necessary that she either stay in her cabin or dress in one of the gowns she kept in a trunk in that small cabin. Even if the *Chameleon* was in port for only two or three days, she could rarely abide to be confined for the length of their stay.

Tommy, as her first mate, handled all business transactions for her. It galled her that she was unable to perform that part of the venture herself, but there was nothing to be done for it. The merchants and Confederates Tommy dealt with had all come to accept the fact that they would never meet the mysterious Captain Sherwood. It was enough that his ship came through the blockade, laden with the goods that enabled them to survive.

"Captain?" Tommy prompted softly, and Lily, lost in her own thoughts, grinned at her uncle.

"I know, I know. Bloody nuisance, hiding below decks." In spite of her objections, Lily turned away from him and disappeared through an open hatch, her feet sure on the ladder. She could find her way around her ship in total darkness, and had been called upon to do just that once or twice. She felt no trepidation as she disappeared into the dark hold, taking the correct number of steps down the narrow hallway with one hand against the wall until she reached her cabin.

Inside, with the door closed, Lily lit a lamp. Already she knew she would not be able to stay there. The cabin was small. There was no luxurious captain's cabin for Lily. Space was critical, and she wouldn't waste an inch simply to provide herself a finer cabin than was necessary.

The bed was small, not much more than a narrow cot. That suited Lily just fine. On board the *Chameleon*, she rarely slept more than three hours a night, even when they were in port. There was a small bookcase built into one wall, filled with a few of her favorite books. A round table was bolted to the floor, with two plain chairs bolted alongside. The only item that might be called indulgent was a saber that hung on one wall, its decorative guard a fouled anchor and leaf design with a twisted rope on the bow-guard. The leather scabbard housed a polished and deadly sharp blade, and the upper scabbard throat was engraved with an anchor. Even the grip was beautiful to Lily—black polished bone that felt smooth and cool when she wrapped her fingers around it.

It was a French naval sword of a kind many Confederate Navy officers carried. Lily had transported a crate of those weapons on her first trip and had instructed Tommy to purchase one for her personal use. She found it to be similar to her father's sword, the one that had been taken from her on the day of his death.

Against one wall, away from the bed, was a large trunk. As of yet, there had been no call for the trunk to leave her cabin, and hopefully there never would be. The trunk was a full three by four feet, and there was a shallow false bottom where she could hide maps, her saber, and gold coins. Piled in the trunk were several gaudy gowns, the special pink one on top. It was hideous, necessarily so, and Lily prayed she would never have to wear it. So far it hadn't been needed, but Lily had planned for every contingency.

Before the hour was out, Lily was pacing her cabin. She should have been able to sleep, but knew she would not. She tried to keep her mind on the business at hand—her business—and to drive all other thoughts from her mind.

Guilt. She couldn't remember ever feeling guilt before. She had clear-cut and important reasons for everything she did, and she never felt guilty over the consequences. Her purpose drove even the prospect of guilt from her mind.

But she couldn't forget Quint's face as he'd sat in the garden and believed that she'd simply been using him to make her Captain Sherwood jealous. He'd been hurt. Really hurt. She hadn't expected that. Quintin Tyler struck her as a man of the world, a man for whom the days fled too quickly because there was so much pleasure to be had. He gambled, he smoked cigars, he drank, and with his looks it would be a miracle if he wasn't a womanizer. He should have been jaded and hard, but he wasn't. She'd hurt his feelings. Maybe he had really liked her after all.

Well, if he had, he certainly didn't like her anymore. And why should he? She'd been heartless and cold, in his eyes.

And in her own eyes as well.

Lily lowered herself to the small cot and closed her eyes. *Sleep,* she commanded. *Sleep and dream of happier times that once were and will be again.* But when she closed her eyes it was Quint she saw. She couldn't afford to remember the hurt expression on Quint's face. She couldn't afford to feel guilty.

"May I wait?" For the second day in a row, Quint was waging a sort of battle with Cora. The little housekeeper was winning.

"No, you may not," Cora said sternly. "Miss Lily does not wish to see you."

"Could I rest my leg for a while?" Quint was growing tired of using his bad leg as an excuse to linger, and from the look on her face, Cora was tired of hearing it.

"You may sit in the garden, if you like," Cora said, frowning mightily. "But Miss Lily will not be joining you." With that she slammed the door in his face for the second day in a row, and Quint followed the path to Lily's tropical garden.

He sat on the wrought-iron bench and looked toward the house. From where he sat he could see only a portion of the second story, two open windows letting in the sea breeze. He stared at those windows, hoping for a glimpse of Lily, hoping she would come to one of those windows and look out at him.

The knowledge that she was baiting him should have angered him, but it didn't. As hard as he tried to convince himself that he was sitting in Lily's garden out of a sense of duty, he knew it was Lily herself who drew him there, not his dedication to the Union. He wanted—he needed—to see her.

Finally, Quint got his wish. He saw Lily. At least, he saw the lavender dress she'd been wearing that first day he'd met her, when he saw her in Terrence's shop and she took his breath away. She stood close to one of the windows, but didn't move close enough for Quint to see her face. She just stood there, stiff and unyielding, a lavender blur through the lace curtains that danced in the wind. She didn't move forward; she didn't move away. She just stood there and watched him for several minutes. Then she turned and disappeared.

Quint waited. Maybe she would join him in the garden, in spite of what Cora had said, but he waited in vain. There wasn't even another glimpse of Lily at the window.

After a tortured wait, Quint left the secluded tropical paradise and climbed the walkway slowly and tenaciously. He allowed himself a wry smile. All the walking he'd done, from his hotel to Lily's house and back again, must have helped his leg to heal. The surgeons had told him to rest, to keep off the leg as much as possible. But immobility was impossible for Quint. He felt the strength returning to his leg a little every day. A few weeks ago, he couldn't have taken the small incline from Lily's garden without working up a sweat.

He turned for a final glance at the house, hoping for a glimpse of lavender in one of the windows, and there it was, a blur of color in an upstairs window. Her bedroom? Captain Sherwood's bedroom? She was watching him, standing back from the window as still as a statue.

Quint stared at the window, watching and waiting. Waiting to see if Lily would come to him. But she didn't, and eventually she turned away and vanished from view.

To hell with her, Quint thought as he turned his back on the house. He wouldn't come back for a day or two. Maybe three. If she was really playing the "come hither, go away" game that Eleanor suspected, maybe she would become anxious when he didn't show himself for a while.

* * *

Cora cursed quietly, borrowing a couple of Tommy's favorite vile phrases, which she would never have dared use were she not alone, as she removed the lavender gown and draped it across the bed. That Quintin Tyler was a persistent devil.

When the *Chameleon* was back in port, she'd have to see if Tommy couldn't dissuade the bloke from hanging about.

Chapter Nine

Quint waited as long as he dared and as long as he could. Days passed, and he had to force himself not to begin the trek to Lily's house. He played the part he had been told to play, the itinerant gambler, lazy and happy-go-lucky, gambling and drinking until dawn, gathering the tidbits of information that were dropped as the bourbon and rum flowed freely.

His favored companions, Dennison and Wright, were absent. Quint wondered if Wright had been captured, or if he had made it safely to Charleston with his cargo. Even with the knowledge of when and where the smaller ship would be, there was no guarantee that the Union blockaders would be able to intercept Wright's steamer. He could move faster and into shallow waters, where the larger ships didn't dare to go, and with skill and a little luck, anything was possible.

Dennison had simply disappeared, as he was wont to do. While he wasn't close-mouthed, neither was he as gabby as Wright. The English captain was moody, sometimes remaining silent, other times grinning and laughing with his companions. He never said a word about his business—at least, nothing Quint could use—and he disappeared on an irregular basis. He would be gone for days, sometimes weeks at a time, and never offer an explanation. Quint knew better than to ask for one.

Some of the captains were more cautious than others, more wary than Wright or even Dennison had been, and they watched everyone suspiciously. Even the Southerner Quintin Tyler. Quint wondered how long it would be before one of them decided to look a bit more closely into his background.

It was early afternoon, a bright and muggy day on the island. Quint decided he had waited long enough. If Lily sent him away again, that was it. He was finished. No matter how much useful information he might glean from her, it wasn't worth this torture.

Why did she do this to him, anyway? And how? She was pretty, that was true, but there were prettier women in Nassau—women who'd made it clear they wouldn't push him away, as Lily did. He barely paid them any attention. They paled next to Lily. Lily, with her affectations and changing moods. Those damn gloves. He wanted to peel them off her hands and kiss her palms and then her fingers, lingering over each one. Quint had never thought about a woman's hands much before, but he couldn't stop thinking about Lily's.

Because she kept them covered. Was that another ploy? Did she realize how obsessed a man could become with that which was withheld from him?

Probably.

As he neared the inviting house with the red door, Quint felt his determination grow. She would *not* send him away this time. He wouldn't leave until he saw her. He knew, deep in his heart, that his determination had nothing to do with his assignment. He didn't care if Lily never mentioned Captain Sherwood or his activities. If Quint had his way, he'd carry her away from this house and away from this island. He would leave the job of spying to those who were more suited for the business. A dirty business, spying on men he was beginning to consider friends. And he would carry Lily away from Captain Sherwood.

To where?

West. San Francisco, maybe. Anywhere far away from the war that had ceased to be noble and grand.

Of course, he couldn't do that, not yet, but it was a nice dream.

He banged his cane against the red door persistently. If he had to push his way past Cora and seek out Lily himself, he would. He wasn't leaving until he saw her.

"Mr. Tyler," Cora said tiredly as she opened the door. "Miss Radford is not receiving this afternoon."

"Tell her I'm here," Quint demanded.

Cora's eyes hardened, and her lips formed a

tight, thin line. "It's none o' my concern, sir, but it seems you would tire o' persisting where you're not wanted." She placed balled fists on her hips and glared at him. "Miss Radford does not wish to see you, sir. Not today. Not tomorrow. Not ever."

Quint leaned forward, placing his cane so that it would be impossible for Cora to close the door. "I want her to tell me that."

Cora sighed, but she did not back away as Quint leaned forward insistently. "Perhaps she will, but not today."

"I'm not leaving." Quint stepped forward, and this time Cora did take a step back. She had no choice as he forced her to retreat. "You can tell Miss Radford that I'm here, or I can commence to shouting at the top of my lungs until she comes to me."

Cora crossed her arms over her chest, as defiant as Quint, in her own way.

"Miss Radford is not feeling well today, sir. She's resting." She used a tone that should have been reserved for naughty children. Next she'd be slapping his hand.

"What's wrong?" Quint asked softly. What if she was really ill?

Cora hesitated, and if he wasn't mistaken, there was an almost imperceptible softening of her eyes.

"Nothing serious," she assured him in a voice that was a bit gentler.

A big man burst into the foyer, a chicken leg in one hand, a mug of coffee in the other. "What the 'ell's takin' you so long, Cora?" He looked first at Lily's servant, and then, with widening eyes, at Quint. "What in the devil are you doin' here?" he exploded.

Quint studied the man from head to toe. A big man, much older than Lily, the man before him was rough, stocky, with hairy arms and broad shoulders. An untended moustache drooped over his mouth, and his hair fell, equally untended, to his shoulders. Was this Captain Sherwood?

Cora smiled at the consternation on his face. "Mr. Tyler 'as come to call on Miss Lily. I tried to explain that she's not receiving visitors—"

"Then why in the devil is he still here?" The man's voice was deep, and he roared the question, wielding the chicken leg as if it were a deadly weapon. "I'll thank ye to stop sniffin' around Lily, you bloody good-fer-nothin' gambler. I could pummel your bleedin' arse into the ground with one hand tied behind me back." His voice was lowered, but still menacing, and he took two steps toward Quint. "You've been told that you're not welcome 'ere."

Quint stood his ground in spite of the threat. "I'd like to see Miss Radford," he insisted. "I'll wait, if necessary."

"You'll get your bleedin' arse out of this 'ouse!"

Lily rolled over and pulled the pillow over her head. All that noise, and that bright light.

The *Chameleon* had docked just before dawn, and Lily had refused to leave until the cotton was unloaded and the crew was dismissed. After more than a week of long days and sleepless nights, surviving on short naps here and there, Lily was exhausted. Tired to the bone. She planned to stay in her big, soft bed for at least three days, if Cora would allow it. She lifted her head and looked across the room to the clock on her dresser, waiting and squinting until she could read the numbers.

There it was again. Tommy, no doubt yelling at Cora about one thing or another. Why wasn't he asleep? He got little more sleep than she did on one of these runs. She couldn't tell what he was saying, but he showed no sign of letting up, and Lily rolled reluctantly from the bed, running agitated fingers through her hair. After a brief moment of silence, she heard Tommy's voice again and, still half asleep, Lily grabbed the emerald green satin robe that was draped over the end of her bed and slipped her arms into it. She didn't bother to attempt to tie the sash; she didn't think she was capable of that small task at this point. She blinked hard three times, trying to clear her mind as she grasped the doorknob and threw open the door, allowing the heavy door to crash against the wall with a resounding thud.

"Bloody hell!" she shouted as she stomped down the hallway and halted at the top of the stairs. "What the devil . . ." Lily stopped suddenly, looking down into the foyer. There were three upturned faces. Tommy's. Cora's. And Quint's. Quint was the only one of the three who was smiling, that crooked grin that revealed his dimple.

"Good afternoon, Miss Radford," he said, not even attempting to hide the amusement in his voice.

Quint looked up at Lily with amazement and growing confusion. The mere sight of her brought a smile to his face. She looked magnificent, her hair in disarray, her robe open so that he could see the plain linen of her nightgown and the way it molded to her body. Her coquettish accent was entirely absent, and until she saw him standing there her face had been flushed with anger. Now she was staring at him with her surprise and embarrassment evident in the way she glared at him, wide-eyed and silent. Finally, she regained her composure and gathered the robe at her waist, tying the long sash.

Cora recovered her senses first. "Did we wake you, miss?"

"Tommy woke me," Lily answered, her Southern accent back. But there was an uncertainty in her voice and in her usually confident stance. "I heard him yelling."

"Tommy?" Quint looked to Cora for an answer, and the housekeeper tried unsuccessfully to suppress a grin.

"Me 'usband, Tommy." She indicated the still angry man with a wave of her hand, and she smiled merrily at the relief that washed over Quint. "I told you Miss Radford wasn't feeling well. Now you've disturbed her much-needed rest."

Quint looked back up the narrow stairway. Lily stood very still, one hand on the banister, her eyes never leaving him. She looked tired, but her color was good. Nothing about Lily looked ill, or in fact anything less than perfect.

"Are you all right? I could bring the doctor . . ."

"No." Lily tried to smile, but it faded quickly and was replaced by a look of indecision. "I'll be all right. I just need to rest for a day or two."

Tommy was still glaring, and Cora had a smug expression on her face.

"I'll come by and check on you tomorrow," Quint promised.

"That's not necessary, Mr. Tyler," Lily said. Quint's gaze rested on the fingers that grasped the white banister. He was too far away from Lily to see those hands clearly, but they were uncovered. There was something odd about the long slender fingers that rested against the rail.

"I insist." He bowed to her slightly, ignoring Cora and Tommy completely.

Lily watched Quint depart through the front door, her stomach in an unfamiliar knot, her hand grasping the banister too tightly. Why wouldn't he simply leave her alone? Why did he insist on staring at her like that? As if he knew her better than anyone else in the world. As if he could see into her very soul, into that part of herself she kept hidden from the world.

" 'E's trouble," Tommy insisted as soon as the door was closed.

"I agree." Cora took her husband's arm and together they faced Lily. " 'E's up to no good. I think you should 'ave a couple o' the lads follow 'im for a day or two."

"Whatever for?"

Cora pursed her lips. "I 'ave a feeling."

Lily rolled her eyes, showing her aunt just how much credence she gave her *feeling*.

" 'E's up to something. I know it," Cora insisted.

Lily relented. She was too tired to argue, and if it made Cora feel better, then so be it. "All right. But he's not up to anything. Is it so hard to believe that a man might simply find me attractive?"

Cora's stern face softened. "It's not that. But you know we must be careful."

"Do it, then." Lily waved her hand tiredly. "But no violence, Tommy," she added curtly. "Have him watched for a couple of days. I'm going to sleep for at least that long."

Lily knew it would be a while before she could make herself fall asleep again, even as tired as she was. He hadn't given up on her. In spite of all that she'd said to him, Quintin Tyler hadn't turned away from her. The thought that he actually cared for her gave Lily a warm, secure feeling, and she hugged it to herself like a treasured lucky charm.

He'd offered to fetch the doctor for her. He wanted to drop by tomorrow to make certain she was all right. She wished there was a time and a place in her life for friends, and even a man who would be more than a friend. But there wasn't. That thought stole away a bit of the warmth that filled her, but even that hard truth couldn't drive it away completely.

"He likes me," she whispered into her pillow as she closed her eyes. "Quintin Tyler likes me." She fell asleep with a small smile on her face.

Quint's frown deepened as he approached the crowded streets of Nassau. *Bloody hell?* In a voice devoid of her whining accent? And what was it about her hands that had caught his attention? Long, slender fingers clutching the white railing. Long, *brown*, slender fingers. Whenever he'd seen her she'd been wearing gloves, but her hands were as brown as her face.

Even her face seemed to have a little more color to it than it had before. Of course, she lived on a tropical island, and it was no surprise that her skin was honey brown. He looked down at his own dark hands. Her hands were not nearly so dark as his own, but neither were his continually hidden from the sun. If only she'd been closer, and he could have taken those hands in his own.

Quint shook his head as he re-entered the hotel.

Bloody hell? What kind of curse was that for a proper Southern lady?

Chapter Ten

Quint kept his promise. He was at Lily's door early the next morning to inquire after her health. When Cora assured him testily that Lily was well, Quint thanked her, turned away, and left the stunned housekeeper standing in the entrance. He didn't give her the opportunity to slam the door in his face or to summon her burly husband to pummel him into the ground. She was obviously disappointed when Quint accepted her assurances and left quietly.

Eleanor Slocum was expecting him. She was sitting at her desk, prim and proper, looking very little like a spy.

Quint had no information to relay that she hadn't already received from another operative, and he related the tidbits he had collected with a cold impartiality. He'd already decided that he wasn't much of a spy, even though what he'd accomplished so far was noteworthy. The information about the marine engines alone justified his presence in Nassau.

He hadn't thought himself a soldier at heart,

even when it was all he'd had, all he knew. But he was not a spy at heart, either. There was, at least, nobility in soldiering. He saw none in spying.

"John Wright is in prison, I suppose?" He sat in his chair and extended his leg, tapping the cane against the floor impatiently. What was left of his good humor left as Eleanor leaned forward, hesitating before she answered. Her face became suddenly stern, and in that moment she did resemble a spy, cold and heartless.

"Captain Wright is dead."

Quint didn't move, not a muscle as he studied the woman who imparted the news coolly, emotionlessly. "What happened?" he whispered in a low voice.

Eleanor leaned back, keeping her visage and voice calm. "He tried to escape and was shot."

"Shot. Goddammit, that wasn't supposed to happen." There was a knot in his stomach that shouldn't be there, and Eleanor's unconcerned shrug only infuriated him more.

"He shouldn't have run," she reasoned.

Quint could barely move. The picture was so clear, so vivid. John Wright, that bear of a man, running away from his captors only to be shot. Probably in the back.

"It's my fault," Quint said, more to himself than to Eleanor.

"What's the matter?" Eleanor asked, evidently irritated with the emotional effect the news was having on him. "Didn't you ever kill anyone in battle?"

"Of course, but that was different," Quint said in a subdued voice. "They were trying to kill me. They were faceless, nameless strangers in gray uniforms. Not friends. Not men I played cards with and drank with."

"You have to put it out of your mind," Eleanor ordered. "You saved lives by stopping those engines from reaching their destination. Hundreds of lives. Thousands, maybe. It's done," Eleanor said sharply. "You have to weigh the one life that was lost against the many lives that were saved."

Eleanor leaned forward, and her face softened. "You can't afford to allow emotions to rule you, Quintin. Winning is everything. Individuals aren't important. Can't be. If you don't learn that soon, you'll never make a decent spy."

"I'll never make a decent spy," he said quietly.

"How are you progressing with Miss Radford?" Eleanor tried to change the subject.

"None of your goddamn business," Quint spat. He didn't want to drag Lily into this deadly game. She was innocent, but he didn't think that mattered to Eleanor. The innocent suffered in war, maybe most of all. A soldier went into battle knowing he might never return, but civilians who were caught up in battle died just as hard, just as bloody.

"As a matter of fact, I've given up on Lily Radford," Quint said coolly. "She doesn't know anything that can help us."

"But the Captain . . ."

"Is as invisible as ever," Quint said as he stood. "Lily can't help us. I'm leaving her out of this."

"We know now that Lily Radford is vulnerable. I'll just assign another operative to take up where you left off," Eleanor warned.

Quint turned and gave her a dazzling smile. "Go right ahead. Wish him luck for me. He's going to need it."

Quint slammed the door behind him and headed back for the hotel. What if Eleanor hadn't been bluffing? What if she really did assign someone to work his way into Lily's life, to try to seduce her? He didn't think anyone would get very far, but what if he was wrong? What if Lily fell in love with a man who was spying on her? Who cared nothing for her? That would be devastating for her. And, he decided quickly, devastating for him as well.

There was something different about Lily, and the thought had plagued him for days. She was no idiot, no silly girl who passed all her time reading poetry and stitching samplers. She was hiding something.

By late afternoon, word of Captain Wright's death was all over the hotel, and the occupants, mostly seamen themselves, were hushed and thoughtful. It might have been any one of them. The blockade was tightening, and the odds of a successful run were not what they had been in the past. John Wright had been a popular man, and everyone mourned the passing of a friend.

But they were living in a time of war, and every man knew the risks he took when he ran the blockade.

Quint didn't feel like playing cards, but neither

did anyone else. He declined dinner and bought a bottle of the hotel's finest rum. Captain Dennison joined him, and the two commiserated silently. Quint felt like a traitor. Hell, he was a traitor, in the eyes of the men who surrounded him. If Dennison knew that Quint was responsible for Wright's death, Quint figured he'd be dead before he hit the floor.

Dennison, almost as drunk as Quint, leaned forward, his elbows on the fine white tablecloth. He was as tall as Quint, but reed thin. His slender form made him appear even taller than he really was, and he handled his height and slight form with a masculine grace. He shaved irregularly, so that he always seemed to be in the process of growing a beard, and he rarely trimmed his fair hair. But his clothing and his manners were always impeccable, and the women loved his easy smile and blue eyes.

"You haven't been chasing after Miss Lily again, have you?" Dennison frowned drunkenly.

Quint nodded his head. "I have, actually, but I'm going to give her up." His words were only slightly slurred. "She's too good for the likes of me, anyway."

"You got that right," Dennison said, nodding. "Smart move. Captain Sherwood would cut out your heart . . ."

". . . and have it for breakfast," Quint finished. "I know. Hell, if I thought I had a chance, he could have it."

"Got it bad, eh?" Dennison nodded sympathetically. "Sorry to hear that. But there are plenty of other ladies in Nassau. There's a whorehouse right across the street, and there's this pretty little redheaded lass . . ."

Quint started laughing. Eleanor's operative must be a fountain of information.

"What's so funny?" Dennison furrowed his brow.

"Nothing." Quint made himself stop laughing. "I'm drunk, that's all. I haven't been this drunk since . . . since . . . hell, I've never been this drunk."

Dennison hadn't yet succumbed to the temptation to drink straight from the bottle, as Quint had. He was still drinking from a glass, and he stared at the amber liquid as Quint lifted the bottle to his lips.

"I'll miss John."

"Me, too," Quint said sadly.

Quint listened as Dennison told tales about Wright, some that might have been true, others that were clearly exaggerations of the dead man's abilities at sea. All the while, Quint continued to drink from the bottle, hoping to find comfort in the fiery liquid, but finding only confusion.

The room, a room that was usually lively and boisterously loud by this time of night, was hushed and subdued. When Dennison had told all he remembered of John Wright, the two men sat in silence for a while. Finally, Quint listed over the table and glared at the English captain.

"Are you married?"

"No," Dennison answered soundly, vaguely horrified.

"Have you ever been in love?"

Dennison returned the drunken stare. "Many times. Are we talking about Miss Lily again?"

Quint nodded and lifted the bottle. There was barely an inch of the amber liquid remaining. He frowned at it, and decided, too late, that he should have had something to eat before he'd consumed so much of the island's favorite drink. When he banged the bottle against the table, Dennison jumped.

"I think I'm falling in love with her." Quint slapped his right palm over his heart as he whispered the confidence. "Isn't that . . . horrible?"

"Aye," Dennison agreed. "Horrible, indeed."

"I can't stop thinking about her," Quint murmured. "Is that love?"

"Or lust," Dennison said gravely.

Quint raised his eyebrows briefly. "That, too, but I don't think that's all it is. Not anymore. But she won't see me. She doesn't like me, and I can't blame her. Why would she want a drunken, crippled . . . gambler." Quint caught himself just in time. He'd almost said the word 'spy'. ". . . When she has the magnificent Captain Sherwood. Why doesn't he marry her?" Quint asked angrily. "Dammit, it's not right. Not fair to Lily."

"Settle down, Tyler," Dennison suggested. "Don't get yourself all worked up."

"Too late." Quint rose, grasping the bottle in one hand and his cane in the other.

"Where are you goin'?" Dennison stood to follow, but he swayed slightly, closed his eyes tight, and fell back into his chair.

"You know damn well where I'm going," Quint said as he walked in an amazingly straight line for the door.

"Lily!" Quint called, his voice a loud, harsh whisper as he looked up at the window that must be hers. In his drunken state, it had taken him several minutes to decipher exactly where her bedroom must be. It was the window he had seen a blur of lavender in as he'd sat in her garden that afternoon and waited.

Was Captain Sherwood in there with her? Damn it all, he didn't care. Quint reached down, laying his bottle aside and grabbing a handful of pebbles and tiny shells mixed with grains of sand. He called her name again after the shower of debris had rained on her window, his voice gruff and much too loud.

He heard her lift the window pane, and he smiled as her head appeared above him. He opened his arms wide, cane in one hand, retrieved bottle of rum in the other. "Lily," he whispered harshly. "Get down here."

"Shhh." She placed a finger to her lips. "Go away. You'll wake the entire household."

"I don't care. If you don't get . . . down . . . here, I'm going in to get you," he threatened, his voice gradually growing louder. "I need to talk to you, Lily. Please."

She disappeared from the widow, and he waited. Either she would join him, or Captain Sherwood would appear and demand his heart. Quint didn't care. He had to see Lily.

"Mr. Tyler." He heard her soft voice before he could see her face clearly, but she stepped into the moonlight and his heart stopped. "You shouldn't be here." Her voice was only lightly chastising.

Quint smiled at her. "Lily, you're beautiful." Her curling hair was loose and fell over her shoulders, and she was wearing that silky dressing gown she had been wearing when he'd seen her on the stairs.

"You're drunk, Mr. Tyler," Lily whispered.

"Quint," he whispered, but his voice was still much louder than hers. "Say it, Lily."

"Quint." Lily breathed his name. "Now, you have to leave."

"Talk to me, Lily," he pleaded with her, and even in the dim moonlight he saw her features soften.

"In the garden." She took his arm and led him down the stone path. Quint leaned against her, not for support but because he could. She was warm, and her hair smelled like sunshine and the sea itself. There was a warm breeze, light and fragrant, and it washed over them gently, the island's own perfume. The moon lit their way, and Lily led him into the wild sanctuary of her garden.

Together, they sat on the wrought-iron bench, and Quint leaned against her.

"What is it that's so important it can't wait until morning?" Lily prodded.

"You won't see me in the morning. You'll send me away, like always," he said petulantly, but his mood quickly changed, and he smiled at her. "So I threw pebbles at your window."

"You threw pebbles *in* my window. It was halfway open, and now most of those pebbles are scattered all over my floor."

"Good. It'll give that hag something to clean up in the morning." Quint narrowed his eyes at her. Why was she grinning like that?

"I imagined you mean Cora."

Quint nodded. "Cora, that hag. Won't ever let me see you, Lily."

Lily laid her hand on Quint's arm. "I told you I couldn't see you again." She whispered, even though they were too far away from the house for anyone to hear them.

Lily knew that if Tommy woke and found Quint here, in the middle of the night, drunk out of his mind and pressing himself insistently against her, there would be hell to pay. Tommy didn't like Quint much as it was.

Quint ignored her protests and laid his hand over hers. He seemed fascinated with her hand, staring at it as he lifted it, twining his fingers through hers. Lily tried to pull her hand away, but Quint wouldn't allow that. He lifted her palm to his lips and kissed it tenderly, than laid the palm to his cheek. Lily tried to draw gently away, but he held her hand firmly, and when he began to kiss each finger, one after another, she felt that undeniable churning in her belly, that fire that had been unknown to her until she'd met Quintin Tyler. She stopped trying to withdraw from him, even when he ran his thumb along the small calluses there on the ball of her hand. Calluses she had tried to hide from him with her gloves.

"I love your hands," Quint said simply, holding them both and studying them intently, memorizing every line, kissing the short fingernails.

"You came out her in the middle of the night to tell me that?"

Quint shook his head. "Did you know John Wright?" His face was somber as he asked, and he continued to hold her hands, running his fingers over her skin as if he couldn't get enough.

"Not very well. I . . . I heard what happened to him. Was he a friend of yours?"

Quint nodded slowly. "Yes. We played cards and had dinner together sometimes."

Lily saw the pain in Quint's face. He was taking his friend's death very hard, and for some reason that pain had brought him to her. "I'm sorry," she murmured. With a little difficulty, she disengaged her hands from his, but instead of moving away, as she knew she should, she leaned forward and placed her arms around his neck. "I'm so sorry, Quint."

She laid her head against his shoulder, telling herself that she was comforting him. But it was more than that. She liked the feel of his body against hers, and she'd use any excuse to indulge herself just this one time. She could feel his ragged breath in her ear, smell the rum on his breath and the smoke from his cigars that lingered in the fibers of the coat he wore.

And she belonged there. It was a searing and painful knowledge, as primal and undeniable as the physical cravings he stirred in her. This was her place in the world.

"Come away with me," Quint whispered, his words only slightly slurred. "Tonight. Leave your Captain and I'll take you anywhere you want to go."

Lily pulled away slightly so she could see his face. "You don't mean that. You're drunk and sad and feeling lonely because your friend died."

"That's not why I'm asking you to go away with me. I'm asking because I love you. I love you, Lily." As he spoke the words, a small frown came over his face. "I love you." He repeated the declaration, even though he was obviously none too pleased.

"You don't even know me." Lily laid her palm against his cheek, and he immediately covered it with his own hand and moved it to his mouth. The warmth of his lips made her tingle from the top of her head to the tips of her toes, and when he flickered his tongue across her palm she almost faltered. "I . . . I'm not the woman you think I am. I . . ."

"I don't care," Quint vowed. "Come with me."

Lily hesitated, but she knew what she had to do. "I can't, Quint. And in the morning, you will care. In the morning, when you're sober, this will all look different."

"Maybe," he conceded. "But I'll still love you." Quint leaned over to kiss her, and she lifted her face to him to accept his mouth. It wasn't the searching, probing kiss of the night of the ball, but a tender, sweet caress. Her heart was breaking. She could love him back, easily, if she allowed herself the luxury of that emotion.

"Good-bye, Lily," Quint whispered as he pulled away from her. "I promise not to bother you again."

But he didn't get up. In truth, Lily didn't think he was capable. He leaned against her shoulder, and in a moment he was asleep. She lowered his head so that it rested in her lap, and in the moonlight she could see his features clearly. Her fingers traced the small bump on his nose, probed the dimples in his cheeks, but he never stirred.

"Dead to the world," she whispered. "I wonder if you have any idea how much trouble you're causing, Mr. Tyler. I think not."

Lily remained on the bench for the better part of an hour, her fingers always in Quint's hair or on his face. He was almost too handsome. He would have been, if not for the broken nose and the tiny lines around his eyes. He must have been an angelically beautiful child, before life had turned him into a devilishly handsome man.

This was dangerous, the feelings he stirred in her. Her life had seemed so clear to her before he'd come bursting into it. Running the blockade was the only way she could satisfy her burning hatred for the Yankees. She was responsible for the Radford family honor, and nothing else mattered. Not friendship, not comfort, not what most considered to be a normal life. And not love. Definitely not love. And then she'd turned around and there he was. He hadn't been completely out of her thoughts since the moment she'd laid eyes on him. Love. Why now?

The noise was so faint that if they'd still been talking she never would have heard it. Lily turned her head in the direction of the sound and lifted her hand, waving the boys in. It had to be the crewmen Tommy had ordered to follow Quint.

They approached hesitantly, and Lily wondered how long they'd been watching, how much they'd seen. She ignored their obvious discomfort.

"Sorry, Cap'n," one of the boys said, unsure of himself. "We was waitin' up by the 'ouse, but it seemed a terrible long time . . ."

"He's dead drunk, Sellers," Lily said tersely. "You two take him back to the hotel. And be careful of his leg, for God's sake," she said when they lifted Quint a bit too roughly, each man taking an arm and draping it over his shoulder.

Quint didn't make a sound as the two young seamen divided his weight between them. Lily picked up the cane from the ground beside the bench and handed it to Sellers with no word of instruction. She sat back down on the bench and watched the two crewmen carry Quint away, and she shook her head. Poor man. He'd probably have one hell of a headache in the morning. She wondered if he'd remember anything that had happened.

She wondered if he'd remember that he told her he loved her.

She wondered if he'd remember that he told her he wasn't coming back.

Chapter Eleven

For the next several days, Quint kept to himself, taking his meals in his room and pacing the streets of Nassau after dark.

Hands. He had awakened the morning after his drunken escapade with a pounding headache, no inkling of how he'd gotten back into his room, and a memory of Lily's hands. That was just about all he remembered clearly. He'd thrown pebbles at her window, and she'd come to him, and he'd touched her hands.

The charm of the island no longer seduced him. He passed enchanting cottages and fragrant foliage and barely noticed. His mind was possessed of one thought.

Captain Robert Sherwood.

Where the hell was the man? If he was as insanely jealous as Dennison claimed, why hadn't he confronted Quint? Lily deserved better than a man who wouldn't marry her, who neglected her and left her to defend herself against wayward gamblers with less than honorable intentions. Damn it all, he'd never felt possessive about a woman before, not even Alicia. Not the way he felt possessive about Lily.

But he hadn't been sent to Nassau to save Lily from a man who didn't deserve her, a man Quint detested even though he'd never laid eyes on Captain Sherwood. Quint would have hated any man who laid claim to Lily, and that was his dilemma.

He'd been sent to Nassau to gather information about the blockade runners, and that was what was tearing him in two. If he hadn't been committed to the preservation of the Union, if he didn't believe with all his heart that what he was fighting for was important, then he would have no qualms about his future. He would grab Lily and take her, by force if necessary, and they would leave Nassau together. West. A man and a woman could disappear out West, in a place where land was cheap and plentiful, and people had learned not to ask too many questions.

He didn't think he would have to kidnap her. Lily didn't love Captain Sherwood. If she did, she wouldn't have kissed Quint the way she had. There was something strong between them, something more powerful than Quint had ever imagined. Whether it was love or lust or some spiritual attraction that he didn't understand, it drew them together inexorably. She was his.

The problem was, he didn't see how he could have Lily and do his job at the same time. He hadn't left his home and joined the Union Army on a whim. There was a deepfelt reason for his commitment. A memory. A memory of one single person that had haunted him through the years.

If only his leg would heal enough for him to return to his company. Then they could leave this island and return to the States, together.

But Lily was a Southerner. How strongly did she feel about the conflict? He discounted Captain Sherwood's involvement in the penetration of the blockade as any sort of evidence of Lily's loyalties. Most of the captains were involved in the venture for the profit, not out of a sense of duty. And was it fair to ask her to wait for him, not knowing if he would survive or not? He was willing to risk his life for what he believed, but was he willing to make Lily love him, and then leave her a widow?

Quint looked up and found himself at the foot of the path to Lily's house. The sun was setting, a glorious sight of brilliance and breathtaking color, but he gave it only a brief glance. He followed the path, not knowing what he would do when he got to the end of it, but realizing the inevitability of facing Lily again.

He rapped the gold head of his cane against the door, and after a few moments Cora threw it open and glared at him.

"Miss Radford is not receiving . . ."

Quint ignored her and pushed his way inside, his cane tapping loudly against the tile floor, his scowl directed at the housekeeper who seemed so intent on keeping him away from Lily.

"Call her, or I'll do it myself," he threatened.

Cora backed away, two small steps. She opened her mouth to speak, then snapped it shut without uttering a sound. She hesitated just a moment too long, and Quint did as he had threatened. He lifted his head and bellowed Lily's name, not once but three times, until she came running into the foyer.

"What's wrong?" Lily looked first to Cora, and then to Quint. When her eyes lit on him, they hardened, and those fiery eyes turned as cold as ice.

"I don't wish to see you again, Mr. Tyler," she said crisply. "If you have once again wandered farther than your leg can bear, then you may sit on the front steps for five minutes. At the end of that period, I will personally see that you are on your way." There was a threat there, and it wasn't even thinly veiled.

"Give me five minutes alone with you, and if you still want me to leave, I will."

Lily sighed. "And this time when you promise not to come back, will you keep your word?"

Quint frowned. Had he promised to stay away from her? "Yes," he said, his voice calmer and more in control than it had been just moments before.

Lily led him into the parlor and sat in the middle of the loveseat. Her positioning left Quint no choice but to take the chair that sat at an angle to the loveseat. He would be close, but not close enough. Apparently it was her intention to keep him at a distance.

Her plans went awry as he sat next to her, his thigh pressing against hers until she drew sharply away from him.

"What do you want, Mr. Tyler?" she asked coldly.

"Back to Mr. Tyler, are we?" He reached out and took her hand, and even though she tried to pull away, he held her fast. She wasn't wearing her usual gloves, and he was glad he'd caught her unaware. Quint lifted her hand to his lips, holding it tightly, his strong fingers gripping her slender hand as she continued to try to pull it away from him. He ran his thumb across the calluses on the palm of her hand and studied once again, in a sober state, the short nails at the tips of her elegant fingers. He wanted to kiss each one of those fingers, but there was so little time. Hell, he didn't understand his own feelings. How could he hope to sort out hers as well?

He lifted his gaze from that hand to her emotionless face.

"I like to work in the garden," Lily snapped, finally yanking her hand away. "That's why I have calluses."

"You could wear gloves when you work . . ."

"I like the feel of the soil in my hands," Lily said sharply.

Quint frowned. Her garden was a tropical paradise, practically growing wild. He saw no evidence of any sort of work she could have done to get calluses on those lovely hands. She was hiding something from him, as she had been since they'd met.

"What's the matter?" she whined artificially, and with a bitter bite in her voice. "Doesn't Eleanor Slocum have brown, callused hands?"

She lifted her eyebrows and gave him a simple-minded look that would have fooled him a few weeks ago. But not now.

"Eleanor Slocum?"

Lily narrowed her eyes as she glared at him, trying to convey her indifference and her iciness. But she was angry. She had no right to be angry. She had no claim to Quintin Tyler.

Tommy had been delighted to share the news. "Quintin Tyler is 'umpin' the Widow Slocum," had been his exact words to her just two days earlier.

"I understand the two of you are . . . very close friends," she said.

Quint sighed and shrugged his shoulders. "Not really. We're just old acquaintances. That's all."

She didn't believe him, though he lied very well. He stared at her for a moment, and then he began to smile.

"You're jealous, Lily? If that's true, then you must care for me, just a little."

"Don't be ridiculous."

Quint leaned toward her, pinning Lily to the back of the loveseat. His face was inches from hers, and his dark eyes delved into her soul. He was looking for answers—for himself and for her.

"There's only one woman on this island—in this world—that I'm interested in, Lily Radford, and I'm looking at her right now. I knew it the moment I saw you, wearing that ridiculous hat and trying to palm me off on Mrs. Greene."

Lily licked her lips nervously. He shouldn't be

able to do this to her. He shouldn't be able to make her heart beat fast and her breath catch in her chest. It made her feel weak, and she didn't like it. Not at all. Still, she didn't push him away, as she very well could have.

"You knew what?"

"That you would be mine. I think I was destined to come here and find you, Lily. I think everything in my life up to this moment has been leading me here." He laid his lips lightly over hers. "Leading me to you, Lily," he whispered, and she felt his warm breath mingling with hers.

"That's the most ridiculous statement I've ever heard," Lily said softly. "I don't believe in destiny. You're just . . . you're just a smooth-talking womanizer, and I shouldn't believe a word you say."

"Come away with me," Quint whispered.

Lily looked up at him, and for a moment she considered what he was offering. He'd never said anything about marriage, and he'd only told her that he loved her when he was drunk. She couldn't consider that reliable. But she did feel something for him. She didn't know what to call it. Love, attraction, a kind of providence . . . and he must return some of those feelings. Damned if he didn't look as confused as she felt.

Tommy could captain her ship. He would make a fine captain. Perhaps even a better one than she. No. She had rejected that notion long ago. This was her battle, and she would finish it. Even if it cost her dearly.

"I can't, Quint," Lily whispered, but instead of pulling away she pressed her breasts to him and wrapped her arms around his neck. "I want to, but I can't."

Her answer made Quint angry. He'd agonized for days over her, and she was ready to dismiss him without a second thought.

"Is it the Captain? Is this what you want?" He backed away from her and lifted his hand. "Are you afraid I won't be able to give you all he can? A beautiful house, fashionable clothes? Well, I don't know if I'll be able to or not."

"Quint, don't—"

"Don't? Don't what? Am I making you uncomfortable?" He rose to his feet easily, the cane in his hand almost forgotten in his anger. "I suppose I should apologize, Lily, but I can't. Why are you willing to settle for your Captain? Where is he, anyway? Dennison said Sherwood would cut out my heart and have it for breakfast if I didn't leave you alone. If you were my woman, and some man came along prowling around your skirts, I wouldn't hesitate to do that. But you're not my woman, are you, Lily?"

"No," she whispered.

"I'm wasting my time." It was a statement meant as much for his own ears as for hers.

"Sometimes there are concerns much greater than what two people feel," Lily said softly.

"Like what?"

"Honor. Duty. Obligation. Two solitary souls in a world full of people really aren't very important." Lily lowered her head. She couldn't or wouldn't meet his gaze. "Emotions change like the tides. You might regret—"

"Never," Quint said, but he frowned. It was as if she'd read his mind and voiced his doubts. The only difference between them was that even though he didn't know what solution he would find to the warring emotions that were tearing him apart, he knew he would find one. If only he could have Lily by his side.

But her words were as final and emotionless as . . . as Eleanor Slocum's. The words were, in fact, quite similar. Two women who were willing to put their personal feelings aside for their beliefs. He knew what Eleanor fought for, but what of Lily?

As he watched, she stiffened her back, took his hand in hers, and sighed deeply. He didn't know what drove her, but she was determined.

"You can't come here again, ever."

"Lily, I . . ."

She met his eyes then, and he could see the pleading in them. "For God's sake, Quint. Stay away from me before you ruin everything."

Before he could reply, Tommy burst into the room. He strode straight to Quint, his hands balled into meaty fists, his intentions clear.

Tommy was a big man, but Quint realized that he was also rather slow. Quint ducked as Tommy's fist sailed through the air where Quint's head had been less than a second earlier.

Quint was hampered by his bad leg, but he hadn't lost any of his skill or speed with his fists. His left hook caught Tommy under the jaw, and the big man dropped to the floor with a thud. Before he could recover his wits, Quint's cane was pressed against Tommy's windpipe, the pressure so great that they both knew any upward movement on Tommy's part would cause serious damage.

"If you intend to ever speak again, you'll lie there until I'm quite finished," Quint threatened.

Without lessening the pressure against Tommy's throat, Quint turned his eyes back to Lily. "Do you mean it? Do you really want me to walk out of your life and not look back?"

"Yes," Lily said clearly. "It's for the best. For both of us."

She was standing almost primly, with her hands clasped together in front of her, her plain dress molded to her torso and flowing about her hips and legs. She'd attempted to pin her hair up, but loose curling tendrils framed her sun-kissed face. He stared at her long and hard, branding her image in his memory; then he lifted his cane from Tommy's windpipe and turned away from them both.

As he left, he heard Lily's infuriatingly calm voice as she restrained Tommy. Quint wished she hadn't done that, because he would love to stomp the burly man into the ground, but good. That, at least, would be a release from the rage that was building inside him. For the first time in years he felt the urge to pound another man's face until he could no longer manage to lift his arms. The problem was, Tommy was the wrong man. It was Captain Sherwood Quint wanted to get his hands on.

And still, he knew that Lily was right. There

were more important things than what two people felt. He knew what his obstacles were, but what were Lily's? What drove a woman to speak of honor and duty as if she were a soldier herself?

Chapter Twelve

Tyler raked his winnings toward him with both hands. Dennison was frowning mightily, and the other three gamblers at the table looked as disgusted as he felt. Tyler had been winning big all week. He always had a bottle of rum or bourbon at his side, though he never again drank so much that he lost control.

Tyler's usually readable face was stony and impassive, and his black eyes gave away nothing. No emotion. No spark of life.

Dennison was fairly certain he knew the reason for the dramatic change in Quintin Tyler. He felt sympathy for the man, though he was puzzled as well. One woman was much like another. Dennison liked them all—blond or brunette, tall or short, plump or thin. They were all soft and sweet, and each woman was possessed of her own beauty, be it remarkable eyes or a devastating figure. One particular woman he had known, long ago, had been considered plain by most, but Dennison had noticed that she moved with extraordinary grace. She was a wonder to watch, as were all females.

But Tyler's problems could be traced to one solitary woman. Lily Radford. Dennison was not blind to Lily's charms, but it seemed futile to dwell on them when another man claimed her, and there were so many other fascinating women on the island.

It seemed that if he ever wanted to win again at cards with Tyler at the table, he was going to have to find a cure for the man's ailment, and the cure, of course, was another woman. Lost in the inviting arms of a willing woman, Tyler would no doubt forget his obsession with Lily Radford. James Dennison definitely believed in love; he just didn't believe it was necessary to confine that love to a single woman. He loved many women, and while he might have a particular favorite at one moment or another, he never forgot that the world was full of those marvelous creatures.

Quint studied the gold and silver coins on the table before him with no joy. His companions, all but Dennison, had deserted him, having lost all they could afford or were willing to part with. He knew that he should be losing, at least a few nights a week. He didn't want to scare away all the potential sources of information. But in the week since Lily had sent him away, he'd approached each and every game as if it were a battle. He didn't face opponents, he faced enemies. It wasn't a game, it was war.

Dennison leaned forward and smiled wryly. He didn't seem to mind losing, but then, his fast little steamer had made him rich.

"Lady luck has been at your side this week, Tyler," Dennison said with good humor.

"So it seems."

"You don't seem particularly pleased." Dennison drummed his long fingers on the tabletop.

Quint didn't want to discuss Lily with Dennison. He knew where the Englishman stood on the subject. Lily was Captain Sherwood's woman, and off limits.

"I'm ecstatic," Quint said woodenly. "It's just that I've developed a good poker face."

Dennison grinned. "Liar." The accusation was delivered softly, and with a warm and friendly edge. "I know what your problem is, and I know how to fix it."

He had Quint's attention, and the grin widened.

"Come with me." Dennison stood, unfolding his long and graceful frame slowly from the chair. "There's someone I'd like you to meet."

She said her name was Marguerite, and she pronounced it with a decidedly French flair. The rest of her speech was definitely American, and even a bit uncultured. Quint decided she'd probably grown up as a Margaret, maybe a Meg. She looked healthy, for a woman of her profession. Prostitutes, in his estimation, seemed to age fast, as if their work sucked the very life out of them.

Marguerite's hair was flame red, curly without being kinky, and it was her best feature. Her face was ordinary, and her eyes were pale gray. She had an hourglass figure that was shown off by the skimpy costume she wore, a brightly colored transparent gown that was cut so low, her nipples peeked over the neckline.

Dennison had presented her to Quint in the parlor downstairs, a large room filled with piano music and cigar smoke and other women of Marguerite's profession. Women of every size and shape and color. Women quiet and boisterous. Quint had left Dennison as the English captain surveyed the scene around him, in what appeared to be his idea of heaven.

Marguerite led Quint up the stairs, taking his hand as if he were a child and coaxing him up the plushly carpeted stairway. She walked with a slow, practiced seduction, her hips swaying beneath the bright gown, the diaphanous material molding to her form as she moved.

Quint followed silently, his face impassive though his mind was reeling. Dennison was certain he would lose his passion for Lily in the body of another woman, and who was to say that was an impossible task? Marguerite was certainly tempting, and he didn't intend to spend his life pining over a woman who didn't love him, a woman who had bound herself to another man.

Marguerite pulled him into her room and closed the door behind them, bestowing upon Quint a seductive smile. The room was dimly lit; the bed that dominated it was garishly decorated in bright green and gold. Tassels hung from the bedposts, thick and gold.

She pressed her body against his, sandwiching him between her body and the door. Marguerite laid her lips against Quint's throat, flicking her tongue over his skin. Talented hands roamed over his arms, down his sides, and finally rested between his legs. She got the response she was looking for, at least physically, but Quint pushed her away with a soft curse.

Marguerite tossed red curls and posed seductively a short step away. "I could lower the lamp," she offered. "You can pretend I'm her. You can even call me Lily, if you like. I often fill in for a loved one who is far away, or unattainable. It's part of the job."

Quint grasped her upper arms, his hands gripping her soft flesh tightly. "Who told you about Lily?" he seethed. "Dennison?"

God, it was bad enough that Lily Radford had his brain and his body so confused that he cared nothing for bedding an attractive and willing woman. How many people on the island knew he was making a fool of himself over Captain Sherwood's mistress?

"You're hurting me," Marguerite whined.

"Then answer my question."

Marguerite's eyes hardened. Gone was the seductive and willing temptress. "Eleanor. It was Eleanor who told me about you . . . Lieutenant."

Quint released the girl abruptly. So, this was the redhead who spied on the captains and the sailors who sought comfort in her bed. He shook his head and dropped to the only chair in the room, a plushly cushioned wing chair. His legs were thrust out in front of him, and he scowled as he studied the tips of his boots. With that, Marguerite sighed and plopped onto the end of the bed, folding her legs beneath her and completely abandoning her seductive air.

"Jamie's already paid for you, you know," she said, defeat in her voice. "And you're a lot better lookin' than most of the scum that comes in here night after night." She lifted her eyebrows in a silent question. "I'm yours for the night, bought and paid for."

Quint raised an eyebrow, and he actually smiled. "You could give Dennison his money back."

Marguerite shook her head. "Honey, I never do that. I did my best."

She rose from the bed with a sigh and headed for the door.

"Wait." Quint stopped her with his sharp command. "I'd like to talk to you."

She shook her red mane and returned to the bed almost reluctantly. "Paid to talk? That's a first." She sat cross-legged on the bed, seeming not to notice that her already daring gown had slipped, and one nipple was fully exposed. "What do you want to talk about?"

"What do you know about Captain Sherwood?"

Marguerite cocked her head to one side and studied him. She looked, for a moment, like a lost little girl, all innocent and sweet, the wonders of the world still ahead of her. It was that naive face, there above a wanton's body, that made Quint close his eyes and shake his head.

"I don't know much about Sherwood. Several sailors from his crew come to Madame Julia's, and there's this one boy in particular who always asks for me." She grinned, obviously pleased with herself. "He's a young fella. Just a boy, actually. Can't be more than eighteen . . ."

"And how old are you?" Quint asked, too obviously disapproving.

Marguerite grinned, and her seductive nature was apparent again. "I'll be nineteen my next birthday."

Her smile turned into a frown at Quint's disapproving glare. "Well," she continued. "At least I've got a roof over my head and food on the table every day. That wasn't always the case, Lieutenant Tyler. What I'm doing isn't all that much different than what Lily Radford's doing, is it?"

The question made Quint's blood boil. He wanted to jump out of his chair and shout at her . . . but she was right.

"Have you ever met Captain Sherwood?" he asked calmly.

Marguerite shook her head. "Never. None of the other girls have either. But the crew of the *Chameleon* talk about him as if he were some sort of goddamn champion."

Quint frowned. It had to be deliberate, the Captain's reluctance to be seen. It was a small island, but Quint had met very few people who actually knew Captain Robert Sherwood. Too few.

"He's sailing tonight," Marguerite added abruptly, as if she had only just decided to share that piece of information. "Soon, if he hasn't already put out to sea."

Quint thought about that piece of information for several minutes. Then he rose from his chair slowly, deliberately, his eyes focused on something far away, some distant point above Marguerite's head.

Lily had tried, in the past week, to push all thoughts of Quintin Tyler from her mind. She wished she'd never met him, never laid his eyes on his dimple or his long lashes or that somehow attractive bump where he had broken his nose. She couldn't forget him, no matter how hard she tried, and she was beginning to believe that she had made the biggest mistake of her life in sending him away.

But the *Chameleon* was making another run, and she had to turn her attention to the matter at hand. The blockade was tightening, and more and more of the fast steamers were being lost, captured, or run aground. Perhaps it was time to give the venture up. One more run, maybe two.

It made sense, but Lily knew she wouldn't stop until the war was over.

She sat at the lone table in her cabin, charts spread before her, the room lit with a lamp that was secured to the wall. Tommy was at her right side as she sat in a straight-backed chair, and her pilot, Cyril, was at her left. He held another lantern over the charts, lighting the maps they studied.

All precautions would be taken this trip, and they even planned to deviate their route. It would take several hours longer, but they wouldn't be approaching Wilmington directly. Hopefully, that would give them a better chance to slip by the blockaders.

That was the reason Cyril and Tommy were bent over the charts with her, as her fingers traced the route they would follow from Nassau to the mouth of the Cape Fear River.

"Captain!" Lily raised her head at the excited voice as one of her young crewmen approached, his footsteps growing louder as he practically ran into her cabin. She'd left the door open, so all he had to do was stick his head into the portal.

"What is it, Simon?" Lily stared at the young man, and her voice was sharp.

"We caught a man trying to sneak on board." Simon was barely eighteen, and the idea of catching a stowaway was obviously exciting. His face was red, and he clenched and unclenched his hands. "What should we do with 'im?"

"Do you know who he is?" she asked calmly.

Simon nodded his head. "That fella Tommy had us tailin' for the better part of a week. Walks with a cane, 'e does."

"Bring him here," Lily ordered.

Tommy and Cyril both stared at her as if she'd lost her mind. She'd gone so far to protect her identity, and now she was jeopardizing everything.

"Just toss 'im over the side," Tommy suggested. " 'E can probably swim."

She heard Quint approaching down the narrow hallway, his cane tapping against the polished wood, that particular sound growing louder with each step as he neared the cabin. She listened, and the next moment Quint was standing in the doorway.

She should have been afraid, but she was not. Perhaps she could believe, just a little, in his concept of destiny.

His eyes fell on Lily, the soft light from a lantern illuminating her face, and he questioned her silently. Why was she here? He glared at Tommy briefly, then turned to the only other man in the room.

The man on Lily's left was as old as Tommy—certainly old enough to be Lily's father. He stood not much taller than Lily herself and was possessed of unruly red hair and a bushy red moustache. The redheaded man was as thin as a reed, but there was strength in that slender body. You could see it in the way he stood, in the way he held himself.

"Captain?" Quint asked, almost viciously. This runt was the infamous Captain Sherwood? The man Lily had committed herself to? Quint had approached the *Chameleon* intent on having it out with Sherwood, but this was not what he had expected.

The red-haired man and Tommy both looked down at Lily, almost as if they were waiting for her to respond. She sighed, never taking her eyes away from him. The young sailor still gripped his arm, and the two of them blocked the doorway. There was no escape from this. Perhaps it was for the best.

Lily lifted her hand into the air, almost an act

of resignation. "What should I do with him? Lash him to the mast and have him whipped? Throw him into the brig?"

"We don't 'ave a brig," Tommy said, and his voice held none of the humor Lily's did.

"Do they still keelhaul stowaways?" She looked to Tommy for an answer.

He shrugged his shoulders. "I wouldn't mind tryin' it with this blighter."

Quint looked at the red-haired man who still hadn't spoken. With an air of discomfort, the man turned to Lily. "I really should return to the wheel."

Lily didn't look at the man as she dismissed him, and the crewman who held Quint pushed him farther into the room to let the thin man pass by.

"There's irons in the cargo 'old," the sailor said excitedly. "Should I fetch 'em, Cap'n?"

Quint looked to Tommy for an answer. So, he was Captain Sherwood, after all. But Tommy just glared at him, and it was Lily who answered. "That won't be necessary, Simon. You're dismissed."

It was evident that Simon wasn't quite ready to leave. He didn't want to miss out on any of the action, but he backed out of the room silently.

Quint stared at Lily, who sat so calmly at that table, while his confusion grew with each passing, silent second. Why had she been the one to answer?

She tried to dismiss Tommy as she had the others, but he was determined to stay, darting glances full of hate in Quint's direction. Finally, Lily turned to him calmly.

"I can handle this myself, Tommy. You know that." She interrupted his further protests. "On land you are my favorite uncle, but on board this ship I am captain, and you are my first mate." She said the words firmly, but with love. "That was the deal we made, remember?"

Tommy evidently didn't like leaving Quint alone with Lily, but he stormed from the room, slamming the door behind him when Lily asked him serenely to close it on his way out.

When Tommy had slammed the door, leaving them alone, Lily rose from her seat. It was only then that Quint noticed what she was wearing. When she'd been seated, all he could see was the simple white shirt, but now he saw that she wore tight black pants, and when she stepped away from the table he saw knee-high black boots as well, well-worn and supple.

"What am I going to do with you?" she asked with a half smile. "Conscript you? Put you to work shoveling coal in the engine room? Maroon you on a desert island?" Most all of her Southern accent had disappeared, and what remained was tempered with proper English and a hint of the Liverpool slums. This was the voice he had heard swearing, yelling *bloody hell!* at the top of her lungs that afternoon he had awakened her. She hadn't been ill. She'd just returned from the sea.

She was Captain Sherwood.

There was no Captain Sherwood.

"I don't understand," Quint said, taking a step

toward her. He was beginning to understand, but it was impossible. She was a woman. She couldn't be captain of any ship, much less a blockade runner.

Lily read the thoughts on his face and laughed lightly. There was a mischievous sparkle in her blue-green eyes, a becoming blush on her cheeks. And he was looking at the real, unreserved Lily Radford.

"Now you see why I had to invent Captain Sherwood. No one would believe . . ."

Quint took a step toward her. "I've met people who claimed to know him."

"Isn't that amazing? Sometimes Cyril or Tommy would wrap up in a cloak and be seen walking from the house, but that was all. The crew perpetuated the myth, as did I, and before I knew it, the nonexistent Captain Robert Sherwood was a bloody hero."

Quint grinned. He couldn't accept it all, but one point was wonderfully clear. There was no Captain Sherwood. "I came here looking for a man who doesn't exist, to convince him that I would be better for you than he's been. That I could take better care of you than he has. And it appears that you don't need anyone to take care of you at all."

Before she could answer, Quint had closed the short space between them and circled his arms around her, lowering his mouth to hers. This was a more powerful kiss than he'd given her before, searching and full of the knowledge that she belonged to him. She parted her lips to accept his probing tongue, relaxing and responding without reservation. Lily's hands were in his hair, against the back of his head, brushing his neck as she held him to her. She pressed against him, the swell of her breasts, her belly and thighs arousing him.

Lily drew away from him reluctantly. "I have to go on deck for a while."

"You're the captain," Quint said as he nibbled on her ear. "You can do whatever you want, can't you?"

"Stay here," Lily said as she pressed her hands to his chest, firmly but tenderly. "Once we're at sea I'll come back to the cabin. We have a lot to talk about."

"That's an understatement, Lily Radford." Quint lifted his head and frowned slightly. "That is your real name, isn't it?"

Lily nodded. "I have to go." She left him standing in the middle of the cabin, confused and stunned and elated. There was no Captain Sherwood.

Like hell there wasn't. Lily was Captain Sherwood!

He had to convince her to stop this insanity. A woman? Running the blockade? Quint paced the cabin and his frown deepened. Not only was it dangerous for Lily, her enterprise was helping to prolong the war. It was his job—his duty—to stop her. He didn't have to arrest her, just convince her to give this up. Captain Sherwood could retire, and Quint's duty would be done.

And what would Lily think when she found out

he was a spy for the Union? Did he really expect that she would forgive him? Lily? She was as passionate about her beliefs as any man he'd ever met. He didn't think she would give up without a fight.

Quint's eyes traveled over the room. The saber hanging on the wall, the large trunk, the small bed. He frowned at that. He would have liked to have Lily lie with him in the big bed in his hotel room, wide and soft and bright with crisp white sheets.

By the time Lily returned to him, it was all he could think of . . . throwing her into the bed and burying himself inside her. But he wouldn't. He wanted to kiss her all over; he wanted to make her as wild for him as he was for her.

He grabbed Lily almost the moment the door was shut, and he gathered her into his arms possessively. He buried his face against her neck, savoring the smell of her. He could smell on her skin the fragrant flowers of the island and the sea air, salty and clean. He could get lost in her arms, lost in a sense he had never dreamed of.

"Quint," she whispered. "We need to talk." Even as she spoke, he felt her melting in his arms.

"Later," Quint said huskily. He lowered his lips over hers and kissed her deeply, searchingly. Lily's lips were as warm as the sun, as soft as the petals of the bright flowers that grew in her garden.

Lily snaked her arms around Quint's neck and smoothed her hands over his skin, the side of his neck, his shoulder as she slipped her fingers under his collar.

Without lifting his lips from hers, Quint placed his hand between their bodies, laying it over her breast. Only the heavy linen of her shirt separated the heat of his palm from her nipple, and he felt it harden as Lily responded to his touch.

"I want you so much," he whispered.

"Yes," she breathed against his mouth, arching against his hand.

Lily felt the growing need inside her, a need only Quint could satisfy. She had denied herself his touch almost from the moment they'd met. Perhaps he had been right, after all. Perhaps it was destiny.

"Yes," she whispered again, pressing her body against his. She loved him. She'd been drawn to him from the beginning, but the last time she'd sent him away, more than a week ago, she'd known, because she'd thought her heart was broken. Love. An emotion she'd thought never to know.

So what could be wrong with this? She lived an uncertain life in an uncertain time. Perhaps, if they had met in another time and another place, conventions would have made her think twice about the yearnings he filled her with. But there was no place in Lily's life for convention. She approached lovemaking as she did everything else in life, with openness and vigor.

She allowed Quint to undress her slowly, his hands lingering, his mouth searching, and with each touch she wanted him more, desired him until she wanted to scream. She didn't fully understand what was driving her to a fever pitch, but she didn't question it either, didn't deny any of her urges.

Lily undressed Quint with the same deliberate slowness he had shown her. Her fingers danced over the crisp, dark curls on his chest, and even over the silken steel of his arousal that proved how much he wanted her. He was amazingly beautiful, with his hard muscles and dark skin. Her fingers found the scar on his leg, the wound that caused his limp. She didn't question him about the lie he had told, but caressed the recent scar with tenderness.

Quint led her to the small bed, taking small steps and touching her lovingly. He lowered his head and kissed her breasts, taking an aching nipple into his mouth and sucking lightly, pushing her beyond reason. Lily didn't try to hide from him, or cower, or douse the light. She was as curious about him as he was about her, and found no place for shame or timidity.

His hands ran over her thighs, fingers lightly kneading the muscles there, and when he touched her between her thighs, there where she was feeling the building pressure that threatened to consume her, she arched against him and moaned into his chest.

Lily lowered her head to the flat pillow and drew Quint to her, wanting to feel his weight on her, knowing now why she had shivered every time he looked at her. Every moment had been leading to this.

His chest pressing against hers was heavenly, his warmth surrounding her like a safe cocoon. She parted her thighs and felt him resting between them, testing, pressing against her throbbing warmth.

Lily wrapped her legs around Quint's thighs, drawing him closer, drawing him inside her. There was a brief burning sensation, a moment of pain, when he finally entered her, and he smothered her surprised cry with tender kisses.

"No more pain," he whispered huskily. He lay very still until her tension subsided, and then he moved slowly, withdrawing and then plunging deep again, bringing her to a state of fiery turbulence as he rocked his hips against her. Lily lifted her hips as Quint thrust into her, impossibly deeper than before, and she pressed her body against his as an explosion racked her. She felt him join her, as he covered her mouth with his and joined with her in a way she had never before believed possible.

They rolled onto their sides, and Lily buried her head against Quint's shoulder. Never had she dreamed that the fluttering in her belly when she looked at him could lead to this. It was a true wonder.

"I'm sorry I hurt you," he whispered, holding her close. She could hear the regret in his voice. "I didn't know it was your first time."

Lily kissed his shoulder. "Still thinking of me as the Captain's mistress? Never mind. The pain was gone quickly, and the rest was beautiful."

Quint smiled. She was so open and uninhibited. That was why he hadn't thought she was a virgin . . . she showed no fear, no hesitation. He wanted to make love to her all night long, then wake with her in his arms. And not just for one night. He wanted to love Lily for the rest of his life. It was a jarring thought. There were obstacles to be thought of.

He ran his hands over her arms. This was no soft and fragile girl. Her upper arms were smooth, but with the strength of a taut muscle beneath. Her skin was like silk, smooth and strong. But Lily was strong because she was a sailor, and that would never do.

"You have to give this up," Quint whispered seriously, and Lily lifted her head.

Tousled, curling hair framed her face, covering one eye completely. "Give what up?"

"No wife of mine . . ." The words were out of his mouth before he gave them much thought, but he liked the sound of them and smiled crookedly.

Lily leaned over and kissed his dimple. "I've always wanted to do that," she murmured softly, and she drew away slightly as she looked into his face. "I don't remember saying that I would marry you. In fact, I don't even remember you asking."

Quint scowled. "All right. I'm asking."

"No," Lily said sweetly, and then she kissed him again.

Quint propped himself up on one elbow and frowned at her. "What do you mean, no?"

The narrow bed sagged in the middle, bringing

them together as they lay side by side, face to face. Quint didn't mind, and Lily didn't seem to, either, as she ran her fingers across his chest. "Not yet, anyway. I'm not giving up the *Chameleon.* Not now."

"Why? Why is it so damned important?" Quint asked softly. "What can be more important than the fact that I love you, and you love me?"

Lily smiled and kissed him again. She brushed the hair away from her face, and when she looked into his eyes there was a mischievous twinkle in her own. "So, you finally say it again."

"Again?"

"The last time you told me that you love me, you were pretty much pickled. Besides, I didn't say that I love you," she teased.

His own smile faded. He didn't want to hear that, even with a teasing lilt in her voice. She saw that and laid her hand over his heart.

"But I do."

"Say it," he ordered gently.

"I love you, Quintin Tyler," Lily said seriously. "I can't believe that this has happened so fast— that you're suddenly a part of my life that I can't do without."

"Then give this up and marry me."

Lily sighed and laid her head against his chest, so he couldn't see her twinkling eyes or her freckles. "I can't."

She explained it to him. Her father's death, her brother's decision to run away. The Yankee captain she hated with all her heart. He could hear the pain in her voice as she relived that day for him. So he would understand.

He was thankful she couldn't see his face as he died a little death. If her passion was driven by revenge, she would never forgive him when she found out he was a spy for the Union. Never. And he wouldn't lie to her. Not about that.

When they returned to Nassau, he would go to Eleanor Slocum and quit. Then he would confide in Lily about everything. Maybe she would forgive him. Maybe not. He was afraid when he heard the hate in her voice as she talked about the Yankees who had invaded her home and killed her father.

He was deluding himself. She would never forgive what he had done. What he was. And he could never desert the cause that had driven him away from his family and his home. Not even for Lily.

Lily sighed and placed her palm tenderly against the scar on his thigh. "This scar is not from a fall from a horse," she admonished with a whisper.

Quint shook his head. "No. I was shot."

"By who?" Lily lifted her head again, her eyes trusting and questioning.

"A scorned woman." He gathered her into his arms and held her tight. "Thank God her aim was off."

"Thank God," Lily agreed, and then she kissed the bump on his nose. "And this?"

"Same woman. Pounded me right on the nose with an incredibly heavy reticule." Quint's voice was light, and his hands were wandering over

Lily's warm body again. Already he wanted to bury himself in her, body and soul.

"Am I supposed to believe that?" Lily whispered half-heartedly, holding her lips a heartbeat away from his own.

"No," Quint said as he rolled over her again. There would be time later for the truth, all of the ugly truth. But for now there were just the two of them and the rocking of the powerful ship, and that was enough.

It was all he had.

Chapter Thirteen

Lily did not remain in the cabin as long as Quint would have liked. She devoted herself to the running of the *Chameleon*, but made the best of the hours she stole, slipping into the narrow cot with him in the middle of the night, waking him with warm lips and curious hands. And when Quint woke in the morning, she was gone again.

Quint couldn't stand to be confined to the cabin alone, so he found his way to the deck and silently watched the blue skies, the fascinating ocean—and Lily.

He wouldn't dare to approach her while she was working, even by putting his arm around her while they stood together on deck. She had to have worked hard to get these sailors to accept her not as a woman, but as their captain, and Quint didn't want to undermine that respect. And he didn't think Lily would appreciate it.

Much of the time he found himself standing alone on deck, but on occasion Lily slipped away and joined him at the rail to look out over the ocean and comment on its beauty. She truly loved the sea. He could see it in her eyes and her smile, in the way she accepted the salty spray on her face as if it were a gift of the finest perfume.

But he could tell that she was also careful to keep her distance from him when the others were watching. Only in the privacy of her cabin did she feel free to touch him. In spite of her blatantly unconventional behavior, in spite of the lack of inhibition she displayed when they were alone, Lily had her own strict moral code. She wouldn't have her crew watch as she displayed her emotions, not even her affection for Quint.

Quint was watching her as she took the wheel from Cyril. It didn't matter that she was captain. She was definitely a woman. She had a slender shape, but her hips swelled slightly, and even the thick, baggy shirt she wore couldn't hide the curve of her breasts. It was no wonder that she had that light sprinkling of freckles, and brown hands, and golden highlights in her dark blond hair. All from her time spent at sea.

Tommy slipped into his line of vision—deliberately, Quint could tell by the scowl on the older man's face. He stood not three feet away, and his eyes glinted with a murderous rage.

"Good afternoon, Tommy," Quint said cordially. He didn't want to get into a fight with Lily's uncle, her first mate.

Tommy grunted. "I've got my eye on you. Slip up just once. Please."

"You love her, don't you?" Quint asked, knowing that if there was to be anything for him and

Lily, he would have to make his peace with Tommy and Cora.

A puzzled expression flashed across Tommy's face. "Like she was me own daughter." He turned angry again. "There's not a man on this ship who wouldn't kill or die for Lily." He lowered his voice. "You'd best remember that."

Quint had noticed the way the young crew treated her, with deference and a kind of awe. "Why? How? I mean . . . it doesn't make any sense."

Tommy grinned, but it wasn't a pleasant smile. "See them two lads behind you?" Quint turned his head and saw two young men working together, their fair heads practically shining in the sun, their young muscles easily accepting the task at hand. "Eddie and Gilbert Farmer. Brothers. When Lily found 'em, they were damn near starvin' to death on the Liverpool docks. She fed 'em, gave 'em a warm place to sleep, and offered 'em well-payin' jobs."

Quint frowned, primarily at the thought of Lily picking up stray boys off the docks of Liverpool.

"Simon?" Tommy continued. "The lad who brought you to Lily's cabin? 'E tried to rob 'er, a poor defenseless woman alone at night." He laughed. "Next thing 'e knew, 'e was in the street on 'is backside, and Lily was offerin' 'er 'and to 'elp 'im up."

"She . . ." Quint still had a difficult time picturing that scene. "She threw him to the ground?"

Tommy nodded, apparently happy with

Quint's discomfort. "Aye. O' course, 'e was three inches shorter and at least two stone lighter at the time."

"They can't all be . . ." Quint hesitated.

"Liverpool dock rats?" Tommy supplied. "No, not all. But many o' them are. Without Lily, their families might be starvin'. Then there's those like Reggie Smythe. 'Er chief engineer. Fine man, years o' experience. 'E was drinkin' 'imself to an early grave over 'is wife and baby's deaths. Lily made 'im stand on 'is own feet and take a good look at 'imself.

Quint craned his neck so he could see Lily over Tommy's shoulder. "I guess I'll never understand." Lily turned to look at him then, as if she'd known he was watching her, and she gave him a small smile. Just for him. Cyril joined her and she relinquished the wheel, stepping quickly to join Quint and Tommy.

"What are you two talking about?" she asked briskly. She was smiling, but she looked from Quint to her uncle with suspicious eyes. "I run a tidy ship," she said in a low voice. "I don't allow the crew to fight while we're at sea, and I can't allow it from the two of you."

"We were just having a . . . a friendly discussion," Quint said, though "friendly" was a stretch.

"Mr. Tyler can't understand why the crew doesn't mutiny, you bein' a woman an' all," Tommy said seriously.

"That's not exactly—" Quint began.

Lily smiled smugly as she interrupted him. "Is that so? Perhaps I should show Quint how I keep the lads in line. How I teach them who's in charge." Her grin was frightening. She was up to something.

Tommy drew his thick brows together. "I don't think that's such—"

"Roger's in the engine room," Lily said, glancing at Tommy. "He smarted off at me this morning. Perhaps I should teach him a lesson."

"It's not necessary—" Tommy began.

"Roger," Lily ordered. "Now."

She turned her head and nodded to Simon, who watched the scene and listened closely. Quint tried to picture Lily throwing the healthy young man to the ground, and could not. He tried to picture Simon as a thin, under-nourished boy, and that made the scene more believable. But still incredible.

Simon disappeared below to fetch Roger, and Tommy headed toward Lily's cabin. Quint noticed that those of the crew who could, crowded around, whispering in small groups and forming a large circle on the deck. At least they seemed to know what to expect. Quint leaned toward Lily.

"What's going on?"

Lily appeared to be composed, but a smile lit her face and her eyes. "You're going to see what happens to men who defy me. It's only fair, after all."

A surly young man climbed from the engine room, sweat pouring from his face, his curly dark hair clinging to his forehead. It looked as if he'd put on a clean shirt specifically for his rise to the deck, because it was the only thing about him that was clean. His trousers and boots were sooty, as was every inch of exposed skin. Especially his face.

"You wanted me, Cap'n?" He presented himself before Lily with a defiant stance, legs braced apart.

"You made an insubordinate comment to me this morning, Roger. I thought I'd give you this opportunity to apologize."

Roger spat on the deck. "I stand by what I said, Cap'n. I'd as soon serve under a monkey as a woman." The man's cockney accent was so thick that Quint had trouble understanding him.

"You know what this means, don't you, Roger?" Lily asked darkly.

Roger gave her a curt and insolent bow, and when he pulled his hand from behind his back there was a wicked-looking knife in it. Tommy had to restrain Quint with one strong hand, while with the other he tossed the saber Quint had seen hanging in the cabin through the air, the sun catching the metal blade and flashing before his eyes.

Lily reached out her hand and snatched the blade from the air, almost without looking at it. She didn't smile, but Quint could tell that the situation amused her, for some reason he couldn't fathom.

Her eyes were on Roger. The sweaty seaman feinted, then lunged forward. Lily stepped aside and Roger stumbled, catching his balance an instant before he fell headlong into the sailors who formed the circle that surrounded them.

Quint turned to Tommy. "Don't you have a weapon?"

"Aye, but Lily will kill me if I use it." Tommy appeared to be more aggravated than upset, and he maintained that iron grip on Quint's arm. Quint searched the crowd. Several members of the crew were grinning, and a few even looked bored. He relaxed, but Tommy didn't release him.

Lily wielded the saber as if it weighed nothing, and Quint remembered the taut muscles in her arms. She would have no trouble lifting and parrying with the weapon, but could she actually stab someone?

As she watched, Lily seemed to toy with the rapidly tiring sailor, and she handled the saber as if it were an extension of her arm. She was light on her feet, moving away from Roger's knife without effort, once stepping on the lower rail, her back to the ocean, and gliding quickly to the other side of the belligerent crewman.

"Do you still say a woman can't be your captain?" she asked, not even breathless with her efforts.

"Aye," Roger replied hoarsely. "To the death!"

Their swordplay intensified, Lily clearly having the advantage. Her saber was much longer than Roger's knife, and he was tiring quickly. But he didn't give up.

Then Lily pointed the sharp tip of her saber at Roger's side. "Yield, sailor," she commanded.

Roger gave her a scowl of pure hatred. "Never."

And then he fell on the saber. His white shirt was quickly streaked with red, sticky blood, and Lily glanced down at the motionless sailor, apparently unconcerned.

"Bloody hell," she muttered loud enough for everyone to hear. "Somebody clean up this mess."

Quint pulled away from Tommy as a few members of the crew bent over Roger, and he ran to Lily, grabbing her by the shoulders. "For God's sake," he whispered hoarsely. "You've killed him."

"It would appear so." Lily smiled, barely lifting the corners of her mouth. "Now do you see why my men follow me?" She handed the stained saber to Tommy, and he took it with a snort of disgust.

"I never doubted . . ."

"Never?" She lifted her eyebrows.

"Lily . . ."

Her eyes softened, and her grin widened. For a moment, Quint thought he had fallen in love with a woman who was quite insane. Then she spoke. "You can get up now, Roger," she said, never taking her eyes from Quint.

Roger rose and turned to the crowd with an exaggerated bow. A small smattering of applause broke out before the crewmen returned to their duties. When Roger came to stand beside his captain, a great smile spread across his sooty face.

"That was a good one, eh?" He was slightly breathless, and his face was flushed.

Quint looked down at the "bloodstain" and reached out to touch the sticky substance on the man's shirt.

"Crushed berries and syrup in an oilskin bag," Lily explained, that satisfied grin still lighting her face.

Quint turned his furious countenance to her. "That's not funny, Lily." He was seething. He had seen enough real death in his lifetime. "Goddammit, it wasn't funny."

Roger removed the sticky shirt to reveal a sooty chest and arms, and he was unstrapping the deflated oilskin bag from his side as he slipped quietly away.

"At least Roger dies like 'e should," Tommy added. "Lily carries on in an awful way, makes such a fuss—"

"You mean to tell me you've been on the receiving end of that charade?" Quint shouted at Lily, not caring who heard. "You could have been killed. You will never—"

Lilt silenced him with a stare. "Don't tell me what I'll never do," she said in a whisper. "It was just a . . . an exercise I dreamed up when Tommy and I were teaching the lads to fence. It holds their attention, and has been known to frighten one or two of the newer crewmen. They need entertainment, you know."

"Entertainment," Quint muttered. "I was worried." His voice was so soft no one could hear him but Lily. "And it wasn't funny!" he added more loudly.

Tommy snorted. "That's one thing we agree on, mate."

Quint turned to the older man, who was suddenly and unexpected an ally. "It wasn't funny."

Lily followed him into the hold, her musical voice drifting down. "Yes it was."

There was a sliver of a moon, and not as much fog as Lily would have liked, though there was a heavy bank ahead of them as they approached the mouth of the Cape Fear River. As always, the crew was hushed, and Lily's heart was pounding as if it might burst from her chest. There was a significant difference on this approach. Quint was beside her, ignoring her pleas to stay below. She couldn't blame him. She never would have been able to confine herself to the dark cabin as they slipped past the Union patrol.

The patrol was tighter than it had been in the past, the Union ships thick. Lily wouldn't rest until the *Chameleon* was safe in the channel where the Union ships, with their deeper draw, would be unable to follow, and she and her crew would be under the protection of the guns of Fort Fisher.

A Union ship on the port side spotted the *Chameleon* first and fired a warning shot across the bow. Lily knew that they would much prefer to take the *Chameleon* intact, but would sink her if that was not possible. She couldn't imagine handing the weapons and ammunition in her cargo hold over to the Yankees, to be used against Southern soldiers and civilians.

"Captain!" A shout went up. There was no longer any reason to remain silent, as a second shot was fired.

There were no guns built into the *Chameleon*. She was not a warship, and as such her crew would be able to return home in a few weeks if they were captured. There weren't even any pistols, except for the ancient cap-and-ball gun that belonged to Tommy. Lily's saber was the most lethal weapon on board.

Another shot was fired, this time from the starboard side, missing the *Chameleon* by mere feet. Their only chance was to outrun the two ships, and with a little luck they could. The *Chameleon* was fast and low in the water. Lily set her sights dead ahead.

There, her bulk emerging from the fog like a wraith, was a third Union patrol ship, and Lily cursed loudly. She wouldn't risk the lives of her crew by attempting the impossible, not for silks and whiskey, or even for the rifles and gunpowder she carried. Lily ran across the deck, Quint at her heels.

"Run up the white flag!" she shouted over the din of yet another shot. This one rocked the *Chameleon*, and Lily steadied herself with her feet planted far apart. Cyril was still at the wheel, calmer than most. But a harried bunch of boys, her crew, looked to her wide-eyed.

"We've talked about this before," she said with no trace of fear in her voice. "You all know what to do. Bloody hell, I'm sorry, boys. Bad luck, that's all it is." Lily turned away from them and disappeared down the hatch.

Quint tried to follow her, knowing that she had to be up to something. In spite of her fearless stance, he had seen a gleam in her eyes that frightened him. Tommy grabbed Quint's arm and pulled him back.

"Leave 'er be," Tommy barked. "If you get in 'er way, you'll ruin everythin'."

Tommy's voice was so anxious that Quint decided to do as he said, and he waited on deck near to where Lily would emerge. The Union patrol was drawing closer and would be boarding in a matter of minutes. Their attack had ceased, and Lily's crew was hushed. The strained silence gave the night a momentary unreal stillness. Lily's short speech had calmed the crew, though they were visibly nervous as they waited for the Union Navy to descend upon them.

Lily was on deck moments later, and Quint could only marvel at the quick transformation. She was Lily Radford, refined lady, once again. She wore an atrocious bright pink dress with satin roses down the front and around the hem, its high neck and long puffy sleeves covering every inch of her skin. Her hair was pulled back with a ribbon, and there were simple white gloves covering her hands. Once on deck, she smiled at Quint dazzlingly, and he realized that she either didn't comprehend or didn't care that she had placed herself in danger. He wanted to hold her. He wanted to shake her. But there was time for neither.

"Follow my lead, Quint," she said curtly, and

she turned to face the officers who were boarding her ship. She didn't move forward, but maintained a regal stance, waiting for them to approach her. She breathed a low curse as her crew was handled roughly. They weren't actually hurt, though, and no emotion showed on her face.

It wasn't long before an officer made his way to them, and Lily placed that vacant smile on her face, the one she'd once fooled Quint with.

Another officer was questioning members of the crew as they were herded onto the Union ship, and Union sailors were taking their places on the *Chameleon*.

"Good evenin', sir," Lily drawled, stepping between the officer and Quint before Quint grabbed her arm and pulled her back to his side. "My, isn't this excitin'? I hope my brother and I aren't in too much trouble. We were just so anxious to get to Wilmington, and this seemed to be the only way. I just thought my little ol' heart was goin' to burst when that other boat shot at us." She spoke fast and wrung her hands in excitement.

"You're in no trouble, ma'am," the officer said in a calm voice. "But I would appreciate it if you could point out the captain of this ship. A Captain Sherwood, I believe?" Evidently, none of the crew was willing to identify Lily as their captain, and the Union officer looked expectantly to the civilians.

"Elliot?" Lily turned to Quint and screwed her lips in a pout. "Did you see Captain Sherwood? I heard a loud splash a few moments ago. You don't think he might have deserted us, do you?

Left us at the mercy of the Yankees?" She looked as if she might cry at the very thought.

The officer turned his attention to Quint, dismissing Lily's lament that she had been abandoned. "Have you seen Captain Sherwood, sir?"

Quint shook his head, and was glad that he could say, truthfully, that he had not. Once they were in custody and he was alone with an officer, he would identify himself. But not in front of Lily. He didn't want her to learn the truth that way. He would tell her when they were alone.

"Excuse me, sir?" Lily plucked at the officer's sleeve. She seemed determined to keep his attention away from Quint. "We haven't properly introduced ourselves. My name is Lily Radford, and this is my brother Elliot. Will my brother and I be remaining on this boat, or will we be moved to that other one?"

"You and your brother will be transferred, ma-'am," the officer said tiredly.

"Could someone get my trunk? It's downstairs in my room. The captain's cabin, actually. He was kind enough to allow me to use it for this trip. All my clothes and things . . ."

"We'll take care of it, ma'am." The officer directed two of his men to bring up the trunk, but when it was on deck, he ordered it opened. The trunk was definitely large enough to hold a man, and the two sailors who carried it to the deck struggled with its obvious weight.

But when it was opened, they found only sloppily folded clothing. The officer delved into the deep trunk, shoving aside silk dresses and bits of lace.

"Please, sir," Lily said, blushing. "I have . . . personal items in there."

The officer's hand was surely to the bottom of the trunk, and still he shifted the clothing aside until he was satisfied. Only then did he pull his hand back and stand.

Quint watched Lily's face. There was something in that trunk besides dresses and "personal items." Small droplets of sweat that had nothing to do with the humidity of the night air had formed on her upper lip as the officer rummaged through the luggage. Lily turned to Quint just once and smiled, and her eyes spoke to him of resignation and disappointment.

The Union naval officer was satisfied and willing to allow Lily to go, but he turned to Quint with hard, suspicious eyes.

"What is your name again, sir?" he snapped.

"His name is Elliot Radford," Lily said, jumping in before Quint had a chance to open his mouth. "He's my brother."

Quint turned to Lily with an exasperated sigh. "I can speak for myself, Lily."

The officer who was trying to interrogate Quint was tiring of Lily's act. "See the lady to the ship," he instructed his men.

Quint breathed a sigh of relief. With Lily gone, he could simply tell the officer the truth . . . part of it, at least. He could reveal who he was, but not that Lily was Captain Sherwood. Her career was over, anyway, with her ship seized. Even if she attempted to have another ship built, it would take months. With any luck, the war would be over by then.

Quint turned toward Tommy's loud curses as the burly man was led, wrists and ankles shackled, by three men. Evidently he had not surrendered as easily as the younger crewmen. As Tommy passed by Lily and Quint and the Union officer, he broke away and faced Quint eye to eye. Toe to toe.

"'Ave you any other instructions, Cap'n?" Tommy asked in a low voice, but not so low that everyone in the vicinity couldn't hear him clearly. The officer's eyes lit up as he turned once again to Quint.

"Captain Sherwood." It was not a question that came from the officer's mouth. It was a satisfied statement.

Lily glared at a gloating Tommy. "He is not!" she said, but she knew as soon as the words were out of her mouth that not only were her pleas sounding hysterical, they were useless. Quint didn't bother to defend himself, and she realized, as she watched the ensign's face, that it would have done no good.

She watched helplessly as Quint was led away, surrounded by a watchful guard that matched Tommy's, and then she was prodded toward the same ship.

"Oh, my!" Lily pivoted suddenly and slipped past her guards, running for the hold. "I'll be right back," she called to the sailors who had been assigned to see her on board the Union patrol ship. In a flash, quicker than she should have been able to move in the cumbersome dress, Lily disappeared into the hold.

She had to move fast, before the sailors followed her into the darkness. With sweaty hands she felt her way down the hallway and did what she had to do.

The sailors were just about to follow when she emerged from the darkness, nothing more than a book in her hands.

"I haven't finished readin' this, and it's just fascinatin'." She gave them each, in turn, a dazzling and flirtatious smile, and all was forgiven. This time she followed them obediently to the Union ship, humming softly a tune her father had taught her when she was just a little girl. She couldn't remember the name of the song, or even very many of the words, but it had a bright and cheerful melody.

On the Union ship, Lily joined the ensign who had interrogated her and Quint, as the man leaned against the bow of his ship and watched over the *Chameleon*. Quint was nowhere to be seen, and Lily tried not to think of him in the brig, or shackled as Tommy had been. The sailors had been attempting to direct her below decks, but she veered, never ceasing her inappropriate humming until she was standing beside the ensign.

"What will become of us, sir?" Lily asked as she leaned against the railing beside him.

"You should go below . . ."

Lily gave him her brightest smile. It had

worked on the sailors . . . and it worked on the officer as well. "What's your name? You know mine, and it's only fair that I learn yours."

She flirted shamelessly, batting her eyelashes and gazing up at the officer with a look she hoped appeared to be awe.

"Ensign Delbert Davis." The officer glanced down at her as if he could see through her act, just as Quint had. Damn! She'd thought she was good at this!

"A beautiful woman, such as yourself, should be safe at home," he said in a low voice. "Not sailing with a notorious blockade runner."

"What will become of us, Ensign Davis?" It didn't take any effort at all for her to look worried.

"After interrogation, you will be released, Miss Radford." He nodded to her in an almost courtly manner. "I would suggest that in the future you choose a safer method of travel or, better yet, don't travel at all. These are dangerous times."

"Yes they are," Lily agreed. "And the crew?"

The ensign shrugged. "They all appear to be British. Unfortunately, we won't be able to hold them for very long. Just until they testify at the prize court. They'll be sent back to England."

"And the captain?" Lily asked softly.

"Prison," Davis said sharply.

Lily thought about trying to convince Ensign Delbert Davis that Quint was not the Captain, but she knew it would be hopeless, and she might damage her chances of helping him later on. She turned to the *Chameleon*, waiting.

"You should go below now, Miss Radford," the ensign said, but his voice was kinder than it had been before.

"Just a moment more," Lily begged. She couldn't stand to be confined, and she wouldn't leave the deck until she saw that her work was done. "Just a few moments more of this lovely night air."

She returned her gaze to the *Chameleon,* trying to hide her impatience. She took a deep breath of the air she had begged for, then placed a puzzled expression on her face as she turned to the ensign.

"I believe I smell smoke. Do you smell anythin'?" She looked up at the ensign and fluttered her lashes.

"No. Nothing unusual." But he turned his gaze back to the *Chameleon,* and a frown marred his face. Smoke was drifting from the hold.

"Damn! She's on fire!" He grabbed Lily's arm securely and dragged her with him. "Get below!"

"Ensign Davis?" Lily jerked her arm away from him. "Are your men on that boat?"

He nodded. "They'll put out the fire."

"You should know," she continued, "the Captain said he had some barrels of gunpowder in the cargo place. Wouldn't they . . . explode or somethin' if the fire reached them?" Her voice was as innocent as an angel's.

The *Chameleon* was soon abandoned, the fire Lily had started when she'd gone below decks to fetch her book hot enough and large enough before it was discovered that they didn't want to risk lives to save the ship and her cargo. Lily was glad of that. She didn't want to be responsible for the deaths of the sailors, young boys not that much different from her own crew. But neither would she allow her cargo to fall into enemy hands.

She was forgotten in the excitement, and still on deck when, as the ship she was on pulled away, the *Chameleon* exploded, lighting the night and creating a wave of heat that washed over her as the blinding fire reached for the stars.

She was watching the end of a part of her life, and she was well aware of that fact as she watched the *Chameleon* burn.

A potent sorrow welled up inside of her, but she pushed it back. That was done. Now she had to think of a way to save Quint.

Get Four Books Totally FREE — A $21.96 Value!

PLEASE RUSH
MY FOUR FREE
BOOKS TO ME
RIGHT AWAY!

Leisure Romance Book Club
65 Commerce Road
Stamford CT 06902-4563

AFFIX
STAMP
HERE

Chapter Fourteen

Lily stood on deck and watched as the Union sailors led her crew from the ship. She had been on the ironclad for three days and nights, long nights during which she had slept little and dreamed of Quint confined to the brig. Confined for her crime.

No matter how much she begged, how pitifully she batted her lashes, how unmercifully she flirted with the guards who were posted at the door of her cabin, they wouldn't allow her to see Quint. She was allowed out of the small cabin only once a day, for a breath of fresh air, and during that time her guards watched her closely. Ensign Davis always seemed to be close by, though he didn't approach her during the voyage.

But as she watched the prisoners disembark, he joined her, standing at her side silently as she tried to study her crewmen's faces from a distance. They were all solemn, but Lily was pleased to see no evidence of abuse. Tommy was still in irons. He was a man not mellowed by his age, but incensed at the injustices that had been thrust upon him. Once, he lifted his face to Lily, but he gave no sign that he knew her, or even that he saw her there.

Lily was holding her breath, waiting for Quint to appear, and finally he did. He was last, and at a distance from the other prisoners. Quint was in shackles, just as Tommy had been, and he limped along without his cane, the weight of the irons making his steps more laborious. His jacket was missing, and the thin material of his shirt stretched across his broad back, the linen wet with sweat and clinging to his skin.

She thought he wasn't going to notice her there, and then he turned his head slowly. He stared through her, and Lily's eyes were riveted to his. How could she let him know that she would somehow find and free him? Did he believe that she would abandon him to pay for her sins?

And then Quint smiled at her, that crooked smile that made him look like a devilish little boy. He had stopped in the middle of the gangplank, and a guard pushed him forward with a heavy hand. Quint stumbled slightly, but recovered and turned his face away from Lily as he continued away from the ironclad.

Lily turned a frown on Ensign Davis. "He might have fallen in the water and drowned, chained as he is," she snapped at the relaxed ensign who watched with relief as the prisoners left his ship.

Two sailors appeared on deck with Lily's trunk

between them. It was time for her to disembark.

"Where are they taking the prisoners?" She directed her question to the ensign, forcing a calmness she did not feel into her voice. If she wasn't careful, she could ruin any chance she had of saving Quint.

Ensign Davis gave her a small smile that seemed to pain him. He would, no doubt, be glad to be rid of her.

"All of them, or just the Captain?" There was a teasing lilt in his voice.

Lily grimaced slightly. By this time she should be better at hiding her true feelings. "Just the Captain."

Ensign Davis relaxed and leaned against the railing, turning away from her to look over the docks. He hesitated, and Lily was afraid he would tell her nothing. And then what would she do?

"I do envy your Captain Sherwood," he said when he turned back to her. "I suppose it would do no harm to tell you where he will be held until his transfer to the prison at Fort Warren. Perhaps the soldiers there will allow you to see him before that departure. Perhaps not. I will tell you that once Captain Sherwood is imprisoned at Fort Warren, you will not see him again until the war has ended."

A knot formed in Lily's stomach as she listened to the ensign's words, and she knew she had to get to Quint before he was taken to that prison.

* * *

Quint paced the tiny cell, the heels of his boots clicking against the stone floor, his jaw clenched. Six days. Six days of inedible food, questionable water, and complete deprivation of sunlight and fresh air.

He could handle the poor rations better than he could the lack of sun and fresh air. The place smelled stale, of sweat and piss and fear, the mingled odors of the other occupants of this jail, men in tiny cells of their own that lined the narrow and dimly lit hallway. They seemed to have given up, these prisoners of the Union. All were awaiting transfer to another place, and no one expected that it would be much better than their present accommodations. They were thin and weary and barely spoke. It was as if even speech was too much of an effort.

Quint knew what time of day it was only by the arrival of his two meager meals, one at midmorning and the other late in the afternoon. Without even a small window to watch the passage of the days, they seemed interminably long.

His black cane had been taken away on the Union patrol boat. He still walked with a slight limp, but no longer needed the aid of the cane. Thank God. He had come to hate the damn thing.

He'd told them, on board the ship and again at the prison, of his true identity. On board the ship he was laughed at, and he didn't try to convince the Union sailors again. It didn't help that Lily's entire crew had taken to calling him Captain. They would protect Lily at all costs.

Quint's claims were taken no more seriously at

the prison, but the warden had reluctantly agreed to send word to Colonel Fairfax in Washington. And so Quint waited, not knowing how long it would take for word to reach Washington and a reply to arrive at the prison in Baltimore. There was no guarantee that Fairfax would be in Washington.

No one would tell him what had become of Lily. Logic told him that if ever there was a woman born who could take care of herself, it was Lily Radford. But still he worried. There was a war raging, and he didn't think she would hide from it. He thought—he knew—that she would walk right into the middle of it all, if she had the opportunity.

The sailors on board the Union ironclad had taken great pleasure in telling him that his ship had exploded and sunk to the ocean floor. They had all heard the massive explosion, and Quint had actually been relieved to hear that the *Chameleon* was gone. By the time they told him what had occurred, he had ceased his efforts to convince them that it was not his ship, and he accepted the news with no visible response. No one was hurt, by all reports, but the cargo was lost. On hearing that, Quint was certain that Lily was somehow responsible for the destruction of the *Chameleon.*

Lily. Damn her, he didn't know if he wanted more to kiss her or to spank her. Perhaps he should do both. He'd had more than enough time to think in the past six days, and the more he pondered the more amazing it was. She was Captain Sherwood. A blockade runner. A soldier as fierce as any he'd ever known, with her own driving motivation. Revenge. A powerful force.

But he loved her. That was an emotion he had thought never to feel again. It was so much more powerful than anything he'd ever felt for Alicia that it boggled his mind. Alicia had been a proper lady, and he had felt an attraction to her. But at the same time his choice of her as a future wife was also based on the fact that she came from one of the county's oldest families, that she was much like him, in many ways. He would have been content, if his life had not taken the turns it had, to marry Alicia and give her children. Content, but not happy. He would have bedded her, but not with the passion he felt for Lily every time he looked at her. His life would have been dull, and comfortable, and bloodless. And he never would have met Lily.

She was a part of him, as though the joining of their bodies had joined them heart and soul. A lifetime with Lily was not so much a choice as an inevitability.

All heads turned when a key rattled in the lock, and the heavy door that separated their hallway from the guards' office was thrown open. It was too soon after the morning meal for any routine visit. That meant they were coming after someone.

It was as though every prisoner in the block was holding an anxious breath. Quint had already learned that being singled out meant either interrogation or transfer, and as bad as their Baltimore prison was, they all knew it was better than most.

Quint had a glimmer of hope that word might have come from Colonel Fairfax or one of his aides, though it was probably still too soon.

The sergeant walked directly to Quint's cell and turned the key with a clang that echoed in the close hallway.

"You've got a visitor." The sergeant spat the words, his voice coarse and full of hate. Quint looked the man straight in the face, refusing to be intimidated by the short, burly man who seemed to take delight in strong-arming the Confederate prisoners.

Quint was relieved, and gave the sergeant a half-smile as he stepped from his cell. Colonel Fairfax had apparently wasted little time in getting word to the prison that he was who he claimed to be.

His first warning was the low mutter of the sergeant behind him. "Cocky bastard."

The sergeant used what was an evident weakness, trying to kick Quint's legs out from under him. There was a low chuckle from the sergeant, but Quint caught himself and turned to face the man, only to find a loaded and cocked pistol in his face.

"Go ahead, Reb," the sergeant said in a low voice. "Give me an excuse to shoot that smug-lookin' face clean off."

The sergeant was disappointed, as Quint gave him a crooked smile and turned his back to the man who held the pistol trained on him, waiting for any excuse to fire.

"I'll be givin' you a thorough search when you're done." The sergeant whispered the warning as he pushed open the door to the warden's office. "Can't be too careful."

Quint barely heard the threat as the door swung open and he saw Lily standing in front of a barred window. The harsh light hurt his eyes, but it was her all right, standing there in that ridiculous pink dress she had worn the night of the *Chameleon*'s capture.

Lily turned to face him as the door opened, and she appeared calm and cool as she clasped gloved hands at her waist. She didn't even smile, but her eyes twinkled with excitement.

"Lily." He whispered her name. What was she doing here? She should be on her way back to Nassau. At least, he had hoped she would be.

Lily didn't move. She stood primly and properly, as any refined lady should. "Sergeant?" At last she smiled, at the sergeant who still held his gun on Quint. "Could we have a few minutes of privacy? Please? The warden has consented."

The sergeant backed out of the room, obviously disgusted with this turn of events.

"Lily, what are you doing here?" Quint stepped toward her, but she looked down and started to push aside the large satin rosettes that decorated the bodice of her gown.

"Getting you out of this place," she said with assurance, her fingers flying through laces that had been hidden by the satin flowers. The laces ran from her neck to below the waist of her pink gown, and in less than a minute she was stepping out of the dress. Underneath, she was wearing her sailing garb—dark pants and white shirt; tall, soft boots; her saber strapped to her thigh. She adjusted the saber, which had been lowered to accommodate the line of her gown, raising the weapon to waist level. Her hands flying, she unwrapped a Colt six-shooter that was strapped to her right thigh.

"It's too dangerous." Quint grabbed her shoulders and was greeted with a smile for his concern.

"I love you, Quint. I can't allow them to keep you here."

Her declaration was so heartfelt, he felt a swelling in his chest. But what he'd said was true. What she was attempting was much too dangerous. She could get herself killed. He didn't waste any time telling her as much.

"I can't die now. I've got too many things still to do." She gave him a wide smile. "Sounds like nonsense, I know, but in my heart I know it's true." She laid a hand on his stubbled cheek. "But I would die if anything happened to you in this hellish place. I should shoot Tommy for this. What was he thinking?"

Lily planted a light kiss on his lips. "I'm glad they don't have you shackled. That would have slowed us up a bit." She placed the Colt in Quint's hand.

"Lily." Quint grabbed her hand and squeezed it. He should tell her the truth now—that in a few days, perhaps a week, word would reach the prison that he was a spy for the Union. He wouldn't die in prison. He had only to survive a while longer. "You can't. I want you to put that dress back on while I—"

The turning of the key in the lock startled them both. It had only been a few minutes. Lily moved to a position behind the door, and Quint held the Colt behind his back. The door opened, and the warden stepped inside his office, a stern expression on his face.

"Miss Smith—" he began, searching the room for Lily. His gaze fell on Quint, then on the crumpled pink dress on the floor. Before he had a chance to call out, Lily was behind him, the point of her saber at his back.

"Thank you so much, sir, for your cooperation," she said softly. "But we'll be leaving now."

The warden stared at Quint with open disgust and balled his fists as if he planned to rush forward and attack. But he didn't. He was an older man, gray-haired and too thin. His hands trembled slightly. Perhaps he had been a great soldier once, but now he was just waiting for the war to end.

"You've had this planned all along."

"Don't hurt him, sweetheart." Quint was reluctant to use Lily's name in front of the warden, even though he could remember saying it as the sergeant led him to her. "This will all be over in a few days. There's no need for this."

"I suppose you're speaking of your bogus claim," the warden seethed. "Don't plan on any help arriving, you lying Reb. Do you think I'm stupid enough to fall for a lie like the one you spun for me? Did you really think I'd waste valuable manpower by sending a soldier off on a wild goose chase? All of my men are here, Captain. There's no way you can escape."

The warden had never sent the message to Washington. That much was clear. He'd thought it a trick, and all of Quint's plans were for nothing.

Heavy footfalls were approaching quickly, plodding and determined steps that Quint recognized. He saw the sergeant behind Lily, and then he saw the pistol in the Sergeant's hand. Before Lily could react, Quint brought around the Colt that had been concealed behind his back. His reaction was quick, and almost unconscious, as he cocked the hammer with his thumb and fired, his aim true, and the surprised sergeant grunted and fell.

Quint ran forward and grabbed Lily's arm as he pointed the six-shooter at the warden. "The key." There was no time to waste. The sergeant who had taken such delight in making Quint's life a living hell was lying half in and half out of the doorway, and another guard could come along at any moment.

The warden grudgingly produced the key to his office, all the while staring at the barrel of the Colt. This had to be every warden's worst nightmare—held by a prisoner bent on escape.

"Pull him into the room." Quint nodded his head at the wounded sergeant, the man clutching a bleeding forearm. The bullet had gone straight through.

Quint's first instinct when he had seen the sergeant aiming a pistol at Lily was to shoot him right between the eyes. Only a last-second impulse had saved the sergeant's life. The warden pulled the wounded man into the office, the sergeant's boots scraping loudly against the floor, and he looked up at Quint and Lily as they blocked the doorway.

"Captain Sherwood," he seethed. "You're no better than a damned pirate."

Quint ignored him. "Are you all right, sweetheart?" he asked Lily without turning to face her. His eyes were on the men on the floor.

"I'm a mite better than these two," Lily answered his question confidently.

Quint watched the warden's eyes as the man studied Lily. There was fear there, and wonder. The transformation from Lily Radford, or "Miss Smith," to the woman he faced now was amazing. Lily looked like a pirate, or a siren sent to lure her victims to their deaths at the hands of her captain. The warden paled as he looked up at her.

"Should we kill them?" There was humor in Lily's voice. To Quint, it signaled that she was trying to scare the warden and the sergeant who had tried to shoot her. But to the men at her feet, it could have meant that she would kill them without a qualm.

"Not if they promise to be very quiet for the next several minutes." Quint tilted forward and whispered, "We have men waiting just outside the door, and if they hear a sound—even a whimper—they'll kill you."

Quint and Lily backed out of the door and closed it solidly. Quint turned the key in the lock and bolted the door. Even if the warden and the sergeant started yelling for help right away, it would take a while for the barrier to be battered down. It was solid oak.

He grabbed Lily and pulled her into his arms. The kiss he gave her was passionate and violent and deep and filled with the frustration of the days they'd been apart. The missing. The wanting. Lily pulled away from him with a smile.

"There will be time for this later, my love. Right now, I've got two horses waiting for us not five minutes from here." She looked down at his leg.

"They took away your cane," she said, anger in her voice.

Quint took her arm and propelled her down the hallway. "Yes. But I don't need it so much anymore."

Quint looked down at her, at the riot of dark blond curls that fell over her shoulder and down her back. Damn. If anyone had told him that he'd fall head over heels for a woman who could do the things she'd done just that day, he never would have believed it. She was beautiful and strong and wily. Strong and wily had never been traits he'd looked for in a woman before. She looked up at him and smiled radiantly.

She loved this. It was all a game to her. The

Chameleon, breaking him out of prison—a prison where he would have stayed until his transfer to Fort Warren, thanks to the warden.

But his heart had stopped when he'd seen the sergeant level his weapon at her. He had to convince her to stay out of this damn war, and that wouldn't be easy.

Lily noticed that Quint was walking with a less pronounced limp, moving at a steady pace with no apparent discomfort. His leg was healing, and that meant his wound had to be much more recent that he'd been willing to confess. Lily wasn't blind. She had seen the scar and knew what that kind of wound meant, but there was no time to question Quint now.

Stepping into the sunlight momentarily blinded Quint, and he raised an arm to block the glare. Lily took his other arm and led him toward the gate.

"The guards?" he asked her in a low voice, unable to see clearly.

"Drugged," she snapped, all her attention on getting Quint and herself away from this place. "They'll wake in an hour or two with one 'ell of a 'eadache, and swear to never again accept a cool drink on a warm mornin' from a British lass." Her voice was an almost perfect imitation of Cora's, and Lily smiled brightly. Everything was going according to plan.

Quint looked tired, with dark circles under his eyes, and he seemed to be thinner. She had arranged everything as quickly as she could, but it hurt her that he'd had to endure even a day in this place. And all because of her.

It was no more than three minutes before she was leading Quint into a dark alley where two horses waited. They weren't fine horses, but they were sturdy and nondescript, saddled and hidden from the street.

Lily mounted the mare she had chosen for herself and watched as Quint stepped into the stirrup to take the saddle with ease. In spite of all that had happened, in spite of the fact that they were still in danger, she glanced across the charged air that danced between them and smiled widely.

She turned her mare and tossed her head to Quint. "Follow me." She left the alley not with cautious prancing of hooves, but like thunder, her body low and her eyes sharp on the road ahead. Without looking, she knew that Quint was right behind her, would follow her until they came to the hideout she had secured for them.

Where they would go from there was undecided. Quint might know exactly where he wanted to go. He'd mentioned heading West, one night aboard the ship, as they'd snuggled on the narrow cot and whispered in the dark. With the *Chameleon* gone, her future was uncertain.

West. Unless they went clear to California, she wouldn't have even a glimpse of the ocean. No salt air, no sand between her toes, no ocean breezes.

But it didn't matter. Not as long as she had Quint.

Chapter Fifteen

No more than an hour later, Lily turned off the well-worn path she had followed faithfully and slowed her mare as they slipped through a bank of tall trees. With close observation, it was clear that the trail had once cut a clear path through the thick expanse of trees, but it was almost completely covered now by encroaching brush and weeds.

The charred remains of a small house sat bleakly in the near distance, its blackened skeleton the only sign that a family had once lived there. The destruction was complete and couldn't hide from the harsh sunlight of late summer. Weeds grew through the charred boards of what had once been a front porch, and vines climbed a broken rail that reached hopelessly upward.

The barn showed the same signs of neglect, but had been spared the fire that had gutted the house. The barn door hung crookedly from the broken hinge, and weeds had taken over the ground on all sides of the structure. There were gaping holes in the roof, and gaping "windows" at sporadic intervals, where whole boards had fallen away.

Lily jumped from her mare and waited for Quint to do the same. When his feet touched the ground, she ran to him and threw herself into his arms. She never would have shown it, but she had been terrified for him. She lifted her face, touched a cheek that was rough with dark stubble, and smiled as Quint threaded his fingers through her hair.

He held her tightly, and Lily pressed her body against his, reveling in his warmth. She had missed him, terribly, more than she'd thought possible.

Reluctantly, Lily pulled away from him. There was feed and water in the barn for their horses, and together they unsaddled the mounts and led them into prepared stables. Quint actually seemed to be surprised that she had prepared their nest so well.

The shade of the barn was comfortingly cool, and shafts of sunlight that fell through the unsturdy roof marked the dirt floor.

Quint had decided that he had to tell Lily the truth. Soon. She deserved the truth, and she deserved to hear it from him. She would hate what he had done, but would she hate him? Did she love him enough to leave behind what she was bound to see as his betrayal?

He stood with both hands gripping the top of a stall, leaning forward with his head hanging slightly, the tension tightening his shoulders and his back. He didn't want to tell her, didn't want to see her face when she learned the truth.

Lily slipped up behind him and wrapped her arms around his waist, laying her head between his shoulder blades.

"We can't stay here long," she said softly. "But the horses need to rest before we head south, and I've got a change of clothes for both of us and a loaf of bread stashed in the loft."

"You didn't forget anything, did you?" he whispered.

"I hope not."

"Jesus, Lily." Quint turned and wrapped his arms around her. "You could've been killed." He'd never forget the fear and helplessness he'd felt when he'd seen the sergeant aim his pistol at Lily, intending to fire. Intending to kill her.

"But I wasn't," she whispered, no anxiety in her voice. "I had to get you out. You didn't belong there."

Quint knew he should tell her the truth before they went any further. Lily was kissing the base of his throat, and if he didn't tell her now he'd lose his nerve, because the thought of losing Lily was terrifying. The thought of losing Lily as she lay in his arms was impossible to comprehend.

"I love you, Lily," he whispered. She had to know that was true. "But I have to tell you . . ."

"I already know," Lily answered, never lifting her head from his chest.

Quint's blood turned cold. He might have been lying on that frozen ground he remembered so well, the chill went so deep. "What do you know?"

"You were a soldier, weren't you?"

"Yes."

"For the Union?"

"Yes." Quint's answer was harsh and low.

Lily lifted her head and stared, unblinking, into his eyes. Her own eyes were as clear and as turquoise as the sea around Nassau. Bright and unflinching. "It doesn't matter."

"How did you know?" Quint asked, realizing that she still didn't know the worst of it. That he was a spy.

"Bits and pieces. The bullet wound in your thigh. It had to have been a recent injury for your limp to have improved so much in the past few weeks. I wasn't sure at first what side you'd fought for, though I suspected you would have told me if you'd been fighting for the Confederacy. But in the warden's office, when he said he didn't believe your claims, that's when I knew." Lily turned her attention to Quint's neck and chest, and she wound her fingers through the hair that curled over his collar.

Quint couldn't think with her lips on his skin, with her fingers brushing against the back of his neck. He lost himself in the sensations of her touch, the smell of her hair. It was impossible, but she still smelled of the sea and tropical flowers, as well as the sun. Any other explanations he had to offer would have to wait for later.

They half walked, half danced, to an empty stall and Quint lowered Lily to the straw-covered ground. They knelt in the broken shadows of the abandoned stall, knee to knee, thigh to thigh, lips bonded together with the reckless passion that had, in a matter of weeks, changed their lives, even the way they looked at the world around them.

Lily slid her hands away from Quint just long enough to disengage the saber from her side and toss it away. The weapon landed with a muted clank in the dirt far behind them. She moaned low in her throat when Quint deepened the kiss, probing hungrily with his tongue.

Quint drew the Colt from his waistband and he cast it away with an unconcerned flick of his wrist, diverting none of his attention from Lily. She tasted as tempting as she smelled, and he closed his eyes to shut out everything else. Everything but the senses she aroused.

They had been apart too long, and their fingers flew to remove the clothing that separated them, burdens to be flung aside. Lily unbuttoned her own shirt and reached for the buttons that held Quint's trousers fastened. His shirt was whipped over his head and dropped to the ground, and he turned his attention to the black boots and tight trousers Lily wore. Her boots flew over his shoulder to land with a thud that startled the horses. Her black trousers sailed through the air to join the saber and pistol, and the remainder of Quint's prison garb landed in a heap almost as far away from them as Lily's boots.

She was smiling at him, then laughing as he tossed their clothing aside. It was a laugh of pure joy and abandonment, and she was silenced only when Quint lowered her back into the straw, towering over her and kissing her deeply and thoroughly.

That was all they needed, and Quint buried himself in her quickly, deeply, sheathing himself inside her warmth as if she could save him.

Lily closed her eyes and sucked her breath in sharply, dazzled by the sheer magic of it all. To feel him inside her, to know that he was as lost in her as she was in him, was the only true magic she had ever known.

He stroked her, slow and fast. Kissed her deep one moment and feathery the next. What had been soothing became turbulent, and Lily wrapped her legs around Quint's hips, lifting herself higher, raising herself to meet his thrust as that sharp release took hold of her body. She cried out his name, no longer forced to stifle her cries as she had been on board the *Chameleon*. And then she felt Quint's completion, felt his seed released within her.

Quint didn't want to leave Lily just yet. It was over too quickly, and he wanted more of her. He knew he would never have enough of Lily.

"Marry me, Lily," he whispered, towering over her and scattering kisses over her face and her slender throat.

"I suppose I should," she murmured contentedly, rubbing her foot against his leg.

"Is that a yes?" Quint asked, his uncertainty making his voice a bit too gruff.

"That's a yes, Quintin Tyler." Lily looked deep

into his eyes. "Bloody hell, married to a Yankee soldier."

"Ex-Yankee soldier," Quint corrected her. With Lily beneath him, her bare skin against his own, he could think more clearly, or so it seemed as he gazed down at her. A sliver of sunlight, peeking through the side of the dilapidated barn, crossed her face.

He couldn't go back. He'd shot a Union soldier. No one would care that the sergeant had been about to kill the woman he loved. To return would mean prison and death. Nothing mattered but Lily.

"Where will we go, Quint, my love?" Lily whispered. Her hands traced the planes of his face.

"Say that again," he ordered gruffly, burying his face against her neck.

"Where will we go?" she teased.

"The other part."

"Quint, my love," she whispered. He grazed his rough beard lightly against her cheek and her neck as he lowered his face to her, contentedly brushing his lips against her soft skin.

"That's the part I wanted to hear again." He cupped a breast in his hand and ran his thumb gently over her nipple. Lily arched her back slightly and pressed herself into his hand, leaning her head back and purring like a kitten.

"It doesn't matter where we go," Lily said, languidly breathless. Her eyes were hooded as Quint continued to caress her body in ways that he knew drove her wild with wanting him. "As long as we're together."

"Do you mean that?" Quint lifted his head to look into her eyes.

"Quint, my love." Lily gave him that trusting and heartfelt smile that could make him forget, for a while, that life outside the abandoned barn went on as before. "You and I, together, can conquer anything."

She meant that. He could read the sincerity in her expressive eyes. He couldn't tell her now. After they were married, after he'd shown her again and again how much he loved her, then he would tell her the truth. All of it.

He grew and stirred within her, and Lily's smile widened. They loved one another with slow tenderness, their earlier frenzy behind them. It was a tenderness born of love and caring and passion—and a knowledge that there was a lifetime of such afternoons ahead of them.

Along with their clean clothes and a simple meal was a small bag of gold Lily had hidden in the loft. She had hated to leave her trunk with the cleverly hidden false bottom, but was practical enough to bring only what she could carry in a satchel that would fit behind her saddle. Besides the gold there were three dresses, one to wear and two that could be rolled up tightly and stored in the bag along with a hairbrush and two clean shirts for Quint.

The bedroll would fit behind Quint's cantle, and there was dried beef and hardtack in the saddlebags. She didn't have any paper money, but in these times that was a blessing. Anyone would be happy to take gold or silver in payment for their needs along the road. A room, perhaps, and certainly more provisions.

They would have liked to spend the night in the ramshackle barn, but they were still too close to Baltimore to be comfortable. So they changed into fresh clothes, shared a portion of the fresh bread Lily had purchased in town, and left the deserted farm. They were headed south. That was as far ahead as they had planned. Virginia. Lily wanted to stop by her home and show it to Quint. And to see for herself how it had fared. Funny, but it no longer seemed like home to her. Home was her house in Nassau, if that was where they decided to go. In truth, home was wherever Quint was, and that awareness warmed her as they rode down the dim path in the twilight hours.

They traveled south, keeping to the back roads and riding until it was too dark to see even a few feet in front of them. They camped a short distance from the trail, keeping a cold camp and sleeping under a thin blanket, snuggled together with Lily's head nestled against Quint's shoulder, her leg thrown over his. It wasn't warmth they were seeking under the stars. The night was mild, with warm air pushed by a gentle breeze. What they sought was the comfort of knowing that they were not alone, that they had become a part of something more than they had been before.

Lily was exhausted and fell asleep almost immediately, but Quint's rest came not so quickly or so deep. He held Lily as though she might slip away in the night if he didn't. The knowledge of his lie nibbled at his conscience, even as he told himself that he had no choice.

They woke while the sky was still gray and came together as naturally as if they had never been apart. They made love lazily, without words, and Lily never even opened her eyes. Quint woke her to a world of physical sensations, following the instincts that guided his body.

When Lily dressed, she donned a full-skirted dress that would allow her to ride astride, though she complained that she'd much rather wear her trousers. One concession she refused to make. Beneath the simple dress Lily wore her knee-high black boots. They were sturdy and more practical than any more feminine substitutes she could have acquired.

Quint was always on alert for Union patrols, but the trails they followed were all but deserted. Only twice during the day did they lead their horses from the trail to hide while others passed. The two lone travelers they encountered were no threat. They were simple people, ragged and weary, and if they had ever been soldiers they'd lost their battle edge long ago. Neither of them stopped to look into the dense forest that lined the road, sensing the presence of others. They simply plodded past at a lethargic pace, eyes on the road, feet kicking up dust as they dragged drearily by.

They stopped before dark, setting up camp in a secluded valley. It would be another cold camp, even though they'd seen no evidence of either army. Quint wouldn't take the chance of alerting the soldiers that were bound to be close by, either Union or Confederate.

Lily handed Quint a strip of dried meat and a piece of hardtack. The biscuit was hard, but edible, and he washed it down with water from the canteen they shared.

Quint sat on the hard ground with his back against an old tree. The small clearing they were in was surrounded by such giant growths, dwarfing the lovers in the dying light. He'd said little since they'd stopped, and a frown creased his brow.

He couldn't run away. That certainty had come to him somewhere on the road, not a sudden revelation but a gradual and sure knowledge. He wasn't a deserter. It hadn't been a whim that had driven him from his home and family, and his motivations were no less clear now than they had been then. He would marry Lily, get her to safety, and return to Washington to face Colonel Fairfax. It wouldn't be easy to explain away what had happened, but neither would it be impossible.

"Quint, my love," Lily said, settling herself between his legs and reclining against his chest. "What are you thinking about? You look positively morose."

Quint kissed the top of her head and wrapped an arm around her. "Nothing."

Lily twisted around and turned her face up to his. She fingered the beard that had begun to grow the night the *Chameleon* was destroyed. His

218

hair was so long that it was beginning to curl over his collar, and Lily trailed her fingers through the long strands.

"You're beginning to look like a pirate, Quintin Tyler." She gave him a mock pout. "The beard is rather dashing, but I don't think I like it. It hides too much of your face from me."

Quint bent down to kiss her softly. His decision meant that he would have to leave her behind, that they would be separated for months, or even years.

When he pulled away from her, Lily reached out and ran a lightly browned finger along his nose. "You never did tell me how you broke your nose."

Quint wrapped both arms around her and held her tight. "It was while I was in the infantry." His tone was light and he gave her a crooked smile. "A sergeant tried to toss me a piece of hardtack. My attention was diverted and it hit me right on the beak. As a matter of fact," he continued even as Lily began to giggle, "I believe it might have been the same piece of sheet-iron cracker we had for supper tonight."

He nestled a breast in one hand and ran his thumb over her nipple, and it hardened beneath the cotton of the plain dress she wore. Lily laid her head back against his shoulder, and her laughter stopped.

"That's not true," she murmured softly.

"No, it isn't." Quint unbuttoned her dress with one hand while the other pushed the voluminous skirt high to reveal creamy thighs.

After he made love to her, he slept in her arms and held her close. Twice in the night he woke with a start, only to find Lily sleeping peacefully against him. She'd found her peace with him, but Quint felt as though he were still searching. It wouldn't be finished until he told her the truth, and the war was over. Only then would he know the peace that was etched on her face.

Quint and Lily were married the next morning, in a small country church that had been long neglected. White paint was peeling, and several windows had been broken. Whether they'd been shot out or broken by vandalous children with rocks, it was impossible to tell. But the church had suffered, as most of Virginia had suffered.

Whatever the reason for the building's condition, the preacher seemed grateful for the gold coin Quint pressed into his hand. There were no questions, even though Quint knew he and Lily didn't look like an especially prosperous couple.

They had spent the morning just outside the small town, bathing in a swift-running creek. Lily's hair was still damp, curling in a pale brown-and-golden cascade down her back.

If he didn't remember anything else about this day, Quint knew he would never forget the way Lily looked. She'd dressed herself in a vivid blue linen gown with just a touch of lace at the collar. The blue made her eyes shine with green fire, and tranquillity made her face glow. That damp hair curled around her face as well as down her back.

Standing before the preacher, repeating the

words with his eyes on Lily's face, Quint committed her face to memory. The light sprinkling of freckles, those perfectly shaped lips. She seemed so sure of their future, so unafraid. She would have fire in her eyes when he told her what he'd done, and what he still planned to do, but by then she would be his wife. She would know how much he loved her.

Quint allowed himself a rare moment of peace. There was so little beauty in the world anymore—real beauty, moments like this one that transcended reality. It wouldn't last, so he savored it, as he savored the love in Lily's eyes, a love so deep, it almost hurt to look at it.

Lily deserved a fancy wedding, with flowers and candles and a church filled with friends and family, but she seemed content with the shell of a building and the preacher's own wife as a witness.

The preacher said a prayer for them at the altar and promised with a small smile to remember them in his prayers again that night.

He pledged himself to remember them in his prayers in the weeks and months to come, a vision of love and faith in a time of hate and hopelessness.

Chapter Sixteen

Lily approached the home she had been born and raised in with growing apprehension. Elliot had employed Joshua Wiggins, a man who used to help out on occasion, to look after the place, but that had been almost two-and-a-half years ago. In her mind the farm was the same. Well-tended and untouched by war, deep green ivy growing over the red brick. Lush grass. The neighing of horses.

But what she had seen since her return to the States had shown her that the war had left little untouched. What if she found her home burned to the ground, like the house they had stopped at that first day?

She looked at her husband and smiled. Her husband. She liked the sound of that, and it felt as natural as if they'd been married years, instead of days. She'd never thought to feel this close to another person.

"Are we almost there?" he asked, pulling his horse up to ride beside her. For most of the morning she had been silently guiding him, her tension building with each step.

Lily nodded and smiled at him, then urged her mare forward.

The ornately carved sign that marked the path to Lily's home was hanging crookedly and was almost completely covered by the ivy that had claimed the post. Lily slid from her mare and brushed the growth away, then she stepped aside so Quint could read the marker.

Sherwood.

"Sherwood?" Quint slipped from his saddle and joined Lily, inspecting the sign more closely. "The name of your home is Sherwood?"

Lily grinned and shrugged her shoulders. "I know. It was probably careless of me to name the Captain after my home, but it seemed so perfect. My father loved the legends of Robin Hood. I grew up hearing the tales of Nottingham and Sherwood Forest. When I ran the blockade for the first time, I felt rather like Robin Hood."

Lily turned her gaze down the lane, a lane that curved snakelike through the dense trees, giving no indication of what they might find at the other end. Sherwood Forest.

They walked slowly, leading their horses down the path. Lily was almost reluctant to reach her destination, and Quint took her hand in his, as if he sensed her disquiet.

"Are you sure, Lily?" he asked quietly. "We can turn back, if you'd like."

Lily gave him a small smile and kept moving forward. She was a little scared, that was true, but she was also determined to see what had become of her home.

When they rounded the bend, they had an unobstructed view of the two-story red brick house before them. There were signs of disrepair—weeds that grew tall at the edge of the porch, a single broken window—but the structure was standing otherwise unchanged, and Lily's mouth curved into a wide smile. She turned to grin at Quint.

"Sherwood." She said the simple word with a depth of emotion that astounded her.

The front door opened, and a thin old man came down the steps, an ancient but obviously well-cared-for rifle gripped in his hands.

"Git, the two of ya," he barked sharply. "I ain't got no extra food for you tramps. The Yankees took it all." He raised his rifle to his shoulder and pointed it at Quint. "Now, git!"

"Mr. Wiggins?" Lily took a step forward. The white-haired man on the front porch of her home looked as if he could have been Joshua Wiggins's father. He had certainly aged more than two-and-a-half years. Wiggins was thin, and even from this distance she could see his hands shake like an old man's.

Wiggins lowered his rifle slowly. "Miss Lily?" He squinted, and eventually smiled as she stepped close enough for him to see her features. "Lord have mercy, it is you."

Joshua Wiggins led them into the house, and that was where Lily saw the changes that had taken place since Elliot had taken her to England. Several pieces of furniture were missing, and her home, which had always been spotlessly clean and well cared-for, was dusty and neglected. Bare spots screamed at her. A table was missing, and her father's favorite chair . . . the bookcase she had tried to climb at three with disastrous results . . . all gone, the books that had once been carefully housed in the bookcase scattered across the floor.

But there in the study was the portrait of her mother, and somehow her father's desk had survived. Too heavy to move quickly, perhaps. Lily looked to her husband and found him staring at the portrait.

"Your mother?" he asked, never taking his eyes from the face in the painting. "It's you, Lily, but without the mischief in your eyes. She was a beautiful woman, almost as beautiful as you."

"I don't remember her," Lily said pragmatically. "She died when I was four. My father tried to tell me stories about her, to keep her alive in my heart, but she was no more real to me than Robin Hood." She couldn't remember ever feeling deprived of a mother, because her father had given her so much love.

Over a meal that consisted of beans and passably fresh bread, Lily related to Joshua some of what had occurred since her departure from Virginia. She didn't tell him that she had spent much of that time as a blockade runner. Joshua was an old-fashioned man and never would have understood or accepted that role for her. But she did manage to shock him by telling him that she had broken her husband out of a Yankee prison.

That caused Joshua to spare a second, thoughtful glance at Quint. Lily didn't bother to explain, but managed to catch her husband's eye and give him a sly smile.

They climbed the stairs to Lily's old room. The room had always seemed small to her, but now, with no furniture remaining but the bed, it seemed huge.

Quint wrapped his arms around her as he kicked the door shut. He wound his fingers through her hair and brushed it aside so he could lower his lips to her sensitive neck.

"Look at this, Lily." He took a step forward, guiding her with a light touch. "A real bed." His voice was low and husky. "I might not let you out of this room for days . . . weeks. We could grow old together in this room."

They worked their way toward the bed that dominated the room. It was tall, the feather mattress covered with a faded green quilt. Quint brushed his hand across Lily's breasts, while the other hand splayed against her belly. Lily closed her eyes and rested her head against his shoulder, a low purring sound deep in her throat. All he had to do was touch her, and she was ready for him, burning with a fierce desire that ruled her body.

Quint reluctantly released her and fumbled with the buttons that ran down the back of her dress. He was cursing under his breath before he was halfway done with the chore. "I want you to get a few more of those dresses like the one you wore to the prison."

"That awful pink thing?" Lily whispered.

"That awful pink thing you can slip out of in a flash."

"Glad you liked it." Lily turned to him as he pushed her dress over her shoulders and down to reveal the thin chemise that barely covered her breasts. "I made it myself."

"Make a few more," Quint whispered. "Never wear anything that takes this long to remove. I'd like to loosen those laces and have you on the bed in seconds, instead of minutes."

"Patience, my love," Lily said, revealing her own impatience as she struggled with his clothing. "We have a lifetime for this."

Quint lowered her to the bed, and they sank into the depths of the luxuriant mattress. He pushed aside all the doubts that assailed him. He should have told her. Now it would have to wait. From here they would go to Wilmington, and he would put her, forcibly if necessary, on the next steamer for Nassau. She still believed that their days together would go on uninterrupted, but he knew that was just another lie.

"I love you, Lily," he said intensely as he kissed her flat belly and trailed his lips upward to take a nipple in his mouth.

Lily arched her back to feel more of him—his warm, wet mouth against her breast, his strong chest against her soft belly. His warmth was her comfort. His love was her strength.

"I love you, Quint. More than you know. More

than I ever thought possible."

They loved one another, fast and slow, desperately and contentedly, with a heat that threatened to burn them with its fire, with a cold and calculated search for pleasure.

For one afternoon and one long night, the war ceased to exist for them. The world ceased to exist but for the small room, the heat of their bodies, and the love that had so suddenly and unexpectedly claimed them both.

They woke to the crack of the bedroom door as it crashed against the wall. The pale light of early morning streamed through the windows, illuminating the blue-coated soldiers who rushed through the doorway and in a split second surrounded the bed, rifles trained on them, by the time Quint had fully opened his eyes.

"The old man was right," one of the soldiers observed as his eyes traveled over the thin sheet that covered Lily's body. "They do match the description."

He turned his attention to Quint and grinned. "Good morning, Captain Sherwood."

Quint's gut impulse was to jump out of the bed and take them all on. He didn't like the way they were staring at Lily as she lay there covered only by the white sheet. In spite of it all, he remained cool. It was the only way to get Lily out of this.

"Actually, the name's Lieutenant Quintin Tyler, United States Army, soldier." The tone of his voice was calm and authoritative. "The lady is my—"

"You got proof?" the same soldier pressed. Out of the corner of his eye, Quint saw Lily's face. She hadn't panicked, and he admired her for that, but she was coldly assessing the situation as if she planned to act. He grabbed her arm under the sheet, his fingers tender but firm.

"If you'll contact Colonel Fairfax in Washington, he will vouch for me." Quint hoped that the colonel still would acknowledge him, after what had happened at the prison. At least he could buy a little time with the revelation.

The soldier, a husky sergeant, drew his eyebrows together. "Colonel Fairfax. I know that name." He looked at the private who stood at his side, and the younger man whispered an aside to the sergeant before turning his eyes back to Lily.

"Colonel Fairfax with the Secret Service?" the sergeant asked the question rather unsteadily, as if he'd stumbled upon something that was over his head.

Quint nodded. "Yes."

He felt Lily glaring at him, and when he turned to face her, he saw the knowledge of his betrayal in her eyes. "I wanted to tell you myself," Quint began, as Lily yanked her arm away from him, the arm he tried to hold under the thin covers. She drew away from him until she was all but hanging on the edge of the bed. "I'm sorry . . ."

"You're a goddamn Yankee spy." Lily whispered, but everyone in the room heard her.

"I'll explain later," Quint said in a low voice, but he could see that she was not listening to him. Anger was flashing in her eyes, and her face flushed pink.

Then, in a flash, the angry fire was gone, and a coldness stole over her eyes. Those lush lips thinned, and the color drained from her face. Her eyes were riveted on Quint's face as the change took place, and it was only after the transformation was complete that she turned to the sergeant, looking up at him as she held the sheet bunched above her breasts.

"He's telling the truth, sergeant," she said boldly. In her fantasies about telling the Yankees that she had been the one to make fools of them all, she had never imagined that her tongue would taste of copper and her heart would beat so hard she expected it to burst through her chest. She made sure that none of the signs of her fear were evident to any of the men in the room—not to the blue-clad soldiers, not to Quint.

"He's not Captain Sherwood," she said icily. "I am."

"Lily!" Quint exploded.

"I should be good for a promotion, don't you think?" She ignored her husband and continued to stare at the sergeant. There were half-a-dozen rifles still aimed at her and at Quint, the muzzles mere inches away. She ignored the deadly weapons as completely as she had ignored Quint. "If you and your men will wait in the hall, I'll get dressed and we can proceed."

She finally turned to face Quint. "To Washington, I suppose. Isn't that where we're headed,

Lieutenant Tyler? Wasn't that to be our next stop?" She had her emotions under control, and the stare she bestowed upon him was icy cold.

The sergeant shook his head. "I don't think I should leave you two alone . . ."

"Dammit, sergeant!" Quint bellowed. "Give us ten minutes!"

The sergeant nodded to his men. "Search the room thoroughly for weapons." The inspection didn't take long. The soldiers had covered every inch of the sparsely furnished room in minutes. They left with Quint's pistol and Lily's precious saber.

After the other soldiers had left the room, the sergeant turned to Quint and Lily. "There are guards posted around the grounds, should you be thinking of going out the window. You have five minutes."

Lily sprang from the bed as soon as the door was closed. She turned her back to Quint as she grabbed her clothes and began to dress. Her stiffened spine was toward him as she pulled the chemise over her head, and she was stonily quiet as she buttoned the high neck and cuffs of a plain sea-green cotton gown.

Quint dressed quickly and tried to step in front of her as she struggled with the buttons. She was trying hard to show no emotion, but her hands trembled slightly. Quint reached out to assist her, but Lily pushed him away with all the strength she could muster.

"I'd sooner prance stark naked in front of the

231

entire Union Army than allow you to touch me again," she seethed.

"Lily, I was going to tell you."

"When?" She lifted cold eyes to him. "When you turned me over to your Colonel Fairfax?"

"I wouldn't have done that," he swore softly, and in vain. She didn't believe a word he said.

"You're a very good liar, Lieutenant Tyler," Lily said in a chilling voice. "What sacrifices you've made for your cause. It's very noble of you, I'm sure, to go to such lengths. Perhaps there will be a medal in it for you."

Quint reached out and placed a hand on her shoulder, but she backed away violently. "Don't touch me again, you bloody bastard," she said in a low voice.

Lily pulled on her black boots. When the full skirt of her dress fell to the floor it was impossible to tell that she wore the same boots she had sailed the ocean with, but when she walked, the sharp report of the heels against the floor echoed crisply. She was headed for the door, where she turned without warning.

"I feel like such a bloody fool." For a moment, she felt tears threaten, but she pushed them away. "Everything was going beautifully. I had my own house, and the *Chameleon*, and Tommy and Cora, and my crew . . . and then I allowed myself to be suckered in by the likes of you. You're a damn good spy, Quintin Tyler."

Heartbreak was new to Lily. She had never suffered the pain of rejection or the despair of an unrequited love. She had never before allowed anyone into her heart, and therefore she was floored by the intense pain Quint's betrayal was causing. She felt as though her heart would literally be torn apart.

Lily pushed away the pain and steeled her heart. She would show Quint none of her weakness. In fact, she managed to meet his look with an emotionless stare of her own.

"Why in hell did you tell them that you were Captain Sherwood? Why didn't you just keep your mouth shut and let me handle it?"

The door opened just as Lily slapped Quint with all her might. Her years of fencing and sailing had given her more strength in her arms than most women had, and Quint's head snapped back. But he returned his gaze to hers almost immediately, with no change of expression in his eyes. She knew he could see all the hurt and confusion she tried to hide, and that only made her hate him more.

"Let me explain . . ."

"I loved you, and you lied to me. No explanation can change that," Lily whispered. The sergeant stood right behind her and could no doubt hear, but she didn't care. "I'll never forgive you . . . I'll never forget what you did."

Their hands were tied in front of them, Quint's as well as Lily's. He would be treated as a prisoner until his identity could be confirmed. Joshua Wiggins was waiting anxiously at the bottom of the stairs, wringing his hands and crying out in dismay when he saw the bonds on Lily's wrists.

"No," he cried out as he blocked the foot of the stairway. "Not the girl. He's the one you want."

Wiggins was unceremoniously knocked aside by a stone-faced private. Lily tried to have some sympathy for the frightened man, but she glared at him, stopping on the bottom stair to look down at him as he lay half sitting, half lying on the floor.

"Why, Mr. Wiggins?" she asked coldly.

He shook his head and dropped his head, as if he couldn't bear to look at her. "I didn't mean for them to take you, Miss Lily. I'm . . . I'm an old man, and as long as I . . . I help these soldiers out now and again, they leave me alone and see that I have food."

His rationalization did nothing to ease her anger. "Make sure you get your thirty pieces of silver as well."

He was another one. She hadn't loved him, but she had felt affection for the old man. His betrayal didn't cut as deep as Quint's, but it added to her burden.

With the assistance of a young soldier, Lily was seated on the saddle of her mare. The reins were taken by another soldier, and Lily stared straight ahead.

She heard the footsteps stop beside her and looked down haughtily. She would show no emotion. Not to Quint. Not to any of them.

Quint was standing beside her. If he'd stretched out his bound hands he could have touched her leg. But he stood very still, staring into her eyes.

Lily stared back hard, refusing to be the one who broke that contact. She swore that she would get even with him, somehow, for his treachery. But as he looked up at her with those dark eyes, she felt herself soften. Surely it hadn't all been lies.

"It'll be all right, sweetheart," he whispered. "I promise." His eyes softened, and Lily felt her resolve begin to melt.

But she couldn't allow that to happen.

Her answer to his vow was to swing out her leg, catching Quint under the chin with her sturdy boot. He practically flew backwards, and was caught by the two guards who stood behind him.

A group of soldiers burst into sporadic laughter sprinkled with colorful curses, as Lily turned her eyes forward and ignored them all.

She hardened her heart then and there. There was nothing that could make her forget what Quint had done to her. He had used her body and her heart against her, and that she could never forgive. She resolved that she would never love anyone again. Ever.

They traveled less than an hour before they joined a huge contingent of Union soldiers. All Lily had thought of was escape. The plans that ran through her mind kept her thoughts from Quint and his deception. She cursed when she saw the number of the troops before her. It would be bloody impossible to escape from this place.

The private who had led her horse, giving her wary glances now and again over his shoulder, helped her to the ground, heedful of her dangerous booted feet.

Lily didn't kick him, as she had Quint. It would have served no purpose. She reverted to her old ways, smiling at the Yankee sweetly as he released her.

Her smile obviously confused the young soldier, and Lily saw that she had not allayed his suspicions. He'd seen too much that morning to dismiss her lightly. She couldn't fool even him.

"Captain Brighton." She heard the sergeant's deep voice somewhere behind her. But she had no time for this Captain Brighton. Eventually they would have to transfer her to a prison, and they wouldn't want to spare too many men for that chore, if they could help it. If she tried to appear harmless, fragile, then perhaps they would assign only two or three the task. She smiled as she thought of that. It would take at least two days to reach Washington. Plenty of time and opportunity to escape.

"Captain Brighton, sir." Lily returned her attention to the sergeant's voice. "Damndest thing I ever did see. According to the description we got, this man's Captain Sherwood. But the woman claims *she's* Captain Sherwood. Probably trying to cover for him, but she's a wild one, so I took them both."

"That's fine, sergeant."

Lily stiffened at the sound of the captain's lifeless reply. She would never forget that voice.

Some nights she still dreamed of it, in her worst nightmares. She made herself turn around slowly. The captain was making his way toward her. He was thinner and grayer. The war had aged him badly, but it was the captain responsible for her father's death.

He stopped several feet away from her, his instant recognition evident on his stunned face. The captain looked her up and down, as if he expected her to change before his very eyes and become some other woman. But she glared at him, let him know that his eyes were not playing tricks on him.

"Bloody hell," she murmured, and that made him smile. "It's you."

"Miss Radford." The captain continued forward after a long pause. "I must admit I'm quite surprised to see you again."

All Lily's plans went awry when she saw him there. "You're still alive, I see. What a shame. Suffered any serious tobacco injuries lately? Cigar bombs? Pipe blasts? Whatever happened to the private who shot my father? Is he a captain, also, or does he outrank you, that fine soldier?" She couldn't keep the anger and sarcasm from her voice. The very sight of the man infuriated her.

Captain Brighton's smile faded. "That young man was killed less than a month after your father's death. You shouldn't be surprised. He was a nice boy, but a poor soldier."

Another private led Quint forward. Quint held his jaw tenderly with both bound hands. A trickle of blood marked his lip, and beneath his dark bristle a patch of his skin was red, and would be purple before long. Lily actually smiled a little. Served him right. He glared at her before she turned her attention back to the captain.

Captain Brighton grimaced at Quint's battered face. "What did you do to him? I thought you said he claims to be one of ours."

The sergeant defended himself stoutly. "We didn't touch him, Captain. It was the girl. She booted him right beneath the chin."

"Ah, Miss Radford. I see you haven't changed at all," Brighton said tiredly.

Quint tried to move closer to Lily, but his guard restrained him. "Do you know this man, Lily?" he asked through clenched teeth.

Lily ignored him, but Brighton answered him with a wry smile. "Miss Radford and I have met."

"And you're wrong, Captain Brighton," Lily said the name hatefully. At least she had a name to put with the face that had haunted her in nightmares. "I have changed. If I held my saber to your heart today, I wouldn't hesitate to run you through."

Captain Brighton turned to the sergeant. "If this woman claims to be Captain Sherwood, then I assure you it's the truth."

The captain approached Quint with the same lazy step Lily always associated with him, as if he'd just risen from a restless night.

"Lieutenant Quintin Tyler, sir," Quint said as crisply as he could through clenched teeth.

Lily broke away from her guard and rushed toward the two men. "He's a bloody spy!" she shouted, her eyes on Quint. The control she had planned to show was forgotten. She would have slapped Quint again, if her hands had been free, but she satisfied herself with a swift kick to his shin. As her guard grabbed her and pulled her back, Quint lifted his bound hands, palms forward.

"It's all right," he said, looking at the anxious private who held Lily so tightly.

"The two of you should be great friends," Lily spat. "You're two of a kind, you are. Deceitful, blue-bellied, lily-livered, egg-sucking bastards. Spineless, back-stabbing, flea-brained vermin."

They all stared at her, the soldiers who surrounded her as well as Quint and Captain Brighton. Captain Brighton sighed tiredly, and Quint raised an eyebrow. He was so damned infuriating! How dare he look at her like that? The charade was over. Why couldn't he simply turn away from her and be done with it?

Captain Brighton turned to the sergeant who dogged him. "Noon meal in my tent for three." He looked from Lily to Quint. "I'd like to get to the bottom of this."

Lily straightened her spine and glared coldly at the captain. "I'll starve before I eat with the likes of you." She shared the cold stare with Quint, including him in her vow. "Quint, my love." She said the endearment coldly, and she could see the hurt on Quint's face. "Be sure to tell the Captain every scandalous detail. I'm sure it will make for an entertaining afternoon."

She turned away from him before he could see the sudden tears that threatened.

Chapter Seventeen

Lily sat cross-legged on the floor of the small tent that had been provided for her. The light of several campfires glowed bright yellow through the coarse canvas, silhouetting the four sentinels who had been assigned to her.

Four guards! If she hadn't lost her senses when she'd seen Captain Brighton, she'd probably have only one or two guards—but four!

Even when she'd politely asked to be excused to tend to her personal needs, she'd been accompanied by the four vigilants. When she'd protested the need for privacy, one enterprising young soldier had tied a rope securely to her waist, the tight knot at her back too difficult for her to disengage without alerting the guard who held the other end of the rope, keeping no slack in the line.

She had tended to her personal business quickly and marched back to her warden's side. The urge was there to deliver to him a kick as sturdy as the one she had given Quint, but that would serve no purpose but to anger them all. So she smiled sweetly and called them, wryly, her four paladins. In response she received confused frowns. The idiots were wondering if they'd been insulted.

If she'd wanted to insult them, she'd make certain they knew it.

So Lily sat alone on the floor of the tent. She would not eat their food. She would not rest on their cot. If the night became chilly, she would accept the chill rather than wrap herself in the Yankee blanket that was neatly folded on the narrow cot.

When the hunger pangs began, she accepted them as well, a sign of her stubbornness and fortitude. She concentrated on the sharp pains. They were a sign of her determination, as was the hard ground beneath her. Her discomfort reminded her that she could rely on no one but herself.

It was after midnight before she laid her head on the ground and slept. She expected to be haunted by dreams that would wake her screaming in the night, and she didn't want that. She would show the Yankees none of her weakness. But her sleep was so deep and complete that she was lost in a black void until morning came.

Lily's escort to Washington consisted of a full dozen soldiers, as well as Quintin Tyler. Evidently Captain Brighton had believed Quint's story, because when he joined the contingent he was unbound.

There was a soldier with Quint, a corporal

younger than Quint; the two of them spoke quietly, heads together, and the corporal glanced at Lily once. Only once.

Quint's clean-shaven face was a lovely shade of purple, and his scowl told her how much his jaw pained him. He spoke to the corporal as they passed her, a low "Watch your step, Candell." Lily gave him a wide smile as he went by, not coming too close to her as she was already seated on her mare and her boots rested easily in the stirrups. Lily's smile never touched her eyes. It wasn't meant to. It was meant to convey to Quint how little she cared for him and his machinations.

She bit her tongue as he passed by silently. She wanted to scream at him as she had the day before, wanted to bestow upon him every sailor's curse she had ever heard, and then some. But Lily simply smiled coldly until he turned his head from her.

"Miss Radford." She looked away from the back of Quint's head and found the captain standing almost beside her. He, too, was cautious of his nearness to her booted feet. "I regret that I cannot accompany you to the capital myself. Sadly, I have other duties to attend to."

"Killing civilians. Stealing horses. Abducting innocent women . . ."

He raised a hand to stop her. "You are far from innocent, Miss Radford. And you've been caught, not abducted."

Lily stared at Brighton for a long moment. He didn't look particularly hateful or dangerous. He looked no different than a dozen merchants or sailors she had known in Nassau. With the proper clothing, he might have appeared to be an English lord, for there was an almost regal air about him, in spite of his constant lethargy.

"Do you know how much I hate you?" The question from Lily was delivered softly, and with much bewilderment. Brighton didn't seem to take offense.

"Yes, and that saddens me greatly, Miss Radford. I don't consider you my enemy. I never have."

Lily looked down at him. He was confusing her, just as Quint had. No. Not as Quint had. Quint had confused her with his hands and his lips and those incredibly deep eyes. Captain Brighton confused her with a kind voice and a sadness on his tired face.

"I sometimes have nightmares about you," she confessed. "About that day."

Brighton sighed. "I have seen your face in my nightmares as well, Miss Radford. I have relived that afternoon a thousand times. I wish I could say that your father's death was the only senseless waste of life I've seen in the past three years, but it's not. He was one of many."

Lily was unexpectedly sorry for the captain, and she realized why he moved with such a slow step, why his eyes were always so lifeless.

"I understand you've been refusing to eat." He changed the subject suddenly, to Lily's relief. He brought a large red apple from behind his back, and he tossed it through the air so that when she reached out her bound hands it smacked her palm smartly. "You must take care of yourself."

Lily squelched the urge to throw the apple back at him, instead taking a healthy bite. The captain smiled as she chewed the juicy apple.

"You'll forgive me for not handing the fruit to you in a more proper fashion. One look at Lieutenant Tyler this morning warns me that would not be smart."

Lily nodded, swallowing the sweet fruit. Perhaps it was foolish to starve herself to spite the damn Yankees. "You're probably wise in that respect, Captain."

Brighton glanced down at the black boot that rested in the stirrup. Her dress was hiked up to allow her to ride astride, but the boots covered any skin that might have been improperly exposed. He doubted very much that Lily Radford would have cared, in any case.

She turned her face front, ignoring him, but he had a feeling that she had, if not forgiven him, then at least found room in her heart for a little understanding. Perhaps her face would stop haunting him in nightmares where she knelt over her father and then looked up at him with that accusing gleam in her bright eyes.

But there were other nightmares more horrible than that one that he would never be rid of.

He shook his head as he walked away. God help the soldiers responsible for keeping that woman in prison, for that was surely where she was headed.

Brighton knew, thanks to Corporal Candell,

that Tyler was indeed one of their own. How ironic, that two soldiers so passionate about their cause should find one another in a time such as this. He didn't find it odd that he so naturally thought of Lily Radford as a soldier. She had the heart of a soldier, the determination of a warrior.

And God help Quintin Tyler. If the man was truly planning to try to win Lily Radford back, as he claimed he was, he had a long and bumpy road ahead of him.

The band of soldiers and their single prisoner moved at a slow but steady pace over the road to Washington. One soldier held the reins to Lily's mare, and she was flanked on either side by stalwart privates who watched her with an almost amusing mixture of caution and wonderment. She wanted to laugh at their amazement. They couldn't accept that a woman who looked no more dangerous than their own wives and sweethearts could be a blockade runner. Women were supposed to be weak creatures who needed their protection—not the enemy. Not prisoners.

Quint rode at the rear of the line. Lily was always aware of his presence; she could actually feel him behind her. But she didn't turn to look at him—not once during the day's journey.

They stopped for a noon meal and to tend to the horses. Since Lily's hands were still bound, one of her more daring guards assisted her as she dismounted. Lily was docile, putting the private's fears to rest. Her thoughts had been occupied with a single thought during the morning's ride. Escape.

She certainly couldn't fight the contingent of a dozen soldiers and expect to make any progress. They were armed and long-legged and extremely wary of her. They expected her to try to escape. No one spoke to her, even after they stopped, but they all watched her carefully.

Even Quint kept his distance as Lily sat beneath the leaves of an oak tree that was in the process of turning red. A few brown leaves had dropped to the ground already and crackled beneath the soldiers' boots. Lily lifted the soft bread she'd been issued in her hands. Her wrists were chafing, but she refused to complain.

Quint watched Lily lift the bread to her mouth and take a dainty bite, her eyes unfocused and turned away from him. His own eyes were narrowed as he studied her, and the longer he watched, the angrier he became.

He continued to watch Lily out of the corner of his eye as he approached the lieutenant Captain Brighton had placed in charge of this detail. Lieutenant Hanson was young, probably younger than Lily, but he was as serious and dedicated as a twenty-year veteran.

"Can't you at least untie her hands so she can eat?" Quint hissed. He didn't want Lily to hear him pleading for her. She was so furious, she'd probably prefer to remain bound than to benefit from his assistance.

Hanson shook his head. "She's handling herself just fine, Lieutenant Tyler." Hanson turned his harsh glare to Lily. "I'd think that you, of all people, would understand why she needs to remain restrained."

Quint placed a hand over his discolored jaw. "She was bound when she did this." He looked to her, sitting close enough for him to study, yet too far away to hear his conversation with the lieutenant. Suddenly, Quint was certain that Lily knew he was watching her, knew he was talking about her, and she was keeping her gaze averted from him on purpose.

He ignored Hanson and strolled toward Lily. He'd tried to allow her enough time to cool off, at least enough for him to explain what had happened. If the look on her face was any indication, he hadn't waited nearly long enough.

He was almost upon her before Lily turned her head and acknowledged him. She lifted her eyebrows slightly and looked him up and down, her eyes sweeping over him with disdain. There was no hint of tenderness in her cold perusal.

"Lily." Quint squatted beside her, his left leg bent beneath him, his still impaired right leg extended. "Are you all right?"

Lily saw it, then, the flash of guilt in his dark eyes. Guilt. It must be a new feeling for Quintin Tyler, she thought as she watched him without responding. And as she watched his face, a plan began to form in her mind. She'd been playing a role for the past year and a half and doing a fine job of it. She could pretend a little while longer, if that was what it would take.

Quint started to work the bonds at her wrists.

The skin beneath the rough rope was red and swollen and tender, but there was no blood yet. Without looking at her face, Quint massaged her sensitive skin.

"Did you . . ." Lily's voice was soft as she questioned Quint, hesitating briefly. "Did you tell them that we're married?" She wished that he would release her hands. It was as if her body didn't know that he was a traitor, even though in her mind she had dismissed Quintin Tyler. She still liked the feel of his hands on hers, his fingers massaging her wrists and hands. For a moment, just for a moment, she felt an odd tightening in her chest as she watched his face. She had come to love that face . . . and then to hate it. But the sight of those dark eyes, that nose with the small bump, the strong jaw that was now a strange shade of purple, still stirred her. Even though she didn't want to feel anything for him.

Quint shook his head. "No. Captain Brighton seemed to think it would be best if we kept that to ourselves for now. It'll be easier for me to get you out—"

"To get me out?" Lily snapped, then grabbed hold of her emotions and calmed herself. "Why would you go to so much trouble to capture me, just to get me out of prison as soon as we get to Washington?"

Quint lifted his head and stared into Lily's eyes. "You have to know that I never expected this. I never expected you to be Captain Sherwood, and I sure as hell never planned to fall in love with you."

For a fleeting moment Lily felt a softening of her hatred for the man who was her husband, a man who still claimed to love her. And then it was gone. "How can you help me once I'm in prison?"

Quint gave her a smile, as if he meant to re-assure her, to soothe her doubts. "I know an officer in the capital who might be able to help. If that doesn't work out, I have a couple of names from Captain Brighton. Names of people there who can assist us."

Lieutenant Hanson joined them, a scowl on his face as he ordered Lily's hands tied once again. Lily lifted her eyes to Quint, and they were wide and trusting. Great tears welled up in her eyes, but didn't fall down her cheeks. Her lips trembled slightly, until Quint turned away from her.

The trembling lips stiffened and the tears dried. Her face hardened, as well as her determination.

She could be as devious and single-minded as Quintin Tyler. She could be as cold and unfeeling as he, and in that she would find her escape.

It was near dark before they stopped again. Enough light remained in the sky for the soldiers to pitch a single tent for Lily and for the cook to begin to prepare their evening meal before darkness fell.

There were never fewer than two guards at Lily's side. She watched them with a grim smile, her vigilant watchmen, as the rest of the camp went about their business.

More than one campfire was built, and a few of the soldiers grabbed a quick bite to eat and settled into their bedrolls. Lily assumed they were the men who would take the second watch. Four soldiers settled into a game of cards, after they had finished caring for the mounts, and Quint was engrossed in an apparent argument with Lieutenant Hanson.

Lily couldn't tell what was being said. They stood too far away from her. But she recognized the stubborn expression on Quint's face and an equally immobile set to Hanson's young features. They were arguing about her, she was certain.

When Quint finally came to her, she couldn't tell who had won their argument. Lieutenants Tyler and Hanson both still seemed extremely put out.

Quint lowered himself to the ground beside Lily and began to loosen her bonds as he had that afternoon. Lily gave him a small smile, even though his eyes were on her wrists and not her face. She lifted her head and saw Hanson glaring at them. So this was what the contention had been about.

Quint removed the rope and began to massage Lily's sore skin as he had that afternoon. It was painful, but necessary, as the blood began to flow freely once again. Then he lifted uncertain eyes to her.

"Thank you," she said reluctantly.

With the setting of the sun, the comfortable air had turned chilly. It wasn't cold. Winter was still months away, but the nippy breeze was a drastic change from the warm winds of Nassau. It pressed wild curls away from Lily's face and made her cheeks burn, and as Quint removed his hands from hers, she shivered. From the chill of the air, she told herself. From the chill of the air.

Lily looked down and straightened her skirt as best she could. She was dusty and tired, and for a split second she almost regretted what she was about to do. But she didn't regret it. She would go through with her plan even if she did.

"Quint." Her voice was little more than a whisper as she pleaded with him. "Is there some way we can talk . . . in private? Just for a moment." She laid her hand on his arm. In the light of the small fires that lit the camp, Quint's face softened.

"Perhaps."

Lily stood and offered her hand to Quint. "Can we walk around the camp for a bit? My legs are cramped from riding all day." That was when she gave him "the smile." She had been working up to it all afternoon, wondering if she was capable of flirting with Quint at this point without him knowing exactly what she was planning.

Evidently, she was. Quint stood and took her hand, placing it in the crook of his arm as they walked around the perimeter of the camp. Her two guards stayed several steps behind, far enough away that they couldn't hear if Quint and Lily kept their voices low, close enough that Lily wasn't going far without them right behind her.

"I'm scared," Lily whispered without slowing her pace.

Quint laid his hand over hers and squeezed it lightly. "I know. I'll have you out of there in no time. I promise." His voice was as low as hers.

Lily knew, at that moment, that the words were true. She was scared. Terrified, in fact. But not of prison. She was scared of returning to a life without Quint. Without love. She would have been better off if she'd never met Quintin Tyler. How could she ever be satisfied with a loveless life again? Now that she knew what it was like to care for another being with all her heart, to lose herself in warm arms and tender lips. The tears that ran down her cheeks were real this time, not manufactured tears like the ones she'd shed that afternoon. She was going back to a life that suddenly seemed cold and lonely. Quint had taught her how vulnerable she was to love, and in the process had managed to ruin her life.

Quint stopped when he saw the silent tears, taking Lily's shoulders and pivoting her to face him. With an agitated wave of his hand, he motioned back the guards who followed them. The soldiers stopped, then took a step back when they saw her tears.

Lily peered over Quint's shoulder. The camp behind him was quiet and well-ordered. A few soldiers were sleeping, a few were playing cards. They were all relaxed . . . all but Lieutenant Hanson, who watched Quint's back with a frown. But he was on the opposite side of the camp. Her two guards were as far away as they'd been all day, and talking quietly. Now was the time.

Lily stood on her tiptoes and lifted her face to

Quint's. Tear tracks marred her face, and her eyes were wide as she kissed him lightly on the mouth. Her hands were pressing lightly against his chest.

Quint began to raise his arms to wrap them around her, but he was too late. Without warning, Lily shoved him with all her might, and he stumbled backward. Quint felt a sharp catch in his right thigh, but managed to remain on his feet.

Lily disappeared into the trees that surrounded the camp, leaving the circle of light that the campfires created.

His first thought was to let her go.

His second, and most frightening thought, was that if he did, he might never see her again.

The rifle fire that echoed all around brought him to his senses sharply, and he ran after her, cutting in front of the two guards.

"Hold your fire!" he shouted, hurling himself between Lily and the barrage. His feet thudded against the earth and dried leaves, every step painful. But he never slowed his pace. He could hear Lily ahead of him, though he could see nothing. He heard her boots against the brittle dead leaves, her body as she brushed against low limbs in her path.

He had to catch her. If the guards got to her first, and she didn't surrender immediately, she could be shot. Shot in the back, just like Captain John Wright. Was this what had happened to him? Had he bolted in the night, only to die moments later with a bullet in his back?

He couldn't allow anyone else to catch her, and he couldn't let her get away. Lily could disappear anywhere in the world. He might never find her if she escaped now. It would take a dozen lifetimes to search the earth for Lily.

His thigh felt as if it might collapse beneath him, but Quint willed it, with gritted teeth, to withstand this test. He had to catch Lily.

The cold air hurt Lily's chest as she ran, but she never slowed her flight. She could see only a few feet ahead of her, but that was all right. That meant the soldiers following her couldn't see either. But she could hear them. And that meant they could hear her. As far as she could tell, only one soldier was close. One of her guards, no doubt. They were the only ones who had been near enough to be so close on her tail. Quint couldn't possibly run, not with his injured leg.

She ran and ran, listening to her pursuer. She could only hear one now, and he seemed to be moving closer. Damned persistent, that one. She was tiring, and that meant he had to be, too. But she kept running; she would run all night if she had to, to get away from the Yankees. And from Quintin Tyler. Quint, most of all.

The soldier hunted her obstinately. He was closing in on her slowly. Lily could hear his breathing, labored and rasping, and still he came.

And then she knew it was Quint. Impossible, but somehow she *knew*. In spite of his injury, in spite of his pain, he pursued her relentlessly. That knowledge only inspired her to move faster, to keep going. Quint was not going to give up easily. He was as competitive as she, and as accustomed to winning. She would never give in to him, never give up.

They might have run all night, but the toe of Lily's boot hit the exposed root of on old tree, and she tumbled to the ground with a startled cry, landing in the dirt face first, the dead leaves crunching beneath her body. Before she could rise, Quint was on top of her, pouncing on her prone form and pressing her harder into the ground.

"Get off me!" she demanded, with as much dignity as she could muster.

For several moments, her only answer was his raspy panting against her ear. When he finally spoke, his voice was harsh and unforgiving. "Like hell I will. I'm not up to chasing you any farther, woman, so you'll stay right where you are for the moment."

How had he been able to keep up with her for as long as he had? She knew his leg, while much better, was far from strong. There was pain in his uneven breathing.

"You're crushing me!" she insisted, spitting a broken dead leaf from her lips.

Once again, Quint was slow in answering her. "Good," he whispered. "Did you really think I would let you run away from me?"

"Why do you care?" Lily felt dangerously close to tears again, and that angered her more than anything else. She was not a sentimental fool, not over a man! She felt as if he were smothering her, truly crushing her with his weight. In spite of the chilly night air, he was hot, and he transferred his heat to her. It melted through the back of her dress, through her skin, burning her very soul.

"I do care, Lily." Quint laid his lips against the tender skin beneath her ear, at the back of her neck. "You must believe me."

Lily scoffed, maintaining her dignity even in such a position. "Believe you? Never. You're nothing but a lying, spineless bounder, with the morals of a snake and the honor of a jackass. I hate you. I hate the day I met you." She had intended to anger Quint, but he remained calm as she herself became more and more incensed. His breathing had slowed, but he took none of his weight off her.

"Let me go," she whispered. In the near distance she heard other soldiers approaching. "Please, Quint. If you ever cared for me . . ."

"Over here!" Quint shouted, and in moments they were surrounded. When Lily tried fruitlessly to beat Quint with hands that flailed wildly backwards, he grabbed them and pinned her wrists to the ground.

Flanked by four winded soldiers, Quint rolled off her. He kept her wrists pinned to the ground for a moment, then he yanked her into a sitting position so that she faced him.

"Tie her wrists and ankles," he ordered coldly.

"But Lieutenant, she has to walk . . ."

"I'll carry her."

The four soldiers looked at one another in disbelief. Quint saw their skeptical glances out of the corner of his eye. They didn't expect him to be able to carry Lily back to camp in his condition. But he would have to, somehow.

"Sir, with the five of us to escort her—"

"Do it!" It was an order, clear and simple and barked with authority, and the soldiers did as they were told.

But not easily. Lily was furious, and she kicked and clawed as the soldiers tied her. Quint released her only when she was in their hands and unable to escape.

"I hate you!" she spat at him. He could barely see her face in the patchy moonlight that found its way through the leaves.

"Don't be redundant, Lily," Quint said coolly. "You already said that." His lazy voice gave away none of his emotions. How was he ever going to get through this? Lily was a spirited woman and not, from what he'd seen, particularly forgiving. If her hate was as volatile as her love, he would never win her back.

Without voicing any of his reservations, he threw Lily, bound at the wrists and ankles, over his shoulder. Her head hung behind his back, and she beat her fists against his spine. He'd only taken half a dozen steps before he tossed her forward, catching her and setting her on her feet half a second before she would have fallen.

His thigh ached, his chest ached, and in spite of the cool air, he was sweating from the exertion of chasing Lily.

"If you hit me one more time, I'll stop . . . find a sturdy limb . . . and truss you to it like a roasting pig." There was no kindness in his voice this time. No hint that he had told her moments earlier that he cared for her. "Do you understand?"

"Yes," Lily said, gritting her teeth as he tossed her again over her shoulder. Her single word was filled with the knowledge of her defeat, and she lay motionlessly against Quint. He held her by the crook of her knees, and she hung over his shoulder like a rag doll.

She could feel the unevenness of his step, the way he struggled with her weight, but he never slowed his step or mentioned handing her over to one of the other soldiers. He'd won again, and Lily felt absolutely humiliated. She wouldn't anger him, not now, but she mouthed the words she longed to scream. *I hate you.*

Quint sighed deeply. "I know."

Chapter Eighteen

The trek back to camp was a long and laborious
one. And quiet. No one spoke. There was only the
rasp of Quint's ragged breath and the shuffling
of five sets of footsteps in the dirt and leaves.
Now and again, Lily would lift her head and look
around her. The soldiers flanked Quint on four
sides and watched him with a respectful awe.
Carrying her back to camp would have been a
chore for any of them, but it should have been
impossible for Quintin Tyler.

Lily dismissed his response to her unspoken
avowal of hatred. Perhaps he had been thinking
of something else, or perhaps he had felt her
breath against his back and realized those were
the only words she would have for him. Perhaps
she had actually spoken aloud.

No. She had mouthed the words. He had
known what she was thinking. Was that really so
strange? Was it any stranger than her realization
that Quint was the soldier chasing her? God, had
they forged a bond so deep so quickly?

They entered a circle of light, leaving the darkness of the forest behind. Quint's breathing was coming hard and broken, and he tossed her roughly forward as he set her on her feet, always careful to keep a firm grip on her. His hand on her wrists or grasping her arm . . . she was never free of his touch.

Lily glanced up into Lieutenant Hanson's smugly triumphant face.

"You were correct, Lieutenant Hanson," Quint said hoarsely. "Miss Radford cannot be trusted. I agree that she should be bound at all times."

Hanson smiled complacently. "After all, it's just for one more day. After that, she's none of our concern. Correct?"

"Correct," Quint agreed shortly. "I don't believe I'll feel safe tonight with nothing more than a length of rope between Miss Radford and freedom. You do have shackles?"

"You wouldn't dare!" Lily had to crane her neck to get a good look at Quint's face. He was pale—almost green—and he was deadly serious.

They were shackled together, at Quint's insistence. His left wrist to her right. His left ankle to her right. Hanson gave Lily an arrogant grin as he watched the proceedings. Of course, this was a victory for him, over her and over Quint as well. She'd proven herself untrustworthy, as he'd claimed her to be.

Quint remained quiet, and after one look into his thunderous black eyes, Lily turned her face away from him. She had more right to be angry than he did, caught by a bloody Yankee spy with a bad leg. He could have allowed her to escape.

He could have let her go. But no. He'd hunted her down and brought her back in humiliation, and now he dragged her toward a tent without so much as a backward glance, limping as badly as he had when she'd first met him.

Quint lifted the tent flap and allowed her to precede him. She did so ungraciously, jerking at the chain that bound them together. There was barely enough room in the tent for the two of them to stand in the center, face to face.

Inside the tent there was so little light that Lily could see nothing but a shadow where Quint's face should be. That was good. She would be more effective opposing him if she didn't have to look at his face.

"Lie down, Lily," Quint ordered sharply.

Lily placed her left hand on her hip, in what she hoped was a defiant stance. "I will not. This was a preposterous idea, Lieutenant Tyler. I don't know what you were thinking—"

"If you don't lie down, I'll fall down," Quint said slowly. "If I fall on top of you, that's where I'll stay all night."

"Is it that bad?" Lily asked, instantly regretting the soft tone she used. She didn't care about his bloody leg!

"Yes, thanks to you."

They lowered themselves together, slowly, to two bedrolls that had been laid out side by side. The breath that Quint released when he was finally flat on his back told her how badly his leg hurt. She pushed away every bit of sympathy that welled to the surface.

"Why didn't you just let me go?" Lily asked desperately. "Is it really so important that I make it to Washington? Will Captain Sherwood really be such a feather in your cap?"

Quint turned his head to look at her. He was so close, and on any other night she would have expected him to reach out and touch her, to kiss her or to caress her cheek with his long fingers. But not now. He kept his hands to himself and moved no closer.

"No," he barked. "You risked your life by running, Lily. That was damned stupid." Then Quint turned away from her and closed his eyes.

Lily shut her eyes tight and willed sleep to come. Beside her, Quint breathed deeply and evenly. His exhausted body had found the rest it needed, pulling him inexorably downward soon after he had laid his head on the blanket. Outside the tent, the soldiers slept or kept watch. She heard their snores and their muffled footsteps, an occasional whisper from one sentry to another.

The shackles that bound Lily to Quint chafed at her, physically and mentally. Her predicament was as confining as if she'd been locked in a small room with no window. Had it been just two days ago that she would have welcomed such closeness with him, even if it meant being chained to the man? Lily turned her head to the side, abandoning all hope of ever finding peace again.

Her eyes rested on Quint's profile, so soft and dreamlike in the dark. In sleep he looked more angel than devil, though she knew there was nothing angelic in his soul. Deception and treachery were the trademarks of a demon, not a saint.

A nagging voice in the back of her mind reminded her that she had been less than honest with Quintin Tyler at one time. With the entire population of Nassau, in fact. She comforted herself with the knowledge that she had not enjoyed lying to him. Had hated it.

Tired of watching him sleep, Lily lifted her hand and rattled the short chain that bound her to Quint. The clank of the heavy links was muffled inside the confines of the tent, and Lily smiled with smug satisfaction as Quint's hand tensed and shuddered, and a frown marred his perfection. The once relaxed rhythms of his breathing turned ragged and uneven, and to aggravate him further, Lily lifted her hand once again and rattled the heavy chain.

Quint turned his head to one side, so that he was looking away from her. She should have been relieved, but somehow she was disappointed.

With the grace of a feline, Lily rolled up onto one elbow. Was he awake? She smiled at the soft noises that reached her ears, muffled bits and pieces that came from Quint's mouth. He was talking in his sleep.

Careful not to rattle the chains again, Lily edged toward Quint. She wondered, as she crept closer to his averted face, if he was dreaming about her as he muttered unintelligibly in his sleep. It would only be fair. She expected he would haunt her dreams for the rest of her life.

Lily laid her left palm, the free one, beside Quint's head, and held herself suspended over his chest as she watched his face and attempted to make sense of the words he mumbled. Her smile vanished when she saw his face. A frown creased his brow and he seemed to be fighting the very demons she accused of possessing him. His mouth moved, but she could make no sense of the words that escaped in a harsh whisper. Determined, she lowered her head. Her hair brushed his face as her ear came close to his mouth.

"Jonah."

It was the only word she could make out. A man's name? Who was this Jonah who haunted Quint?

In spite of her intentions, Lily felt herself softening towards the man beneath her. He had betrayed her, but he was no monster. He was a man—a man who had nightmares and laughed and made love to her until she was certain the stroking of their bodies would start a fire that could consume the entire world.

The woman in Lily wanted to comfort him, to ease his pain. He was asleep. He would never know that she had relaxed her resolve to hate him. Just for one night.

Lily lowered herself so that her head rested against his chest. Her hand caressed his face, brushing back the errant strand of hair that fell across his forehead. His reaction was almost immediate. His frown disappeared, and his frantic breathing slowed gradually. Lily wound the fingers of her shackled hand through his, afraid to admit to herself how comforting the touch of his hand on hers was, how much she needed the warmth of his body against hers.

Quint's arm moved sluggishly but surely until it was resting against her back. The weight of his arm pressed her closer to him, the warmth penetrating her icy armor.

"It's all right, my love," Lily whispered into his chest, amazed at how quickly her plan to disturb his irritatingly sound sleep had turned into an urge to comfort him. What would it matter if she spent one last night sleeping in his arms?

The sleep that had eluded her came quickly, surrounding her with a safe and warm cocoon that nearly swallowed her whole. Her last conscious and disturbing thought was that she would never again know the contented warmth that came from sleeping beside the man she loved.

For a moment, Quint almost forgot where he was. His fingers were wound through Lily's soft curls as she slept on top of him, her head over his heart, and exhaled her warm breath onto him. One of her slender hands was resting against his neck, and the other lay in his. It was when he tried to lift that hand to his lips that the memories came flooding back. Memories jarred by the clank of the shackles that joined them, and by the pain in his thigh.

He didn't move, afraid that he might wake her and ruin this almost perfect moment. Almost. If the moment had been truly perfect, he could have awakened Lily with a kiss and made love to her languidly, bringing her to full consciousness in a leisurely fashion.

Today was the day he would help deliver his wife into the hands of a warden who would lock her up. Lily cherished her freedom. She would never forgive him for his part in her capture, even if he did eventually manage to get her out of the federal prison.

And could he blame her? He had never been a particularly forgiving person himself. If she was leading him right now to a Confederate prison, would he understand?

No.

Would he still love her?

Yes.

Quint pulled her up, bringing her face to his. He dragged her sleep-warmed body across his so slowly that it was almost painful, a sweet torture he allowed himself. Lily moaned softly, licking her lips as they neared his, her still closed eyes fluttering delicately.

"Good morning, my love," she murmured faintly, lost in the memories of mornings he had awakened her just so, with wandering hands and anxious lips.

Quint finally held her face above his, and pressed his mouth against hers. It was a tentative kiss, tender and sweet, and she parted her lips slightly, sighing contentedly.

"Good morning, sweetheart," Quint whispered, and that was his mistake.

It was the sound of his voice that brought Lily to instant awareness, and she jerked back from his chest with startling clarity in her eyes.

"How dare you?" Lily asked coldly, smoothing frenzied hair away from her face with her one free hand.

Quint couldn't help but smile at her. Her eyes sparkled with anger and confusion, and her cheeks colored enchantingly. Her lips were pink and moist, and her skirts were twisted around her thighs. She was as beautiful as always.

"I'm not the one who couldn't stay on my side of the tent," he said calmly, making no move to sit up.

Lily pursed her lips. "I can't help it if I move around a lot in my sleep. If I ended up on top of you—well, that was entirely accidental." She tried to forget her tender feelings of the night before, the empathy that had driven her to try to comfort him. She didn't care, in the light of morning, what demons haunted his dreams.

Quint rolled to his side and rested on his elbow to watch her closely. The chain that joined them prevented Lily from moving away, as she would have liked.

She wanted to move away from those probing eyes, those eyes that looked at her as if Quint knew everything she was thinking. As if he knew that she had laid her head on his chest and twined her fingers through his of her own volition, and not in some sleeping search for warmth.

"Are you going to behave yourself today?" he asked suddenly, breaking the strained silence that stretched between them. He lifted his hand to massage a jaw dark with stubble and a purple bruise.

Lily lifted her eyebrows haughtily. "Probably not."

Quint smiled as if he had expected no other answer.

All eyes were on them as they left the tent. Lily ignored the stares and held her head high, behaving as if it was perfectly normal to arise in the morning shackled to one's traitorous husband.

After a quick, cold breakfast, the soldiers prepared to depart. Lily took no small pleasure from the fact that Quint's limp was decidedly more pronounced as they walked around the camp.

Lily glared down at the shackles, waiting for them to be opened so she would no longer be chained to the man she detested. If nothing else, she simply had to make a quick trip into the privacy of the forest that surrounded them. She'd be damned if she'd do that while she was chained to Quintin Tyler.

As always, the soldiers tied a rope at her waist and stood much closer than she would have liked. It was mortifying, even for Lily. Her complaints only brought her an assurance from Lieutenant Hanson that if she tried anything, her next request for privacy would yield her a six-man guard.

When she stepped from the shelter of the trees, she saw that Quint was mounted on his horse and staring straight ahead. Several other soldiers were mounted and ready to ride as well, their gear compactly stored and all but the smallest signs of their campsite erased.

Her own mare was near the rear, rather than directly behind Lieutenant Hanson, as it had been the previous day. Her heart skipped a beat when the soldiers who guarded her turned her toward the waiting soldiers without tying her hands, then led her straight to Quint.

"What the bloody hell is going on here?" she asked as they stopped at Quint's side.

Quint smiled down at her and offered her a hand.

Lily scoffed and crossed her arms across her chest.

"Like hell I will. I'd sooner walk than ride with the likes of you, you bloody bastard."

Quint continued to smile, but one eyebrow cocked itself in mild surprise. "There's no time for that, darling." His hand was still extended.

A docile mask spread over Lily's face. They hadn't bound her hands with that damn rope. Maybe, if Quint felt confident enough, she would be able to slip from his grasp, jump to the ground, and disappear before they knew what had happened. Her escape would have to come at just the right moment . . . along the road, near a thick forest. She couldn't stop the wide smile that stole across her face as she took Quint's hand and he lifted her into his lap.

And then Quint offered the guards his left hand, and hers as well, and the shackles were fastened, chaining her to her husband once again. Her smile faded.

"You'd think you bloody well had John Mosby in your custody, instead of a helpless woman."

Her declaration brought a scattered and hearty bout of laughter from the troops.

Quint leaned forward so that she had no choice but to look at his bruised face. "Sweetheart, no one here thinks of you as a helpless woman. Least of all me."

Lily couldn't think of a sharp enough retort, so she fastened her eyes on the road ahead and ignored Quint's remark.

Chapter Nineteen

They traveled quickly, and still it was dark before they arrived at their destination. Throughout the day Lily had ignored Quint as he attempted to talk to her, to assure her that he would find a way to get her out. Lies. All lies. He was doing nothing more than assuaging his own guilty conscience. She would be happy to be rid of him, even if it meant prison.

Lieutenant Hanson himself loosened the shackles that joined Quint and Lily, wary eyes on her and her conniving husband as they dismounted. Quint stayed with her as she was led into the huge brick building. With Quint at her right and Hanson on her left, there was no opportunity to escape.

Prison. Lily shivered as she was led into the building. It didn't look like a prison, except for the barred windows and the sentries placed at the entrance. A small part of her, the part of Lily that was frightened and unsure, wanted to turn to Quint and beg him not to leave her there.

But she didn't even look at him as she walked

down the dimly lit hallway with her head held high and her eyes straight ahead. Silently, she accused him of deserting her and acknowledged the fact that she was afraid. This wasn't the way it was supposed to end.

With two sentries behind her and Quint at her side, Lieutenant Hanson stepped away from Lily and presented himself to the warden. It was then that Quint leaned toward her slightly and whispered in her ear.

"I will come back for you."

Lily turned to stare at him then, trying hard to disguise her fear, not certain that she was succeeding. Quint looked awful. Guilty. Torn. A little afraid himself. But she could find no room in her heart for sympathy for Quintin Tyler.

"Liar," she whispered as she turned away from him again.

Quint departed with Hanson, and Lily was left in the company of a sour Yankee warden and two sentries. She gave the warden her coldest glare as he recited to her the rules she would be expected to obey.

She heard not one of them. Her blood was rushing so that all she heard was a roar in her ears. Lily was afraid that she might faint for the first time in her life, but she didn't. She would not give them the satisfaction.

She put on a stony, impassive mask for the Yankee warden. Lily would not allow herself to weep, or beg, or even to tremble. She'd always known capture was a possibility, and she had been prepared for that prospect every time she ran the blockade. But she had never expected to feel so utterly helpless.

The sentries led Lily to her room. And it was a room, not a cell, though there were bars on the window and a sturdy lock on the door. One of the sentries lit a lamp for her and reminded her curtly that lights out came in less than an hour.

When the door was closed and bolted, Lily sank to the narrow bed. Her bones had turned to butter all of a sudden, and her legs were shaking visibly. In wonder, Lily held out her trembling hands.

"Get hold of yourself, Lily Radford," she said softly. "You're no coward."

Immediately, her mind turned to the possibility of escape. Her prospects were dim. She had no money and no weapon, and the prison seemed well guarded. Lily dismissed Quint's final avowal that he would come for her. That was just another lie.

Lily jumped from the bed and went to the small window. Silently, she lifted the glazed pane, wrapped her fingers around the iron bars, and tugged hard. The bars were firmly secured. One look out the second-story window told her that with a little luck, she would be able to work her way to the ground—if she were able to loosen the bars. She yanked again, then pushed against the bars, but there was no play in the obstacle. None at all.

But that didn't stop Lily from planning her escape. The bars would eventually work loose, somehow. She set her mind to work on the problem.

It could be done. Lily knew now that nothing was forever.

When a sentry returned to knock on Lily's door and shout a loud "light's out!" she doused the lamp and undressed in the dark. She ignored the nightgown that had been laid across the end of the bed for her and slid beneath the covers in her chemise. She still wanted nothing from the Yankees.

Although her heart was broken and she felt a gnawing pain deep in her gut, Lily was true to herself. She told the interrogating Union officer nothing more than she had told the burly sergeant as he'd stood over her bed, aiming his rifle at her and Quint.

She was Captain Sherwood. That was all she would say. When she was questioned about those who had helped her along the way, her contacts, the supplies she carried, and most especially the other blockade runners and their schedules, she closed her mouth and smiled at them—the same insipid smile she had perfected in Nassau.

More than three weeks had passed, and she hadn't seen Quintin Tyler once. She was imprisoned in that small room, and yet she knew her fate was much better than that of her male counterparts. Her prison on the outskirts of Washington D.C. appeared to have once been a boarding school, with large classrooms on the first floor and small bedrooms on the second and third floors. The exterior of the prison reminded Lily of Sherwood, the red brick stately and elegant, the ancient trees now turning burnished gold and bright orange.

The bars on the windows and the sturdy bolts on the doors looked to be relatively new additions to the facility.

Her prison was as comfortable as one could expect a prison to be, but it was incarceration just the same. Silent guards escorted her to almost daily questionings. Occasionally Lily heard delicate footsteps in the hallway, surrounded by the heavier footfalls of the soldiers, and twice she had heard a woman sobbing, but she met no other prisoners.

She took a small amount of satisfaction in the knowledge that her captors so obviously didn't know quite what to do with her. No one had expected Captain Sherwood to be a woman. She couldn't be sent to prison camp, but they were understandably loathe to release her.

Lily had resigned herself to the fact that she might well spend the remainder of the war confined to the small room. Her room on the second floor was larger than her cabin on board the Chameleon—and had a window to boot, bars and all—but the idea of spending months, maybe even years, confined to the room made her break out in a cold sweat. No salty air. No sea. No sand between her toes. No sun warming her skin. Just the four plain walls that surrounded her, a narrow but comfortable bed, a dresser, and a chair.

Try as she might, she couldn't stop thinking

about Quint—Lieutenant Tyler, she reminded herself when she remembered him with a trace of warmth. She could recall every moment they'd spent together, every scene etched into her memory. Her first sight of him in Terrence's shop. The ball at the hotel. Playing chess. Loving him on board her ship. Their wedding. Every moment was crystal clear . . . up to the moment the Yankees had burst into their bedroom.

Had there been a sign of his betrayal that she had missed? If he had given himself away at any time, she had been too blinded by love, or passion, or sheer stupidity, to see it.

She cherished the satisfaction of knowing she'd had him fooled for a while. Obviously he had been using her to get to Captain Sherwood. She didn't believe for a moment that he'd known before he'd seen her on board the *Chameleon* that she was captain of her own ship. It didn't ease her pain any. Perhaps he had been caught in his lie. Maybe he really had cared for her and had been trapped by his own deceit.

But if that was the case, why hadn't he told her the truth? She had been willing to leave everything behind for him. A foolish mistake she wouldn't make again.

Nothing could drive him from her dreams. She woke in the middle of the night with the blood running as cold as ice in her veins, scared and reaching out for him. It always took a moment, a disoriented moment of total fear, before she realized where she was, and remembered what Quint—Lieutenant Tyler—had done. That was when she was forced to face the worst part of it all.

She still loved him. If he were to come to her at night and climb into the narrow bed with her, she would let him love her. She would welcome him with open arms—and hate herself for it by the light of day. And that was the worst of it, acknowledging a part of herself that she couldn't control.

Lily paced the small room. There were books, a few well-read volumes of poetry, on the dresser. She had tried to read them, but her mind wouldn't stay on the printed word. Her mind invariably wandered, and the book was discarded.

She heard the familiar sound of the key turning in the sturdy lock, and the door was pushed open. Sergeant Hughes was the least favorite of her guards. He sometimes openly leered at her, when he thought no one else was watching, and once he had dared to lay his sweaty palm against the bodice of the gray wool dress she had been issued.

Lily had responded with a boot to his shin, and he hadn't dared to touch her again, though the look in his eyes warned her that he would like to make her pay for her unladylike response.

"Let's go," he said curtly, waiting impatiently in the open doorway.

Lily stood, as still and cool as a marble statue in the middle of the room. In truth, Sergeant Hughes still frightened her, but she refused to allow him to see her fear as she stared him down.

"Where am I being taken?" she asked frostily.

"Interrogation."

Lily sighed and moved with a lethargy she copied from Captain Brighton. The lazy steps, the slow pace, even the slant of her head infuriated the sergeant. He was a military man, efficient and deadly. Lily knew this was a duty he viewed as beneath him, guarding women. And still he ogled her, his beady eyes lingering on her breasts. She was tempted to give him another swift kick.

Lily walked down the familiar hallway. More bloody interrogation. She couldn't tell them anything that would be helpful, and even if she could, they should know by now that she wouldn't. She took short, slow steps, purposely infuriating the sergeant. Even the walls of the hallway seemed to close in on her, suffocating her slowly. When she tried to take a deep breath, she seemed to feel a heavy weight on her chest.

Lily stepped into the room, ignoring the two sentries who stood on either side of the door. She was familiar with the routine, and with the room. It had probably been the office of the headmaster, or the headmistress, before the war had closed the obviously exclusive school. Bookcases lined three walls, and a massive walnut desk sat in the middle of the room. The chairs were covered in burgundy leather, and a cream-colored rug softened her steps as she entered the room.

She expected to see the white-haired naval officer who had questioned her so frequently over the past two weeks. He had pale skin, and her refusal to speak so frustrated him that he had occasionally turned an alarmingly deep shade of purple. She had brought him, more than once, to his feet with a shout of exasperation.

But this man was new. She could tell even though she saw only his back, the blue of his uniform stretched across broad shoulders as he bent forward to study something on the desk before him. As soon as the door opened fully, he turned slowly, and Lily had to fight to keep from screaming.

Lieutenant Quintin Tyler, with his hair cut short and his cheeks shaved smooth, stood before her. His uniform was perfectly fitted, and he looked wonderful. It was a shocking sight, her Quint in the uniform that had haunted her dreams for years.

Lily did an about-face and ran into the sergeant, butting her head into his chest before she could make herself stop. "I have nothing to say to this man," she muttered, her eyes on the shiny buttons of the sergeant's uniform, her stiff back to Quint.

Hughes didn't move. He looked over her shoulder to Quint and then closed the door.

"Sergeant," Quint said crisply. "Wait in the hall."

"Sir, beggin' your pardon, sir, but I wouldn't recommend bein' shut up in a room with this one, and no protection."

"Protection?" Lily could hear the smile in his voice. "From a woman?"

"Yes, sir."

Lily turned to Quint, once again composed.

The shock of seeing him was over. She had pushed it away. "He's only saying that because I gave him a limp that lasted a day or two." She smiled coldly. "And he knows that if he tries to maul me again, I'll cripple him."

She wanted Quint to know what kind of situation he'd left her in. She wanted him to feel guilty, and it worked. Quint was glaring at the sergeant as the red-faced Hughes finally backed out of the room, closing the door quietly behind him.

"Did he hurt you, Lily?" Quint moved toward her, but she quickly evaded him.

"I'm capable of taking care of myself," she said calmly. "What do you want?"

Lily turned her back to him, unable to continue to look into that face and show no emotion.

Quint sighed. Had he expected her to forget? "I'm going to get you out of here," he said softly.

Lily spun on her heel to face him. "A prison break? Won't that hamper your career?"

"Not an escape." Quint picked up a sheet of paper from the desk beside him. "Sign this document, and you'll be released."

Lily took the paper from his hand, being careful not to touch Quint's skin. Being in the same room with him was powerful enough. She couldn't allow herself to touch him. With a strength of will she summoned from deep inside, she grinned as she read the document, then laughed as she tossed it back to Quint.

"Bloody hell," she said brightly. "Do you really expect me to sign that?"

Quint leaned on the desk, placing his face close to hers. "You damn well will sign."

"No. I will not swear allegiance to the Union, and I will not swear not to resume my business."

"Why not, for God's sake?" Quint was clearly exasperated, and Lily loved it.

"Because I wouldn't mean it. It would be a lie. Some people may be able to take a vow lightly, but I do not." She wondered if he knew that she wasn't speaking only of the oath before her. "I have my pride, and my honor—"

"Damn your pride to hell," Quint seethed. "It's what got you here in the first place. You never should have been on that ship." He was angry, not only because she refused to sign the document, but because she looked so pale, and even thinner than he remembered. "It took me all these weeks just to get the government to agree to this. It wasn't easy. I had to explain away the soldier I shot when you broke me out of prison. Don't think they dismissed that incident without a second thought. If the man had died, I never would have made it back here. I'd be in a cell of my own, or hanging from a gallows."

Lily's face was impassive, infuriating him further.

"Damn it, Lily! I went to the president himself for you!"

"I'm still not signing." To prove her point, she picked up the offensive document and tore it in half.

Quint had been careful not to touch her, not to anger her, but when she ripped the paper in half, he reached out and grabbed her arm, pulling her against him. "Why did you do that? Do you like it here? Do you want to stay in prison until the war is over?" His voice was low and threatening. "War was never meant to be fought by women . . ."

"What should I have done?" Lily glared into his eyes, staring hard, refusing to back away even though they stood thigh to thigh. "Should I have stayed in England with my spineless brother? Stayed at home and wrapped bandages and danced with lonely soldiers home on leave? That wouldn't have been enough."

Lily closed her eyes.

"I want you safe," Quint said. She had her eyes closed tightly, like a child shutting out the world, and he never wanted to let her go. He expected her to pull away from him, but she stood very still, and finally he rested his cheek against the top of her head. She held her body rigid, but he found great hope in the fact that she didn't move away. "I love you too much to—"

"Don't say that," Lily whispered. "You don't mean it. You never meant it."

Quint pulled away just enough that he could see Lily's face, her full lips, the dusting of freckles on her flawless nose.

"Open your eyes, Lily Tyler," Quint commanded gently, and she did. He was a little surprised that she responded so quickly. His heart broke a little when he saw the tears in her eyes, tears she fought to hide. "I wish I could tell you that I've never lied to you, but that's not true. But

I never lied about the way I feel for you. You don't have to forgive me. I don't expect you to. But I want you to know that I never lied about loving you and needing you, and in time I would have told you the rest of it myself."

Lily searched his eyes, and he knew that she was searching for some sign that he was telling the truth.

"Now, sign the paper," he said gently, "and I can get you out of here."

Lily broke away from him suddenly. "Bloody hell, I almost let you fool me again—all for the sake of your bloody allegiance." She glared at him, her eyes like blue-green ice. "I'll die in this place before I sign anything."

Quint gathered up torn pieces of the document that could set Lily free, the document he had worked so hard to get for her. Damn it all, he couldn't leave her here! She talked tough and acted tough, but he could see the pain and the fear in her eyes and in her too-pale face. So much of Lily was in the sea and the sun that he feared she very well would die in prison if he didn't get her out of here soon.

"I'll be back tomorrow," Quint said, the warmth in his voice replaced by a cold determination. "And the next day, and the next. You will sign this, Lily. I don't care if you mean it or not."

"But I do," Lily whispered. "I care very much about the commitments I make."

Quint strode out of the room, leaving Lily behind. But at the door, he grabbed the waiting sergeant by the collar and placed his face close to the wary soldier's.

"Touch that woman again, and you'll have more than a temporary limp to worry about."

Lily watched Quint's retreating back as he walked down the long hallway to the front entrance.

She was in for a fight. Quint was not one to give up easily, and neither was she. God help her, she could face anything . . . but Quint, every day?

Her beloved Quint, dressed in blue, glaring at her with those dark, deceptive eyes. Lily wanted to believe him when he said that he loved her, but she couldn't. He would only hurt her again.

Sergeant Hughes was still staring down the hallway. He'd watched Quint's retreat just as she had. What had Quint said to the soldier?

Lily quietly approached Sergeant Hughes, and when she was right behind him she let her foot fly, kicking him in his rock-hard calf. She wished they hadn't taken away her boots after the last time she'd kicked the man and replaced them with soft slippers.

With a scowl, Hughes turned to her and grabbed her arm. "What's your problem, Miss Radford?"

"You're in my way, you bloody oaf," she snapped. "Take me to my room."

He scoffed at her. "You make it sound as if I'm your escort and this is a fine hotel rather than a federal prison." Hughes tightened his grip on her arm and pushed her forward.

"No supper for you again tonight, Miss Radford," the sergeant said as he propelled her forward.

Chapter Twenty

Quintin kept his word. For the next two weeks he came to the prison every day. He insisted that Lily sign the allegiance to the Union. She refused as adamantly as he insisted.

Lily watched Quint's growing frustration with a small kernel of satisfaction. She had initially refused to sign the oath because it was against her principles. She continued to refuse because it infuriated Lieutenant Tyler.

Every afternoon Sergeant Hughes led Lily to the same room, where she found Quint waiting for her. He no longer carried a cane, though he continued to favor his right leg. Lily tried to convince herself that she didn't care—about his leg or anything else—but the truth was, she looked forward to walking into that room every day. The sight of Quint made her heart stop, and she decided that love had turned her into a bloody fool, a sniveling twit.

Apparently, no one at the prison knew that they were married. The guards always addressed her as Miss Radford, and if the dense sergeant was puzzled by Lieutenant Tyler's evident interest in her, he didn't show any sign that he found it odd. The white-haired, purple-faced naval officer stopped coming; but for her guards, Quint was Lily's only contact with the outside world.

Quint seemed as cautious as she about touching. She noticed that he sometimes placed his hands behind his back and glared at her with murder in his eyes, his feet planted far apart as if he had to will himself not to rush at her. Perhaps he was afraid that if he touched her, he would wring her stubborn neck. Lily rather liked that thought.

But the unfortunate fact was that when she saw him, she had the urge to throw her arms around his neck and sob like a little girl. The image disgusted her. She had never been given to sobbing, even when she *was* a little girl, and she certainly had no intention of allowing a man to drive her to such lengths. Even a man she dreamed of at night and wanted desperately to hold in her arms just one more time.

Sometimes, when that stubborn lock of ash-brown hair fell over his forehead, she wanted to reach out and smooth it back. To combat her urges, she clasped her hands behind her back and planted her feet as Quint had, and they stood face to face, no more than a few feet separating them, the air between them charged and crackling.

It took every ounce of strength Quint possessed not to grab her. Not to hold her and force her to sign the damn papers, then throw her over his shoulder and march away from the prison with her. And then what? Just allow her to go? Watch her sail for ports unknown, knowing that he might never see her again? No. There had to be some peace between them before that happened.

He was worried about her. She was pale and thin, and some days she had dark circles under her eyes, as if she hadn't slept at all. Prison hadn't hurt her spirit. Her eyes still flashed green fire at him, and sharp retorts rolled off her tongue with no apparent effort. But physically, confinement was wearing on her. She looked tired and thin, with only the sparks in her eyes unchanged as she challenged him, daring him to best her.

Quint wanted to see Lily in one of her fussy gowns and silly hats, with a wide grin plastered on her face. He wanted to see her in her captain's garb, unconventional trousers and boots, her saber dangling from her side. He wanted to see her with a pink flush on her cheeks from a windy day in the sun.

Instead he saw her grow paler every day. The gray woolen dress she had been issued had been ill-fitting to begin with, and now it hung on her, bagging at the waist. He was afraid that soon there would be nothing left of her, that she would waste away before his very eyes.

Only once had they gone so far as to end up shouting, Quint accusing Lily of being a stubborn, ignorant child, and Lily calling him a bloody bastard, along with other inventive curses even he had never heard. The curses of a Liverpool dock rat.

Sergeant Hughes had burst into the room, another guard at his heels. It was clear that they were frightened, though whether they were concerned for him or for their prisoner was unclear. They had been reluctant to leave the room, even when Quint shooed them away with an impatient wave of his hand. They hesitated for a moment before they left, and Quint knew they would be listening just outside the door, waiting for another outburst.

He was running out of time. In a matter of days he was to report to his new regiment. The leg had healed well enough for him to resume his military career, but he couldn't. Not with Lily in prison.

Quint arrived at the prison late in the morning, having made the familiar trip from Washington in less than an hour. The red brick building didn't look like a prison—except for the iron bars on every window—but more like the girls' school it had once been. On this particular morning there was an unfamiliar wagon in the yard. It was a rough-looking conveyance, the wooden seat splintered and warped, the bed of the buckboard haphazardly filled with rags and straw and flour sacks and a single water barrel.

He knew there were at least seven other female prisoners in the building, though he had never seen them. Spies, all seven, or so they'd been accused of being. Perhaps one of them was being released and would be going home in the less-than-sturdy wagon pulled by a single gray mare.

Sergeant Hughes and two other guards were posted outside the door of the office where he always met with Lily. One of the other prisoners was probably being interrogated—or wisely signing the oath of allegiance to the Union.

"Good morning, sir," Sergeant Hughes greeted Quint curtly, straightening his spine and lifting his chin.

Quint grunted and paced in front of the closed door. He'd never been a patient man, and he most especially disliked waiting to see Lily.

"Go fetch Miss Radford," he snapped. "I'll question her in another room today, since this one is occupied."

Hughes frowned. He didn't appear particularly bright to begin with, and his puzzlement made him look downright stupid. "Miss Radford is in there"—he crooked his head toward the closed door—"with her brother. Shall I put an end to the visit?" Hughes reached for the doorknob, more than willing to interrupt Lily's private moment with her brother.

"No," Quint said quickly. "Let them talk. She hasn't seen her brother in a long time, and I imagine she has a bit of explaining to do."

Quint couldn't stand still, so he paced the hallway outside the closed door. The other three soldiers stood perfectly still, their eyes following Quint's agitated steps.

"You might be glad to know that Miss Radford has been much better behaved for the past several days," Sergeant Hughes offered. "I haven't had to withhold her supper for almost a week now, and the bruises on my legs . . ." He became silent when Quint glared.

"Damn it all, is that why she's so thin? You've been withholding her food?" His voice was soft but menacing, and he watched the color drain from the sergeant's face.

"Only when absolutely necessary, and as I said, she's been quite tame this week. To be honest, I think she's a bit under the weather, and as soon as she's all better, she'll be battering my poor legs again for no apparent reason." The sergeant's face regained its color as he defended himself. "I have every right to punish the prisoner, and keeping back her supper is mild compared to . . ."

"You will see that she's fed, Sergeant," Quint seethed. "If I look at her and think that she's lost even a single pound, I'll beat it out of your hide. Is that clear?"

There was a short pause before Hughes answered. "Yes, sir," he murmured, his normal military crispness absent.

Quint stared at the closed door. "How long has he been here?" He didn't want to interrupt Lily and Elliot, but he was anxious to see her.

"About an hour, sir," Hughes replied. "Yesterday he stayed for about that long before I made him leave. Put up quite a fuss, with that funny accent of his. Called me a bleedin' arse, he did. I can see that Miss Radford's temper is a family trait—." Hughes stopped dead as Quint lowered his face to stare at the sergeant.

"When yesterday was he here?"

The sergeant frowned, then resumed a more military stance. "Late in the day, sir, after you left."

"Tall man? Older than Lily? Bushy moustache?" He could just see Tommy now, passing himself off as Lily's brother, plotting a way to get her out of her comfortable prison.

But Hughes was shaking his head. "Not at all. Young fella. Dark curly hair . . ."

Quint backed away, cursing his imagination. Still, what the sergeant had said didn't fit what Lily had told him of her brother. Elliot Radford was supposedly a refined gentleman, meek and temperate, but Quint could imagine that finding one's sister in such a predicament would incite the fire in even the mildest man's blood.

"Well," he muttered to himself, "I can hardly wait to meet this Elliot Radford."

"Wrong brother, Lieutenant," Hughes answered. "This one's name is Roger. Roger Radford."

Quint stared at the closed door. Roger Radford? There wasn't any Roger Radford. . . .

He heard the faint murmur of raised voices through the door. Lily's he recognized, even as it rose to a new level. The mysterious Roger answered her in kind, as the two of them shouted curses at the top of their lungs. Quint threw open the door and stepped inside first, already suspecting, but not quite prepared for, the scene that was unfolding before him.

Lily stood with her back to the desk, hands

clutching the desktop on either side of her. Quint was looking at her profile—and at Roger's. Not Roger Radford, but Roger of the engine room, sans coal dust and sweat.

"Yer a disgrace, Lily Radford," Roger shouted, ignoring the four soldiers who crowded in the doorway. His hands clenched and unclenched in apparent anger—or anticipation. "It shames me to call ye me sister."

He spared a quick glance to the doorway, and to his credit he showed no surprise at seeing Quint there. "This is between the wench and me, mates."

Lily ignored the soldiers. "And I am ashamed to call you my brother. You are a spineless coward, a liar, a shiftless bounder." She reached behind her, and her hand fell on a crystal paperweight. Pale fingers curled around the smooth surface, and she swung it forward.

Roger ducked, and Lily's heavy hand missed his head by no more than two inches. Quint saw Roger reach into his boot, the movement graceful and amazingly fast, and withdraw a knife smoothly, grasping it tightly in his left hand.

"'Old on there, Lil. Ye'll be 'olding yer temper." His voice was menacing, but he didn't threaten Lily with the knife. He held it before him like a shield.

Lily cast a furtive glance at the stunned soldiers who flanked Quint, and then her eyes lit on him. He stepped forward to stop her—and that was a mistake. She wasn't going to allow him to stop her. He should have realized that sooner.

Lily fell forward and the knife Roger clasped in his hand pierced the gray dress she wore, staining it with dark crimson that turned the gray to black.

"'Eaven above us," Roger whispered, suitably shocked and pale. "I didn't mean . . . I just wanted to scare 'er. To make 'er back away." He knelt beside her body. "Lil," he groaned most convincingly. "I'm sorry, Lil."

Quint shoved Roger out of the way. He knew what was happening. He had seen a version of this particular play on board the *Chameleon*. But still, the sight of Lily pale and motionless on the floor scared him, and he knelt beside her, touching the tear in her dress and pulling his hand away. This was no mixture of crushed berries and syrup—it was real blood.

"Lily." Quint's voice was low as he lifted her head and cradled her in his arms. "For God's sake . . ."

Lily's eyes fluttered open, and she fixed her gaze on him. He was kneeling on the floor, supporting her weight as she rolled against him. "Quint, my love," she whispered in a raspy voice. She raised a limp hand and touched it to his cheek. "I loved you, once." Her eyelids quivered and then closed, just as the guards came to their senses and rushed forward.

Quint lifted a blood-soaked hand and held it to the pulse at her throat. Thank God. There it was, strong and steady. She'd lied too well. For a moment, he'd actually believed she'd been stabbed.

"Blimey! She's dead!" Roger shouted. "I've killed me own sister!"

Hughes tried to kneel over the body, his bulk close to Quint, but Quint shouted for the man to back away. The sergeant stood, and the other guards moved to their positions by the door, their faces white and solemn.

Quint struggled to his feet. His leg ached with the effort, but he lifted Lily and walked toward the door. Roger was directly behind him, and the young seaman was amazingly believable in his distress.

Damn, she was still! And her head lolled against his arm, her hair falling in a golden waterfall as he strode toward the guards.

Hughes stared down at the large puddle of blood on the floor, at Quint's blood-stained hands and the black blood on Lily's gray prison dress. Decisively, he stepped in front of Quint.

"I'll take charge of the body, sir. It's my duty." The sergeant obviously found it an unpleasant duty, but one he considered to be his own.

There was no sign of life from Lily. No rise and fall of her chest. What if something had gone wrong, and she was really dead? Perhaps she'd been distracted and fallen on the knife so that it pierced her skin rather than the oilskin bag he knew had to be strapped to her side. Quint lifted his head to glare at the sergeant.

"You will not touch her." Each word was a crisply spoken command. "I'll bury her myself."

"But Lieutenant Tyler, there are regulations. . . ."

Quint leaned forward, and the sergeant backed away from Lily and the golden hair that swung forward. "She was my *wife,* you idiot! Get out of my way!"

Hughes did as he was ordered. "Wife?" The shock showed on his face, then faded to understanding as Quint rushed past him and through the door with Roger close behind, wailing and moaning convincingly.

Quint could hear the echoing footsteps as Hughes and the other two guards followed him down the long hallway. They were all silent, still in a state of shock.

He was halfway down the hallway before he heard Lily's release of air. Still she didn't move. Quint wanted to lean over and kiss her, he was so relieved to know that she was alive. He wanted to speak to her, to shake her, to kiss her again and again, but he didn't dare.

He carried her to the wagon, knowing now why the bed was cushioned with rags and hay and flour sacks. He ignored the soldiers who watched his procession across the yard, and they kept their distance.

It was the blood. On his hands, on Lily's neck where he had felt for her pulse, on her dress and his uniform. The soldiers saw blood and death all too frequently . . . but not here. And not a beautiful young woman like Lily. They all stood back as Quint gently laid her on the wagon bed, smoothing her skirts and reluctantly moving away from her to hitch his own horse to the back of the wagon.

Roger rushed past and vaulted into the driver's seat, still distressed but much less vocal about it. Quint jumped into the wagon bed and sat beside Lily, touching her hand to reassure himself that it was warm, laying a single finger against the pulse at her wrist, assuring himself that it still throbbed.

As they pulled away from the prison, Quint lifted his eyes from Lily only once, to watch the stunned guards gawk as he took his wife away.

"Pig's blood!" Quint shouted at her, repeating her answer to his question. Instead of being appalled, as she should have been, Lily laughed.

She turned her back to him and unbuttoned the gray wool dress, reaching inside to remove the sliced oilskin bag. Using a dampened rag she washed the blood off her skin, her side, and her neck; then, with an unconcerned flick of her wrist, Lily tossed a damp rag to Quint, and he wiped the pig's blood from his hands.

"Well, even the dimwitted Yankees wouldn't have been fooled by berries and syrup." She said the words with a small grin, but she could force no joy into her voice. She turned to Quint once again, her dress fastened to the neck. "Why didn't you give us away?" Her smile faded.

Quint shook his head. He was leaning against the back of the wagon that lumbered down the bumpy road, the top of his head at Roger's back. Lily sat beside him, carefully holding herself away from his swaying body.

"I don't know," he admitted. "It was a decision

I had to make quickly, and I followed my instincts." He looked into her eyes, and Lily turned away from him . . . too quickly, she knew. "I wanted you out of there, Lily. If not my way, then yours."

Roger laughed. "That was great, mate. *She's me wife!*" He mimicked Quint's cry and was rewarded with a swift slap across the back, and he jerked his head around just in time to see Lily's arm swinging away.

Lily stared down the road they'd just traveled over, the dust rising and falling in a red-brown cloud, while Quint's bay kept pace with the lumbering wagon. There was a nip in the air, but her wool dress was warm, and only her nose seemed to feel the cold. Finally, she summoned the courage to look at Quint again.

"You were early."

Quint met her stare, and she saw the moment of complete understanding mirrored in his dark eyes. Anger . . . amazement . . . the hurt she couldn't take away or apologize for, were all evident.

"You would have allowed me to believe you dead?" His whispered words were chilling. "If I had arrived as usual . . . Roger would have absconded with you, and I would have believed . . . how could you do that to me?"

Lily wished that she could blind herself to the pain in Quint's eyes, but she couldn't. "I thought it would be best, for both of us, if you believed I was dead."

Quint reached across and took her hand, holding her tightly as if he expected her to try to pull away, to snatch her hand away as soon as his fingers touched hers. But she didn't. She twined her fingers through his, hungry for the touch of his skin against hers. She parted her lips to speak, to defend herself, but there was nothing she could say. Nothing adequate. So sne closed her mouth and turned her face away from him.

"To believe that you were lost forever would be the worst pain you could possibly inflict upon me," Quint said softly. "I'd like to think that someday . . . when this is all over . . . you and I . . ."

He couldn't finish. Lily was staring away from him, her hair gleaming in the autumn sun, her profile showing him an impassive face. How could she so easily close off her emotions? Did she feel nothing of his pain?

"Are we really married, Quint?" she asked softly. "I mean, is it legal, or was that nice old preacher a Yankee in dis—"

"Of course we're really married!" Quint snapped. "Dammit, do you think I would stoop so low?" The expression on her face answered that question for him. Lily believed him capable of any deceit. But still, she clutched his hand.

Roger hit a deep rut in the road, and the wagon danced, tossing Lily about until she ended up nearly on Quint's lap. He expected her to move away quickly, but she stayed where her quick flight had taken her. After a few moments, she laid her head against his shoulder, and he wrapped his arm around her, pulling her to him.

She was skin and bones beneath the rough woolen dress, and his heart ached for her—and for himself. She might never forgive him.

"Will you tell?" she finally asked, her voice a husky whisper. "Will you bring the entire bloody Yankee army down on my head?" Her voice displayed more exasperation than anger.

"No," Quint answered curtly. "But I want your promise."

Lily snuggled against him, and Quint was painfully aware that her warmth was a luxury he would have to learn to live without . . . at least for a while.

"Promise of what?"

"That you'll keep yourself safe. That you'll stay out of this damn war and away from the blockade." His voice was firm, demanding. He lifted her chin and tilted her head so that he could lock his eyes to hers. "Promise me, Lily."

"You have my word." She breathed her answer, the truth of it in her eyes, and relief washed over Quint, as tangible as any wave. He sighed and returned her head to his shoulder, threading his fingers through her hair. Lily would never break her word. It was her code of honor that had gotten her into this mess.

Lily closed her eyes as she buried her head against Quint's warm shoulder. No, there would be no more blockade running, no more late nights sailing past the enemy. She would return to Nassau and stay there. But not for the reason Quint believed. Not because he demanded it of her.

She still loved him. There had been a time when she'd believed that nothing could penetrate her anger and deep feelings of betrayal. But she'd been wrong. She knew that, as she drank in Quint's warmth and listened to the beat of his heart. Did that make her weak? Perhaps. Perhaps it wasn't weakness she feared, but vulnerability. Quintin Tyler had the power to hurt her far more than any Yankee army or summer storm.

"Quint?" she whispered his name, a soft question caught on a cool breeze.

"Yes?" He sounded oddly content, for all that their lives were a shambles at the moment.

"Would you kiss me?" It was a tentative question, although she knew what his answer would be. She lifted her face to him, wide-eyed and serious, and Quint lowered his mouth over hers. At first his lips were gentle, barely brushing over her sensitive lips, but he gradually intensified the kiss, his tongue teasing against her own.

It was the involuntary low moan deep in her throat that seemed to break the last of the barriers between them, and Quint pulled her to him, tightly, possessively, melding their bodies as they were meant to be.

Lily wrapped her hands around his neck, pulling him closer, knowing he could never be close enough. She could no longer hear the sounds around her—the horses' hooves against the road, the rattling of the wagon as it creaked along, the wind in the brittle leaves. All she heard was a roaring in her ears, something akin to the roar of the ocean, that impossible sound in her ears driving away everything else but the ecstasy of Quint's mouth against hers, his hands against her breasts and at her back.

They slumped to the wagon floor, progressing an inch at a time until they were writhing in the straw. Quint ran his hand along her leg, slowly lifting the skirt that twisted around her legs. His hand rested against her knee, against her thigh. When she worked her hand between their bodies and laid her palm over the swelling at his crotch, Quint groaned and whispered her name again and again, his breath and hers mingling. She could almost smell the sea and the tropical flowers that grew outside her window.

Roger glanced over his shoulder, intrigued by the muffled sounds that were emanating from the wagon bed. He quickly returned his eyes to the road ahead of him. Gor! Tyler was on the Captain like a starving man at a kidney pie.

Moments later he saw the turn he had been searching for. "Captain?" he called, tentatively at first, and then louder. "Captain!"

Blimey, he couldn't drive into camp with the two of them at it like that! Gibbon and the rest of the crew would be anxiously awaiting the Captain's arrival, but they wouldn't be expecting Tyler at all. They certainly wouldn't expect to find the Yankee pawing their captain like that. "Mr. Tyler!" Roger shouted to be heard above the horses and the rumbling wagon. He glanced over the seat, his eyes finally resting on the only loose object at hand. He tossed the half-eaten apple over his shoulder, and listened as it landed with a thud.

He risked another peek into the wagon bed. The apple lay not far from the Captain's head, but if she had heard it fall, she had ignored it.

Roger turned onto a narrow road, and in moments the wagon was surrounded.

The lurching wagon stopped so suddenly that Lily felt as if she'd been awakened from an intense dream before she was quite ready to give it up. She studied Quint with narrowed, lazy eyes.

"Blast it all, girl!" Tommy bellowed as he gaped into the wagon bed. He wasn't alone. Half a dozen young faces, crewmen from the *Chameleon,* stared at her in evident astonishment.

Lily glanced at Quint briefly, and then turned her eyes to her red-faced uncle. Roger could have warned them! Tommy was staring at Quint with murder in his eyes, and this time it was her uncle who had the upper hand. She would've felt much safer if Tommy was shackled, as he had been the last time she'd seen him.

How could she have lost all control so quickly? All she'd wanted was a quick kiss, an assurance that what they'd once had wasn't an impossible fancy she'd constructed in her love-muddled mind.

She bit her lip as Tommy held her eyes with a furious glare. He'd kill Quint if he got the chance. Suddenly, Lily smiled, and she turned to face Quint with that victorious grin in place. His mouth was just inches from hers and he watched her expectantly.

Lily gave a little squeeze of her hand that was still between their bodies, as she smiled at Quint. "Checkmate."

Chapter Twenty-one

Quint lifted his hand from Lily's thigh as if her skin were scorching him. Her full skirt covered her limbs, all but her shapely calves. As he slowly withdrew his hand, his eyes delved into hers. Damn it all, her blue-green eyes sparkled mischievously, even as she squeezed him between the legs.

Eleanor Slocum had been right all along. She'd been leading him around by that appendage for months.

"Very good, Lily," he said coolly. "I've always known you were devious, but you've outdone yourself this time."

"Why, thank you, Lieutenant Tyler. How very kind you are." She lapsed into her Southern accent as she withdrew her hand from between their bodies. "That's quite a compliment, coming from the likes of you."

As they sat up, Lily reached across and took Quint's Colt from its holster. He started to protest, saw that there were several firearms pointed over the side of the buckboard, and lifted his arms in supplication as Lily lifted the weapon and tossed it to Roger.

"How does it feel?" Lily asked.

Quint gave her a mocking smirk. "How does what feel?"

Lily blushed prettily, like an embarrassed schoolgirl. "To be a prisoner." To further make her point, she shoved him easily onto his back and sat on his belly. Quint placed his hands behind his head and closed his eyes.

"Quite cozy, actually."

"Shackles," Lily said plainly. "I need shackles."

Quint opened his eyes to no more than narrow slits that allowed him to watch Lily as she looked up at her uncle.

Tommy grinned. "It will do me soul good to see this blighter in shackles again." He sent Sellers on the errand, and returned his attention to Lily, knitting his massive eyebrows together in concern.

"Damn them," he muttered, "What 'ave the Yanks done to you, girl? You're downright puny." He shot a hate-filled glance Quint's way, raking his eyes over the blue uniform—what he could see of it with Lily sitting on his stomach.

"Nothing, really," Lily assured him, "I've been sick, that's all."

"Gor, and that's the truth," Roger exclaimed. "She lost 'er breakfast all over me shoes."

Lily's head snapped up, and she glared at Roger.

"Sorry, Cap'n," he muttered.

Lily turned to her uncle. "Roger tells me we

have less than two days to make it to a rendez-vous point on the coast."

Tommy nodded. "Aye. A ship'll be waitin'."

Lily looked down at Quint, and he closed his eyes quickly. Beneath the peaceful countenance he fought to display, he was seething. He was, to use Lily's favorite curse, a bloody fool. He'd fallen right into her trap. She'd seemed so innocent, so sincere when she'd turned her face up to him invitingly and asked for a kiss. Had Roger signaled her that they were close to her uncle's camp? Had she been familiar with the area? Either way, he'd been beguiled by Lily once again . . . and for the last time.

"Come on down here, girl." Tommy offered Lily his meaty hand. "The lads can watch the prisoner."

Lily sighed, almost wistfully. "No," she said softly, drawing the word out. "I don't trust him. I'll wait for the shackles."

Quint heard them, the clanking of the heavy irons, as Sellers approached the wagon.

"His right wrist to my left," she snapped. "His right ankle to my left."

He couldn't ignore her any longer. His eyes flew open and he sat up, dislodging her from her seat. "The hell you say!"

Tommy's response to her request was as loud and belligerent as Quint's, but Lily would not be swayed. She was still the Captain, and Sellers did as he was told.

"Sellers," Lily said calmly as the seaman fastened the irons to Quint's wrist and then to hers.

"You are to keep the keys to these shackles. They are to be removed only on my command. If I die, perhaps strangled in my sleep, then the chains will never be removed. Toss the keys into the deepest part of the ocean. Lieutenant Tyler will just have to haul my dead carcass around with him for the rest of his days."

"Mighty short days they'll be," Tommy muttered under his breath.

Lily and Quint stepped down from the wagon with more than a little assistance. The chain that linked them was no more than a foot in length and made of heavy iron.

With a watchful guard, they walked into the camp. Several small tents were set up in a half circle of men—boys, most of them—and Lily smiled. "Thank you, lads. Tommy. It's nice to know that I wasn't forgotten." She shot Quint a meaningful glance.

The group dispersed, and Lily and Quint faced one another. Her face was defiant, her chin lifted and her eyes hard. With great effort, Quint kept his own features set in an impassive mask. That seemed to make Lily even more resolute.

"Are you hungry?" she asked snappishly.

Quint shook his head.

"Well, I am." Lily sent a flaxen-haired crewman to fetch her a snack. The young man returned moments later with an apple and laid it in her free hand.

"It could be worse, you know," she said sensibly between bites of the fruit. Quint stared at her wordlessly as if he couldn't imagine how that was possible.

"Cora could be here." Lily's eyes sparkled. "She never did like you. She saw through you when I could not. She knew all along that you were up to something."

"Smart woman," Quint growled.

Lily nodded her head in agreement. "I should have listened to her."

"I wish you had."

Lily led him around the camp as she visited with each and every sailor who had accompanied Tommy on his quest to rescue her. Quint was quiet, listening to every word Lily said. She knew not only every crewman's name, but the names of his family, who had been ill, who had had babies or died or changed occupations. He felt like a monkey on a leash, led about as he was with nothing more than an occasional "Come along, Quint."

The lads, as Lily called them, were very careful not to look directly at him. They kept their eyes on Lily's face, answering her questions solemnly and acting as if to look at Quint meant death itself.

As dusk fell, Lily stifled a yawn and stretched her right arm over her head. She acted as if there were nothing unusual about their situation, yet she ignored him at the same time. She ate a plateful of pork stew and a hunk of soft bread, balancing her supper on her lap much more gracefully than he could manage. He cursed under his breath as he struggled to balance the tin plate and eat with his left hand.

When they were finished, Lily rose, dragging him to his feet. It occurred to him that in the dead of night he could pick her up and run. He doubted that any of her crew was a good enough shot to be confident of hitting him without harming their Captain. What he would do after that, he couldn't say. Sellers had the keys. He would have to lift the keys from the boy first or stay shackled to Lily until he could find someone to remove the manacles. Perhaps that wasn't such a bad idea.

He looked down at Lily's compelling face, lit by the flickering fire and almost serene in its victory. Almost. And he spoke the first words he'd managed all evening.

"I gotta take a piss."

Lily raised her eyebrows. "You've lost none of your charm, Quintin Tyler. Very well." She turned toward the darkness of the trees that surrounded the camp.

"Not with you!" he nearly shouted.

Lily lifted their manacled wrists. "Not without me," she said calmly. "Don't worry, I'll keep my back turned. Not that I'm likely to see anything I haven't seen before."

In the near black of the forest, Quint relieved himself while Lily kept her back to him. When he was finished, they left the shelter of the trees as Quint wondered if Lily had kidneys of iron.

Back in the circle of light, Lily walked directly to her uncle. "Did you bring me a change of clothing? I really must get out of this horrid, filthy dress."

Quint didn't say a word as Lily motioned for Sellers to join them, and Lily's shackles were transferred, at her insistence, to her uncle's wrist and ankle.

"You boys behave yourselves," she ordered sweetly as she took the calico dress and soft brown boots Tommy had brought for her and disappeared into the shadows of the forest she and Quint had just come from.

Quint swore under his breath. He'd missed his opportunity. He should've grabbed Lily and run when they'd been hidden by those trees. Lily could have screamed all she wanted, but if he'd been fast enough, her crew would never have caught them. But he knew there was no way he could run that fast—not with Lily's weight and his bad leg. "Dammit," he muttered. "She's the most difficult woman I've ever met. And I've never met a woman who wasn't difficult."

Quint glanced up to see Tommy glowering at him, hate in the older man's eyes. In truth, Quint couldn't blame him. The responsibility for Lily's predicament fell on his shoulders, and no one knew better than he how protective Tommy Gibbon was of his niece.

Without warning, Tommy's fist flew into Quint's gut, and Quint doubled over. He held his free hand over his midsection and took a deep breath.

Slowly, Quint returned to an upright position, a grim smile on his face. That was all he needed.

An excuse. He brought back his left fist and hammered it with all his might into Tommy Gibbon's massive belly.

The older man doubled over as Quint had, but his years caused him to delay in rising. There was not a sound from the crew as they watched, standing well away from the shackled pair.

When Tommy did finally rise, it was with a scowl that Quint met with relish. His hand shot out and gripped Quint's throat. "I could kill you right now, you blighter."

"Please don't," Lily said calmly as she emerged from the shadow of the trees. She had combed her hair and washed her face, and changed into a calico dress of deep rose and pink with a scattering of tiny green leaves. Every man in the clearing turned to stare at her, and Quint realized as he noticed the stunned faces around him that none of these boys had ever seen their Captain in a simple dress. Never before had they seen her as lovely as she was right now, with her hair loose and waving down her back, and her figure undisguised. In the past, they'd seen Lily dressed in ruffles and lace and silk flowers or in clothing not much different from what they wore themselves. Quint knew he shouldn't be standing there thinking how beautiful she was, but he couldn't help it.

Lily positioned herself before him and Tommy and waited for Sellers to reattach the manacles. Tommy tried to stop her.

"Yer not intendin' to spend the night shackled to the bastard, are ye?"

"Of course," Lily answered calmly as Sellers returned the shackles to her wrist. "Which tent is ours?"

"Bloody hell, Lily Radford!" Tommy shouted. "I'll not allow it!"

Lily smiled at her uncle calmly. "Actually, it's Lily Tyler. Quint is my husband, and I'll bloody well do with him as I like."

She couldn't have said anything to quiet the camp more quickly or thoroughly. Suddenly the crackling of the fire and the cool breeze through the trees was clearly audible. Brittle brown leaves brushed together as the wind pushed them across the campground, hissing around their feet.

Lily stared at Tommy, waiting. Half a dozen young boys were mesmerized, their wide eyes turned to their Captain. And Quint studied them all with a stoic countenance that disguised his anger at the lot of them.

"Married?" Tommy finally said softly. "To 'im?"

Lily gave her uncle an easy smile. "Yes."

Roger was the first of the crew to recover his senses. He stepped forward and slapped Quint on the back. "Congratulations, mate!" he said heartily. "So ye weren't tellin' a tale when you told the Yanks ye were wed to the Cap'n." He nodded, evidently relieved to learn that his captain had not behaved inappropriately in the bed of the wagon that afternoon. "Why, yer just newlyweds."

That bright smile faded as Roger's eyes fell to the shackles that bound them together. He stepped back into the throng that surrounded Quint and Lily.

Lily turned her back on them all with a curt good night and stepped into the tent Tommy had grudgingly indicated was to be theirs. Quint was right behind her, bending over to step into their small shelter for the night. Without looking at him, she laid out the blankets that had been piled in one corner. Quint realized, as she fussed unnecessarily with the bedding, that she was nervous and quite diligently avoiding looking directly at his face. That realization brought a sardonic smile to his lips.

"That's good enough, Lily," he rasped. There was little light in the tent. A faint glow from the fire that continued to burn in the center of their campsite lit her face for him, and as she looked up from the bedding he felt a twinge of guilt. And she was the one who was holding him prisoner!

But she was scared. He could see it in the set of the lips he knew so well, in her wide eyes. Scared. Of him?

Lily lay on her back and stared at the black expanse above her. She couldn't look at Quint. She'd seen him angry before, but not like his. He looked as though he really wanted to kill her with his bare hands.

Her intentions had been good. First, to keep Quint out of Tommy's hands, to keep him alive. And then, damn her stubborn pride, as revenge for the weeks she had been a prisoner herself. She wanted him to know how humiliated she had felt, how furious she had been with him for his part in the scheme.

And now he was looking at her as if he could eat her alive. She turned her head to look him full in the face. He was lying on his side, watching her intently, his black eyes riveted on her face as if they might burn through her. He drummed his fingers slowly in the narrow space between their bodies—long brown fingers that were masculine and at the same time graceful.

"Well, Lily," Quint finally said softly, his voice menacing in its dark silkiness. "What now? Am I to forever be your slave? Are you going to shanghai me and throw me in the brig? Lash me to the mast and whip me into submission? Do they keelhaul disobedient husbands in your world, Lily dear?"

"Quint, I . . . I . . ." Lily stammered. His stare was unnerving her, making her quake.

"Don't go soft on me now, Lily. That's not your style." With slow calculation, Quint reached out and traced her face with a single finger, brushing her skin so lightly that she shivered in spite of her determination to show no reaction to his touch. That same finger traveled in a leisurely pattern across her throat and down to the edge of the scooped neckline of her calico dress, where it hooked possessively in the rose-colored fabric.

Lily almost expected a violent yank that would tear the fabric from her chest, but instead that indolent finger rocked back and forth, brushing against her tender skin.

"I suppose I could grab you and make a run for it." Quint seemed to be thinking aloud rather than discussing a viable plan of action.

"You wouldn't get far," Lily snapped. There was a tremble in her voice that she could not disguise.

Quint held her captive with his shadowy eyes, and she knew, in that moment, that he was not her prisoner. She was his. Perhaps it would always be so, even when they were hundreds of miles apart, separated by the war and their stubbornness and the vagaries of fate.

Outside the tent that separated them from the rest of the crew, a new sound joined the wind and the leaves and the soft murmur of lowered voices. A guitar strummed, expertly played, and the strains of a haunting melody reached through the chilly night air and wrapped itself around her, around Quint, as they faced each other with slowly melting hostility.

"Roger," Lily said softly.

Quint's finger was still hooked in the bodice of her calico dress, warm and alive against her skin. "Roger," he repeated.

"Playing the guitar," Lily added. "He's very good, don't you think?" It seemed suddenly necessary to fill the air between them with words, spiritless words with little or no meaning. "His mother was an actress, you know. She must have been quite talented. . . ."

Lily stammered to a halt. Quint was tugging at her dress with that damn finger, pulling her closer, shifting his own weight as he inched toward her.

"When I first saw Roger he was pulling a clever con in London, standing in front of a carriage and jumping away at the last minute. The poor blokes in the carriages would give him a coin or two, and he would limp away." Quint was right beside her now, his heat reaching through her dress. "He's quite agile, that's why—"

"Shut up, Lily," Quint said harshly, yet placidly, his lips so close to hers that they were almost touching.

Lily laid her palm on the side of Quint's face. No matter what had happened, no matter what was yet to happen, when he touched her she lost all reason. That was her weakness, a scar on her soul, but she had come to accept it.

Roger's music and the sheltering darkness of the night wrapped around them, and with a shared sigh they accepted the unalterable enchantment that brought them together. Their lips met with a fire that scorched them both, that burned their hearts and their souls and melded them together, until there was no distinction between Quint's spirit and Lily's.

Quint pressed his hand against Lily's back and crushed her to him, felt her surrendering tremble as she grasped the back of his head and pulled his lips harder against hers, thrusting her tongue into his mouth and releasing a muffled cry from deep within her. Their mutual surrender was explosive, all-consuming, and as predictable as the stars.

The chains that bound them together clanked loudly as Quint pressed Lily to the blanket and towered above her. Lily didn't seem to hear, or to care, as Quint shifted his weight onto his forearms. Those arms rested on either side of Lily's head, as Quint lost himself in her kiss and led her into oblivion with him.

There was no hesitation in the way she offered her mouth to him, lips parted and hungry. Quint was lost in the soft surrender of a woman who could be so hard. Lily wound her fingers through the hair at the back of his head, pressing her lips to his and brushing the tip of her tongue against his. She could make him forget anything—everything—with those lips, and he knew as he looked into her passion-clouded eyes that he had the same effect on her.

Quint pushed her skirt up with his knee, refusing to release her mouth even for an instant. And then his hand was there, pushing the full and cumbersome skirt to Lily's waist, touching her where she throbbed for him as he throbbed for her. Lily spread her legs wider, and he rested between her open thighs with the comfort and the pain of knowing that she was his wife, his soul-mate, and that he had no control where Lily was concerned. No control over his body or his soul.

Lily slid her hand between their bodies until she reached the buttons of his trousers, loosening them one at a time until his swollen shaft was free and grasped within her hand. He pulled his mouth away from her slightly, so that their lips barely touched, and he groaned as he closed his eyes.

Lily moaned into his mouth as he kissed her again and again, waiting until he was certain she was yearning as he was to be joined, body and soul.

She guided him to her, pressing the tip of his shaft against her wet center. Quint entered her in one swift movement, burying himself inside her with a groan that she caught with her mouth.

Lily lifted her hips, rested her hand against his back, and moved against him as he stroked her again and again, thrusting deep inside her until she shattered beneath him and he felt the spasms of her tight muscles. He sheathed himself inside her one last time, releasing his seed deep within her, clutching the hand that was chained to his as a convulsion rocked him to the core. With gradual reluctance, the world returned, gray and smoky, the only sound he heard the mournful strumming that continued outside their shelter.

And then another sound intruded—A sound close and yet hushed. Quint buried his face against Lily's neck and located the source of the tender noise. Her throat quivered as she fought to control the tears that threatened, and her breath came ragged and broken.

Quint lifted his head. Silent tears ran freely down Lily's cheeks, and when he frowned at those tears her resolve melted and she began to sob. Lily released long, heart-wrenching sobs that tore from her as if they'd been held prisoner for too long.

"I'm sorry, sweetheart," Quint whispered, wiping away warm tears with his thumb. He kissed her wet cheeks, tasting the salt of her tears on his lips and his tongue. "I'm sorry."

He hadn't meant to make love to her, to lose all reason as he seemed to when she was near. Obviously, she hadn't meant to either, and now she was regretting what had happened. He didn't. He couldn't. It was too right, too perfect to hold Lily in his arms and forget everything that stood between them.

Lily didn't push away from him, but let him hold her, let him cuddle her as she wept.

"I'm sorry," she said when she lifted her head to look at him, tears falling like rain from her turquoise eyes. "I don't know why . . ." She stopped, and Quint drew her against his chest. He rocked her in his arms and murmured into her ear, long into the night, even after the tears had stopped and she settled into a bout of sporadic gasps for breath, hiccup-like catches that seemed to take her by surprise as she buried her head against him.

He held her long after she fell asleep, listening to her even breathing and holding her with all the tenderness he felt for her.

His woman. His wife. She was so much a part of him that it seemed she had always been there, deep inside. When he finally drifted off to sleep, it was with Lily snuggled against him, her tears damp on his uniform, his heart in her delicate hand.

Chapter Twenty-two

Lily woke slowly, becoming aware first that Quint's warm and deeply even breath was in her hair and that his unbound hand was at her back. His body protected her from the chilly morning air, with his arm and one leg thrown over her.

She was momentarily content, in spite of the manacles that bound her to her husband. Perhaps because of them. And then it hit her—a roiling, unpleasant churning of her stomach. And she hadn't even moved yet!

"Quint," she whispered, tugging at his sleeve. "Wake up, Quint."

Her husband only growled sleepily and held her tighter, rubbing his leg up and down hers in a drowsy motion.

"Quint!"

He opened his eyes one at a time, and then he smiled at her sleepily, planting a kiss on her forehead.

"Good morning, sweet—"

"Get up," she ordered uneasily, pulling herself and Quint into an upright position. As she stood, the tent seemed to tilt and spin, and she slapped her hand over her mouth.

Lily ran from the tent, dragging a half-drowsing Quint with her. With her hand clamped over her mouth and her stomach rebelling, she rounded the tent and stopped only when they were out of sight, away from the rest of the camp.

She emptied her stomach onto the ground, retching until there was nothing left. She stood very still until the waves of nausea had passed, and only then was she aware that Quint was holding her up with the arm that was bound to hers and holding her hair away from her face with the other.

"Are you all right?" he whispered huskily into her ear.

Lily turned her head. She was mortified that Quint had been there when she'd gotten sick and terrified that he might guess the reason for her infirmity.

"I'm fine," she said weakly. "It must have been the stew. I . . . I shouldn't eat pork," she lied.

He accepted her explanation easily, much to Lily's relief, and they walked back into camp. All eyes turned to them as Quint placed a tin cup of water to her lips, but no one dared to stare. Not even when she and Quint began to walk around the camp in a comfortable sort of symmetry, the clanking of the heavy chains between them. Lily didn't view the manacles as a burden any longer, and Quint didn't seem to either. There were harder possibilities to contemplate—harsher fates than being chained to the man she loved.

Lily stopped in the middle of the camp and signaled silently to Sellers. The crewman jumped from his task of taking down the tents to rush to her side, ready to do whatever she asked.

Quint remembered Tommy's words of warning. The men of Lily's crew really would kill or die for her. He could see that reality on the young man's face.

Lily lifted her manacled hand, and Sellers fished the key out of his pocket, releasing his Captain.

"You're not chaining me to that uncle of yours again, are you?" Quint asked, frowning as Lily was released, wrist and ankle.

Lily's answer was to turn and call for her uncle, and Tommy grudgingly approached his niece, leaving the chore of packing and saddling the horses to the crew.

"You're not fastening me to that bloody bloke again!" Tommy insisted.

Lily remained calm. "No. I'm going to release him, and I want your word that you won't do him any harm."

"I'll do 'im 'arm, all right. I'll take 'is bloody 'ead off." Tommy took a step closer, and Lily stepped between her uncle and Quint.

Quint smiled, a maddeningly joyful smile as he realized what Lily had done. Chaining herself to him had been her way of protecting him from Tommy. He knew he should be angry that she believed he needed protection from her irascible guardian, but that anger was lost in his relief.

The shackles fell away from his wrist, then from his ankle. Lily still stood between him and Tommy, and Quint took a step forward to place both hands on her shoulders. He wanted to lean forward and kiss her, but he didn't. He stood directly behind her, his back as straight as hers, his eyes meeting Tommy's over her head.

Tommy couldn't take them both on, that much was clear. Lily's uncle turned away from Quint and Lily, from their combined strength. "All right," he muttered. "But 'e better not give me a reason to shoot 'im, because I will if it comes to that."

Lily stepped away from Quint, and his hands fell from her shoulders. When she turned to confront him, he was presented with the same stony countenance Tommy had faced.

"You're free to go, Lieutenant Tyler," she said calmly.

Quint cocked his head and stared at her. "I'm free to go," he repeated.

Lily nodded her head.

"Like hell I will," he shouted. "I'm not leaving until I see you on a ship sailing away from this place."

Lily's expression never changed. She folded her hands almost primly at her waist. "You needn't worry. I give you my word that I'm leaving and I won't come back."

Quint felt as if the ground had dropped out from under him. Life with Lily was like riding out a storm at sea. One minute he was riding the crest of a wave, on top of the world and soaring through the sky, and the next minute the world threatened to swallow him whole.

"I'll see you on that ship," Quint said, his voice deceptively calm. He stared at her for a full minute, a silent minute in which no one spoke. Then he turned on his heel and stalked away from her.

They traveled toward the coast, taking a southeasterly road. Lily was flanked by Quint and Tommy, her husband on his bay, her uncle on a tired gray mare. Lily's own mare wasn't in much better condition, nor were any of the lads' mounts, though they seemed more than capable of the single day's travel that was required.

The wagon had been left behind, hastily covered with limbs cut from the trees that had surrounded their camp. It would be discovered eventually, but by that time Lily and her crew would be long gone.

In front of her, Roger rode with the flaxen-haired Farmer brothers, and the three of them were constantly engaged in a spirited conversation. Roger emphasized his arguments with a single animated hand, as the other hand held the reins of his own less-than-magnificent steed.

A glance to the rear showed Lily that Sellers and his two quiet companions were vigilantly watching the road, peering ahead and back the way they'd just come, anxious to return to the sea where they belonged. Sellers held the reins of the packhorse that carried blankets, three tents, and Roger's guitar.

Quint was fuming, his silence a controlled and

almost tangible entity. When Lily dared to look sidelong at him, she saw a stoic face, but Quint's jaw twitched as he fought to maintain that apparent apathy. As far as she could tell, Quint hadn't looked at her since they'd left camp, though he had remained at her side throughout the morning.

Tommy rode at her right, and tried to be as austere as Quint. But occasionally he broke into a litany of curses just under his breath, as he swore to himself and stared at her with disapproving eyes.

The morning seemed to last forever, and Lily, whose energy had always been boundless, was exhausted by the time they stopped for a cold noon meal. Sellers and his companions saw to the horses, while Roger and the Farmers unpacked a store of fruit and bread and filled tin cups from the clear spring the horses drank at.

Lily sat at the base of an oak tree, its trunk wide and weathered and rough. But it provided support for her back as she lowered herself to the ground. It made no sense for her to feel so tired. She had always been active and strong, rising early and staying busy throughout the day. She'd never had much patience with frail women who resorted to afternoon naps to maintain their negligible energy.

As these thoughts ran through her mind, she closed her eyes and allowed the exhaustion to sweep over her.

Quint stood several feet away, ostensibly brushing the layer of road dust from his uniform.

He even removed his hat to beat it against his leg, creating a cloud that formed quickly and then fell about his feet. All the while, he had one eye on Lily as she settled herself in the dirt and leaned back against the tree.

"What the 'ell 'ave you done to 'er, you bleedin' Yankee bastard?"

Quint turned his head and raised a quizzical eyebrow to Tommy, as the older man practically growled at him. "Are you speaking to me, or is there another bleedin' Yankee bastard around here somewhere?"

"Look at 'er," Tommy whispered as he studied his niece. She had fallen asleep moments after she'd closed her eyes, and the hand that rested in her lap slid to the ground as they watched.

"I know." Quint frowned. "I think being in that prison was harder on her than she's willing to admit." For a moment his anger at the old man was forgotten. "Once you get her home, she'll be all right." He hoped that was true, that once Lily was in her house, surrounded by the sea air and the gentle breeze that wrapped itself around the island, she would regain the vitality she'd lost.

It was Roger who woke Lily, kneeling before her and handing her a tin plate and a cup of water. Quint watched as Lily smiled wearily at the young man, and he felt a twinge of jealousy.

When the horses had been watered and the travelers fed, the lads mounted up, ready to get on the road again. Lily trudged toward her mare, fatigue in her step. If only she could sleep for an hour or two, she was certain she would be all right. Tommy mounted his gray with an ungraceful grunt, and only she and Quint remained unseated.

Quint stared at her with those damn dark eyes, and his jaw worked impatiently. Why hadn't he simply returned to Washington where he belonged? She didn't want him to see her tired and sick, and maybe start to wonder . . .

With an impatient step, Quint moved to her mare, grabbed the reins, and tossed them to Tommy. Without a word, he took Lily's arm and led her to his bay. Before she could protest, he had lifted her into his saddle and vaulted up to sit behind her.

"What do you think you're doing?" She had only to glance up to see his stern visage, so close. Too close.

"You're too tired to ride," Quint snapped. "I'd rather you didn't fall out of the saddle." With his long arm, he held her close to him, though he managed not to look her full in the face. "Just lean your head back and take a nap." His voice softened slightly, in a kind of resignation.

"I'm perfectly capable . . ."

"Not today you're not."

"I can't possibly sleep . . ."

"Of course you can."

Before Lily could protest further, they were moving forward. She'd expected a protest from Tommy, but none was forthcoming. She couldn't see her uncle's face at all, sitting as she was with her back to the man who was her favorite relative and her first mate. But he was silent, and Lily sighed with an uncommon passiveness and laid her head against Quint's chest.

She could hear Roger's lively voice ahead of her, and she could hear Quint breathing just above. That sound alone was oddly soothing. The horses' hooves beat against the road in a steady cadence that relaxed her as if it were a lullaby, and in a matter of minutes, she was sound asleep.

It was a sudden change in pace that woke Lily, almost two hours later. Quint had pulled his bay to a standstill, and Lily heard the prancing of nervous hooves instead of the relaxing rhythms she had slept to.

They had rounded a curve in the road and found themselves face-to-face with a Yankee patrol. Tommy's hand was on the pistol at his waist. Eddie Farmer snaked a hand behind his back and closed his fist over the knife that was sheathed there. Roger was uncommonly silent.

At least her crew had the sense not to draw their weapons, though they were certainly prepared to defend themselves, should it come to that. They had been prepared for this, as they had been for most everything else.

Quint moved forward, forcing Eddie's and Roger's mounts to part for him. Lily stirred in his arms, looking ahead to the patrol of twenty or more men.

"Major," Quint greeted the officer at the head of the column, an older man covered with road dust and scowling at the inconvenient delay he faced.

He raked his eyes over Quint, and over Lily as well. "Lieutenant. What are you doing in this neck of the woods?" He took off his hat and wiped the dusty brim. His too-long hair was not completely gray, but silver was predominant in the almost shoulder-length curls.

"I'm escorting my wife and her family home," Quint said, not bothering to mention that "home" was Nassau.

The major scowled. His suspicions were clear on his lined face, in the narrowing of his eyes and the flaring of his nostrils, as if he smelled a traitor. Sharp eyes took in all the members of her party, her crew too young and healthy not to be soldiers. And then his eyes landed on her. She met his gaze and finally gave him a faint smile.

Quint reached inside his coat and withdrew a neatly folded sheet of paper. He wasn't blind to the major's suspicions, any more than Lily was.

"I have a letter from Captain Brighton," Quint said calmly, passing the paper to the major.

The officer snapped the missive open and read the brief note. His fine eyebrows lifted slightly as he read, and the mistrust cleared from his eyes. He refolded the note and passed it back to Quint. "I see." Then he gave Lily a smile. "So you're a friend of Peter Brighton? Good man."

Lily simply nodded.

"Shame about his wife, though. She was so young." The major's smile faded. "You favor her a little. Were you related to her, Mrs. Tyler?"

Lily perked up. They were going to have to bluff their way past these soldiers, and that was something she was very good at. "No, Major. This is my family." She waved her hand to indicate the men around her. "My father, Thomas Gibbon." She smiled at Tommy and nodded in his direction. "And these are my brothers. "Eddie and Roger and Gilbert." They each nodded when their name was called, and Lily looked to the lads at the rear. "Phillip and Johnny and Timothy."

The major replaced his hat and narrowed his eyes suspiciously at the "family" before him. Except for Eddie and Gilbert with their fair hair, there was little resemblance among the boys.

"Where's home, Lieutenant?"

Quint hesitated before replying. "On the coast."

The major nodded slightly. "You going home to stay?"

Quint shook his head. "No, sir. I report to General Sheridan in three days' time."

Lily looked up at him, wide-eyed and dizzy. It was true. She could tell by the tone of his voice. He was going back to fight again.

"Your leg," she said softly. "You can't possibly . . ." Lily glanced back to the major. She had forgotten for a moment that he was there.

"I'm transferring to the cavalry," Quint directed his comment to the major. "I was wounded last year and have just recently been declared fit for duty."

"Fit for duty," Lily repeated, squirming in her seat. "I think . . ." She squirmed until she started to slip from Quint's grasp, and for a second she thought she might actually fall. Quint caught her and pulled her closer to him, but not before they all heard Roger's excited cry.

"Cap'n!"

All heads turned to the young man.

Lily grimaced at him and turned to the major. "You'll have to forgive my brother," she said in a loud whisper. "Roger's a bit daft."

Roger guided his horse forward until he was close to Quint and Lily. The expression on his face was dignified and disdainful, eyebrows arched and mouth puckered.

"I 'eard that," he said calmly. He turned to the major, chin high. "I'll 'ave you know, General, that I am not daft."

"Major," the Yankee corrected Roger.

"O' course, General," Roger said reasonably. "You wouldn't, by any chance, 'ave a few sweet-cakes in your saddlebags?" He moved close to the major, leaning to the side so as to be close to the saddlebags.

"No, I'm afraid I don't." The major's attention was diverted from Quint and Lily and centered on a fidgeting Roger who sidled closer to him.

"Oh," Roger sighed deeply. "I do so like sweet-cakes, and it's been ever so long." His face transformed into one of longing and sadness. "Are you most certain you don't 'ave no sweetcakes?"

The major backed away, his horse retreating two steps. "I might have a bit of hardtack . . ."

"Gor, no!" Roger shouted. "I 'ad some 'ardtack once. Tasted almost as tough as one o' me sister

Lily's biscuits." His body slid slowly to the side, until he was almost parallel to the ground. Only his strong thighs were keeping him from dropping to the ground as he reached for the major's saddlebags.

With flailing arms and a surprised yelp, Roger fell to the ground and landed flat on his back. "Would you look at that," he said dryly. "Fell out o' me saddle again."

One of the major's men jumped from his horse to check on the civilian in the dirt. Roger glared up at him serenely. "Do you 'ave any sweetcakes, Cap'n?"

"No." The private backed away, assured that the man on the ground wasn't hurt.

Roger leapt to his feet and vaulted into the saddle, as agile as a cat. "Well, if you're absolutely certain that you 'ave no . . ."

"Roger!" Tommy's bellow made Roger straighten his back and glance over his shoulder.

"Yes, Admiral?"

Tommy simply crooked his finger, and Roger hung his head and plodded away from the major. Once he was beside Tommy, the older man punched Roger lightly on the arm, and the former con artist fell to the ground as smoothly as silk on silk.

The major turned to Quint with sympathy in his eyes.

"Good luck to you, Lieutenant Tyler." The major tipped his hat, and the sun glinted off of his silver hair once again. "And to you, Mrs. Tyler."

Quint and Lily moved to the side of the road,

and Lily's crew followed suit. They allowed the Union patrol to pass, then returned to the road silently. That could have been a disaster, if the major had asked too many questions, or if Quint had not had that letter from Captain Brighton.

Lily found herself wondering about Captain Brighton, the man she had hated for so very long. What had happened to his wife? What was his tragedy?

They were miles down the road before Roger fell back and gave her a dazzling grin.

"Daft, am I?"

Chapter Twenty-three

The sun was setting at their backs. Lily could smell the sea, though she could see no sign of the ocean, could hear no lapping surf. The land they rode across was sparsely green, and they passed what remained of a huge summer garden, a plot in the ground now overrun by weeds and scraggly plants that would continue to reach for the sun until the first frost wilted their tough leaves. That wouldn't be long, Lily thought as a cold wind nipped at her nose.

Quint had grudgingly returned her to her own horse not long after the run-in with the Yankee patrol. Her nap had energized her greatly, and that combined with the excitement of their encounter kept her wide awake.

She'd felt Quint's probing eyes on her all afternoon, but rather than stare back, as she'd been prone to do in the past, she kept her eyes on the road or on Roger's back.

The cottage they stopped at had once been white, but more raw wood showed than whitewash. Still, the neglected home showed some signs of care. The weeds that grew with wild abandon elsewhere had been pulled from along the path that led to the front door. There were curtains and drying herbs in the windows, and two sturdy-looking rocking chairs on the front porch.

Sellers and his mates took the horses to the barn, and the rest of the crew entered the cottage.

The house was cold, and there was no sign of occupancy—no fire in the fireplace or welcoming pot on the stove. The chill went through Lily's calico to her skin. Without the sun to warm the air, the damp chill was icy and penetrating.

"The folks who own this place won't be back until late tomorrow." Tommy spoke to Lily, ignoring Quint, as they stepped into the large room. There was a huge fireplace at one end, and a kitchen built into the other. An opened door led to the single bedroom.

"Are you certain?" Lily walked around the room, stretching her legs and working out the kinks that had settled in after several hours in the saddle.

"Aye. They've been well paid. They looked as though the bit o' gold I 'anded them was the first 'ard money they'd seen in years."

Roger and the Farmer brothers built a blaze in the massive stone fireplace and started another fire in the stove. Quint paced the room, his boots clicking against the wood floor, his hands clenched behind his back. Tommy's eyes followed his movement, hard and unyielding. Lily knew that in those eyes Quint was responsible for every hardship that had befallen her—her capture, her imprisonment, her apparent illness.

Quint muttered something almost unintelligible about a breath of fresh air and stormed through the front door. A rush of cold air blew in before he could close it, and Lily shivered as the chill reached her. Her eyes were on the door he had disappeared through.

Tommy decided to check on the lads who were tending to the horses. Sellers and the other boys had learned quickly, but they weren't horsemen. They were sailors.

After a few silent moments, Roger sent both Farmer brothers in search of more firewood, as he gathered together the ingredients for the evening meal. More stew. He'd said it was the only thing he knew how to make, and none of the others would own up to knowing how to cook.

Lily was sitting at the table, drumming her fingers nervously as she stared at the front door. She was so lost in her own thoughts that she didn't know Roger was near her until he stood directly in front of her, leaning down to place his face close to hers and claim her attention.

" 'E doesn't know, does 'e?" Roger asked solemnly.

Lily looked up at Roger with innocent eyes, as wide and clear as she could manage.

"Who doesn't know what?"

"Tyler," Roger said, backing away. " 'E doesn't know that yer preggers, does 'e?"

Lily stared at the boy—no, he was a young man on the verge of true manhood. The look he gave her was lightly condemning, pensive for Roger, and knowing.

"What makes you think—?"

"I 'ave nine brothers and sisters," Roger snapped. "I should 'ave known the moment you retched all over me shoes, but when I saw you sleepin' in the middle o' the day, I knew fer sure."

"People can simply get tired."

Roger shook his head, sending dark curls bobbing. He would make a handsome man one day, when he lost the still-smooth prettiness of his fine features.

"Mind your own business, Roger," Lily added, tired of looking at his censuring face.

She'd hurt his feelings. She could see that in his eyes before he turned away from her and returned to the stove and his stew. "O' course, Cap'n."

Lily drummed her fingers on the table, faster and faster. Her foot was tapping nervously against the floor, and as the chill nipped at her toes she wished for the warmth of Nassau.

She looked away from the door to Roger's back. His head was bent over a large, bubbling pot.

"Just out of curiosity, Roger," Lily began nonchalantly, "when your mother was expecting . . . was she sick the entire time?" Try as she might, she couldn't hide the despair in her voice.

"No." She couldn't see his face, but she could hear the smile in Roger's voice. "Just the first two or three months. With little Amy, she was hardly sick at all. But she was tired the whole while and slept like the dead, she did." He turned around, a sharp knife he'd been stirring the stew with still clutched in his hand. "But she always said it was worth it, in the end, to 'ave a little baby to 'old in 'er arms."

Lily had never really thought of her condition as anything more than that. A condition. But a baby . . . tiny and squalling . . . That was all she knew about babies, that they were tiny and fragile and cried a lot. A boy or a girl? Quint's dark hair or her fair?

Roger crossed his arms across his chest, a triumphant smile on his face as he watched her. "So, you're goin' to tell 'im?"

Lily's face was stern and determined. "No. And you're not to tell anyone, either. Is that clear?"

She gave him a look that would have put him in his place a few months ago. But the *Chameleon* was at the bottom of the ocean.

"Why not?" he asked insolently.

"Please, Roger." Lily's voice softened. "I'm asking you not as your Captain, but as your friend. I don't want Quint to know."

"Why the 'ell not?"

Lily didn't have a chance to answer, as Gilbert and Eddie returned, their arms full with more than enough firewood for the evening. But Roger's last glance told her what she wanted to know. He might not approve, but he would accede to her wishes . . . unwillingly.

She had her reasons for not telling Quint that she was going to have his baby. Perhaps it wasn't fair. Perhaps it was even heartless. But she wouldn't become a clutching woman who tried to hold a man through his child. She didn't want Quint to bind himself to her because she carried his baby.

She wanted him to love her, and she didn't know if that was possible. Not the way he had once loved her. Not the way she wanted him to love her again.

They gathered around the fire like a large and imperfect family, the lads of Lily's crew sitting on the floor with bowls of Roger's stew cradled in their laps, speaking softly over the steaming bowls, trying to ignore the tension in the room.

Tommy glared at Quint with silent rage. It was easy to see that the old man would gladly kill him but was bemoaning the fact that he would likely never get the chance.

Quint ignored the man's hate-filled perusal. He turned all his attention to Lily, as she picked at her food and stared into the fire. When she wasn't staring into the flames that blazed in the stone fireplace, she was looking at Roger, a veil over her eyes, a new tension in her face.

It was a restive silence that settled over the room as their meal was finished and the crew cleaned the kitchen area. Roger was a good cook, but a messy one, and the crew, all but Roger, bumped into one another as they wiped the stove clean, washed the bowls, and swept the floor. Their silence grew heavier as they progressed— almost, Quint decided, an extension of their Captain's discomfort.

Roger stretched out in front of the fire. He had done his part in cooking the meal and had declared loudly that he had no responsibility for cleaning up the mess that had resulted from his efforts. He lay on a tattered rug, casting what he obviously thought were furtive glances at his Captain, her first mate, and occasionally Quint.

Quint decided he could almost see the boy's mind at work, as Roger pursed his lips and narrowed his eyes.

When the clean-up was done, the rest of the crew joined Roger in front of the fire, but the agile young man jumped to his feet before they could lower themselves to the floor and relax.

"Well, mates, we're off to the barn," he said with a smile.

They all looked at him as if he were as daft as he had pretended to be that afternoon.

"What for? It's cold out there," Gilbert Farmer whispered loudly. Several heads nodded in agreement, but Roger would not be swayed.

"It smells o' pork stew in 'ere. I can't sleep with that odor in me nostrils all night. Them onions were a bit strong, and I can still smell the pepper." He wrinkled his nose.

"I can't smell anything."

"Doesn't bother me at all."

Roger sighed, evidently disgusted. He looked to Lily, cutting his eyes to her and then back to the boys who still watched him expectantly. Finally, he whispered softly to the Farmer brothers, and they spread the word.

In a matter of minutes they were headed for

the door, red-faced and clutching blankets in their hands. Roger let them all out, then turned back to the warm room.

"Aren't ya comin', Mr. Gibbon?" His face was all innocence, but Tommy wasn't fooled. He glared at the dark-haired young man in the door-way.

"I'll be sleepin' in front o' the fire, if you don't mind," Tommy growled.

With the crew gone, and only Lily, Quint, and Tommy in the room, the tension increased ten-fold. There was no sound but the crackle of the fire and the click of Quint's boots against the floor as he paced. Lily sat at the table and drummed her fingers lightly against the wood, and Tommy pulled a chair close to the fire and leaned forward, offering his palms to the blaze and drinking in the warmth.

There was a lingering odor from the evening meal, a spicy and somehow comforting smell that filled the house. It reminded Lily of warm evenings spent with Cora and Tommy . . . before Quint had burst into her life. But would she have it any different? Knowing what she knew now, would she have sent him away?

When a log split, sending the flame high and filling the room with a loud crackling noise, Quint stopped pacing, Lily's fingers were stilled, and Tommy nearly jumped out of his skin.

"Bloody 'ell!" Tommy leapt out of his chair, sending it flying backwards to land with a crash against the floor. He glared at Quint, then turned his eyes to Lily.

The harshness in his eyes softened, and Lily found herself smiling wistfully at her uncle. Everything he'd done, he'd done out of love for her—attacking Quint in the parlor of her little house, having him watched on the island, calling him "Captain" in the presence of the Yankee ensign.

And he found it so hard to believe that she'd fallen in love with Quint. She'd seen that disbelief in his eyes as he'd watched the two of them.

But Tommy knew love, in spite of his rough appearance and harsh speech. He knew love, thanks to Cora.

Roger burst through the front door. "Mr. Gibbon! Johnny and Eddie are brawlin' somethin' fierce. I tried to stop 'em meself . . ."

Tommy turned away from Lily and gathered up the single blanket that was folded neatly by the fire. "I can see I won't be able to leave you bleedin' idiots alone tonight. I'll whip the lot o' you, if I 'ave to."

The cold air that came through the entrance as Roger stood in the open doorway filled the room, touching every corner with a bit of winter and making Lily hug her arms to her body searching for warmth. The door slammed as Tommy followed Roger, leaving Quint and Lily alone. Quint stared into the fire, and Lily watched his back, her mind filled with the same disturbing thought that had been haunting her all evening.

He was going into battle. Lieutenant Quintin Tyler was going back to the Army that had cost him full use of his leg. Lily had never seen battle, but she had seen the effects—men crippled, women widowed. Blood flowed in the thick of a battle, and she suddenly realized why Quint had said her impromptu play on board the *Chameleon* wasn't funny. He had seen real blood shed, and he would be facing that again.

And he would be facing rifles that might have been delivered into the hands of his enemy by her own ship. Ammunition she had made a profit from. Sabers she had gladly put into the hands of the Confederate Army. Her revenge could play a part in Quint's death, in the cruelest twist of fate imaginable.

"Quint." She whispered his name and saw his shoulders straighten and his back tense.

"Yes, Lily." He didn't turn to face her, but continued to stare into the blaze before him.

"Don't go. You don't have to fight anymore. . . ." Her words trailed off slowly as he turned to face her.

"Yes, I do," he said solemnly. "Remember your promise. I want you to stay out of this."

"I will, but you . . . you could come with me."

Lily hadn't intended to deliver the suggestion with such a wistful voice. Quint locked his eyes to hers and she didn't turn away, didn't avoid that gaze as she had all day.

"Back at the prison—when you were *dying*— why did you say what you said?"

Lily smiled sadly. "That I loved you, once?"

Quint nodded.

"Because I thought it would sound very dramatic, for the guards' sake . . ." Lily hesitated.

What if she never saw him again? How much should she tell him? "And because it's true."

Lily laid both hands on the table, one palm over the other. She was trembling slightly, so slightly that she was certain Quint couldn't see the tremors. At least, she hoped that he couldn't.

"Do you still love me, Lily?" He whispered the question, as if he were afraid to ask, as if he were afraid of what her answer would be.

Lily studied him before she answered. His dark eyes were hooded, his face impassive, but without the cockiness he sometimes wore as a shield. There was no hard set to his mouth, as there sometimes was when he was stubbornly determined. He looked a little lost . . . almost as lost as she felt.

"If I say yes," she said softly, hesitantly, "will you come back with me? Back to Nassau?"

"No." He answered so quickly Lily knew it was true. She took little comfort in the sound of defeat in his voice.

"Then it doesn't matter, does it?" Lily lowered her eyes and stared at the tabletop, concentrating on the grooves in the wood. She would not cry in front of him again, dammit. She *would not*.

"Go to bed, Lily," Quint ordered gruffly, turning back to the blaze.

Lily stood slowly, pushing back the chair and laying her hands against the table. She could tell him that she loved him, could beg him not to leave her. Would that make a difference to Quint? Or would he break her heart again and tell her that it really didn't matter?

346

With slow deliberation, she crossed the room until she was standing directly behind Quint. She laid her hands on his shoulders, pressing her fingers into his flesh, feeling his heat through the uniform. She heard the rush of air that escaped his lips, a sigh of surrender as her hands touched him.

And then she was in his arms. He pulled her against his chest and buried his head against her shoulder, holding her as if he never wanted to let her go.

His eyes were piercing when Lily lifted her face to him. No words would bridge the gulf between them, so there were none. Quint lifted her and carried her to the single bedroom, burying his face in her tousled hair, quivering at the touch of her lips against his throat.

The bedroom was as plainly and sparsely furnished as the rest of the house, but a large bed dominated the room. There was a well-worn quilt neatly covering the bed, and Quint laid Lily in the center of it, bracing himself on one knee as he leaned over her. He undressed her slowly, easily, as if she were a fragile doll, one he was afraid he would break. Each button on the rose calico dress was unfastened with simple calculation, each step revealing a little more skin, the swell of her breasts.

Quint swept the dress over her head and sat back to look at her, his eyes seeming to take in every inch he had uncovered.

Lily's unruly hair fell over her shoulders, and the thin chemise she wore hid nothing from him.

The nub of her nipples pressed against the thin fabric, the linen almost transparent. He reached out and touched her lovingly, his fingers brushing against one nipple and then the other, while one hand rested at her waist.

Lily pulled him to her, hungry for his mouth against hers, for the feel of his skin against hers. The heat of his chest against her breasts made her want him even more, and she moaned low in her throat as his tongue thrust into her mouth, greedy and possessive.

Her hands were at his chest, working the buttons of his uniform, the jacket, the shirt, until she could rest her palms against his skin. She wanted to drink in his warmth, absorb as much of Quint as she could in the brief time they had left.

She wanted him inside her, wanted the union that made her whole. Once they were separated, she didn't know if she would ever see him again, ever hold him in her arms.

Quint removed the chemise hastily and ran his hands over the bare skin he exposed. He lowered his mouth to her breasts, sucking gently and pressing his tongue against one hard nipple. She felt a tugging at her center, a wrenching feeling that warned her she would ache forever if she didn't have him. She arched her back and moaned out loud. His name escaped her lips, a hoarsely whispered plea.

Lily protested when he moved away from her, but he shed his uniform and returned to her moments later, pressing his body against hers. Mouth to mouth, chest to chest, thigh to thigh, they knelt in the center of the bed. Lily's hands trailed along Quint's muscled back as they waited, prolonging the sweet torture that swept over them.

He was in her blood, in her soul, a part of her that no number of miles could take away. She ran her hands over his body, memorizing every line, every muscle. Her hand slipped between their bodies and she grasped the heat of his swollen shaft.

Quint pushed her back onto the bed with a groan of abandon. He entered her in one ardent thrust, then held himself very still.

Lily clutched him to her with all her might. It was so right, so fine, to bond herself with him, to marry their bodies and their hearts.

He began to move again, so slowly that Lily was certain he meant to torment her. For now, there was only this, the entwining of their bodies, the dance of their hearts, the driving beat of blood that thrummed through their veins.

Her body reached for his, and Quint drove himself into her again and again, until she reached a climax and shattered in his arms.

It was then that he let himself go, and as her inner muscles tightened around him he plunged into her one last time, convulsing over her again and again. Lily was calling his name, calling him *Quint, my love*.

"Lily, my love," Quint whispered. He had drained every bit of her energy, and apparently his own as well. It was an effort for him to roll off her, keeping her in his arms and pulling her on top of him.

Lily pressed her lips to his chest and laid her head against his bare skin. What if she never saw him again? What if he were killed, or simply never returned to her? That last thought shouldn't have occurred to her, not after what had just happened, but it did. Making love to Quint was so very special to her, so magical. But what if he didn't feel the same way? She couldn't ask. Not now.

He rubbed his hands possessively up and down her back, and it was a curiously comforting touch. She melted into his chest and closed her eyes.

No matter what, she wouldn't regret anything that had happened. No matter what, she had a part of him that would be hers forever.

"The ship will be here early in the morning," Lily whispered.

"Before dawn," Quint said, and she could have sworn that there was regret in his voice.

Lily lifted her head to look down at him. The room was lit with a hint of the yellow glow from the blaze in the other room and a slice of moonlight that cut through the window. She reached out and brushed back the lock of ash-brown hair that had fallen over his forehead. He grabbed her hand and kissed her fingers, lovingly, one at a time.

"So . . . we have tonight?" Lily asked, almost

shyly. Only Quint could make her feel insecure. What if he didn't want her again? What if he . . .

Quint allayed all her reservations with a smile. "Yes, Lily. We have tonight."

Chapter Twenty-four

Lily rolled against Quint's side and snuggled there, drinking in his warmth. The second time they'd made love, he had come to her languidly, driving her crazy with wanting him, moving slowly and tenderly until all she could think of was the pleasure he would bring her to.

But, being Lily, she realized what he was doing and responded in kind. It became another test of wills, although a more pleasurable test than their battles of the past.

And now she had only enough strength to snuggle contentedly against him, one arm flung across his chest.

"It's strange to imagine," Lily whispered hoarsely, "that if it were not for the war, we never would have met. I hate this war, and now it's pulling us apart, but I wonder . . ."

"I would have found you, Lily." Quint held her firmly nestled in his arms, his fingers trailing lazily down her back and up again.

His certain statement intrigued her, and she lifted herself up on one elbow so she could see his face. The fire in the main room had died down, and only a hint of moonlight lit his face.

"How?"

He gave her a smile and brushed the hair away from her face. "I would have gone to Virginia to buy a horse. Something would have drawn me there. Of course, someone would have told me that your father's horse farm was the best, and I would have been directed there."

"But you wouldn't have liked me," Lily said certainly. "None of the boys my father and Elliot brought home liked me."

"I'm not a boy, Lily. I'm a man. And I damn well would have liked you." He seemed adamant. "You might not have liked me, of course."

"Probably not," she teased, smiling down at his face.

"I would have won you anyway."

"I actually had a suitor tell me once that I was more of a man than he was. Of course, I had just beaten him in a horse race, and he was a petulant sissy." Lily traced a finger along Quint's chest. "He meant it as an insult, but I smiled and thanked him. It hurt though. I can't help the way I am."

"I like you just the way you are," Quint said brusquely. "Who said that to you?"

Lily smiled. He was angry at the insult, not at her. "It doesn't matter. How would you have won me?" She wanted to imagine what it would have been like to fall in love with Quint without the war between them. Would he have tried to court her as her unsuccessful suitors had?

"First I would have challenged you to a game of chess," Quint declared.

"I would have beaten you."

"Perhaps. Perhaps not," Quint said dreamily. "Then I would have grabbed you and kissed you."

"How unchivalrous." Lily tried to sound shocked, but she laughed. "Just like that?"

"Just like this." Quint pulled her against him and kissed her thoroughly, until she melted in his arms. With a sigh, he pulled away slightly. His lips were close to hers, almost touching, but not quite. "And then I would have said, 'Damn, I'll never find another woman like this one. I guess I better marry her.'"

How could he break her heart so easily, with a smile, with a word? How could she walk away from this?

"Come with me, Quint," Lily begged. She forgot about her stubborn pride and pleaded with him. "I'll worry about you, and your leg—"

"My leg is fine. I've just got a little limp, that's all." Quint kissed her again to quiet her protests, but Lily pulled away.

"Please." There was a ragged pain in her voice.

"I can't," Quint whispered as he laid his palm against her cheek.

"Why not?" Lily pushed against him angrily.

Quint ignored her anger and gathered her in his arms, pulling her head against his shoulder and burying his face in her hair. She felt his warm breath against the top of her head, his insistent hands at her back.

"Because I believe that what I'm doing is right. Important."

"Why?"

"Because it's not right for one man to own another. Because it's not right for a man to be beaten because he dares to look at another man without fear in his eyes. Because . . . because it's not right for a thirteen-year-old boy to be sold away from his family because he was playing with the master's son when the clumsy boy fell out of a tree and broke his nose." There was such raw pain in Quint's voice when he spoke that Lily lifted her head to look into his eyes. That was the truth. She kissed the bump on his nose.

"I'm sorry," she whispered. "He was . . . your friend?"

"Yes."

"What happened to him?"

"I heard that he died a few years later, whipped to death because he tried to run away."

Lily laid her head there in the crook of his shoulder where it fit so perfectly.

"I was always glad that the break healed badly. I wanted my parents to feel guilty every time they looked at me. I wanted them to be reminded of the cruel thing they'd done."

"Were they?"

Quint managed a hoarse laugh. "No," he answered with pain in his voice. "That was the worst of all. They never gave Jonah another thought."

Jonah. Lily closed her eyes and tried to comfort Quint with a kiss to his shoulder, her fingers twined through his. Jonah. The name Quint had cried out in his sleep as they lay shackled together. His demon.

"I still wish you would come with me," Lily said, already certain of what his answer would be.

"I can't," Quint whispered.

Lily accepted his answer. How could she ask him to abandon his honor when she had been so damned inflexible about her own? But she would miss him, and she would worry about him, and she would love him, deep in her heart, for the rest of her life.

It was still dark when Quint roused Lily from a fitful sleep. It was time to go. He helped her dress in the rose calico, buttoning the tiny buttons for her, tying the ribbon at her throat. He even brushed her hair, and she allowed him to do all these small things for her.

She was silent, too silent for Lily. Quint found that he couldn't find his voice either. It hurt too much. And he knew there were no words of comfort that would change what was about to happen, no words to ease the pain.

He ran his hands over her shoulders and down her arms. She was as smooth as silk and as hard as steel. Strong and soft, vulnerable and intractable. And she was his.

His, and not his.

He wanted so much to tell her that he loved her, but he was afraid. So much had happened. He had betrayed her, but that didn't mean he loved her less. She wouldn't believe him. Not now. Not after all she'd learned about him. Their night together had been an enchanted slice of time, suspended and separate from the other trials they'd been through. But that couldn't last forever. Only for a few short hours.

He moved away from her, and when he glanced down and caught her staring at him, she smiled sadly, poignantly, and Quint tried to smile back.

He couldn't.

His face was like stone, and he couldn't pretend for her anymore.

Lily wanted to tell Quint that she loved him, but she remained silent. She didn't want him to go into battle burdened with her love. That was certainly how he would see it. A burden. If he was determined to be a soldier, then he had to give all of himself to that task if he was to survive.

He was so distant, Lily thought as she watched him dress in his dark uniform. She sat on the edge of the bed and drank him in with her eyes, memorizing his face, the way he held his hands, the stern lift to his shoulders. It was over, whatever had brought them together for that final night. She was glad of it, though. Glad to have more memories of Quint to carry in her heart.

The beach was a short walk from the house, over a weed-covered hill and again over jagged rocks. Quint held her hand, and they followed Tommy and the crew as they made their way toward the beach. The sky before them was gray as morning approached, and Tommy and the lads were silent silhouettes against the sky.

Lily dragged her feet, clasping Quint's hand as a gust of wind caught her unaware. The chill of the wind couldn't match the frost that was building in her heart as he led her toward a ship that would take her away. Their fingers intertwined as they slipped silently through the early-morning mist.

She steeled herself, pushing back the tears that threatened. Her spine was stiff and unyielding, her face untouched by emotion.

Quint continued to hold her hand even when the jagged rocks were behind them and they walked across the sand. The ship waited in the distance, and already the full skiff carried all her companions but one to the waiting ship. Tommy stood near the water, his arms crossed over his chest.

Not a word was spoken on the beach as Tommy stared away from them and Quint and Lily stood apart, their hands still clasped. The sky lightened slowly, the gray turning to a soft lavender shot with pink.

It was worth it all. The pain, the heartache, the tears. All for love, for the chance to be—perhaps just for a short time—a part of something more than any one person could ever be.

The skiff was coming for her, rowing toward the shore quickly. Lily was surprised to see Captain Dennison step from the skiff, leaving two of his men behind.

Tommy stepped through the waves and into

the skiff without a backward glance, as Dennison advanced.

"Tyler," he said in soft voice. There was surprise in his voice as he studied Quint and his uniform from head to toe. "Miss Lily." He bowed to her briefly, "I'm here to take you home."

"That's right," Quint snapped. "You get her back to Nassau, and then you make certain that she stays there."

Dennison looked bemused. "And Captain Sherwood?"

"There is no Captain Sherwood," Lily said, a touch of melancholy in her voice.

Quint squeezed her hand. "Actually, *she's* Captain Sherwood."

"The devil you say." Dennison's eyebrows shot up, and he stared at Lily without even attempting to hide his shock.

Quint escorted Lily to the skiff, lifting her easily when they neared the water to keep her feet and skirt dry. If any other man had attempted to do that, she would have been insulted. But she wasn't. This was Quint.

She didn't protest until he moved away from her, taking Captain Dennison's arm and pulling the captain out of her range of hearing. Once or twice Dennison turned to look at her, and Quint was stating his case heatedly, arguing with Dennison. Whatever it was, he didn't want her to hear.

Lily didn't move from her seat. The chill of the air penetrated her thin dress and nipped at her nose. He was really sending her away.

Before Tommy or the two sailors knew what was happening, Lily jumped from the skiff and splashed through the surf. She didn't feel the chill of the water or the dampness of her skirts as the gentle waves soaked her calico. She paid no mind to the sting of tears in her eyes and the bite of the cold air that tossed her hair about her head.

She ran to Quint and threw herself into his arms. "I love you, Quint," she whispered. "I didn't want to tell you, but I can't leave without saying it. I love you. Please don't let me go."

Quint gathered her into his arms. God, why did she have to do this? It would have been much simpler to watch her sail away without knowing how she felt.

"Our timing is bad, Lily."

She pulled back and looked up at him. "Our bloody timing is bad? Is that all you can say to me?"

Quint kissed her one last time. He didn't allow her to argue or chastise him or say again that she loved him. He kissed her so hard and so deep that she couldn't breathe, and when he released her, he pushed her into Dennison's arms. Then he turned his back on her.

He heard her muffled protests as Dennison carried her away. Her voice faded, and he heard the oars slapping against the water. Lily called his name, one last time, and then she was silent.

He turned to watch the skiff carry his wife away, standing stock still with his arms crossed over his chest and his feet planted far apart. The wind whipped his hair away from his face.

It was the wind that put the tears there, he decided, that caused that unfamiliar stinging in his eyes. A grain of sand that troubled his eyes the way Lily troubled his heart. He hadn't shed a tear since he was twelve years old and had broken his nose. He'd cried when he'd fallen, and again when he'd watched Jonah carried away from his family. He still had nightmares about Jonah's tears, the chains that had bound a thirteen-year-old child, and Jonah's mother's screams.

Just as he would have nightmares about watching Lily sail away from him. It was for the best, he tried to convince himself. She would be safe in Nassau.

"I love you, too, Lily." He whispered into the wind the words he didn't dare say to her face.

Lily boarded Dennison's ship, the *Sally-Anne*, and refused to go below as instructed. She stood at the bow of the ship and looked toward the beach. He was still there. From what she could see, he hadn't moved at all.

"It's cold, Miss Lily," Dennison said kindly. "You really should go below."

"No," she said shortly. "Not yet." She wouldn't take her eyes from the figure on the beach until she could no longer see him. "What did he say to you?"

Dennison shrugged, reluctant. "That the two of you are married. Is that true?"

"Aye, it is." If he was confused by the loss of her Southern accent, he didn't show it.

Dennison shook his head. "I should be surprised, but I'm not. He was taken with you the first time he saw you."

"Did he say anything else . . . just now?" Why did she insist on torturing herself?

Dennison hesitated, humming under his breath for a moment. "He said I was to protect you while you were on board my ship. And he said if I touched you, or if any of my crew touched you, he would cut out my heart and have it for breakfast."

Lily smiled sadly. Maybe he did love her a little. Maybe he was just possessive, like a small boy who was afraid to let anyone else touch his favorite toy.

Dennison left her there, unable to convince her to go below. She stood at the bow of the ship, and when Dennison was gone she stepped onto the lower rail and grasped the top rail with her cold hands. The wind lashed her hair back and pressed the calico to her body, whirling the damp skirt around her legs.

"I love you, Quint," she swore confidently. "I'll always love you." The wind snatched the words from her mouth and whisked them away to be lost in the frigid surf and howling gusts.

Lily moved around the deck as the ship turned, always watching the beach. Quint never moved, even as the *Sally-Anne* sailed away. She watched until he was nothing more than a dark speck on the beach that was finally bathed in a golden morning light, and still she couldn't tear herself away.

Chapter Twenty-five

With the seizure of Fort Fisher in January and Fort Sumter in February, the business of blockade running died. As the activity which had fueled the prosperity of Nassau ended, the island town underwent a speedy and inevitable change.

The hotel that had once housed the captains of the fast steamers and their crews was quiet. A few residents remained there, but the ballroom was silent and the dining room no longer reverberated into the night with the shouts of drunken sailors and gamblers.

Tommy kept Lily informed of the changes, and it seemed that every day he had news of a new departure. The new serenity of the island seemed to agree with him.

He took up fishing, an activity he had disdained for years, and he provided the household with fresh fish every day. Uncle Tommy, a fisherman.

Shops closed; the merchants who had come to Nassau to make a quick profit were gone with the blockade runners. Those who remained had been there for years and would be there for years to come. Their profits were not so great any longer, but they earned enough to get by. That was all they had been looking for when they'd settled on the island of New Providence, in the town of Nassau.

Lily stayed in her white house, as reclusive as Captain Sherwood had been. She had Cora and Tommy with her and the ocean outside her window, and she told herself again and again that she needed nothing else.

The climate in Nassau was always mild, but Lily knew that March meant a promise of spring for Quint. She had followed the progress of the war closely through newspapers that were weeks old before she saw them, and she couldn't stop herself from wondering, as she read of battle after battle, if Quint had been there.

She'd had no word from him, not a single letter in the five months they'd been apart. Neither had she attempted to send a message to him. The temptation to tell him that she carried his child would have been too great, had she put pen to paper.

She sat in the parlor, where she and Quint had played chess. She rested on the serpentine-backed loveseat where he had held her hand and kissed her and asked her to run away with him, and she laid her hands over her swollen belly as she remembered.

Life since her return to Nassau had been so quiet that when she heard someone knocking at the front door, she started, and her heart skipped a beat. Her first thought was that it might be Quint, though she knew he wouldn't knock so timidly. Besides, the war wasn't over, and she didn't expect to hear from him until all his battles had been fought and all his ghosts put to rest.

If she heard from him even then. If he still wanted her.

Cora led the visitor into the parlor, and Lily rose awkwardly. She couldn't have been more surprised, even if it had been Quint.

"Mrs. Slocum." Lily remained standing in front of the loveseat, her hands resting on her belly, her head cocked to one side as Cora backed out of the room.

Eleanor Slocum was dressed in a silver-gray gown; it was the first time Lily had seen the widow in anything but black. Her mourning was over, then, Lily decided, though Mrs. Slocum looked anything but cheerful with her high-necked gown and that dark hair pulled back into a severe bun.

"Mrs. Tyler," Eleanor Slocum returned the greeting solemnly. She tried to hide it, but there was surprise in her eyes as she stared at Lily's distended midsection that was covered with draping green calico.

Lily felt the blood drain from her face. "How did you know?" She had told no one but Cora and Tommy that she and Quint had been married. No one else on the island knew. Captain Dennison had left the island for good in January, taking Roger and the rest of Lily's crew with him. They had sworn not to tell.

"I received a letter from Quintin several months ago, through a mutual friend." Mrs. Slocum regained her composure and moved with slow, graceful steps to stand near Lily.

Lily offered her guest a chair and returned ponderously to her own seat. Quint had found the time to send a letter to Eleanor Slocum, but not to her. That fact told her all she needed to know.

"What brings you here, Mrs. Slocum?" Lily felt huge and clumsy next to the elegant woman who lowered herself into the chair like a queen taking her throne. Suddenly her stomach seemed larger than before, grotesque even, and her hair too untidy, her dress too plain.

"I'm leaving the island this afternoon," Eleanor Slocum explained indifferently. "I wanted to see you before I departed. The truth is, I should have left weeks ago, but . . ." She faltered, and her lips trembled slightly. "I don't really know where I'm going."

Lily frowned at the woman's reticence. "Your family?"

"Disowned me when I married Henry Slocum." A sad smile, but the composure was once again intact. "But that's a long and very boring story."

Lily wondered how close Eleanor Slocum and Quint really were. He'd said that his relationship with the widow had been one of friendship only, but had that been a lie? One of many? He'd written her a letter, and Lily was as jealous of that fact as of anything else.

"Your letter from Quint . . . is he all right?" Lily hated to have to ask, but not as much as she needed to know.

"Last I heard, he was just fine."

"You've heard from him . . . more than once?"

"Three times." Eleanor Slocum's eyes were on Lily's face. "The first letter explained some of what happened, *Captain*." She smiled as she said the word aloud. "Then there were two letters which consisted of four words. 'Is she still there?' "

Lily felt a rush of relief. He hadn't forgotten her. "And your response?"

Eleanor Slocum lifted a finely arched brow. "I responded in kind, with a single word. *Yes*. I'm surprised he didn't ask about your health, considering your condition."

"He doesn't know, and I'd prefer to keep it that way," Lily said curtly.

"Is it his child?"

Lily felt her face grow warm. "Of course it's his child!"

"Then why on earth—forgive me, Mrs. Tyler. I didn't mean to pry into your personal affairs."

Lily glared at the woman, and her imagination ran wild. Quint and Eleanor Slocum in her little cottage. Quint and the attractive widow together, back in the States.

"Are you all right, Mrs. Tyler?" Eleanor Slocum leaned forward, a concerned frown on her face. "You've gone quite pale."

Lily stared into the widow's dark eyes, searching for the truth. "What is your relationship with

367

my husband, Mrs. Slocum?"

"I cursed Quintin Tyler as a fool for becoming so besotted with Lily Radford, the Captain's mistress." Eleanor Slocum smiled. "But it seems he wasn't the only one bedeviled."

Lily waited silently for her answer.

"Purely business, Mrs. Tyler."

Lily released the breath she had been holding. Eleanor Slocum was telling the truth, she was certain. "So, you're a spy as well?"

"I was. There's no need for me to be involved in such activities any longer. The war is almost over, Mrs. Tyler." There was sad relief in her voice. "Too late for me. Perhaps not too late for you."

Lily laid her hands over her belly, unconsciously caressing her baby. "I hope that's true."

"You're very lucky," Mrs. Slocum said wistfully. "You have that baby, no matter what happens. I wish that I . . . that Henry and I . . . but we'd been married only a year when he was taken from me. He joined as soon as the war began. Two years later he was dead. My mother cursed me for a fool, because I waited for love. Love, she said, was for poor white trash, not for the aristocracy of the South."

There was a sad, mocking tone in her husky voice. "I was nearly thirty when I met Henry and we married. My mother was mortified. A Yankee!" She smiled poignantly. "If I'd had a baby to hold, perhaps I wouldn't have been so lost, so angry when he died."

"I'm very sorry." Lily's voice was little more

than a whisper. A year ago she wouldn't have understood, but now she understood all too well. What if she had found Quint in peacetime, and they had planned a future together only to have it ripped away?

"Perhaps, since I've bared my soul to you in a most ungracious fashion, you will share with me the reason you haven't told Quintin that he is about to become a father." She sounded a bit sheepish about her request, and she was blushing just a little. Lily was certain that was rare for the composed widow.

Lily sighed deeply. She had wondered a thousand times if she'd made the right decision in not telling Quint about the baby. "I love Quint very much, Mrs. Slocum. But we came together in uncertain times, on opposite sides of this conflict. Sometimes I wonder if his feelings for me were real or a mirage. When this is all over, when the war comes to an end, I'll know. If Quint comes to me, I'll know. If he doesn't . . ." Lily shrugged her shoulders, trying to appear nonchalant. "If he doesn't, then it was all a fancy and I'll have to get on with my life as best I can."

She lifted her eyes to Eleanor Slocum and buried the emotions that roiled inside her. "I won't trap Quint with a baby. I'll love him for the rest of my life, but I won't hold him that way. You know how damned noble he can be."

The widow smiled. "I'm beginning to see what Quintin saw in you. There was a time when I wondered, but you're not the witless girl you pretended to be. He saw through that, you know."

"I know."

"If you and I weren't enemies, Mrs. Tyler, we might have been friends."

Lily smiled sadly, but her smile faded as she laid a hand over her stomach.

"Are you all right?"

"He's kicking." Lily held her hands over her taut belly, wondering how on earth she was going to get any bigger. By her calculations, she had almost two months to go.

Eleanor Slocum rose from her seat, rising like a silver-gray cloud. She floated across the floor to stand before Lily, and to look down at her stomach. There was such a look of longing in the widow's eyes that it broke Lily's heart.

Lily reached out and took Eleanor Slocum's hands. Without thinking, she placed the woman's hands over her belly, and they waited silently. Then the baby moved again, and Eleanor's gloomy look changed to one of wonder.

"I think that's an elbow," Lily whispered.

They stood in that position, Lily seated on the loveseat, Eleanor Slocum bent over her with her hands pressed lightly to Lily's distended midsection, Lily's hands over the widow's, for several minutes. It was as if time were suspended, and the soft light that danced through the window lit Eleanor Slocum's face. Lily saw hope beneath the sorrow and felt a wave of serenity wash over her.

And then the spell was broken, and Eleanor Slocum pulled away as Lily lifted her hands.

"I'm terribly sorry, Mrs. Tyler." The widow actually blushed a bright red. "That was most improper of me."

Lily smiled. "I've never cared much for what was proper and what was not, Mrs. Slocum. I don't intend to start at this late date."

Eleanor Slocum turned to leave, composed once more.

"Well," she said in a surprisingly strong voice. "I've seen what I came to see, Mrs. Tyler, though I must admit you've managed to surprise me."

Her back was ramrod straight, her shoulders thrust back as she walked away from Lily.

"Mrs. Slocum." Lily rose slowly, one hand on the arm of the loveseat, one on her belly. "If you see Quint . . ."

Eleanor Slocum spun around, and her appearance was calm once more. But Lily saw fire in her eyes. "I won't say a word to anyone, Mrs. Tyler. Your secret is safe with me. But when Quintin Tyler comes for you—and he will come for you—hold onto him for dear life. Don't ever let him go."

Lily felt a grain of hope when she heard the widow's confident words. At least one of them was certain of Quint's intentions.

"If he does come for me, you can be assured that I won't ever let him out of my sight again."

"If, if, if." Eleanor Slocum waved a delicate hand in the air. "Really, Mrs. Tyler, insecurity does not become you."

With that, Eleanor Slocum turned on her heel in a swirl of silver gray and marched through the door. Lily heard the front door open and close, then heard the widow's retreating footsteps on the walkway.

"I'm not insecure," Lily whispered to the empty room. "I'm just . . . practical."

Quint sat his bay and surveyed the line of soldiers snaking along the road ahead of him. It would soon be over. Richmond, the capital of the Confederacy, would soon be in Union hands. The Rebs they'd been fighting were hungry, and poorly clothed and armed. They were an army on its last legs.

There was a customary frown on his bearded face. He'd tried to leave Lily behind, but she was always with him . . . in battle and in times like this, when his thoughts turned to the future.

He reached into the pocket of his uniform jacket and withdrew the sheet of paper that had been folded and refolded a hundred times or more. He looked down at the single word, written in a well-formed script of sweeping letters.

Yes.

The ache in his heart longed for more. Was she well? Did she think of him at all? Why did she remain on the island when the venture that had taken her there had ended?

Still, the single word told him all he needed to know. Lily was there.

"Captain Tyler." His name and the pounding of quickly approaching hoofbeats roused him from his reverie, and he returned the letter to his pocket.

The private who drew up beside him handed

over a plain envelope. "From Colonel Fairfax, Captain," the young private said as he placed the envelope into Quint's hand.

Quint dismissed the soldier and looked down at the missive. What now? He'd done his part for the secret service, and wanted no more of it.

He tore open the envelope and whipped out the single sheet of paper. Quint's grimace turned into a wry smile as he recognized Eleanor Slocum's handwriting.

Yes, yes, and yes, you fool. I hope you make a better husband than you did a spy.

There was no signature, but the sweeping penmanship was unmistakable. Did this mean what he thought, what he hoped it meant? Was Lily waiting for him?

He folded the letter neatly and placed it in his pocket with the others.

Yes, yes, and yes.

Chapter Twenty-six

It was over.

Quint had been present when Lee surrendered, had watched as that general's troops had laid down their weapons and gone home. There had been no shouts of victory that day, nor any cries of defeat. Rather, the field had been cloaked in a reverential stillness, a hush that had touched even the most hate-filled soldier.

That had been more than one month past. The Union was preserved, but Lincoln was dead. The Rebel soldiers had been sent home, and Quint was filled with relief that it was over, and with uncertainty as well. There was still a lot of hate between the two sides.

There was an advantage to being an ex-secret service agent, Quint discovered. Colonel Fairfax was able to discover for him the fate of his brother, Dalton. Colonel Dalton Tyler, C.S.A., was alive. The plantation still stood, though it was likely not the home he remembered. There had been too many changes.

Alicia was there, along with both of Quint's sisters, waiting for Dalton's return. Perhaps she had fallen in love with Dalton after all.

And perhaps one day, when old wounds had healed, Quint could take Lily to Mississippi to make peace with his family. A year ago, he wouldn't have thought it possible, but now it seemed important.

Colonel Holt, a barrel-chested officer who was fond of foul-smelling cigars and cheap whiskey, stopped in front of Quint's tent, where Quint sat on the ground, lost in thought.

"Still determined to leave us, son?" the colonel asked in a booming voice. "Can't convince you to come out West with me and fight the Injuns?"

Quint leapt to his feet. The colonel had caught him by surprise, and he felt as if he'd been yanked to the present, leaving behind thoughts of Lily and plans for the days to come.

"No, thank you, sir." Quint ran his fingers through his shoulder-length hair, sweeping the strands away from his face. There had been little time for the amenities in the past several months, and he had neither shaved nor cut his hair since the morning he'd put Lily on Captain Dennison's steamer. "I've had enough of fightin' for a while."

Colonel Holt looked as if he'd expected no other answer. He'd been trying for several weeks to convince Quint to stay with the cavalry, but the answer was always the same.

"Man like you, Tyler, you'll be bored in six months with no one to fight with but the missus."

Quint grinned, a rare smile. "Bored? I don't think so, sir. Lily fights back."

The Colonel laughed and slapped his leg. "Good for her. So, what do you plan to do with yourself, besides fight with Mrs. Tyler?"

"I was thinking of getting into the shipping business, sir. A base in Nassau, one in San Francisco, maybe one in Liverpool."

"Grand plans, Captain," Colonel Holt said with a nod. "But I still say you'll be bored in six months."

Quint knew better than to argue with the Colonel. The cavalry was Holt's career, and the gleam in his eyes told of his excitement at the prospect of heading west. Quint couldn't imagine anyone looking forward to more violence after what the country had just been through, but Colonel Holt was not alone.

"You got a brood, Captain?" Colonel Holt leaned forward, hands clasped behind his back. "Little Tylers?"

"Not yet, sir." Quint smiled crookedly again. Children. His and Lily's. He wondered, not for the first time, if either of their last nights together had resulted in a child. He would love to go home and find Lily sitting in the parlor, her stomach swollen and her face glowing. He shook his head. Of course, that wasn't meant to be. Eleanor would have mentioned it to him in her letter if Lily had been in the family way.

Colonel Holt gave up on him with a dismissive wave of his hand. Quint was damn tired of Army life. In another month he would be discharged, and then he would concern himself with starting that family.

Quint crawled into his tent and lay on his back, hands behind his head, ankles crossed. He had such plans for the future, such dreams. Eleanor's last message had given him hope, but there was no assurance that Lily would still be in Nassau when he returned, no assurance that she would want him back.

But deep inside, beneath the doubts and the fears, was the unshakable knowledge that Lily was his wife, his woman, and with the war behind them, the future was clear. So he closed his eyes and dreamt of her. He dreamt soft, comforting dreams of Lily.

Lily paced slowly, despite Cora's repeated attempts to force her to lie down. It was time. The pangs had started that morning, spaced far apart and mild in nature, but as the day progressed, the pains came closer together and became much harder. Even now, as Lily stopped to wait out a contraction, beads of sweat formed on her face.

Soon she would have no choice but to lie down.

The war had been over for more than a month. The news had reached them weeks after Lee's surrender, and since that day Lily had been waiting for Quint to appear at the door.

"Where the hell have you been, Quintin Tyler?" Lily asked under her breath.

"What's that?" Cora nearly jumped out of her skin when Lily spoke. The great aunt-to-be was more visibly nervous than Lily herself, wringing her hands and holding her breath with each contraction Lily suffered through.

"You can send Tommy for Mrs. Pratt now," Lily conceded. Cora had wanted to send for the midwife hours earlier, but Mrs. Pratt, a mother of eight who had delivered countless babies in Nassau, had told Lily what to expect. Hours of waiting.

Each pain was sharper, harder, and in spite of herself, Lily began to worry. Could she do this? Alone? Quint should be here, beside her, holding her hand, sweating with her.

Lily was in the bed, bolstered by a mountain of pillows, when Mrs. Pratt arrived. The midwife could have been forty or sixty, with her soft gray hair and lean frame. She held herself like a younger woman, back straight and shoulders back, but there were deep lines etched in her face, lines that spoke of years of sun and many days of wide smiles.

"There now, Miss Lily," Mrs. Pratt said as she directed one of those wide smiles at Lily's distended belly. "How are you feeling?"

Lily gave the woman a look that would have made a lesser person step back. It was a look she had once reserved for her crew and, on occasion, Quintin Tyler. Sweat dripped down her strained face, and with an impatient hand, Lily brushed back the hair that fell forward and stuck to her forehead and her temples.

"How the hell do you think I feel, you moron?"

"Lily!" Cora gasped.

But Mrs. Pratt continued to smile sweetly.

"That's all right, Miss Lily. I've been called worse. Much worse. And I imagine you'll call me something more menacing than a moron before the night is done."

Within minutes of the midwife's arrival, Cora had to leave the room. It was too much for her to bear, to see Lily in such pain. She joined Tommy, who was pacing in the hallway, and they waited, listening with pounding hearts and withheld breaths as Lily screamed. Again and again.

Tommy cursed between screams. He vowed to find Quintin Tyler, wherever he might be, and rip the man's liver out. See how he liked it. He swore that if it had not been for that man, Lily wouldn't be in such pain, and if she died . . . if she died, he would hunt Quintin Tyler to the grave, if need be.

They stopped pacing as another scream filled the house. It couldn't go on much longer. Cora didn't know how Lily found the strength to scream, after the day she'd been through. The cry died away, and they heard Lily shout at the top of her lungs,

"Bloody hell!"

"Bloody hell!" Quintin woke as he cried out in his sleep, shooting up into a sitting position in the darkness of his tent. For a moment, he sat there, dazed. What had awakened him? His own voice?

He had been dreaming of Lily. That was all he could remember. Her face. Her voice.

Sweat ran down his face and trickled down his

back. His heart was thudding hard, threatening to burst through his chest. It was too damn hot to sleep well, and even outside the tent there was no breeze to make the heat bearable.

With a frown, Quint lowered himself to the bedroll, resting his head in his hands. Whatever had jerked him from a sound sleep had brought him to such a level of awareness that he knew he would get no more sleep that night. His only consolation was that soon he wouldn't have to rely on dreams of Lily to see her face.

Chapter Twenty-seven

The island was more serene than he remembered. The water shimmered as jewel-like as the year before and the sun shone as brightly, but the docks were quieter and the people on the street moved at a slower pace.

But then, the war was over, and the frantic pace that had driven Nassau when the blockade runners infested her port had naturally slowed.

Quint brushed a thumb over his freshly shaven jaw. He felt surprisingly bare without his beard and long hair, but one look in the mirror had told him that Lily wouldn't have liked it.

He walked past shops he had once frequented, never even looking through the open doors and windows to see if the familiar faces of merchants he had known peered back. Some of the buildings were boarded up, giving the street a deserted look even though some shops remained open. He passed the cottage where he had met with Eleanor Slocum, not even giving the place a second glance.

His limp was so slight now that it was barely

noticeable. He still had his bad days, now and again, but as he walked down the familiar street, he wouldn't have noticed even if the old wound had been bothering him.

There could be nothing more pleasant than June in Nassau. The sun warmed his face, and a balmy breeze washed over him, filling him with the smells he associated with Lily—salt air, perfumed tropical flowers, the sun baking into the cobblestones.

What would Lily say? Was she even there, in the little house he had pictured her in for the past eight months? Eleanor had left the island in March. Anything could have happened in the three months since then. The slumberous atmosphere of the town scared him, and doubts he had pushed aside assailed him, as fresh as a new wound. Had she waited? Knowing Lily, she could be anywhere in the world. Maybe she hadn't bothered to wait for his return.

As soon as he'd been released from the cavalry, he'd made his way to the coast and caught the next ship for Nassau. The little steamer he'd sailed on carried mail and newspapers and a small supply of manufactured goods. It would sail back in a few days, stocked with rum and return mail.

His heart was pounding in his chest when he stepped onto the shaded path. There was nothing for him back in the States. The North was not his home, but he couldn't return to the South. That left West, and a career as an Indian-killer with Colonel Holt.

Quint cursed himself for the last-minute burst of doubt. He'd been so certain of Lily and their future togethcr, but now he felt like a nervous bridegroom on his way to the altar. Would his bride be there, waiting for him?

The house looked the same, neat and bright, the lace curtains dancing in the light summer breeze. On the outside, nothing had changed.

Cora opened the door to his knock, and the look on her face said it all. She was stunned to see him there. Her face turned a pale green, and her eyes widened. For once, Cora was speechless.

"Is she here?" Quint asked, unable to force his voice to a normal level. His words were gruff and low.

Before Cora could answer, Tommy's bulk filled the doorway. His meaty fist flew out, and Quint didn't have a chance to react as the big man's fist rammed into his stomach, sending Quint flying to land on his backside in the dirt by the stone walkway. Tommy was leaning over him, obviously intending to hit Quint again, but Quint swept his leg out and Tommy's feet flew out from under him. Lily's uncle landed in the dirt beside him.

"Stop it!" Cora screamed, planting her feet between them. She was her old self again, Quint noticed, sour and demanding. But this time her anger seemed to be directed at her husband.

She glared at Quint, a question in her eyes. She must have been satisfied with what she saw there, because she smiled, almost kindly.

"Lily's in the garden," Cora said, offering her

hand to Quint. He ignored her overture and rose to his feet under his own power.

"Dammit, Cora," Tommy whispered hoarsely as he slowly regained his footing.

Quint glanced over his shoulder and saw Cora restraining her husband with a light hand on his arm and fiercely spoken soft words. Tommy wanted to come after him. He wasn't finished with what he'd begun, but it was clear that Cora had no intention of allowing her husband to interfere.

He followed the stone path, a path lined with dark green foliage and bright flowers. What would he find in the garden? Lily in trousers and flowing white sleeves, fencing with a sailor? Lily dressed in a frilly gown, with white gloves and a book of poetry in her lap? There was so much he didn't know about the woman who was his wife. He wanted a lifetime to figure her out. It would surely take that long.

Quint stopped when he could see her. Lily was sitting on the wrought-iron bench, a thick book in her lap. Her dress was simple, and her hair was pulled away from her face. Those unruly tendrils curled around her face just the same, refusing to be tamed. She looked almost serene, and that was definitely a new look for Lily.

As if she could feel his eyes on her, Lily lifted her head slowly and set her book aside. He tried to gauge the expression that came over her face—surprise, shock even—and then she gave him a smile touched with tenderness.

She stayed where she was, seated on the

bench, as Quint approached her. He didn't stop, didn't hesitate at all, but took her in his arms as she rose from the bench to greet him. Lily wrapped her arms around his waist as he held her tight, and she laid her head against his chest. She was real, and warm, and her heart was beating as hard and as fast as his own.

"I love you, Lily," he whispered. In his mind he'd gone over their meeting a thousand times, planning what he would say to her. He'd planned to be witty and evasive until he was certain of her feelings. But when he'd touched her, all his determination had disappeared, like fog burned away by the sun. She was his wife, and he would never let her go again.

"Quint, my love." Lily lifted her face and met his eyes. "What took you so long?"

Quint covered her lips with his and kissed her hungrily. He had dreamed of kissing her, of having her in his arms. "I came as soon as I could. Jesus, Lily, I wasn't even certain that you would still be here."

Lily smiled. "I could have gone to England, but I was afraid you'd never find me there."

All Quint's doubts and fears disappeared with that smile. "I didn't know if you would have me or not . . . not after . . ."

Lily stood on her tiptoes and silenced him with a kiss. When she pulled away, she stayed on her tiptoes, holding her mouth close to his.

"I think we should start all over, Lieutenant Tyler. How do you do? My name is Lily. I love you."

"Actually, it's Captain Tyler now."

Lily raised her eyebrows slightly. "It seems I'm destined to be the Captain's woman."

Quint smiled. Lily reached out a finger and lightly touched the dimple in his cheek.

"Captain Tyler," Lily whispered. "Do you play chess?"

Quint touched his lips to hers. "Why, yes, I do. Are you challenging me to a game?"

Lily pulled away from him slightly, and he saw a flash of uncertainty in her dancing eyes. "No more games, Quint. From now on, I want nothing but the truth between us."

Quint sighed with relief. "Nothing but the truth."

"I love you," Lily whispered. "I didn't know if you would ever come for me."

"I can't live without you, Lily. When I sent you away, I knew I was doing what was best for you, but I didn't know it would hurt so goddamn much. In my heart, you were always with me."

Lily laid her head against his chest again. She would never let him go, not now that she had him in her arms again. How many times in the past eight months had she cursed him, and cried for him, and talked to him as if he were right beside her?

She had forgotten how heavenly it was just to have him hold her, to lay her hands against his strong back.

She didn't hear the footsteps on the path, and evidently neither did Quint. But Cora was there, clearing her throat loudly. When Lily lifted her head and faced her aunt, she saw that Cora's face was bright pink. Still, Quint held her tightly, refusing to let go.

"Pardon me," Cora said in a low voice. "But Jamie's awake, and 'e's 'ungry, and 'e's screaming for you, Lily."

Quint stiffened. "Jamie? Who the hell is Jamie?" He looked down at Lily with a scowl on his face.

"Bring him to me, Cora," Lily said calmly, and her aunt turned and ran up the stone path.

Slowly, Quint released her. "Jamie?" A fire burned in his dark eyes. Lily realized, with a slight smile, how very much she had missed those dark eyes—fathomless, but so expressive.

"Not James Dennison!" Quint thundered.

"No," Lily answered him calmly. "Captain Dennison left Nassau months ago."

She didn't know exactly how to tell Quint that he had a son. Right out? Or should she lead up to it gently?

Quint didn't like the look on Lily's face. Was this Jamie responsible for the serenity and tenderness in her eyes? That was what was different about her. It gave her an aura of tranquility.

"Do you love him, Lily?"

"Oh, yes." She glowed when she answered. "Very much."

"You just said that you loved me!" He grabbed her shoulders, and Lily leaned into him.

"I do," she whispered. "I love you both."

Quint spun away from her, and when he spun back around he saw that Lily was unfastening the buttons of her bodice, as calmly and casually as if she were simply taking a deep breath of sea air.

"Dammit, Lily . . ." It hit him a split second before he heard the first hint of the squalling that grew closer and closer. He didn't know what to say, wasn't even certain that it was real until Cora entered the garden with her screaming bundle.

Lily took the child from Cora with sure hands and folded back the blanket he was wrapped in. Quint was presented with a red face and a mouth opened in a furious scream.

"He looks like you, don't you think?" Lily asked with a devilish smile. "Demanding and defiant."

Quint was speechless as he stared down at the tiny baby. For a moment, no one moved. It seemed that no one but the baby was even breathing.

And then Quint reached out a finger, a finger that was suddenly fat and awkward, and the baby grasped it tightly with four fingers and a tiny thumb to draw it to his mouth.

"Your son, Quint," Lily said softly. "James Quintin Tyler."

There were tears in his eyes when he looked at Lily. "How old is he?"

"Almost seven weeks."

"You knew when you left . . . when I put you on that ship . . ." He couldn't finish.

Lily nodded and sat on the wrought-iron bench. She freed one breast and Jamie fastened his mouth over her nipple, resting one delicate and impossibly tiny hand on the swell of her breast.

Lily sighed heavily. "I didn't tell you because . . . I wasn't sure how you felt about me. It was a confusing time, Quint. I was certain of my love for you, but . . ." She avoiding looking directly at him. She gazed down at the baby instead and smiled. "I wanted you to come back because you loved me, because you wanted me. Not because you felt obligated. If you had known about the baby . . . I never would have been certain if you came back for me, or for him, or because of your blasted honor."

Quint sat hesitantly beside her and watched his son contentedly suckling. Jamie's hand opened and closed against his mother's soft skin, a tiny fist so very small against Lily's breast.

"Are you angry with me?" Lily whispered.

He shook his head. "How could I be angry with you? You don't still doubt me, do you?"

"No." Lily shook her head. "I knew the moment I saw you standing there that everything was going to be all right."

When Jamie was sated, Lily wrapped him in the blanket and laid him in Quint's arms. He was awkward with his son for a moment, but then he handled the baby naturally and easily. Jamie seemed to feel safe in his father's big hands, clumsy as they felt to Quint at the moment, and was asleep in minutes.

Lily sighed as she buttoned her dress. "That's all he does. You've seen it all. He cries and eats and sleeps, and occasionally he gurgles. And, of course, he has his more unpleasant moments." She wrinkled her nose.

Linda Winstead

Quint wasn't ready to let Jamie go when Cora returned for him. He had a lot of catching up to do. But he finally laid the child easily into the woman's arms, with the care reserved for precious and fragile objects.

"Planning on staying a while, are you, Mr. Tyler?" Cora asked with a puckered smile.

Quint grinned. "A very long while, Cora. Do you think you can convince your husband to allow me to enter the house without a fight?"

"Aye," she said softly. "I think I might be able to do that."

Quint pulled Lily into his lap as Cora returned to the house with their son. "I wish I'd been here with you, when Jamie was born. The next time I will be."

"Good. I can curse at you instead of Cora and the poor midwife." Lily grinned wickedly. "After all, it wasn't their fault."

Quint pulled her head against his shoulder. His life would never be dull, of that he was certain.

"I'm glad you came to me, Quint," Lily whispered. "There were so many times when I wondered if I'd ever see you again."

Quint kissed the freckles that were sprinkled across her nose. "I suppose I will have to tell you every day that I love you."

"Of course."

"And show you every day how much I love you."

"Naturally."

"And maybe even allow you to beat me at chess, now and again."

Lily lifted her head and smiled at him, her eyes twinkling. "Quintin Tyler, I can beat you fair and square."

"I look forward to it," Quint said as he drew her lips to his.

WEST WIND

Linda Winstead

Annabelle St. Clair has the voice of an angel and the devil at her heels. On the run for a murder she didn't commit, the world-renowned opera diva is reduced to singing in saloons until she finds a handsome gunslinger willing to take her to safety in San Francisco.

A restless bounty hunter, Shelley is more at home on the range than in Annabelle's polite society. Yet on the rugged trail, he can't resist sharing with her a passion as vast and limitless as the Western sky.

But despite the ecstasy they find, Annabelle can trust no one, especially not a man with dangerous secrets—secrets that threaten to ruin their lives and destroy their love.

_3796-3 $4.99 US/$5.99 CAN

Chase The Lightning

LINDA WINSTEAD

"A captivating tale not to be missed!"
—Raine Cantrell

Renata Parkhurst can't believe her luck. The proper daughter of a Philadelphia doctor has run away to her cousin's Colorado spread hunting for love, and the day she arrives, a wounded rancher falls right into her arms.

Although everyone in Silver Valley believes that Jake Wolf is a cold-blooded murderer, no one would accuse him of being a lady-killer. Yet even as he grudgingly allows Renata to tend to his healing, he begins to lose himself in her tender caresses.

The townsfolk say that Renata has a better chance of being hit by lightning than of finding happiness with Jake. But to win the heart of the man of her dreams, the stunning beauty will gladly give up all she possesses and chase the lightning.

_52002-8 $4.99 US/$5.99 CAN

Dorchester Publishing Co., Inc.
65 Commerce Road
Stamford, CT 06902

Pleasc add $1.75 for shipping and handling for the first book and $.50 for each book thereafter. NY, NYC, PA and CT residents, please add appropriate sales tax. No cash, stamps, or C.O.D.s. All orders shipped within 6 weeks via postal service book rate. Canadian orders require $2.00 extra postage and must be paid in U.S. dollars through a U.S. banking facility.

Name_____

Address _____

City _____ State_____Zip_____

I have enclosed $_____in payment for the checked book(s).
Payment <u>must</u> accompany all orders.☐ Please send a free catalog.

Guardian Angel

Linda Winstead

Despite her father's wish that she marry and produce heirs for his spread, Melanie Barnett prefers shooting her suitors in the backside to looking them in the face. Then a masked gunman rescues her from an attempted kidnapping, and Mel has to give him the reward he requests: a single kiss.

Everybody in Paradise, Texas, believes that Gabriel Maxwell is a greenhorn dandy who has no business on a ranch. Yet he is as handy with his pistol as with a lovely lady. To keep Mel from harm, he disguises himself and protects her. But his brazen masquerade can't hide his obvious desire. And when his deception is revealed, he will either face Mel's fierce wrath—or her fiery rapture.

_51970-4 $4.99 US/$5.99 CAN

Bestselling Author Of *Blind Fortune*

Wealthy and handsome, Reese Ashburn is the most eligible bachelor in Mobile, Alabama. And although every young debutante dreams of becoming the lady of Bonne Chance—Reese's elegant bayside plantation—none believes that its master will ever finish sowing his wild oats. Then one night Reese's carousing ends in tragedy and shame: His gambling partner, James Bentley, is brutally murdered while Reese is too drunk to save him.

Entrusted with the care of James's daughter, Reese knows that he is hardly the model guardian. And fiery Patience Bentley's stubborn pride and irresistible beauty are sure to make her a difficult ward. Still, driven by guilt, Reese is bound and determined to honor Bentley's dying wish—as well as exact revenge on his friend's killers. But can he resist Patience's enticing advances long enough to win back his pride and his reputation?

_3943-5 $4.99 US/$6.99 CAN

Yesterday & Forever

Victoria Alexander

SHADOW of THE STORM

DEBRA DIER

Bestselling author of *Surrender the Dream*

Although Ian Tremayne is the man to whom she willingly surrendered her innocence, Sabrina O'Neill vows revenge on him after a bitter misunderstanding. Risking a daring masquerade, Sabrina plunges into the glittering world of New York high society, determined to make the handsome yankee pay. But the virile Tremayne is more than ready for the challenge. Together, they enter a high-stakes game of deadly illusion and sizzling desire that might shatter Sabrina's well-crafted fascade—and leave both their lives in ruin.

_3492-1 $4.50 US/$5.50 CAN

Futuristic Romance

Don't miss these dazzling futuristic romances set on faraway worlds where passion is the lifeblood of every man and woman.

Golden Prophecies by Pam McCutcheon. Even though she is the most accomplished oracle on the planet Delphi, Thena can't foretell the danger Lancer will bring to her world—or the storm of desire he will arouse in her heart. But soon Thena and Lancer are besieged by deadly enemies who stand between them and the sweet, sensual delight of golden prophecies.

_52005-2 $4.99 US/$5.99 CAN

The Crystal Prophecy by Janice Tarantino. He comes to her in visions—a golden-eyed warrior astride a charging black stallion. Yet Susan doesn't dare hope her fantasies will come true—until she is drawn to a faraway world full of danger and desire. From their first meeting, Susan and Jared share a bond that soars beyond mere love. But forces of darkness will stop at nothing to destroy the rapture that is their destiny.

_52020-6 $4.99 US/$5.99 CAN